"'The Spellbinder's Sonata' is a beautifully written piece weaving the everyday together with the supernatural. The world building is superb and the reader can almost see the musty old estate, now the Byrons' School of Music."

— BELINDA WILSON, IND'TALE MAGAZINE

The greatest strength of this story is the development of the relationship between Pippa and Finn. "Internship" is the journey of two characters as they learn to trust and love despite emotional roadblocks and self-sabotage. "The Internship of Pippa Darling" is a great start to the Summer Abroad Series and leaves the reader craving more!

— GWENELLEN TARBET, IN'DTALE MAGAZINE

"Each turn of the page brought something different, and I found myself sometimes laughing out loud; other times, I wanted to crawl into the book and follow these beautiful characters to the end of their story. The Internship of Pippa Darling will leave you ready for more hot Irishmen and lots of laughs."

— MOLLY EDWARDS, READERS' FAVORITE

Printed in the United States of America

Second Printing, 2020

www.stephaniekeyes.com

ISBN 978-0-9998467-8-0

This is a work of fiction. Names, characters, businesses, places, events, locales, and incidents are either the products of the author's imagination or used in a fictitious manner. Any resemblance to actual persons, living or dead, or actual events is purely coincidental.

Cover Design by

Najla Qamber, Najla Qamber Designs

Editorial Services by

Laura Parnum

the Fallen Stars

STEPHANIE KEYES

DEDICATION

To Gran, who taught me everything I know about playing make-believe. I'll miss you forever.

Dusk crept up on the Irish countryside. Despite Cana's anger at her brother Lugh for his inability to save herself and the rest of the Children of Danu from their imprisoned fate, the pristine beauty of the lush green hills, even as day faded into night, was not lost on her.

Cana had once been a goddess, with extraordinary beauty designed to bring any man, mortal or immortal, to his feet. Everyone loved her. Everyone adored her. Until Arawn had captured Cana and her brothers and sisters. Then they'd lost everything. People no longer looked *at* Cana, they only looked away.

When Kellen St. James, the American teenager destined to save the world from darkness, destroyed Arawn, Cana had expected that both she and her family would instantly be freed, and that her beauty would be restored. There'd been a time when she'd championed St. James in her mind, though she would never have admitted it aloud—Cana didn't believe in standing up for anyone other than herself.

She'd been patient, waiting for the moment when the dreadful single eye in the center of her forehead would disappear. Each of the Children of Danu had been cursed with a physical characteristic, a reminder of a weakness that he or she demonstrated in their former lives—though it seemed to Cana that hers was the worst.

Cana sighed. She wanted nothing more than to look into the mirror and again see two blue eyes resting on porcelain skin, not the single eye on the frog-like green skin that currently covered her body.

But alas, she'd peeked into the mirror and nothing had changed.

Still, she and the other Children of Danu were enjoying their newfound freedom. Under the cloak of darkness, they'd snuck out the past two nights and played all sorts of vile tricks on the mortals. It had been amusing, but in the back of Cana's mind she kept questioning: Will I ever be able to go home?

Cana had come out that morning to hunt for the herbs she hoped would boost her beauty's return. She held out little hope, yet it could not hurt to try.

Coming aboveground during the mortal daytime was a luxury she wouldn't have been permitted to indulge in under Arawn's rule. She shuddered as she thought of The Call, the method Arawn used to ensure that the Children of Danu always returned to him.

Tugging the thick cloak about her, one of the few that was effective at hiding her single eye, she stepped out onto the mortal road. Movement ahead made her halt. She pulled the cloak's hood tighter around the sides of her face. She refused to tolerate humiliation from the unwelcome stares of passing mortals.

But then a familiar figure stepped onto the path. A man who wasn't a man.

Cana placed a hand to her throat. "You startled me, Wil'k."

"I don't believe that for a minute," Wil'k said, never moving, forcing her to walk to where he stood if she desired conversation.

But Cana wasn't interested in being social. She had a mission, and the sooner she completed it, the better. Cana continued, unwilling to be deterred by Wil'k's arrival.

"I know why you have not yet seen your loveliness return." Wil'k remained in his spot, as though willing Cana to stop walking.

She did just that, twisting and returning to where he waited.

"We are prisoners. Kellen St. James has the item that controls us all, and he is closer than you think."

Her interest piqued, Cana immediately brushed aside all plans to dismiss him. "I am listening."

"If we work together, we can end him, but it has to be done in a certain way. No random killing."

Cana drew back. "Random killing? How can you even suggest—"

"I do not need to suggest anything, Cana. Your exploits from last night are proof enough." Wil'k's voice managed to sound accusatory despite its even tenor.

Cana sighed. "How was I to know that hurled livestock would crush the men? It was an accident."

Wil'k's smile was quick, as though they shared an intimate moment instead of discussing the murder of twenty mortal men. Cana hadn't meant for the men's deaths to happen. Surely, if their families knew this it would dispel any grief they experienced. If Cana cared enough to tell them.

As if reading her thoughts, Wil'k continued. "You do not care about anyone but yourself. Everyone knows that."

She raised an eyebrow, saying nothing. She had never taken to Wil'k. He had developed an attitude while she,

Cana, had retained her perfectly pleasant personality without fail.

"Besides, if you kill the St. James boy, you'll lose any chance at regaining your looks forever." Wil'k grimaced as though this would be the very worst thing in their world. To Cana it was.

"What is in it for you? Why would you care about my existence?"

Wil'k glanced around as if to ensure they weren't being overheard. "Let us say that I have an interest in what happens to the boy. We need to capture Kellen St. James, and we can do it if we work together."

Cana sucked in a breath. "Keep talking."

CHAPTER 1

KELLEN

The sun shone brightly on Gran's lawn in County Clare, Ireland. The combination of the sea air and the rain that had come down in a fine mist that morning washed everything clean. The purity of it burned my lungs with each breath, making me lightheaded, though that might have had something to do with it being my wedding day.

We'd kept things low-key, only inviting our families, my best friend, Gabe, and his parents, the Stewarts, who'd been more like a family to me than my own these past few years. Then there was just Father Winslow, me, and of course Calienta.

As if my thoughts cued her entrance, Calienta, my bride, exited Gran's cottage through the French doors and made her way across the lawn toward me on the arm of her father, Lugh, the Sun God. Calienta's gown flapped behind her in the breeze, its shimmering skirt covered in a million tiny gemstones.

Gabe waited beside me at the altar we'd set up at the cliff's edge. The stairs leading to the cove where Calienta and I first met stood behind me. This spot was a testament to our past, present, and future, for we planned to live on this very land.

It was a glorious October day filled with sunshine and foliage, though the classic Irish chill still managed to work its way in there. I would've felt bad for my bride-to-be in her sleeveless dress if Calienta wasn't a goddess.

Calienta's mother, Brigid, took a seat in one of the garden chairs. Next to her, Gabe's parents sat hunched together conspiring, secret smiles on their faces that people desperately in love after thirty years often wore. On the other side of them sat Alistair, my grandfather, who winked at me. His thinning salt-and-pepper hair lifted in the breeze, the strands a perfect match for his bushy moustache.

My father, or Stephen as I'd chosen to call him, because he never deserved the title of "Father," and my turd of a brother, Roger, hadn't made the guest list.

"K, I can't believe you're getting married. You're seventeen, dude." Gabe, my best man, stood beside me. "Not that you've ever done things based on age. You always seem to find your way—even when the odds are stacked against you."

Gabe wasn't just referring to my wedding. I'd graduated from Yale last spring at the age of seventeen. True, most guys my age wouldn't have been getting married, but things with Calienta and I had never been normal.

There'd been little point in pretending that we weren't going to end up together. It didn't matter that I'd only reached my seventeenth birthday and she'd turned four hundred fifty last year. Truthfully, she didn't look a day over eighteen.

Calienta even planned to give up her immortality to be with me. She had voluntarily chosen to relinquish a shot at a never-ending life in exchange for a short blip of time. With me. Her father would be performing the ceremony that would change her into a mortal immediately after our wedding.

"She's the one." I sounded like a cliché from every romance novel ever written, or so I'd heard. Calienta had found an endless offering of romantic paperbacks on Gran's bookshelves. She'd been reading through them, along with binge-watching Gran's action DVDs. It had never made sense that my Irish granny loved *Kung Fu Theater*, but then again, people were never one thing. Calienta certainly wasn't.

As if she could read my thoughts, Calienta beamed at me across the grass. Her delicate lace veil whipped around her thick locks. Braids ran through her hair in all directions, culminating in a fancy creation with a clasp in the back that held it all together. In the two weeks since our engagement, Brigid had immediately gone into wedding-planning mode and I was certain that hairstyle had not been Calienta's choice.

Still, she took my breath away.

"And what's up with her having one name?" Gabe whispered in my ear. "Calienta. That's like . . ."

I couldn't take my eyes off her. My thoughts scattered so that I only half listened to Gabe's verbal vomit.

". . . Beyoncé." Gabe made that wondrous proclamation in his usual surfer-style cadence.

Turning, I stared at him and shook my head. "Gabe, man. Do you mind? This is my wedding."

Besides, Calienta would have a last name soon enough. Before the day ended, she would be my wife. Calienta St. James.

Gabe lowered his head as if in prayer. "Sorry, man. That was way uncool."

Calienta came to a stop directly in front of me, her face flaming and highlighting the red in her hair. "Hey." She'd been trying to speak like a mortal. Sometimes it worked out and sometimes it didn't. In that moment, it was perfect.

"Hey, you." An involuntary smile lifted the corners of my mouth. Before she existed, I'd been alone. Now Calienta was my home.

Lugh took his seat next to Brigid and gave me a thumbs-up. Father Winslow, the round, balding man with a halo of hair and a pink nose, began the ceremony with a brief introduction. We'd opted for the shortest version of the ceremony. Only one part mattered to the two of us.

I should have been paying attention, possibly even absorbing some of it to help me along my way in married life, but I couldn't stop staring at Calienta. Her impossibly blue eyes connected with mine and her emotions, something I was far better at reading than the average fiancé, practically poured into me. I was marrying the girl I loved, and I had no doubt how much she loved me back.

Finally, after what felt like an eternity, the good Father turned to me. "Kellen, repeat after me. I, Kellen, take you, Calienta."

I took Calienta's hands in mine. Her smile crinkled a little, as though she might cry. I squeezed her fingers. It was all I could do to reassure her since she wasn't as good at interpreting my feelings yet. "I, Kellen, take you, Calienta."

Father Winslow led me through the vows as I promised to have and to hold, for better or for worse. The small group of guests faded away until there was only the two of us. As wave crashed against rock, I promised her everything. Tears pooled in Calienta's eyes, but they didn't dare fall unless she wanted them to.

My eyes held hers and chills ran through me. That was nothing new—they always did when I looked in her eyes—but this time the air around us cooled instantly. My breath transformed into a smoke-like cloud. Goosebumps rose on my flesh as the sun vanished behind the clouds.

A crash of thunder shook the ground. The clouds, which as recently as ten seconds ago had been uncharacteristically absent, rapidly regrouped into pre-storm mode. The sea growled, a hungry monster inching its way up the cliffs, though it should have been low tide.

The good Father's prompts faded to nothing as our guests looked up. The next voice that spoke wasn't Father Winslow's. It was menacing, yet with a girlish whine.

"Sorry to interrupt, but there is little point in continuing this wedding. You will all be dying today."

I tore my eyes from Calienta's and spotted a hideous green faerie with a single eye in the center of her forehead.

CHAPTER 2

KELLEN

Dressed in a red leather skirt and a tight black leather bustier that revealed way too much sickly green skin and an unappealing wart-covered cleavage, our unexpected guest stood no more than four feet tall. She was hideous. Although she reminded me of Yoda, something told me this creature wasn't one of the good guys.

Gripping Calienta's hand, I leaned in close. "Who is that? And how am I going to explain a one-eyed wedding guest to Alistair?"

Calienta squeezed my fingers. "No idea. I've never seen her before."

Lugh positioned himself between the stranger and us. The muscles in my future father-in-law's back strained through his suit. "Leave the mortals alone, Cana."

The mortals. No. I whipped my head toward Alistair, but he sat beside Gabe's parents, frozen, as if magick had locked them into a single moment in time and thrown away the key.

"I froze them," Calienta whispered in my ear. "They are better off if they don't know what's going on."

But just as she said this, Gabe nudged his way in between us. "K, is this some crazy cosplay thing? I can't believe you didn't let me in on it. I would have worn a costume."

Any reply I could have fabricated faded into the background as an army of a hundred or more faeries spilled into the space behind the one Lugh had called Cana. They ranged in size from Lugh's height to a foot off the ground.

Our attackers were all members of the group known as the Children of Danu, or the C.O.D., as I had taken to calling them. They were a family of gods and goddesses who'd been forced underground and turned to the Dark Side.

Although I'd killed Arawn, the evil Lord of Faerie who'd imprisoned them, I'd also trashed the realm of Faerie and torn the fabric of time, which had caused a significant amount of turmoil in the realm. Since they hadn't come bearing wedding presents, I could only guess that the C.O.D. were pissed about the aftermath.

"Kellen, Gabe, get behind me." Lugh threw his arms out at his sides. In the next instant, he began to grow taller, changing in shape and form until he stood at his full height, ten feet tall. With the mortals at risk, he'd abandoned all efforts to hide his identity.

"Dude, this is insane." Gabe clutched my arm as though it were all a brilliant show. "How did he do that? Special effects?"

"Yeah, you could say that." Better he thinks that because I had zero idea how I was going to explain this later.

"I said, leave the mortals alone, Cana," Lugh repeated. This time the ground trembled and many of the C.O.D. faltered, turning to Cana.

She let out a macabre laugh that stabbed my eardrums, making me cringe. "You would like that, dear Brother, but we have come to take the St. James boy."

"What? What do they want with me?" I muttered the question to no one as Calienta ran toward the mortals, palms outstretched, ready to defend them.

Lugh inched forward. "Whatever revenge you seek is with me. It is not with him. He has done nothing to you."

"Even you cannot be so foolish as to think he has done nothing. Surely you know what he has in his possession. Or not?" The woman called Cana simpered, her whining voice sending my nerves jangling.

The only thing I had in my possession right then was a Snickers bar, a small Swiss Army knife, and my cell phone. I didn't even have Calienta's ring—Gabe took that honor.

"Let us converse about this." Lugh raised a hand to the sky and the clouds above us parted.

"I have finished speaking with you, dear Brother!" Cana drew back her hand to attack.

Calienta sprang into action. With a wave of her hand, Gabe's parents and Father Winslow disappeared, I assumed to somewhere safe. My girl had serious powers.

Gabe gripped my shoulder. "Kellen, what happened to my parents?"

"It will be okay. *They'll* be okay—"

Before I could cobble together some kind of explanation, Alistair popped into place beside me, eyes wild as he gripped my arm. "Kellen, what is the meaning of this?"

I ducked as a wall of fire flew directly over our heads, just missing us. "Listen, there are some things I haven't told you, but can the two of you give me a minute? We've got a few things to sort out here."

The skies rolled and the clouds formed a single dark mass, creating a barricade that seemed to separate us from the rest of the world. Calienta backed up, aligning herself with Lugh and Brigid to stand between the C.O.D. and Alistair, Gabe, and me.

Cana jabbed a short green finger in my direction. "The boy! He's there!"

The C.O.D. advanced, armed with nothing but magick. Light shot from their palms in every color of the rainbow. It rivaled the one Fourth of July fireworks display I'd been allowed to see as a child.

Cana shot fire from her palms. Lugh thrust his hands outward, pushing the flames away from us. Still, the heat from them warmed me, and the pungent smoke sent tears pooling in the corners of my eyes.

Gabe grabbed my arm and Alistair's, whose balding head was now covered in soot. "Come on, we need to get out of here."

Gabe was right. There wasn't much shelter at our makeshift altar. Better we run for cover than force Lugh to take all the heat.

We raced toward a nearby series of boulders at the edge of the lawn. Faerie fire pummeled the earth behind us as the ground blew up in our wake. Finally we took cover behind the rocks.

Gabe faced me. "This is *so* not a cosplay. What the H is going on, K?"

"Yes, Kellen . . . what Gabe said." Alistair's complexion had shifted to maroon.

Guilt sank into my chest to meet up with the fear lodged there. I should have told Gabe and Alistair the truth when they'd first come to Ireland for my wedding. Yet I'd kept Calienta's identity a secret. I thought it would be safer if neither of them knew about her family, about Faerie, about any of it. I should have known better. Keeping secrets never ended well.

I peered over the rock and jerked aside as a portion of its top exploded, missing my head by inches. "This really isn't the best time."

A familiar group of tiny faeries on horseback tore into the fray, heading straight for Calienta. Palms out, she shot a wall of water in their direction, sending the little Trooping Faeries flying from their mounts and dousing many of the small fires from Cana's offensive tactics.

Yet Cana was ready with more flames. The next round transformed midair into a glowing volley of molten arrows. Before they could strike Calienta, she conjured a raging river of rapids. The water poured from Calienta's hands and rushed to meet Cana.

Calienta's defensive tactic appeared to be working—until Cana froze the water. Instantly it exploded into hundreds of jagged pieces. In seconds, the one-eyed faerie redirected the shards at Calienta.

Calienta knew how to protect herself. I understood that. Still, I was done hiding behind a rock while she risked her life. Leaping from my hiding place, I tore across the space between us and grabbed her hand. Before she could argue, I yanked her from the path of ice and back toward the boulders just as the shards sank into the ground.

Alistair and Gabe scrambled to make room for us. Calienta puffed a strand of hair from her eyes and scowled as her wave of annoyance washed over me.

"I had a plan, Kellen." She sounded ticked, despite the soft lilt of Ireland in her voice.

I pressed a kiss fast and hard to her lips. "Maybe, but I have plans too, and they all involve you. Let's cut the Indiana Jones routine for the time being, if that's okay."

Gabe snorted, but Calienta's brow furrowed as she peeked out from behind the rock.

"You speak in riddles sometimes."

I decided to let that one go. "Why are Gabe and Alistair here? Can't you send them home? That's what you did for the others, right?"

"No way, man." Gabe took off his jacket and rolled up his shirtsleeves—like that was going to help him in a faerie attack. "Whatever the heck this is, I'm not going anywhere."

Alistair patted his forehead with a handkerchief. "Me either." Mud trailed up the legs of his Savile Row trousers.

"Look to the sky." Calienta gestured upward. "Cana and her clan have set up a barrier. No one else can leave until it is dismantled."

My eyes flashed upward. The sky had taken on the appearance of a blurry photo or the air on a muggy day. Great. Unless there was a miracle, we were outnumbered and unable to escape.

"What about my family?" Gabe's voice wavered.

"I got them out safely, Gabriel." Calienta took Gabe's hand. "They think they've returned from a wedding. They can't remember whose. I wanted to keep the lie as realistic as possible. I did the same for the man of the cloth."

"Thanks, C." Gabe smiled as Calienta released his hand, but when he faced me his expression changed. His eyes met mine and narrowed, anger sparking within them. "At least someone is telling me the truth around here. Why did I have to hear it from Calienta?"

A knot of fear built at the base of my spine. Gabe had never looked at me like that. He'd always been on my side, but when he put it that way . . .

"Gabe—"

Before I could craft an explanation, the sounds of fighting stopped and silence filled the lawn. The four of us peered above the boulder. Lugh and Brigid had been captured, their arms bound with a golden cord that squirmed snake-like along their bodies.

Cana's voice rang victorious. "Dear Brother, it seems as though we have won." Her evil grin slid over her face like olive oil on a plate at one of those Italian restaurants back in New York. "I will take the St. James boy after all! He—"

"Will not be harmed!" A familiar voice rang in the clearing, as Calienta's uncle, Dillion, popped into place. Standing three feet tall and wearing a pair of black leather pants, a faux fur pink vest, UGGs, and a pair of aviator sunglasses, he would have drawn all eyes to him, even without his clothing choices.

Raising both hands, Dillion blasted the entire C.O.D. off their feet, barely jostling the red leather beret sitting askew on his snow-white hair. With a wave of his hand, he froze the entire army of C.O.D.

Dillion was one of the C.O.D. himself, the only one I knew of that hadn't turned into an evil, freaky mess. Calienta's uncle had been one of the few to help us in Faerie, so his arrival was the mythological equivalent of the cavalry rushing in.

The little man turned to Lugh and Brigid and raised his palm. A bolt of purple light shot at Calienta's parents, freeing them in an instant. His white beard barely quivered with the effort. Without hesitating, he jogged to where we'd taken cover.

Whipping the sunglasses from his face, Dillion looked me in the eye, something that would have been impossible if I hadn't been kneeling. "Kellen, you must get out of here." His words grated with an unfamiliar raspiness, not his usual high-pitched voice. He also looked older. Much older.

The angry spiral of dark clouds began to diminish as the sun peeked out again.

"What do they want? They said that I had something, but I don't know what they're talking about."

Dillion turned to Calienta, dismissing me. "Niece, get them out of here. You are free to go, but not for long."

Calienta nodded once.

Before I could ask where we were going, Gabe, Alistair, Calienta, and I were sitting in the back of a moving taxicab in the Piccadilly Circus section of London.

Cars zoomed around us in every direction. A symphony of horns penetrated the inside of the cab. We'd been transported from western Ireland to London, England, in the time it took for me to blink. I could still smell the salt-infused air. Freaky.

I looked to Calienta. "Piccadilly Circus?"

She shrugged. "I thought the noise and iron from the cars would put them off. Bad choice?"

"No. It was a good one." Iron was a C.O.D. repellent, along with salt, but I didn't know how long either would work to evade an army of pissed-off faeries.

"C, dude, you beamed us here. This is like . . . *Star Trek*." Gabe's eyes widened, and he stared at Calienta as if she were a circus escapee.

"Hey! How'd you lot get in 'ere?" the cab driver yelled while trying to turn around and keep his eye on the road at the same time.

"Don't you remember?" Calienta gushed. "You've picked us up. You are an excellent driver, Mark." Calienta's sugar-coated tone complemented her heartbreaking smile.

The cabbie scratched his head, searching for a memory he'd never find unless Calienta decided to plant it there. "Sorry about that. My mistake, miss. What's your destination?"

Calienta's forehead wrinkled. Turning to me, she spoke in quiet tones. "I don't know where we should go. They can track me here, and I can't take you to the Green Lands."

The Green Lands, or the heavens as I called it, was Calienta's home. Although it was perfect for her, the place had been designed for gods and goddesses. It exhausted any mortals that spent too much time there.

"Got it. We need to stall." I leaned toward the front seat and patted the driver's shoulder. "Just drive for now, Mark."

"It's your money." But Mark grinned, thrilled at the prospect of a large fare to round out the afternoon.

Gabe faced front, scowling. "It would have been nice to know I could expect this at your wedding, K."

"Gabe, *I* didn't expect this at my wedding."

But I'm not sure I would have told Gabe even if I had. There was too much danger involved. Still, that did nothing to erase my guilt.

"How could I ever have warned you about the hot mess this day would turn into?"

The driver frowned, giving up all pretense of paying attention to the road. "Hey now. My cab's not that bad. I just cleaned in 'ere. Are you tourists? Want me to point out the sights?" A horn blared from somewhere beside us and he righted the car.

"He means no disrespect. Your vehicle is quite lovely, Mark. Well done!" Calienta clapped, beaming. The driver turned three shades of red.

"London?" Alistair's voice sounded far away. "We're in London?"

Turning to Alistair, I touched his arm. "I know. We have a lot of explaining to do."

He looked older. More tired than usual. A small string of worries made their way into my mind. After losing Gran eight months ago, I didn't want to think about Alistair dying.

Alistair shifted in his seat, his moustache turning down at the sides with his frown. "Cut the crap, Kellen, as you Americans say. Tell me what's going on."

Calienta leaned in so that her lips were inches from my ear. "Not here. They could be listening."

The car began to shake then. Its steering wheel jerked first one way and then the other. We slid into one another on the crisp black leather seats, crushing Gabe on the one side.

The driver whirled around, panic etched onto his face. "I can't steer the car! What's happening?" He practically stood on the brake pedal, which couldn't have been easy given the enclosed space. The wheel twisted and turned, weaving us in and out of oncoming traffic. The shifter jerked from second to third gear.

"That's what I'd like to know. C, what's going on?" Gabe asked.

Calienta bit her lip. "They've found us. I hoped we'd have more time."

We were in serious weekend traffic. People and cars were everywhere. Pedestrians poured into the streets from a nearby Tube station. If something went wrong, there were more lives than our own at stake.

"Can you do anything to stop them, or at least slow them down?" I asked.

Calienta shook her head. "It's too risky with so many mortals." She closed her eyes. "Leave it to me."

The car jerked forward at about twenty miles over the speed limit then switched lanes, steering us into the path of an oncoming double-decker bus. None of us wore seatbelts—

there hadn't been time. Gabe and Alistair scrambled to put theirs on. Reaching over, I buckled a seatbelt across Calienta's thin frame before fastening mine.

When the bus drew closer and we didn't move, my stomach lodged itself into my throat. "Calienta. There's a bus. We need to do something."

Her eyes remained closed, her chin tipped up in a regal air. The bus let out three long blaring beeps.

"Hold on, folks. I can't seem to stop this thing." Mark frantically shifted gears to no avail.

"Calienta. The bus." I shook her arm, speaking with greater urgency.

Her emotions swarmed around me—calmness—the opposite of the anxiety that had quickly risen in me. Yet she didn't respond.

Beep! Beep! Beeeeeeep!

Passersby stopped on the sidewalk and cried out in warning.

Gabe patted Calienta's arm. "Come on! You have to wake up. Snap out of it!"

The bus was only a few feet away. Alistair's eyes widened. At some point, all three of us leaned toward Calienta with our hands outstretched, powerless. The bus filled my peripheral vision. This was it, the last moment of my life.

"I'm so sorry!" the driver cried, holding up his hands to shield his eyes.

Calienta opened her eyes and extended her hands out in front of her. Thick fog shot from her palms, surrounding the car and each of us. The sounds from the street dulled. It was as though we were hearing things from the inside of a building instead of a vehicle. White mist swirled through the car and out one open window in the back, enveloping us.

"What's happening?" The driver repeatedly slammed on

the brakes, but they'd decided to stop working. His white-knuckled hands gripped the steering wheel.

Calienta leaned forward. "You'll be going home to your wife now, Mark. It's your anniversary. Buy her flowers. You'll forget all of this." Her voice remained even, without a trace of the anxiety that would be permanently lodged in my mind after this joy ride.

"Dude, this isn't *Star Trek*, she's like . . . a Jedi." Gabe's eyes lit in wonder. Hopefully we'd stop the car before Gabe ran out of sci-fi franchises.

Mark tilted his head. "What was tha—"

But before he could finish his question, he disappeared from the front seat. No silent trailing off, but an abrupt pop. The car drove itself.

I stared at Calienta. "You are amazing."

She turned, first to me and then to Gabe and Alistair. "It's a trick. It won't last, but it will get us somewhere safe until we can think up a plan."

"What are you, young lady? A witch?" Alistair's eyebrows rose nearly as high as his receding gray hairline.

Calienta smiled. "All you need to know is that I love your grandson. That will have to be enough for now."

"If an explanation is coming, I'll wait," Alistair said, though he spoke in a way that indicated he didn't want to wait much longer. "We need to get off this road. My house—"

"Is too dangerous," I said, shaking my head. "We'd lead them straight to you. You can't mess with these people, trust me."

Calienta focused on the road as if she herself were steering. "Kellen's right. We need someplace safe. Somewhere they can't follow."

My brain began its own internal scan, cross-referencing everything I knew about the C.O.D. with possible safe places. "What about Leeds Castle?"

"Leeds Castle? In Kent? Whatever for?" Alistair had a death grip on the arm rest of the car door.

"Because Leeds has one of the finest moats in all of England." I tried to catch Gabe's eye as I spoke. He wasn't looking at me, but he was listening.

Calienta cupped my cheeks and kissed me firmly on the mouth, a move that sent my head spinning. "You're a genius, Kellen."

Technically she was right, but I preferred to think of myself as an average guy. "Thanks. You're not so bad yourself."

"I don't get it," Gabe said. "How's that place supposed to keep us safe?"

"Faeries can't bear to cross running water, and the Leeds moat is fed from an external water source, the River Len. We need someplace where we can safely regroup."

Gabe narrowed his eyes, making him look the part of a stranger again instead of my best friend. "Finally, the truth. Was that really so hard?"

"Faeries. Is that what those things were? I'll be damned." The wrinkles deepened in Alistair's forehead as the seconds passed. "And how do you know this?"

"I took an advanced geography class last summer." It seemed better to explain the castle than the faeries. Fortunately, he didn't argue. Perhaps he'd even written it off as my unusual memory, something he often forgot about until I recalled a fact that no one had ever heard of.

"They're closed on Saturday evenings. Most historic locations are." Alistair's voice was flat.

I met Gabe's eyes at the opposite end of the back seat. Instead of grinning the way he normally would have, he only looked away, leaving me to answer my grandfather.

"Then we'll just have to break in."

I only hoped there'd be no one there to greet us.

CHAPTER 4
KELLEN

The driverless car came to an abrupt, shuddering halt on the circular drive in the barren courtyard at Leeds. Three buildings stood on the tiny island that was Leeds, and a well-manicured lawn stretched out before us. I opened the car door and stepped outside.

It was after six p.m., and though it was the perfect time for a wedding—a Saturday in October—the place was deserted. But something I'd learned from my time in Faerie? Looks were deceiving.

The silence suffocated me. No sounds pierced the night, not even the call of the occasional bird or cricket. The quiet gave the dramatic setting an even more eerie quality. It reminded me too much of Faerie itself. Goosebumps ran across my skin. My suit hadn't been made with the changeable British weather in mind, and the October chill seeped through my clothes.

"Are there guards? What about a security system?"

I offered Calienta my hand, which she took as she climbed from the car.

Calienta took two steps ahead of me, seeming to scan the

perimeter. "No one can see us. For the time being we are safe, but we can't stay here."

Gabe hopped out of the car and bounced up and down in place, reminding me of a fighter before a match. "Okay, wait. This is not *Star Wars*, it's *Mission Impossible*!" Excitement lit his eyes as he helped my grandfather from the vehicle before I had the chance.

"Except we're not in bodysuits and suspended by a cable fifty feet in the air." I grinned, almost forgetting Gabe was angry with me.

Gabe apparently didn't have the same problem. His forehead creased in a way that made me think I'd taken all the fun out of it for him. He glanced away.

"We should get inside." Calienta took my hand in hers, leading me from the taxi.

"What about the car?"

"Leave it to me." Calienta waved her free hand and the cab vanished before my eyes. Probably returned to Mark's driveway, wherever that was.

Alistair swallowed as though trying to digest dinner in a place that served up insects as its main course.

Gabe, on the other hand, seemed energized, as though he'd been waiting for this moment his entire life. He stalked toward a nearly darkened area of the courtyard. "Let's try and access the building this way." He stopped before a plain door. "I'm betting this door isn't secure. The outside is fortified. Why bother setting an alarm on the interior buildings?"

Alistair raised his eyebrows. Though Gabe so often sounded like a stoner, he'd been hailed as a legal mastermind by his Yale profs and had begun his first term at Harvard Law last month. Not too many people got to see that side of him. I, on the other hand, was all too aware of the power of Gabe's mind. I once thought I could argue my way into getting the last slice of pizza. Not only did I not win, but I also ended up cleaning the bathroom for a month. I still had no idea how that happened.

"Good idea." I patted him on the back as I reached for the Swiss Army knife. When I was a kid, I'd gotten good at picking locks. It was more out of boredom than anything else. But before I could unsheathe the knife, the door swung open.

"Coming boys?" Calienta breezed past us and moved into the building.

Gabe smirked, but kept his thoughts to himself. "Whatever you say, C." Without a backward glance, he followed her inside, dipping his head to avoid smacking it on the doorframe.

Alistair was about to follow when he turned back to me. "So this is what's been going on with you?"

"Some of it," I admitted. He needed to hurry up and get inside. The moat should protect us, but I wasn't sure for how long. This wasn't the time for a tell-all.

He nodded. "That explains why you didn't return my calls for so long. Tell me something . . . Calienta . . . do you trust her?"

I remembered Gran holding my hand and urging me to believe in the girl I'd once thought existed only in dreams. "With my life."

Again, he gave me a curt nod. "Then I shall too." He turned and walked through the door and I followed, taking care to lock up behind me.

Our tentative steps led us into a darkened hallway. Alistair and I followed the soft sounds of Gabe's and Cali's voices toward a room up ahead. We'd barely made it over the threshold when Alistair stopped short and I had to grab the doorframe to avoid running into him. Then I froze in my tracks. Lugh stood at the head of a dining table, a grim smile on his face.

"Father!" Calienta rushed into the circle of Lugh's arms.

Giving them a moment, I took in the formal dining room where we'd ended up. There was a large rectangular table made of what looked to be cherry. A set of fine china had been laid across it with a complex assortment of sterling silver place settings. The crystal goblets had been polished to gleaming and placed at the ready, and the white high-backed chairs were drawn from the table as though waiting for guests to take their seats. At one end of the room, an ornate fireplace with a mantle of white waited for someone to throw on a log.

Calienta pulled back to look at Lugh. "Father! Is everyone all right?"

Lugh smoothed her hair, staring as though trying to memorize her face. "We are fine. Dillion ended the attack, but most, including Cana, escaped."

"Where's Mother?" Calienta stood on tiptoe as though expecting to find Brigid hiding behind him.

"She stayed behind to help. I came to warn you and to see how all of you fared." Lugh rested his hand on his daughter's cheek.

Gabe pulled out a seat for Alistair, but my grandfather walked to the other side and selected his own. "I'm not a senior citizen, Gabriel."

That was exactly what he was, but I wasn't going to be the one to bring it up. Gabe smirked but had the good sense to keep his mouth shut and take a seat.

Lugh released Calienta and met my eyes over the table. "Now, I think we owe Alistair and Gabe an explanation. They are Kellen's family, and they have a right to know what he's gotten himself into."

"Yes, that is what I've been asking for all along." Alistair's eyes narrowed as he regarded Lugh.

Gabe remained silent, but he waited, his eyes trained on Lugh's face.

Lugh walked to the wall of windows and waved his hand. The glass shimmered—the same type of shimmer I'd seen in Ireland when Cana put up the barrier. At the time, Cana had intended to keep us from leaving. Lugh probably planned to keep the C.O.D. out.

Job done, he gestured to the dining table. "Why don't you all sit down."

Calienta and I took seats beside one another at Alistair's side. Lugh moved to stand at the head.

"Forgive me as I think about how to explain this." Lugh lowered his voice as he adopted a secretive tone and leaned in toward us, his coconspirators. "It's rare that we reveal our true selves to mortals. My family and I are descendants of the goddess Danu."

Gabe swallowed hard and loosened his tie. "The goddess—"

"We are gods and goddesses," Lugh interrupted in soft tones. "Immortals. We play a pivotal role in this universe. We bring light to the Earth."

Gabe's jaw dropped and then he closed it abruptly. Alistair sighed, his face impassive. They hadn't even heard the whole story yet.

"When I was young, about six hundred thirteen years old, I first visited Earth. In my explorations, I found a cave with drawings depicting a prophecy that named Kellen as the savior of my family and of Earth as we know it."

Lugh rested a hand on my left shoulder and squeezed. I tried not to cringe as my bones cracked. Unintentional chiropractic adjustments were a casualty of hanging with immortals who didn't know their own strength. Seconds later he released me. "There's more to it, but that was the part that stood out."

The prophecy had decreed not only that I would save Earth, but that I would become a god and marry Calienta. To say I experienced a bout of skepticism when Calienta told me didn't even begin to cover it.

"We are here today because of Kellen. He destroyed the Lord of the Underworld, Arawn, but he also helped my son, Cabhan, see the error of his ways. Kellen saved my family, and he fell in love with my daughter."

Lugh's words rang true, but I couldn't take sole credit for killing Arawn. I hadn't done much of anything. After all, I'd wielded a sword that couldn't fail.

"So, Calienta is . . . immortal?" Alistair's eyes widened and his voice strained.

Standing, I moved behind Calienta's chair and put my hands on her shoulders. "She is a Star Child. Her responsibility has always been to light the stars at night. She's immortal." I twisted a lock of Calienta's hair between my fingers.

"And what about you, Kellen?" Alistair swallowed. He hunched in his seat. Perhaps he didn't want to know the answer. "Do you have any special powers?"

I'd played my part on the journey through Faerie, but there was nothing special about me. "I have no gifts. Just a masochistic sense of honor."

Gabe snorted, but when I tried to meet his eyes, he quickly returned to his earlier scowl.

"Kellen is being modest." Calienta reached up to squeeze my hand. "His bravery saved us all."

"I see." Alistair removed a handkerchief from his breast pocket and dabbed it against his forehead. His voice had lost its grouchy grandfather sternness. "Why do they want my grandson?"

"They said I had something." I unbuttoned the top two buttons of my shirt and withdrew the pendant my mother had left me. I'd used it to open the Ellipse, the back door to the heavens. It had even been the catalyst for Cabhan breaking his alliance with Arawn. "Did they mean this?"

Lugh shook his head. "I don't think it's worth their time. We sealed the portal to the Green Lands permanently after you killed Arawn. Your pendant is a family heirloom now. Keep it, though. It holds meaning for you."

I nodded and tucked my mother's gift inside my shirt where the metal warmed my skin.

"No. They claimed to be looking for Danu's amulet." Lugh's grim expression said it all. Whatever this amulet thing was, he couldn't imagine anything worse.

Calienta gasped beside me. "But Kellen doesn't have that. Arawn does—or did. Beyond that, it's cursed."

"What does it do? Give the wearer ultimate power?" Now I sounded like I was quoting something from the movies.

"That's exactly what it does. Arawn used it to control my brothers and sisters all this time. Though I was never sure how. Why they believe you would have such a thing, I have no idea. I tried reasoning with Cana, but she has never been one for conversation."

"So, Kellen and Calienta need to go into hiding then? Find somewhere low-key to stay until all of this is resolved?" Gabe trailed his fingertips over the base of the saltshaker in front of him as he spoke.

"That's right. Since my brothers and sisters won't speak with us, there's little we can do to vouch for Kellen." Lugh stared off across the room as though imagining that very conversation. "Unfortunately Calienta is making it easier for them. Immortals stand out like a beacon on Earth. They have an inner light inside of them that is brighter than everyone else's. That's how I found you all today. I could have used other means, but Calienta's light was the simplest." Lugh spoke the words that crushed me.

"Which means they'll be able to follow us anywhere too.

As long as she's immortal," I added, wishing this was one time I didn't have an answer at the ready.

But instead of agreeing, Calienta tugged her hand from mine.

Her reaction confused me. If our wedding had taken place, she'd already be mortal. I hadn't asked her to give up her immortality—she'd been the one to make that choice.

Slowly, she met my eyes. We both knew I'd sensed her hesitation. All I had to do was be near her and her feelings hit me as strongly as if they were my own. It's how I first recognized that her love for me carried the same weight as mine did for her.

Focusing on Calienta, I let out a slow breath and reached out to her with my senses again. I imagined my mind connecting with hers and Calienta inviting me inside to share in her true thoughts. Often, when her feelings were powerful enough, I didn't need to try to pick up on her emotions— they came to me. Today was not that day. This time when I reached out to her, nothing came back. It was as if she'd blocked me. Calienta had never done that before.

Despite the internal wall, she didn't protest. "Kellen's right. I want to do this."

"You don't have to." But even as I said it, I knew what her argument would be. I'd had the chance to be an immortal and I'd turned it down. If Calienta didn't change now, we couldn't be together. We had to stay together.

"You need to make me a mortal, Father." She squeezed my hand with such force that the bones in my fingers cracked. Unlike Lugh, Calienta usually took greater care with me, which told me all I needed to know about her state of mind. "Then we have to go into hiding. I just don't know where."

Alistair inclined his head to Calienta. "It needs to be somewhere with no ties to Kellen, or to you, my dear."

"I know where we can go." Gabe's expression turned grim

as he pushed his chair back from the table. "It's the safest place I know."

Lugh and Gabe exchanged glances. Whatever understanding passed between them must have been good enough for the Sun God, because he nodded. "Then let's not speak of it, Gabe. You will oversee the plans. Tell no one of your destination."

A mask of seriousness covered Gabe's face. "Understood."

I didn't know how Gabe planned to get us out of our situation, though he wouldn't have volunteered for the job if he didn't have a strategy. Yet one thought that kept springing up in the back of my mind was that we'd chosen to entrust our lives to a guy who'd once put a gallon of milk in the dryer by accident.

CHAPTER 5

CALIENTA

It was all happening so fast. I'd originally made the decision to become mortal after witnessing Kellen's misery at being immortal. At the time, I hadn't thought much of it. I'd only wanted to be with my love. Now, as Father turned to me and we locked eyes, I realized how cavalier I had been with my forever life.

"Are you sure you want to go with him?" Father jerked his head in Kellen's direction as though the man I loved were an annoyance that could be swatted away. He continued as though no one else were in the room but the two of us. "We can hide him on his own. I can take you home. You'd be safe there." His voice, usually so confident, turned pleading.

I wrapped my arms around him and held him close. He'd already lost two children to mortal loves. How could he handle losing a third? Yet our home, the Green Lands, wasn't meant for mortals and I wasn't meant for Earth. But I *was* meant for Kellen.

Alistair crossed his arms in front of his chest. "And why wouldn't she want to go with him? He's a brilliant boy, after all."

How nice. Kellen hadn't had that many people stand up for him in his life. It warmed my heart to see Alistair doing so.

Swallowing hard, I forced myself to meet Father's eyes. I could not speak, could not look at Alistair or Gabriel. The thudding of my heart reverberated in my ears. In the span of several moments, I would become a mortal. Regardless of whether I'd chosen the fate, things were about to change between my father and me, and I needed a moment.

Kellen shifted in my side vision, perhaps anxious that I would change my mind. Yet, there was never a decision to be made. It had always been Kellen.

From the time of my creation, I'd known about Kellen. I'd waited anxiously for his birth and for the time when he became old enough for me to meet him. When we finally came face-to-face, I had known that he was meant for me. Years of spending time with his consciousness, when wardings he himself had not put in place kept us apart, had given me the opportunity to see Kellen St. James for who he really was: a lost, kind-to-a-fault, brave soul.

Kellen was not looking at us. Instead he seemed fixated on the dishes that the castle staff had used to set the table. He wanted me in his life. He had said as much on the day he asked for my hand, and on every day since.

Before Kellen, I had lived in an isolated world far above the one where technology and people buzzed. In the past few weeks, Kellen had shown me so much, and we had not yet left Ireland. He would not bear me any ill will if I asked to walk away from him and declared I wanted to remain immortal, but I needed to be with him.

Good-bye, Father. My whispered good-bye in a voice only my father could hear rang inside my brain like a bell in an empty, forgotten hall.

"Then so be it. We will proceed at once." Father pulled

me to him for one final hug, my last as an immortal. I held him close for several long moments, but when I pulled back, my eyes found Kellen's.

"Wait." He leaped from his chair. "You can't do this."

Panic rose within me. "You don't want me anymore?" My words hardly reached my own ears, fear barely allowing me to utter them.

Father stepped back as Kellen bridged the space between us. He intertwined his fingers with mine. "Of course, I want you, but you're giving up too much. How can I ask you to give up who you are for me?"

The intricate hairstyle Mother had insisted on saddling me with had not held up. The braids were as limp and worn as I felt. Kellen tucked a lock of my hair behind my ear.

What was this nonsense about? I had already made the decision. Should we not just get on with it?

"You did not object when we discussed it before."

"It didn't seem real before. It's real now. I'm afraid of what will happen to you. You'll be able to get hurt, injured, die—" His voice broke.

Suddenly the phrase "'til death do us part" took on a whole new meaning and my annoyance vanished. "Do you think I don't know you can get hurt? Besides, you need me."

A lopsided grin filled his face and I would have sworn I fell deeper in love with him. "I do need you, Calienta, but you have to want this for yourself. I've had enough people control me in my life to know that I'm not going to do that to you." He cradled my cheek in his palm, tracing my bottom lip with his thumb. "If this is what you want, then I'll support you."

I leaned against him, finding relief and comfort in his touch. "It is." It has to be.

Kellen held my gaze for a moment longer, then closed his eyes, reaching out to me with his mind and searching my emotions, checking to see if I meant what I said. Forcing myself to relax, I thought of him, of how much I loved him, and the desire he had awoken within me during our private moments. Slowly, he opened his eyes, his pupils widening. He had picked up on all of it.

After several moments, he lowered his hand and turned to Father. "Do we have to do anything specific for this? Make a circle?"

Father stepped forward, so familiar and so kind. "Surprisingly, the most draining ceremony for an immortal is the simplest."

Dearest Danu, I'd never been so afraid.

Hesitating, Father lowered his hands. "Daughter of my heart, I want you to know that you will always be my daughter and you can always ask for me. Your mother and I will always love you." Tears sprung in his wise eyes, built on years of sorrow and loss.

My own tears trailed down my cheeks. I hated myself for being emotional at a time when I should have been a pillar of strength, an example for the mortals. Yet my world was ending and I could not stop the silent tears that insisted on escaping.

Father led me into the center of the room. Cupping my head in his hands, he spoke one simple word: "*Faoiseamh*."

Then Father's voice filled my head with words for me alone. *Daughter of Air, of the wind that lifts the trees, of the air that breathes life to the world, your bond to Air we sever.*

Memories surrounded me. Calming a hurricane that threatened to take down a fleet of ships, guiding the wind from coastal villages where it might have caused harm, flying in the air with Kellen over Faerie . . .

"Air, I release thee." Father's gruff voice vibrated somewhere deep inside me.

Fresh air encircled us, lifting my hair, ruffling my clothes, like a friend. My lungs filled with its purity, untainted by mankind, as clear and fresh as when Danu herself first fed life on Earth with it.

As quickly as Air had joined us, it dissipated, leaving us once again in the quiet of the room. I trembled as though a piece of my soul had been ripped away. I couldn't have moved from my position if I'd wanted to.

Father's voice returned to my head. *Daughter of Fire, of the heat that warms our hearths, of the warmth that sustains our lives, of the passion that fuels our love, your bond to Fire we sever.*

Reminders of my time with Fire rushed forward: calming a forest fire that had gotten out of control, creating fire for a homeless family on the coldest night of the year, warming Kellen when he grew cold as a child.

"Fire, I release thee," Father continued.

Fire burst into life in the hearth at one end of the room, bright and wonderful. My skin warmed as though I lay on the sand on a hot summer's day. Fire chased away the cold, keeping my immortal soul comfortable at any temperature. Then, as suddenly as it began, the warmth subsided and the cold set in. My teeth chattered.

Good-bye to you too, friend.

Daughter of Earth, of the dirt that feeds our trees, of the ground beneath our feet, of the soil that grows our sustenance, your bond to Earth we sever.

Memories of dancing on a hillside, of standing on the sea cliff in the glorious tall grass, of creating a moat around Kellen's home to protect him . . .

I had an affinity for Earth, and I would miss her. She'd always helped me to remember Ireland, to remember home. My tears built, blurring my vision and lodging themselves in my throat as though they would never leave me.

"Earth, I release thee." Father's kind voice held a hint of sadness.

The room filled with the scent of a spring meadow and

damp earth, and the sensation of sand beneath my toes, scratchy, damp, and somehow soft, ran over my skin. The whip of the salt-water–laden air made my eyes water, though I couldn't blame that solely on Earth. Earth left us then. The sharp, fresh scents were replaced by a cold, musty smell.

Father squeezed my hand as he addressed the final element. *Daughter of Water, of the element that grows the fields, of the rain that breaks from the skies, of the force of all things in life, your bond to Water we sever.*

My memories of Water danced through my head— splashing in a stream, guiding the rain to the parched earth, shepherding the ocean waves from Kellen as he slept in the cove as a boy . . .

This is it, my daughter, came Father's words in my head again.

How will I go on without them?

They will always be with you in spirit, but you will receive a distinctive gift from the element that holds you closest to heart. It will come in the time of your greatest need. Only time will tell which one.

Then Father's quiet thoughts were silenced as he spoke again to the room. "Water, I release thee."

Water began to leak in through the corners of the windows, then suddenly burst from the fireplace and flowed into the room. Gooseflesh rose on my arms as it swirled around me, a whirlpool that gradually built.

But as Water flowed over my skin, it grew warm and calming. It eased the tension in my muscles and swirled around me in an embrace.

Good-bye, my friend.

Then Water began to slow, to lose power. Eventually it evaporated, leaving the space dry, as though it had never been there at all.

The pain shifted from emotional to physical as my immortal life-force left me, and I held myself, rocking forward and back. My skin had been ripped open and parts of me simply taken, as if I'd been cut in quarters. Yet I didn't bleed, couldn't speak, couldn't move or cry out.

Four luminous golden strings rose in the air, winding their way from my chest. I looked on in rapt wonder as they levitated before me. My immortal life-force. The shimmering light left me and broke apart, flitting out of the building through the seams in the windows and cracks under the door and up the chimney. As the last remnants of it left the building, so did my immortality.

All the light, the same light that lit the stars in the sky, had gone back to the heavens.

The room held the reverence of a tomb. I couldn't speak. No one understood what I had lost, what I had sacrificed. Not even my father, for he'd always been an immortal.

Bells rang in the distance, the sound harsh and foreign.

"My family can't see or hear us, but I think the mortal security guards can." A rushing sound filled my ears, making Father's voice sound far away. Perhaps that was how all mortals heard—not with the sharp senses I'd grown used to, but through ears that reshaped sounds until they'd dulled. "We need to get you all out of here. I'll seal the doors."

"Calienta?" Kellen's voice broke through the haze. It sounded scratchy—as if it hadn't been used in quite some time—and filled with worry.

Still, I was unable to answer. A million thoughts competed for attention as my world crashed down around me and the blackness took me. My immortal life, all that I had known, had ended.

CHAPTER 6

KELLEN

I caught Calienta before she could hit the hardwood floor. With care, I lowered her down, cradling her head in my hands as her eyes drifted shut all the way.

"Calienta. Wake up." I shifted her head to my lap as I eased into position beside her.

I hadn't realized the ceremony might weaken her. I'd witnessed it once, when her brother Cabhan had been made a mortal, but I hadn't gotten the chance to catalog the aftereffects. She would be fine, but that didn't ease the ache in my heart. She'd been forced into giving up who she was. I would've preferred she'd made the choice willingly.

A pair of feet stopped in front of me. "Kellen?"

Unexpected tears burned the backs of my eyes as I looked into Alistair's. "I'll talk to you as soon as I can," I said. "I'll call you."

Alistair's entire expression changed. "Kellen, I'm coming with you. I never had a relationship with my own son, your father, though God knows I tried. I don't want to lose you too."

I understood how he felt. After all, I'd spent part of my

childhood with Stephen. There'd been so little love in my life. I'd experienced it only in small pockets of time, after which I'd stored the memories like a miser. This moment would be one of those.

"Thanks." I swallowed my own emotion. "But it's too dangerous. I've been through this sort of thing before. You haven't."

Alistair's brow wrinkled, and he appeared torn between his need to be a grandparent and common sense. Though perhaps both arguments were the same.

"I don't want anything to happen to you. You're the only one I have left. Without you, I'll be alone. Again." My voice cracked on the words. I was still mourning Gran. My mother and Granda had died years ago, and I'd never been close to Stephen and Roger. I honestly didn't think I could stand to lose Alistair.

He reached out and squeezed my shoulder. "No, my dear boy. I think you are many things, but you are not alone." He smiled and the corners of his eyes crinkled.

Worry pressed down on me. "You should call Percy and James—to check in." At least his other sons lived close, and he had Jonas, the butler. He would be all right.

"I'm going to send you home now, Alistair." Lugh traced what I now knew was an invisible protection charm directly above Alistair's heart.

"Thank you." Alistair stared up at Lugh in wonder. "Is this going to hurt?"

Lugh chuckled. "Only if you land on your buttocks, mortal. Safe travels." Once more, the Sun God touched Alistair, this time on the forehead. In a flash my grandfather was sent home.

Sounds of shouting and barking dogs grew near. Lugh walked over to Gabe, and the pair of them held a whispered conversation, heads bowed. Gabe pulled out a notebook and pen. Just as quickly, Lugh shook his head and placed a hand on top of the notebook. Gabe returned it to his jacket pocket. Gabe always had to write everything down, otherwise he'd forget it. Hopefully whatever information Lugh was sharing had enough importance that it would be committed to Gabe's long-term memory. Lugh must have picked up on the same, because he eventually handed Gabe a tiny sliver of paper, which Gabe placed in his pocket, followed by several envelopes that appeared as if they'd just been picked up at an average office supply store.

"This is everything you'll need," Lugh said to Gabe. "Remember, it needs to be a secret. Don't tell anyone where you're going. Not even Kellen."

That wouldn't be hard. Gabe hadn't spoken to me directly since we'd been attacked. He must have felt the same, because my best friend nodded without meeting my eye.

I scooped Calienta up in my arms and pressed a kiss to her forehead.

Lugh moved to stand before me. "I can transport you three from here, but it's best if you have as little traces of my magick on you as possible. You'll be on your own once you leave this place." He nodded to Gabe. "Gabe is in charge."

Gabe stood at attention. "I'm on it, sir."

Lugh placed his hands on my shoulder and Gabe's. "Take care. All of you. My brother Cian, you all know him as Dillion, will find you as soon as he can."

I looked up into the face of my almost–father–in–law. He'd been more of a father to me than Stephen ever had. "Lugh, I—"

"If you hurt her, I'll cut out your internal organs by hand and hang them up to dry." His tone was cutting, but then he softened the warning by squeezing my shoulder.

I swallowed and cleared my throat. "Good enough."

Lugh brought his fingers to Calienta's forehead. Her skin,

which had become ashen, quickly took on a warm golden glow.

Calienta turned to me with vacant eyes, then blinked. "Kellen?" Her voice was weak, like the voice of someone getting over the flu. But that didn't matter. It was familiar. It was Calienta's.

"You're safe. Mortal, but safe."

Her skin felt so much colder now, so different from the heat that had emanated from her before.

"Oh." Then Calienta came to herself. Taking my hand, she slid from my arms as a furious pounding began at the door. The jingling of keys pricked at my ears. The security guards' shouts reverberated throughout the room.

Calienta looked to Lugh and whispered, "Good-bye, Father."

Those were the last words I heard as Lugh beamed us from the castle grounds. Our life as fugitives had begun. I could only hope we'd be able to stop running one day.

Before I could blink, we were in a hallway that reminded me of the cafeteria at my old boarding school. The stark white walls blended into tiles that ran from the middle of the wall down to the floor. The walls were marked up from the times they'd been struck, possibly with utility carts. Large swinging double doors dominated both ends of the hallway. The doors to my left hung dirty, white, and windowless with a kick plate at the bottom. The other doors matched but had windows. Through them, workers moved about, though I couldn't tell what they were doing.

Scuff marks ran across the borderline-clean floor. I went to move and realized I'd been beamed onto a piece of gum. Using the wall tiles as leverage, I did my best to get it off.

"Where are we?" Gabe seemed to be running through the same inventory.

That's when I smelled the food and my stomach rumbled. "A food court or a cafeteria, I think. Where, I'm not sure." I couldn't even remember the last time I'd eaten anything. Calienta would start to get hungry too.

As if in answer, her stomach grumbled. She looked at me with wide eyes. "What is this odd mortal sensation?"

I bit back a laugh. "Are you hungry?"

"I think I might be." She looked down at her stomach as though a beast might live inside.

Gabe turned away, but I caught the grin he clearly didn't want Calienta to see.

Just then, the doors at one end of the hall swung open. A man burst through them and halted, the door continuing to swing in his wake. He wore a chef's outfit: a white hat and a white jacket unbuttoned to the navel, revealing a T-shirt that read *Burn This Mother Down*. An apron and black-and-white–checked pants completed the ensemble. Despite his clothes, the stranger had a couple of inches on Gabe, who was already six foot three, which meant the chef made for an intimidating presence when he placed his hands on his hips.

"Who are you three? Are you the help from the agency?"

Gabe turned on the charm, grinning at the stranger. "We got lost."

The man scowled. "Lost, huh? You better get out of here. I'm calling security if you don't."

Playing along with Gabe's approach seemed the best bet. "No problem. Can you show us the way out?"

The man rolled his eyes as if I'd asked him to cook a five-course meal for us. "Come on, out you go. Follow me."

Without a word, he led us through the doors and into a food court.

"You'd better get on your way before you get into trouble." The man stared us down for several more seconds before turning and stalking back in the direction of the hallway.

"He was *most* unpleasant." Calienta frowned, as though she could see no reason for Chef Happy's attitude.

"That he was. Now, if we can figure out where we are . . ."

Panning the area, I searched for a sign. We'd been set down in the middle of chaos, which made figuring out our location easier said than done. People bustled about with trays. Many of the shops appeared to be cleaning up and winding down for the day as their grates slid into place. Gabe, Calienta, and I stood in the middle of it all, resembling a trio of lost schoolchildren. It seemed as though all eyes were on us.

"I know where we are. Heathrow Airport, London." I'd flown in and out of Heathrow on my last visit to see Alistair.

Great. It looked like we'd be flying today on top of everything else, and I was not a fan of flying.

How was this supposed to help us, anyway? Did Lugh think the C.O.D. wouldn't know how to find the airport?

Gabriel, Kellen, and I stood in the middle of the large, bright area filled with people. It was a space Kellen called the air-o-port. I was not certain what transpired in such a place. Mortals surrounded us, and there were many sounds and scents, not all of them pleasant. Kellen held my hand, grounding me. My head spun from the intensity of it all.

Kellen tugged at the black tie thing around his throat until it loosened and then shoved it in his coat pocket. He turned to Gabriel. "We need to get Calienta out of this dress, otherwise we can forget about going in disguise."

"Agreed." Gabriel nodded as he shot furtive glances around us.

Shopkeepers lined the area. The smells emanating from their stalls made my mortal body rumble. Especially the part right below my belly button.

Belly button? How was it possible that I knew that term? I'd never been mortal before. Yet, as I glanced down and considered my new body, the name for each part echoed in my mind.

Foot, leg, knee, hips, stomach . . . and it continued as knowledge poured into me. How to brush my teeth. How to tell exhaustion from energy. When to wake up and when to fall asleep.

"There's a Starbucks!" Gabriel shouted, his eyes shining with unshed tears as he pointed to a place with green lettering.

It did indeed read Starbucks. So many important words that I would need to learn in the mortal language. I found myself drawn to the place Gabriel had gotten excited about. Maybe it was because it had the word star in the name, but this place seemed magickal. Many delightful smells wafted from within that very place. Was it faerie magick? Danu help me, but I wanted to go inside. "What's a Starbucks?"

"Of course, this would be the place you'd be interested in." Kellen moved in beside me, taking my arm.

"Dearest Danu. Is this the work of the gods? The lights are so pretty, and it smells nice."

Kellen chuckled. "No, it's the work of some people from Seattle. But we do need to go. Everyone's staring. Most people don't wear a wedding dress to the airport."

That's when I remembered my beautiful gown. There shouldn't have been anything special about it. As an immortal, I could have conjured thousands of them in the blink of an eye, but Kellen had bought it for me as a wedding present after I had fallen in love with it. I glanced down. The dress was covered in dirt and stains from the grass. Mud caked the hem.

"Your gift. My beautiful dress. It's ruined." My eyes burned—actually stung—from tears as they built up. The stares of passersby made my face heat. All I could see were people, lights, and movement.

Kellen gently guided me back to him, cupping my cheek so that the most natural thing to do was meet his eyes. "It's a dress. I don't care about the dress. I care about you. We will get married and it will be even more special."

I kept my eyes locked onto his to avoid the other stares. Ones that weren't as kind. "Changing clothes does seem prudent."

He removed his jacket and rested it atop my shoulders so that I could slide my arms in. The heavy material didn't hide much, but it felt better.

A woman's voice filled the large space, announcing a final call for someplace called Bos-ton. Oh, Boston, the mortal city. Air-o-ports had the flying things, air-o-planes. We were flying somewhere. How odd when I could have once taken the three of us there in an instant.

"Kellen, we don't have time to go shopping for Calienta. We have to get on that plane to Boston. You know, the one that's having its final boarding call?" Gabriel glared at Kellen, all enthusiasm at finding the star place forgotten.

Kellen shoved his hand through his hair. "Oh, crap. Where do we have to go."

"Follow me." Gabriel took off at a run.

Kellen's hand clamped down on mine. "Come on, Calienta. Run with me."

My body obeyed as Kellen helped me pick up my skirts and we ran after Gabriel, who never let himself get too far ahead as we navigated through the maze of people.

If I had been alone and mortal, I wasn't sure I would have managed. Thank goodness I trusted Kellen and Gabriel to help me.

And yet you can do nothing to help them. My inner voice rose in my mind, a whispering menace. I detested the sound of it. What I despised even more was that it spoke the truth.

CHAPTER 8

KELLEN

In the end we made our flight, but Lugh hadn't bothered with first class. We'd gotten stuck in the last row on an overbooked flight. I glanced to the darkened window. No lights winked at me from below, which meant we were over water. My stomach flipped in response. I longed to shut the blind but I sat in the middle, and Gabe and Calienta had fallen asleep on my shoulders so the pull was just out of my reach. Sweat beaded on my forehead and the back of my neck. I'd have to deal with the answering blackness for the time being.

Calienta slept soundlessly, though every once in a while she would snuggle closer. I still hadn't gotten used to her lack of warmth.

Gabe snored into my ear, doing a pretty good imitation of a freight train—the ultimate nightmare passenger. "Mmph." He moved closer to me, putting his hand on my chest, a mirror of Calienta.

I shoved at him. "Get off."

He rolled over and then fell back against me, snuggling

into my shoulder. "Mom, I don't want to go to school," he mumbled. "I have to find him before it's too late."

"I'm not your mother and I don't know who you're talking about." My hiss jarred him, and I managed to push him off for good this time and back into his own seat.

Calienta shifted beside me but didn't wake.

My jacket rested across her shoulders. Her passport peeked out from the inside pocket. She'd been given a US passport, but Calienta had no last name. Curious, I slipped her passport free, taking care not to disturb her. Flipping open the firm navy cover, I read her name: Cali St. James. A smile broke across my face. We hadn't gotten married, but she'd still be traveling as my wife.

Calienta stretched and then opened her eyes. Blinking, she looked first to me and then to the open passport in my hand.

"Hey, you." I pressed a kiss to her forehead, forcing my worries aside. "Cali St. James, huh?" When Calienta blinked in confusion, I lifted the passport to reveal the first page.

She took the passport and sat up straighter, running her index finger over her name. "Cali. That's what my sister and brother used to call me when we were younger." She looked up from the passport and into my eyes, her smile spreading across her face. "I think you should call me Cali. It sounds more mortal."

"Cali. I like it." Silently I pondered what age they would have been considered "younger." Fifty? Seventy-five?

With care, I pulled her close and let my questions go unasked.

"We shortened our names. I was Cali, Rowan was Row, and Cabhan was Cab. Nothing elaborate, but we considered it exciting. We could be anyone that we wanted. My mother scolded us. She didn't think immortals should shorten their names." Slowly, her smile began to fade. "I miss them. Especially Rowan."

"I know you do. I'm sorry things had to end up the way they did."

She didn't seem to hear me but stayed lost in thought. Calienta—Cali—hadn't told me much about her sister, Rowan, other than that she'd married a famous musician and lived in Connecticut. I didn't know his name. I had no idea how long ago the wedding had happened either, because Cali's concept of mortal time was definitely skewed.

Cabhan . . . well, his story had been a different one. He'd loved a mortal woman once, but Lugh had refused to grant him mortality in order for Cabhan to be with his love. After years of brooding alone on a star, Cabhan was approached by Arawn, Lord of Faerie, who wanted to partner with him. Their plan? A simple one. They'd kill Lugh and steal all the light from the Earth so that it fell into chaos.

It turned out that the woman Cabhan loved was my great-grandmother squared. When he learned that, he didn't want to kill me anymore, he only wanted to be with Clare. Lugh finally consented to making Cabhan a mortal and helped him travel back in time to Clare. She died several generations ago, which unfortunately meant so had he. He was now an angel in the mortal heavens.

Both Rowan's and Cabhan's paths had led them from Cali. Had she remained immortal she would have been the last true Star Child. Yet even she had left her past behind for mortality and a future with me.

There were a million reasons I'd wanted to marry Calienta, but it boiled down to two main ones. First, she was the one I'd been waiting for my entire life. She'd been in my dreams every night and knew me like no other. There couldn't be anyone else. The second, and the reason I'd moved so fast, was that I was afraid she'd leave me behind, another mortal down on Earth. Time passed differently in the immortal world. An immortal could hang out for a day and an entire mortal life would pass by, or something like that. No one had gotten the time difference down to an exact science.

Of course, Calienta had never given me any indication she'd leave me behind. However, I had a history of being forgotten. I'd wanted to make sure Calienta was always in my life, so I'd proposed. Me, the guy who planned everything he could in advance, had been spontaneous. Too bad we hadn't been able to see the wedding through.

As though reading my mind, Cali's eyes remained on the passport and she touched her name again with one slim finger. "St. James. I like having your name beside mine."

"I like it too." As I spoke, she reached up and touched her hair, as though trying to free it. That weird hairstyle of Brigid's had been falling apart for hours and couldn't have felt great. "Here, let me help."

"Please."

She turned from me to face the window. I ran my fingers through her hair, loosening the braids, massaging her scalp, and freeing the curls. Cali's eyes met mine in the window and my throat ran dry. Once all of her curls had loosened, I gently guided her back to me.

The other passengers were sound asleep. The woman across from Gabe, who'd been complaining about the lack of leg room, snored gently, her jacket draped over her like a blanket. The man who'd been praying loudly throughout most of the journey—making part of me fear an even more imminent death than the one that Cana and company had planned for us—rested his head on his Bible against the window.

Before I realized what was happening, Cali and I were kissing. Our lips sought one another's in the dim light of the airline cabin with nothing but the white noise of the engine surrounding us. Cali sighed against me, pressing closer, sending my thoughts scattering.

"Dearest Danu." Cali's whispered words sent a thrill through me as I lost myself in her eyes. I liked knowing I had the same effect on her as she did on me.

Cali and I hadn't had much time alone since we'd saved the world. Other than our kisses in Faerie and the few that we'd shared since we'd returned (snuck in away from Brigid's watchful eye) we hadn't been close.

This night would have been our wedding night. Had we married, we would have been together. I rested my forehead against hers. "I'm sorry we didn't get married today, Cali."

Her emotions flooded me, a ball of concern and sadness expanding inside my chest. "It's not your fault."

That was kind, but after everything that had happened, I wasn't on board with that line of thinking. "I'm not so sure. The green woman, Can—"

Cali placed her finger to my lips, silencing me. My skin tingled where she touched me. "Don't say her name. We must not speak it."

Nodding, I sat back against my seat, causing it to hit the wall behind me. One of the cardinal rules in dealing with faeries was to never mention them by name. It was known to attract their attention, particularly at night when they roamed the mortal world.

"Do you think they know where we are?" I wasn't sure why I asked. Cali had no more insights than I did now that she was mortal.

She rested her head against my chest and we stared out the airplane window into the darkness. "No. They couldn't possibly. We're safe for now."

Maybe she knew what I wanted to hear, or maybe she

needed to say the words for herself. Either way, I desperately wanted to believe Faerie jurisdiction didn't extend to the Atlantic.

CHAPTER 9
CALI

The cold seeped into my bones, sneaking through Kellen's jacket as the endless flight continued. Kellen and I attempted to rest, but I could not stop shaking, the tremors making the muscles in my arms and legs ache from the stiffness.

"Are you cold?" Kellen's sleepy-sounding voice rumbled from beneath my ear.

My teeth chattered as I wrapped my arms around myself. The dress without sleeves had been a poor choice. I realized that now. Even the jacket wasn't thick enough to protect me. "I think so. I have never felt the cold before. It is *most* unpleasant."

Cali, calm down. You make it sound as though you are lodging a complaint. He'll think you're odd.

Kellen's lips twitched. "Yes, it's very unpleasant, but the good news is . . ." he reached over and extracted a parcel from the back of the seat in front of me, then tore off the covering before shaking out a piece of fabric, "you get a blanket."

He spread the material over my lap. Instant warmth flooded me. The chill remained, but it wasn't anything like it had been. Next, he held up a tiny pillow, which he positioned behind my head. "Better?"

Snuggling under the blanket, I felt a thousand times warmer—a delicious sensation. "Much better."

Kellen took out a blanket and pillow for himself. "You're mortal now." He lowered his voice as he spoke, positioning the fabric over his own long legs and the pillow behind his head. "Many things will be different, but we'll take them one step at a time. I'm with you."

Again, tears welled up in my eyes. *Intolerable*. Did mortals always want to cry? I felt as though that was all I'd done since I'd become one. Yet, try as I might, I couldn't force my tears to dry up. Besides, there was little point in trying to hide my feelings from Kellen.

I took a breath and spoke quickly. "I'm afraid. I don't know how to do anything. I'm . . ." Try as I might, the right words eluded me.

"Vulnerable. Almost like you have to trust someone totally and you're afraid to take the chance?"

As usual, it was as though Kellen had plucked the words straight from my mind. "I'm not used to relying on others."

"And that's exactly how it felt when we met." His ever-patient eyes locked with mine. Their haunting green had always seen into my soul.

That explained so much. When I first appeared to Kellen, he had refused to believe who I was. It was foolish. After all, who else would I have been but me? Still, I had no desire to revisit that time, those moments when he hadn't wanted anything to do with me.

"I had to make a choice to trust you. To take a chance. Though between you and me there was never a choice—it was always you." The green in his eyes intensified, making my face heat.

Kellen pressed his lips to my forehead, breaking the

connection, even though I could have stared into his eyes for the rest of the flight.

"It takes time and patience."

"I can be patient." I smiled at the irritation in my own voice.

His lips quirked as he drew back, settling himself against the seat. "That's something I'd like to see." He expelled a breath and closed his eyes.

After a time, his breathing evened out and he relaxed his grip on the blanket. When I glanced up, it wasn't into Kellen's eyes, but into Gabriel's, who had finally awoken.

"C, what will they do to him if they catch us? If they catch *him*?" Gabriel's voice sounded strained from the effort of whispering.

I opened my mouth to explain that I didn't know, but there was one part I was certain of. "They'll keep him, Gabriel. Forever."

Gabriel blanched, but there was little I could do to comfort him. Once you became a prisoner of Faerie, you never escaped. At least that's what I'd always been told.

CHAPTER 10

KELLEN

When I woke, Cali and Gabe were chatting in low tones over me. I stretched my arms to the ceiling and the pair sat up as I unintentionally ended their discussion.

"Sorry, guys." I looked to Cali, then to Gabe, who quickly looked away.

Cali brightened. "I am glad you rested."

"Rested is generous." I checked my watch. We were about five hours into the flight. With the time change, though, it was only around eight o'clock at night.

Though I'd slept, no dreams had come to me. After so many years of vivid dreams with Cali at center stage, I half expected to see her whenever I closed my eyes. Yet she no longer needed to haunt my dreams. She'd moved into my reality.

Excusing myself, I got up and headed for the facilities. Walking felt good. Even taking the three steps to reach the bathroom represented some movement.

I shut the door behind me and slid the lock into place. Out of habit more than interest, I examined myself in the tiny mirror under the dingy lighting then splashed cold water on my face. I needed coffee. It seemed easier to focus on such a mundane thing as caffeine than on the freaks following us.

When I was finished in the bathroom, I opened the door and found Cali standing outside. It occurred to me that she probably didn't know about basic mortal necessities. Yet she brushed past me with confidence and shut the door. I stayed behind for a moment to make sure she was okay. After I heard running water, I left her to it and returned to my seat.

Gabe stood up to let me pass. "I bought breakfast." He grumbled the information and faced front, his profile stony.

A too-small cup of coffee steamed in invitation on my tray table. A cold bagel with a packet of cream cheese sat on a small square napkin with the airline's logo printed across the front.

"Thank you so much. I owe you one." I lifted my breakfast from the tray, locked the tray in place, and drank down my coffee in a single gulp before sitting. I bit into the bagel and the coldness hit my tongue. It had probably been stored in a freezer somewhere. Toasted bagels were a favorite of mine, though I could guess what names I'd be called behind the flight attendants' curtain if I asked them to toast my breakfast. Swallowing, I turned to Gabe. "Boston, huh?"

Gabe bit into his food. "You'll see where we're going. I'm not supposed to talk about it." His words were mumbled as he chewed.

"I know you're not, but what's up with you? And since when have either of us ever done what we were told?" I leaned in, careful to keep my voice down. "You've done nothing but give me the evil eye since we started this trip. I promise to tell you everything when we get somewhere more private, but there hasn't been any time."

"I know, but it doesn't mean I can't be pissed at you in the meantime. Drop it, Kellen." Gabe kept his attention centered on his bagel.

This was a strange side to Gabe. Though he was five years older than me, I'd always been the one in charge. He'd looked to *me* for guidance.

Pushing my thoughts aside, I took the last bite of my bagel. I waited, watching out of the corner of my eye for Cali's return, but there was no sign of her.

"Cali's been gone too long."

Gabe was instantly at attention, searching the aisles. I climbed over him and went back to the bathroom. A line of several annoyed people had formed outside the restroom door. My heart pounded. Had they gotten to her? Had she been kidnapped?

Gently I pushed to the front of the line. "Excuse me. I'll check on her." I placed my cheek against the door so I'd be able to hear if she was hurt. "It's me. You okay in there?"

"I don't know how to open the door." Exasperation shaded Cali's voice.

I tried not to laugh as relief filled me. "Um, did you unlock it? Pull the handle to the left."

Minor shuffling ensued. "Where is the handle?" She uttered the words with short, crisp articulation.

"You could always read the directions." But then another question popped into my mind. Did she know how to read? I needed to understand what Cali did or didn't know.

Another moment passed and the door opened. Cali emerged looking annoyed as she stepped aside to let the next occupant pass through. When he shut the door behind her, part of her gown caught. As Cali moved forward, a distinct ripping sound broke through the white noise in the cabin. I reached down and ripped a small part of her gown off to free her. The other passengers waiting in line gasped audibly as their faces transformed into pictures of shock.

"It's not real. We're going to a concert."

Without waiting for their reactions, I placed my hand on the small of Cali's back and led her to our seats. She climbed over Gabe, picked up her bagel, and started eating it as she sat down.

"Not a word, Kellen," she whispered as she glared at me.

"What?" A laugh escaped me, but her annoyed look made me regret it instantly. I turned to Gabe, who normally would have taken my side, but he remained stony.

The flight attendant picked up the microphone. "Ladies and gentlemen. We're—"

He didn't get the chance to finish. The plane shook and swerved. Tray tables rattled, and people walking about the cabin stumbled. Luggage slammed around inside the overhead compartments. The plane accelerated, abruptly taking a nose dive.

Passengers screamed, grabbing for their families. Around me, people frantically scrambled, probably trying to remember the safety instructions they'd studiously been ignoring for years. The praying man in the corner increased the velocity of his prayers, which only served to up the amount of drama in the cabin. We were stuck in the middle of every traveler's greatest nightmare.

Gabe and I looked to one another. We didn't need to speak because we already knew.

They'd found us.

I tried not to think about all the passengers on the plane. They would all die, every one of them—because of me.

CHAPTER 11

CALI

My knuckles whitened as I gripped the air-o-plane seat with every ounce of my mortal strength.

Panic filled Kellen's face as we sped toward the sea. "We have to do something." He stared at me, pleading, yet I was as vulnerable as I had predicted.

"Kellen—"

I couldn't finish the sentence out loud, but he seemed to hear the ending nonetheless. *There's nothing we can do.*

Gabriel shuffled through the papers Father had given him. "Dammit. Where is it?"

"What? What are you looking for?" Kellen sat up straighter, searching the floor for whatever item of Gabriel's had gone missing.

"The paper. Lugh gave me a paper." He continued his search, checking his pockets frantically. "Hold this." He handed Kellen the white papers we'd used to board the plane and returned to checking his jacket.

Alarms had begun to sound. Frantic whispering and crying filled the cabin. The scent of fear, indescribable yet immediately identifiable, filled the air.

Then finally, after his third search, Gabriel withdrew a small strip of parchment from his jacket. Holding it close to his face, he scanned it repeatedly before clearing his throat. He spoke his next words with an unfamiliar authority. "*Glaoim ar mo theaghlach.*"

"What did you say?" Kellen gripped Gabriel's arm.

Gabriel ignored him and continued staring ahead, radiating an air of calmness. "*Glaoim ar mo theaghlach.*"

The screams grew louder, rising to a fever pitch until suddenly the air-o-plane leveled off. The shaking stopped, the alarms silenced, and a shocked hush filled our cabin. A feeling of lightness washed over me then, as though I'd been carrying twenty weights and finally had the chance to set them down. The air-o-plane flew smoothly once more, and we continued our descent.

All the color drained from Gabriel's face. He stared at the paper then tucked it inside his pocket with one hand as he gripped the arm of the seat with the other.

"What did that say?" Kellen asked.

"I have no idea." A scowl distorted Gabriel's normally sunny expression. "Lugh didn't tell me. He just handed me this piece of paper and said it was for emergencies." Gabriel faced me. "Do you know, C? He's your father."

His eyes lit with hope as if I might know what had been written on the paper. I didn't. Without even looking at it, I knew that I didn't. Even when I'd been a goddess, I hadn't needed to rely on spell work, except for the occasional protection charm.

"I don't know what would have possibly had that effect."

The flight person's voice returned with calm words for the passengers. "Sorry about that, folks. We're not sure what happened there, but everything's fine now. We're now making our descent into the Boston area. The local time is nine forty-five p.m., and the temperature is forty-four degrees Fahrenheit. For those of you with connecting flights, we'll review the gates . . ."

Ignoring the rest of the announcement, I continued to watch Gabriel. "Can I see that piece of paper?"

He shook his head, his mouth flattening. "No."

Kellen tried again. "We're going to Boston?"

"Trust me, K and C. I'll tell you when I can. I don't lie to my friends."

A pounding sound echoed in my ears. The air-o-plane prepared to land, and the noise drowned out Kellen's words, but Gabriel seemed to have heard him.

"You know what it's about. You're a liar. You don't tell me what's going on, and now Lugh gives me this piece of paper and I steer the freakin' plane!" Gabriel forced the last word down so that it came out in a whispered hiss.

"What does that piece of paper have to do with me?" Kellen's voice hardened. "And I never lied to you, okay? I was just trying to protect you."

"What if I don't want your protection?" Gabriel hissed.

Mortals nearby were now watching us. The last thing we needed was to draw attention. Kellen and Gabriel's behavior fell under the category of "careless."

"You kept things from me, Kellen. You haven't spoken to me in months! Then you're all like, 'Gabe, come to my wedding on the other side of the ocean.'" Gabriel punched the upright tray table in front of him to enunciate the word ocean.

Kellen stared. "We told you what happened, why—"

"No, you didn't tell me anything. Lugh did. You're supposed to be my friend." Gabriel and Kellen had leaned over in their seats so that they were now almost nose to nose.

"I *am* your friend. That's why I didn't call you and drag you to a party in hell. I didn't think you'd be interested."

I took off my belted seat—after a couple of tries—and stood, glaring at them. "Please stop!"

"Young lady, please take your seat," the flight person warned me from his place in the back of the cabin.

My eyes shot to him but found him limited in the muscular department. I remained standing. I could defend myself from him if needed.

"Gabriel. Kellen. Stop this at once." I sounded like my mother, which I hated, but there was nothing for it. Either way, it worked. Kellen sat back in his seat and Gabriel did the same.

"Young lady, if you don't take your seat this instant, I'll call security," the flight person threatened.

I stared at the flight person. Yes, I could have bested him, but I didn't want to call any more attention to myself than I already had, what with getting stuck in the bathroom and all. "I am sitting. My apologies."

Gabriel and Kellen both seemed to calm themselves, though the air between them remained like a mental battlefield.

"Can we call a truce?" Kellen asked.

Gabriel's almost imperceptible nod dissipated some of the tension.

We sat in silence as the air-o-plane drove down the runway to the gate. After an interminable amount of time passed, during which no one spoke, Kellen finally broke the silence. "Where are we staying in Boston?"

Gabriel didn't look at him. The air-o-plane came to a stop and a light went off. People unbuckled immediately and stood up in their seats.

"We're not." Gabriel stood, and we waited for the passengers in the many rows in front of us to disembark. Then he looked down, meeting my eye. "We've only just started."

Kellen stretched and then righted himself, a grim smile on his face. "Then let's hope we make it to wherever we're going alive."

From the look in Gabriel's eyes, we shared the same fear.

CHAPTER 12

KELLEN

Gabe's shoulders hunched as the airline herded us off the plane and down the jetway. The gray carpet on the floor had probably once looked trendy and new, but had since worn down, the result of countless footsteps from the thousands of passengers who'd come before.

Despite our safe landing, I couldn't help but look over my shoulder as we walked. The C.O.D. obviously knew we'd gotten on the plane. Yet there was no sign of them now. The airport looked like any airport at night. Vendors had closed, weary business travelers hauled laptops with overnight bags.

Forcing the worries from my head, I tried to focus on the present. I tapped Gabe on his shoulder. "Should we rent a car?"

"Let me handle it." He didn't turn around, only kept walking.

Cali touched my arm before I could respond. She didn't need to say anything. This wasn't the place.

My almost-bride seemed sleepy but otherwise okay. Her dress had wilted, and the train was absolutely wrecked from where I'd torn it earlier. I'd reckon even Cali was past the point of caring on that one.

We made it through customs, and I plastered a smile on my face, trying not to look shady as we went through immigration. Please don't let there be a problem with our passports. If we were stopped, I'd crash right then and there. Yet there were no issues. We breezed through as though we weren't presenting magickally manipulated passports to Homeland Security.

Cali got stuck on a turnstile before the exit. She stared at the metal barrier as if deciding whether to go over or through it. I intervened when Cali lifted her skirts.

"Let me help." I pushed the handle, moving it forward and freeing her.

She glared at the offending turnstile and then at me.

"It could have happened to anyone." I deliberately made my voice solemn and forced all traces of humor from my face.

Gabe didn't meet my eye, though I could have sworn I glimpsed the ghost of a smile there.

"Let's go." Cali swept down and picked up her torn skirts.

The airport wasn't crowded, but the people that were there gaped at Cali as if transfixed. It wasn't every day that they got to see an exceptionally beautiful girl walking through the airport in a filthy wedding dress. Cali wasn't helping matters by gawking at everything in wonder with her mouth agape.

Gabe led the way, consulting signs as he navigated the airport. He kept ahead of us, never meeting my eye or interacting as we bypassed baggage claim. None of us had brought luggage.

One long walk and a short shuttle ride later and we stood outside the rental car section of Ground Transportation. Gabe left us beside a large round support with a number one on it and walked over to the counter. Smiling, he held up his phone.

Cali pulled my jacket more firmly around herself and hugged her arms. Her teeth chattered audibly. She all but sagged against me. Hopefully we'd get where we were going soon so she could rest.

I wrapped my arms around her and drew her close. "They know where we are, don't they." I pressed my lips to her forehead and did my best not to think about how we'd almost died on the plane.

"They did know before, but I think my father's spell may have cloaked us."

I stilled against her. "Spell? What do you mean, spell?"

"The piece of paper my father gave to Gabriel. The writing on it had to have been a spell." Her brow crinkled in concentration. "That's the only way I know of that he could have conceivably stopped the plane from crashing."

"So it wasn't just a coincidence?" Part of me still thought if I plugged my ears and closed my eyes that the magick would simply vanish. I'd never had any such luck.

Cali laughed, and somehow, even without her immortality, it still sounded like bells tinkling. "You should know by now there are no coincidences."

Gabe returned after about ten minutes, and Cali and I followed him, scanning the empty garage for anything out of the ordinary. We didn't have long before we reached a mid-sized teal-colored SUV.

I offered Cali the front seat, but she asked to take the back. Shadows had begun to form beneath her eyes. I helped her inside and buckled her in as Gabe started the car. Cali shivered.

I climbed into the passenger seat beside Gabe. "Would you mind turning on the heat? Cali's freezing."

"No problem." He switched on the heat and twisted the

dial to full blast. Then he adjusted the mirrors and seat to accommodate his height.

Peering over my shoulder, I found Cali already asleep. Heat flooded the front of the car. With Cali settled, I could focus on Gabe.

Gabe muttered something under his breath. It sounded like the words he'd spoken on the plane.

"What did you just say?"

He rubbed the back of his neck. His collar stuck up on one side, his tie long ago loosened. He met my eyes as he spoke. "I don't know, but it seemed like what I said . . . helped. I figured it couldn't hurt to say it again."

"Good idea." I stared out the window, my own reflection looking back at me. "We do need to get Cali something to eat and clothes for all of us. Unless you want to hang out in this suit for however long we're going to be on the run."

"Agreed. Just let me get out of here first." Gabe put the car into reverse, shifted into drive, and headed toward the exit. We drove out of the airport lot and after about fifteen minutes merged onto I-95 North. We were going farther into New England.

CHAPTER 13

CALI

The journey was not uncomfortable. The seating in the vehicle Gabriel had acquired was marginally better than that of the air-o-plane. Still, I could not seem to get warm despite the heat pouring into the vehicle.

Gabriel pulled to a stop outside an immense building. Lights were ablaze on the interior, and cars dotted the parking lot at intervals.

"Is this where we're hiding?"

"No, C." Gabriel grinned at me from the front. "This is Walmart. We need to get supplies, like new clothes and food, among other things."

"And all the table salt we can find." Kellen winked at me and my heart fluttered inside my chest for a million reasons I couldn't put into words.

Inside the building we came to a large section of what appeared to be women's clothes. The options seemed to go on forever, and I found myself quite overwhelmed at the choices.

"I'm not sure I know where to begin."

Kellen's quick smile didn't disappoint, and he guided me

in between the racks. "I'm at a disadvantage myself since I don't know where we're going, but we seem to be headed north. That means we pick out lots of warm things. I don't think we can go wrong with a sweatshirt and sweatpants." He tugged some items from the rack and held them up as though comparing them to my body.

"Sweatshirt. Must one perspire while wearing it?" I didn't like the sound of that. I'd never once broken a sweat as an immortal. I didn't plan to begin that odorous habit now.

"No. Not exactly." He selected a pink sweatshirt and a matching pair of sweatpants that read I Love Boston. "Will these do? I've never picked out clothes for a girl before. Heck, I haven't had much experience buying clothes for *me*. I have no idea what size you wear, so I'm guessing."

"Those are satisfactory. Thank you." I beamed at him, clutching the clothing to my chest.

"You need to try them on. You'll need to get out of your wedding dress first though." He gestured to my gown, his eyes not quite meeting mine.

"So it would seem." I sighed and removed Kellen's jacket, handed it to him, and then began tugging down the shoulder strap on my dress.

Kellen's eyes widened and he threw his hands out at his sides as though to shield me.

I froze, releasing the strap. "I'm doing something wrong again, aren't I."

"It's all right. Most people change clothes in private." He led me into an area marked Fitting Rooms and pointed to a nearby open doorway. "You go in there."

Of course. Mortals were much more comfortable covering up their nudity! As a goddess, I'd rarely worn clothing and had always been at home in my natural state. Perhaps Kellen wasn't prepared for such views? Shrugging, I spun on my heel and headed toward the small room.

"Wait." Kellen caught up my elbow. "We need to unzip the back of your dress."

I'd always been comfortable with my body, yet the moment Kellen's fingers graced my back it was as if every part of me had come alive. He dragged the zipper down, and though the cool air hit my exposed back, I felt flushed.

I turned to Kellen and he, too, seemed undone. His voice had gone hoarse and his eyes filled with something unfamiliar. "When you get in the stall, pull the zipper the rest of the way down to get out of the dress."

"Thank you." My voice came out in a whisper. After a moment I turned and made my way into the fitting room. Once I'd shut the door, I leaned against it, my heart pounding.

Kellen and Gabriel's voices reached me, and I shook my head and forced my ruined dress off the rest of the way. My beautiful gown. Yet it did no good. It wouldn't work for where we were going. Even I knew that.

I changed quickly after that and found, to my surprise, that Kellen had guessed my size correctly. The new clothes were not only infinitely warmer, but a perfect fit.

Scooping up my dress, I exited the room and stuffed my gown into the bin of garbage by the door. Only magick could save it now, and I no longer possessed any. Pushing aside the wave of sadness, I went out to meet Kellen and Gabriel.

"Better?" I held my hands out at my sides.

"Much. What did you do with the dress?" Kellen asked, taking my hand as Gabriel walked ahead.

"I left it behind." Tears welled in my eyes. "Your beautiful gift."

"You'll have another one that you'll love even more at our next wedding. Next time we'll really get married. Not that this practice one wasn't entertaining."

Warmth flooded my chest. "At least we can say it was that."

We shopped as quickly as possible, always staying together. Since we'd determined my size, Kellen merely held up things for me to approve. Clothes, outer garments, undergarments, and shoes and boots for all of us went into the basket with wheels. It took longer than necessary as Kellen kept wandering down the aisle of books. Finally I had to admonish him as he perused a volume on birds, of all things.

Kellen paid a sleepy-looking young woman for our purchases. She didn't so much as blink when we shared that Kellen, Gabriel, and I were wearing our new things out. Gabriel's and Kellen's suits received the same treatment as my gown—the bin. The fabric had been torn and couldn't be saved.

When we returned outside, the cold didn't seem as bad as it had before, thanks to my new fleece pants and something called a poufy coat.

Our mountain of clothing bags formed a small pyramid on the rear seat, while more bags packed with dry goods and other food supplies filled the rear of the vehicle.

"Here. Why don't you eat something?" Kellen handed me a package labeled Trail Mix.

"Thanks." Yet, try as I might, I couldn't get the package open, even when I pulled at the words "Tear here."

Kellen held out his hand and I relinquished the mix. He smiled as he handed it back, open. "Here you go."

"Thank you." I narrowed my eyes, ready to admonish him for teasing me, but his smile seemed reassuring. Perhaps the bathroom incident was the last of it. *Or perhaps you should stop being so sensitive about all of this. Dearest Danu, I had been moody about it all, hadn't I?* "The mix of trails is . . . awesome." I smiled at Kellen as I found myself shaking the last bits into my palm.

"Good." In a flash he'd opened another and offered it to me. "Have some more. You need to eat, and it will be a while until we can put together a normal dinner."

"Thank you." I accepted his offering and dug into the bag filled with nuts and chocolate wonders.

Gabriel met my eyes in the mirror, his own smile widening. "You all right back there, C?"

"Yes, thank you, Gabriel." I finished my food and then added the empty wrappers to the bag Kellen had set upon the floor for garbage.

With my belly full, exhaustion washed over me almost instantly. Kellen unearthed a blanket from one of the bags and tucked it in around me from the front seat. Warmth enveloped me, and no matter how I tried, I couldn't keep my eyes open. The world around me winked out.

Cali slept hard as we sped down the darkened highway, headed for who knew where. There was a small chance that she'd only closed her eyes to give Gabe and me privacy, but the soft sounds she made periodically said otherwise.

Which meant the conversation I'd been dreading could no longer be avoided. It was time to come clean with my best friend.

"Gabe, I am sorry. I should have told you about Cali. About all of this." It wasn't hard for me to apologize. I wanted Gabe to know the truth.

I searched his hard exterior for any signs of a crack as he stared at the road ahead. There were none.

"Cali showed up and then everything . . . happened."

Gabe looked down at the wheel and then out to the road. "You're pretty young to be getting married, Kellen. Have you ever even been on a date?"

Ouch. That was a slam.

It would've been easy to lash out with something caustic, but that wouldn't win back Gabe's friendship. As Gran used to say, fighting is easy, it's keeping the peace that's difficult. Pushing my resentment aside, I continued. "No, I've never been on a date, but there's a reason for that. It has to do with something I've been wanting to tell you."

There'd been many things that I'd kept from him. The journey through Faerie, the duel with Arawn . . . Where could I begin?

"Cali and I met when I was a kid."

"You've never mentioned her to me." His tone twisted his words into an accusation, but he kept his focus on the road. "Didn't you trust me?"

"I knew I could trust you. That wasn't the reason." The car had grown painfully quiet, save for the constant hum of its engine. Darkness pressed in on us from outside. The only light came from highway lights hanging overhead at every quarter mile. The next one illuminated an exit and Gabe swerved off the highway without warning.

I squinted at the sign. "Peabody. We're going to Peabody?"

"No, it's a diversion." Gabe kept his voice even.

"If they even have a clue as to where we are, then we're better off sticking to the main roads. No point in getting lost on a bunch of rural routes."

Gabe seemed to consider my opinion for a split second before coming to a stop at the end of the exit ramp. We sat there for a moment, then he looked first left, then right before he drove straight onto the ramp across from us and merged back onto the highway.

"Then what was the reason?" Gabe's voice still had a hard edge to it. "If you trusted me, what was the reason you didn't tell me about Cali?"

I tried to figure out how I could word my thoughts so I didn't sound insane, but in the end all that mattered was that I shared them. "I didn't want you to think I was crazy."

There, I'd said it, and my geekiness was out there on display. I had no choice but to continue. "You don't know what it was like, okay? I was the only guy my age at college. It never mattered that I aced every class or was ranked the best in each. The only thing that mattered to other people was my age. No one would even talk to me."

Gabe frowned, his hands gripping the steering wheel tighter. "People liked you. I never saw you have any trouble."

"You wouldn't have because they were all paying attention to you. Everyone loved you, Gabe. You were the best—you *are* the best friend I could ever have."

"Thanks." His response was barely audible over the engine.

"When I stood beside you, no one noticed I was there, but they didn't tell me to leave either. I belonged. That's something I never had before. College would have sucked for me without you, but instead, it was great."

My years at Yale had afforded me an unprecedented amount of freedom. Stephen had had an easy time keeping tabs on me when I was at boarding school, but college allowed me to do whatever I wanted with Gabe as my friend.

Delaying the inevitable, I leaned into the back seat and grabbed the package of Snickers candy bars from the bag next to a sleeping Cali. I opened the outer package and took out a Snickers. "Want one?"

He shook his head. "Nah, I don't eat that stuff anymore."

"Since when?"

"Since I started watching what I eat, dude. Gimme a granola bar."

"Granola? What are you, an old man now? You watching your fiber?" I laughed for the first time since Gabe had stood next to me at the altar, and it felt good.

Gabe snorted, but knowing him as I did, I had no doubt

that a full cross-examination would follow. I handed him a granola bar and then tore into my Snickers.

"As I said, I met Cali when I was six. I'd gone to my gran's in Ireland with Stephen and Roger."

Gabe grunted. He hated it when I called my father "Stephen."

He knew of my brother but had never met him. Roger could be best described as a loser and a younger version of Stephen. I often referred to him as "The Turd." The presence of the word *the* implied Roger had reached a certain status as a turd—the highest level possible.

My stomach rumbled greedily as I polished off the rest of the chocolate. I considered another, but instead balled up the wrapper.

"Did your mother go with you? To Ireland? You only mentioned your father and brother." Gabe bit into his granola bar.

"My mother had already passed by then." Or at least that was what I'd been told.

"Yeah." Gabe's voice softened. He knew about my child-hood: my mother's death, my trip to boarding school and early admission to Yale, and even some of Stephen's cruelty, yet Gabe had always insisted that I should make more of an effort with Stephen. I doubted he would have if he'd known the latest.

Earlier that year, pre my fantastical journey through the world of Faerie, I'd inherited Gran's cottage in Ireland and a substantial amount of money. After graduation, I'd decided to move there and focus on my writing. My degree in literature had been the first stepping-stone toward getting my work published.

Cali had been the one to help me find a stack of letters from my mom, as well as the truth. My mother hadn't died in my youth as I'd been told.

Stephen, tired of caring for her progressing cancer, had had her committed to a mental hospital. Not because she was insane, but because of her illness and short life expectancy. Apparently that combination made my mother a *messy inconvenience*. She died in an institution in Northern Scotland, hidden by Stephen's money and influences. But one thing at a time.

"Cali showed up with Lugh on the beach, and I felt a connection to her. I wanted to go with her, but she wouldn't let me. It was like, from the instant we met, she was all I could think about. Gran told me Cali was a legend—a Star Child. As much as I'd wanted Cali to be real, I figured she must have been a dream."

"Why did it matter whether she was real or not?" Gabe seemed less angry now and more curious.

"She made me feel like everything would be okay. Like I had a friend." I forced my confession. Sharing that side of me with anyone, even Gabe, went beyond my comfort zone. I'd been taught that emotions were a weakness. A vulnerability. Relationships were battlefields, with each side choosing their own strategies. If your opponents knew your weaknesses, they could take you down. Destroy you. It was better to keep my feelings close.

At least that had been my approach until recently. When I decided to trust Cali, something inside of me let go. I didn't want to lock parts of myself away anymore. Being alone had become exhausting.

Gabe's features softened from their rigid state of a few moments before. "How did you two find each other again?"

"I'm not sure we were ever apart. After we met, I dreamed about her every night for eleven years. It was always the same dream, about our first meeting. Then after Gran died, Cali showed up."

The car hit a bump in the road as Gabe slowed for a

construction zone. No one was working, and abandoned signage sat positioned at various angles, ghosts along the highway. The car's lights bounced off the reflectors on the bright orange cones as we passed.

Another bump in the road jostled us. Cali was still out cold. A ball of warmth filled my chest as I watched her sleep.

"So, these past few months, K. What happened then?" Gabe reached for another granola bar and I held up the bag for him.

"Cali showed up at Gran's place when I got to Ireland. She told me about this prophecy and my part in it. That we were destined to end up together."

Gabe let out a low whistle. "Dude. That must have been a lot to take in."

Dizzy with relief that Gabe sounded like Gabe, I continued. "You have no idea. I didn't get a lot of processing time though. Lugh got kidnapped and Cali needed my help, so we went into Faerie. I had no choice."

"You could have walked," he began, but he ended up responding to his own comment before I could. "Nah, you wouldn't have done that." He shot me a sideways glance.

"She needed me. No one really knows why the prophecy is about me, but if there was a chance that I could help her, I had to. Besides . . . I'd already fallen in love with her by then."

Even that explanation didn't do justice to what I felt for Cali. She'd taken hold of my hand, taken over my heart, and turned everything I'd ever known on its side.

Gabe nodded. "I'm not surprised you love her. I guess I've always known that."

I whipped sideways, jamming my knee into the console. "What do you mean, you've always known?"

"You kinda talk in your sleep. Every night you'd say her name. Mostly I just heard 'Calienta, don't go' or 'Calienta, please don't leave me.' I thought she was an ex-girlfriend or something. I wanted to ask but didn't want to interfere."

Wow. "But you've never held back before."

Gabe inclined his head toward me, still being careful to keep his eyes trained on the lonely road. "Kellen, you've had so many things happen to you, man. You can tell when someone's really been through it. You were damaged goods. My life has been happy, normal . . . like a Norman Rockwell painting. I figured there was a reason you weren't telling me. I would have listened, but I didn't want to force you to talk about it."

Gabe understood beyond what I'd given him credit for. That left me feeling more than a little guilty for underestimating him. Shame weighed me down. "I'm sorry I didn't talk to you about any of this."

"It's over." Gabe patted my shoulder. It didn't matter what had or hadn't happened before. I'd been forgiven. "Tell me the next time something freaky happens. Oh, and K?" He reached into the front pocket of his jacket and pulled out a small yet familiar box, which he pressed into my hands. "I know you still want to marry Cali, so I thought you might want to hold on to these for the time being."

With care, I popped the lid. There, resting on a white velvet backing were our wedding rings. I quickly snapped the box shut and added it to my own pocket.

"Thanks."

The interior of the car grew silent, and the part of my mind that longed for normalcy wanted to pretend we were a car full of friends on a journey.

After we put another three miles between Boston and us, Gabe cleared his throat. "So, K, tell me all about this creepy Faerie place and killing that bad dude. Did you, like, get to use a sword?"

For the first time since Cana had gate-crashed my wedding, I genuinely laughed out loud. "Oh, yeah."

But even as I told the story, I kept one eye trained on the side mirror. The road remained empty, though I doubted very much that the C.O.D. would travel by car. I had no clue where they were and how much time we had. Only one thing brought me any degree of comfort: Old Gabe was back.

CHAPTER 15

KELLEN

Gabe continued to drive as the hours passed. He wouldn't accept my offer to take over, no matter how much I insisted. We kept going, through Massachusetts, New Hampshire, then straight into Maine. I glanced back at Cali for about the hundredth time. Her hair had fallen along the seat beside her, the strands ending in soft curls that bounced as the car moved over the pitted asphalt.

Though Gabe and I had kept diligent watch, we hadn't seen anything strange. Throughout the night, there had only been one other car behind us, and it had exited about a half hour earlier.

"I haven't seen anything, though it's not like they need cars." I reminded Gabe. "They could be watching from a distance."

"You're right. So stop looking and get some sleep. One of us has to be rested, besides Cali." He inclined his head to the back seat and grinned at me.

Gabe turned on the radio to signify that our conversation was over. It blared rock music before he turned down the volume and switched it to an eighties party station. He started singing along in a soft voice to the Human League.

Eventually, unable to fight the heaviness of my own drooping eyelids, I gave up. The image of Cali's hair bouncing on the seat kept replaying in my mind as sleep claimed me.

Hair. Someone combed his or her hair. Parted it down the middle, rigidly. Not Cali, but a man. Then he looked up and into the mirror and I recognized my father, Stephen St. James.

Dark circles rimmed each of his eyes. Lines I didn't remember seeing before stood out on his face. He'd lost weight and his color was anything but healthy. He'd grown pale to the point that he could be compared to a corpse.

If we'd never met, I would have assumed that this man hadn't slept well in weeks. Though I hadn't spent much more time than that under Stephen's roof in the last ten years, I knew something was up.

I couldn't figure out where we were. The warm and toasty room couldn't have been more of a contradiction to the environment I'd known as a child when Stephen insisted on keeping the house unnaturally cold. Either he'd remodeled or he was traveling. Though it just as possibly could have been the home of a one-night stand.

"It's like Kellen has disappeared. I can't find him anywhere." Stephen sounded uncharacteristically worried.

When had he ever been worried about me?

I tried to see who Stephen was speaking to. Probably one of the many women he dated. There had been a revolving door in our house since my mother died. All the potential contenders for her replacement left as quickly as they arrived.

An unfamiliar male voice answered, surprising me. "He'll

turn up. You know how kids are. Besides, we'll be the first to know when he surfaces."

I tried to see the other person. A foot extended out from a pair of crossed legs, but the bed hangings blocked the other man's face.

"He has to. I need him!" Stephen punched his fist on the desk.

In an instant, I snapped out of the dream and looked around. My heart pounded. Cali and Gabe were talking. She'd leaned forward, her head resting sleepily on the back of my seat. I sat up straighter and sucked in a breath.

There hadn't been a time in my life when dreams weren't part of my normal sleep pattern, however I'd never once dreamed about Stephen. It had been weird. He'd looked different, so worn out in the dream. Who had he been talking to?

"Hey, it's about time you woke up, K. We're here, man." Gabe seemed tired but pleased.

I rubbed my eyes with the heels of my hands and peered out the window as we rolled to a stop. The rental's headlights illuminated a small parking area, but not much else.

"Where are we?"

"A bar." Cali yawned at the end of this exclamation so that the word "bar" stretched out for two extra syllables.

Gabe chuckled. "No, I said Bar Harbor, not a bar."

"Bar Harbor, Maine?" My brain fog lingered, and I struggled to recall any attachment that Gabe might have had to Maine. Then it was there. He'd told me once that his family had some beach vacation homes. His favorite was in North Carolina. The other was in Maine.

"Why didn't we just fly here, man?"

Gabe turned the ignition off and the car silenced. "We had a connecting flight for later today, but I didn't want to wait around in the airport or be in the air any longer than necessary. It seemed risky with all that's been going on." Gabe undid his seatbelt and climbed out of the car.

"Yeah, I get that. I'm not sure I could have handled another flight anyway after that last one." I got out and opened Cali's door. I offered her my hand, which she accepted, and drew her into my arms. "How are you doing?"

"Good. Adjusting." She sagged into me despite her words.

The wind blew Cali's hair sideways and up so that it tickled my chin. The ocean sounded close, a roar that filled the otherwise quiet night. The salt from it clung to the air.

I reached my arms to the sky in a much-needed stretch. Cali never moved from her position, leaning forward as I leaned back. After a moment, I scooped Cali up. She was the weight of a feather in my arms, almost nonexistent. Since I didn't have Gabe's six pack and pecs, this surprised me. Then again, I had changed physically during my time in Faerie. I couldn't explain it exactly, but I'd gotten stronger and bulked up more than I ever had before. When I looked at myself in the mirror, I no longer resembled the pasty runt of a litter, but a healthy guy most wouldn't bother to pick on. That was a casting change I hadn't anticipated.

Gabe walked around to the back of the car and opened the trunk. He shoved most of our bags into a large duffle he'd bought, but we'd need another trip or two to get it all.

Once he'd gotten as much as he could carry, he slung the bag over his shoulder and shut the trunk. He shook his head when he spotted Cali sleeping in my arms.

Gabe switched on his flashlight and a beam of light cut into the darkness. He aimed it in the direction of the house. "Follow me, but be careful. There's a footbridge."

Mimicking his tentative strides, I followed, taking care

not to bang Cali's head or feet against the railings. The darkness on either side dropped off into nothingness. It reminded me of the black void I'd fallen through in Faerie and I fought back a shudder.

We reached the front door and Gabe stretched his hand up, feeling along the top of a massive doorframe. With a start, I realized he was searching for the key.

People still hide keys on the ledge? Amazing.

The key clicked in the lock and soon we were inside, though it was so cold that it was hard to tell if we'd made any progress.

"Sorry about the cold. It's the off-season." Gabe peered at a glowing thermostat on the wall. "The water's been shut off to keep the pipes from freezing when winter comes, but we'll have heat." A beat later, the welcome sound of a furnace coming to life greeted us from somewhere in the house. He flicked a switch and the entryway lights kicked on. He grinned in answer. "We'll have to rough it at first. You up for it?"

"It's fine." I wanted nothing more than to crash. Judging by Cali's deadweight against my shoulder she already had.

Gabe walked over to a dark corner of the room. For a moment he became engulfed in the shadows, then his quiet exclamation broke the silence. "Yes!"

My lips curved into a wry smile. It was three thirty in the morning and Gabe still appeared happy and upbeat. At least now that he wasn't angry and he'd had his granola.

A moment later, a crackle and light pierced the quiet darkness as a fire came to life in the fireplace. The small flames soon illuminated Gabe's face. "Why don't we stay in here tonight and we'll sort out rooms tomorrow?"

In the center of the room there was a large sectional that could easily have accommodated fifteen.

"Sounds good."

I set Cali down on the part closest to the fire. I took off her coat and tossed it along with mine onto the floor of a little alcove by the door. Gabe disappeared and then returned moments later with a stack of blankets. I spread one of the quilts on top of Cali while Gabe made himself comfortable on the other end of the sofa.

My stomach grumbled, but snacks didn't appeal to me. I wanted real food. Pushing images of a ginormous cheeseburger and soda from my mind, I kicked off my shoes and removed Cali's. I added another layer of blankets on top of the quilt I'd placed over her and then curled up against her. The fire would chase the cold away eventually, but in the meantime, the warmth from the blankets enveloped me. Contented, I laid my arm over Cali and buried my face in her hair. She smelled incredible.

She snuggled back against me, pinning me to the sofa. As tired as I was, I should have been able to crash and not wake up for a week. But with Cali pressed against me, I couldn't. I wanted her in a way that I'd never wanted a girl before. Sure, I'd paid attention to the opposite sex. I'd imagined . . . well, what most guys imagine. But those moments never amounted to more than random fantasies.

Here, on the sofa, in the dead of night, my brain flashed to the curves that I'd only gotten the briefest of chances to explore. If it hadn't been for the C.O.D., the pair of us would be as close to one another as it was possible to be.

Lifting myself up on my elbow, I pressed my lips to her cheek, then smoothed back a lock of her hair. "I love you, Calienta. It will all be okay. You'll see."

All we needed to do was get through this and we could start our life together. We could be alone then.

But memories of that green woman with the eye in the center of her forehead stuck with me. How exactly did I think our happy-ever-after would come true? I had no idea how to stop the C.O.D. or what our next move should be.

Despite my own fears, my heart rate settled into a slightly less erratic pattern out of sheer exhaustion. Sleep overcame me before I could add to my list of worries.

CHAPTER 16
CALI

When I opened my eyes after only a few hours of sleep, they immediately focused on the water outside. The early morning sun hit the waves, and the light reflected so that it sparkled like diamonds. It reminded me of Ireland and my family. I missed them both with a fierce ache that spread across my chest. I supposed that was heartache, though I couldn't say for sure. Either way, my thoughts made going back to sleep impossible, even with Kellen's warmth at my back and his hand under my breasts.

With care, I slid out from under the blankets and stepped into my snuckers. (Was that the word Kellen had used?) After a few moments of fumbling with the door leading outside, I had it open. I had no idea where my coat was, so I grabbed a blanket from one of the nearby chairs and wrapped it around myself.

I stepped outside onto a balcony and pushed the door shut behind me. The water was even more breathtaking as it lapped at the cliffs. There was no beach behind Gabriel's parents' house. Instead, there was a sharp drop-off where rock plunged into water. It gave the impression that one sat at the entrance to the sea itself.

"I'm mortal." I whispered this secret to the ocean, as though we were coconspirators and I expected an answer. Maybe that was because I once thought of Water as a dear friend, one that was always with me.

But she was silent now, as she would be forever more. Never again would she speak to me as she once had. Still, that did not mean I couldn't speak to *her*.

Flinging open the blanket, I let the frigid wind blast my body. "I'm mortal!"

A gust of wind hit me and chills wracked me as the reality of the changes settled. I would never be a goddess, would never again visit the stars or light them at night.

The first set of tears began to fall quite without my knowledge. I yanked the blanket around me, tucking it tight around my neck. The damage had been done, however. Once the chills began, I couldn't fight them.

The glistening sea blurred. It shouldn't have worked this way. Kellen and I planned to be married first and then we would have gone away together. I could have slowly gotten used to my mortal bones with only the two of us. He would have taught me everything I needed to know in that patient way of his.

My existence as I'd known it had ended, and I was left with a choice: embrace my mortality or give up. I refused to give up on Kellen. I refused to give up on me.

I reached for Cali, hoping to pull her closer. I'd somehow
grown colder, and I missed her warmth. But as I reached
and I reached, I realized I lay under the covers alone. I bolted
upright, panic sinking a hole deep in my chest.

Something flashed in the corner of my eye and I spotted
the edge of a blanket flapping in the wind outside. Cali stood
on the balcony, a large blue quilt wrapped around her.

She's okay. Relief flooded me, but it would be short-lived if
she didn't put something warmer on. I scanned the massive
great room for our coats and spotted Gabe, fast asleep, all
four limbs spread out around him like a giant lopsided
starfish. He let out a snore that could have rivaled a bear's in
hibernation.

I shoved my own blankets aside and stood. We'd arrived
so late that I hadn't seen much of the house. In the light of
day, I took in the great room with its tall ceilings. The
comfortable living area blended seamlessly with the informal
dining room and a kitchen that looked like it could have
accommodated a restaurant. An outside balcony spanned the

length of the entire room, with three sets of glass French doors opening out from various points.

I retrieved our coats from the area near the front door and slid mine on as I padded across the cold hardwood in my socks. Seconds later I stepped outside and a cold blast of air met me, its chill contradicting the sunshine. The door clicked when I shut it behind me.

Cali didn't notice my arrival. She leaned against the railing, shivering in the cold. She'd always been beautiful, beyond what my mortal eyes could comprehend, but on this morning her beauty went beyond imagination.

The sun kissed her chestnut hair, making it appear more of a fiery red than a flame-colored brown. Her eyes were closed against its rays, as though soaking up the warmth on her porcelain skin.

I slid her coat over her shoulders. She tensed but quickly sighed and leaned into me.

"Good morning." I wrapped my arms around her, hoping to warm her.

"Mm. Thank you, and good morning." She rested her head back against me and we stood like that for many moments, staring at the bay while the sea gulls dipped and dove over the water. Their cries greeted both of us, as if they deemed us a worthy audience for their first show of the day.

Scanning my memory, I searched for a time when I'd come across a view to rival this one. Certainly some of the places that I'd visited in Ireland had been breathtaking, but Maine set its own standard. The landscape had been described to me as rugged, both in geography classes as well as in magazines and coffee table books that I'd skimmed over the years. No explanation could have been more accurate. The rocky, jagged coastline simply fell into Frenchman Bay as it led out to the rough seas of the Atlantic. Pine trees dotted the landscape, jutting out at odd angles. The smell of salt water and pine and not much else filled my lungs as I took a slow, deep breath. I could only sum it up in one word: extraordinary.

"How are you feeling this morning?"

She gave me a small smile. "You already know."

"Yep, but I was trying not to pry." I closed my eyes and, focusing solely on her, I reached out for her emotions and found them mixed. Sadness clashed with elation and regret in a jumbled-up ball of feeling.

We'd never tested out exactly how close I needed to be to pick up on them, but we'd been separated in Faerie once and I'd sensed her through time. That must have meant that little ability of mine was robust. Though it worked best when I focused on her. Touching her made it easier.

Still, sometimes I picked up on things I didn't want to know. This was one such occasion. I wanted Cali to only feel happiness. Yet when it came to being mortal, she was decidedly *undecided*.

Cali rested her head against my chest, hugging me close. She shivered beneath the blanket like a normal girl. A mortal girl.

"We haven't had the chance to talk much about being mortal. Do you . . . know how to do everything?" Please let her know about the female *things*. I didn't want to have to be the one to explain that.

She smiled, enjoying my discomfort. "Whatever do you mean?"

My cheeks burned. "There's this thing that happens—" That was the instant I caught the laughter in her eyes. She was messing with me.

"When I changed, my mortal body came with the basic knowledge that I need to care for myself. You don't need to explain."

"That's a relief." I let out a breath. Conquering Faerie was easy compared to talking about feminine hygiene.

Cali frowned, the little crease in her forehead that was so familiar returning. "There is one other gift that Father gave me. I'm not sure what it is yet. He said that it would reveal itself when the time was right."

"Since I'm assuming it will be a time when we're under attack, let's hope that doesn't happen for a while. I'd much rather have some time alone with you." I grinned down at her, still feeling very much like the lovesick boy I'd been when I first met her.

Standing on tiptoe, Cali pressed her lips to mine. Her lips were so soft, and they melded to mine like a promise. In that moment I forgot where I was and that we were hunted. Everything around us faded like it always did when we were together, like it was the two of us against the world. The kiss didn't last long and probably would have been considered chaste by most. Still, I gripped the railing to steady myself when she drew back.

"Is there breakfast? I'm starving." She craned her neck, as if waiting for breakfast to magickally appear. It was a logical move. After all, she'd conjured bacon for me once. Unfortunately we were a tad short on magickal bacon at the moment.

Pressing my lips to her forehead, I gave her my best smile, one I hoped would convey we had nothing to fear. A look full of lies. "No, but I think we can change that. Follow me."

And just like that, the darkest parts of our dire situation seemed to evaporate. It was a beautiful day, and I was with Cali. Maybe we weren't in danger. We were so far from Ireland, and we hadn't seen any faerie action since we got to the states. Surely, they'd never find us here.

But a small voice in the back of my head warned: They can find you if they want to.

CHAPTER 18

KELLEN

There was one small problem with my promise to Cali. I had no idea how to cook anything that could even remotely be categorized as breakfast. Gabe was another story.

"Gabe." I shook Gabe's arm. Our trip to Walmart had provided us with nonperishable snacks, but Gabe had polished off the granola bars and I was already running out of Snickers. "Come on, man, wake up."

Gabe groaned, pressing the heels of his hands against his eyes. "Noooo." He rolled over and started snoring.

"Cali needs to eat." I shook him again. "If we want to eat real food, you're going to have to get up."

Cali laughed. "Maybe we should let him sleep longer. I'm sure I can wait. Probably. I mean, I'm not exactly sure, but I'll try."

Gabe opened his eyes and glared at us as if we'd ruined his day. Slowly he sat up and then leaned back against the couch. "Gosh, man, like, give a guy a minute."

"Okay. Come here, Cali." Together we walked to the pile

of bags we'd left by the door last night. After some shuffling, I found Cali's things. "Why don't you pick out something to wear. You can change in the bathroom." I turned to Gabe. "Where's the bathroom?"

"Down the hall, you pain in the ass." He wiped his hand over his face while yawning, a superb feat of multitasking.

When I faced Cali again, she was holding up a pale blue bra and matching underwear. Damned if I didn't wake up then and there.

"These go on under the mortal clothes, right?" The crease in her forehead was back as she considered me with all the seriousness of a specimen under a microscope.

I wanted to point out that she was already wearing under-wear from the wedding, but I had no idea how Brigid had dressed her. It was better not to comment. Odds were, I couldn't handle the truth. "Yes. *Under* the clothes."

She brightened and headed in the direction of the bath-room, her clothes scooped up under her arms.

As if a switch had flipped, Gabe's eyes popped open and his normally buoyant personality returned. "Hey, there's this great pancake place in town. Let me get my stuff and we'll go."

"Isn't there someplace that delivers?" I began flipping through a binder about the house and the Bar Harbor area from front to back and then back to front. "I don't know if going out is such a great idea. We're supposed to be in hiding." I sounded like somebody's parent, but someone had to be the voice of reason.

"Yeah, but we need more supplies. I know it's only Octo-ber, but the weather is dicey here. We don't know how long we'll need to stay, so it's important to make sure we're prepared for whatever might come. Plus, we don't have any cream for the coffee." Gabe waggled his eyebrows.

"Ugh.

Gabe shrugged. "If we go into town, no one needs to know where we're staying. If we have food delivered, the local people will know the house is populated and they'll talk."

The windowpanes rattled as a gust of wind kicked up. Outside a tree blew almost sideways in the wind. It was pretty darn cold, and it was only the beginning of October. What if we ended up staying through the winter? If we found ourselves trapped in the house, we didn't have enough food to last the three of us a week.

"I think we should go, but we need to be quick about it." Cali smoothed her sweatshirt and zipped up her coat as she returned from the bathroom. She held the pink sweatsuit she'd changed into last night in one hand and added it to one of the empty bags. "Gabriel gave us time when he read those words on the plane. But not much. Let us eat, get what we need, and come back here as quickly as possible."

I didn't like it, but I couldn't argue with Cali's stomach and the dropping temperature.

Bags crackled as Gabe and I dragged out the scarves, gloves, and boots that we'd purchased the previous night. Once we were ensconced in several layers, we left the house and stepped out into the magnificence that was fall in Maine. The smell of burnt wood clung to the air while leaves swirled, forming little eddies around us. A patchwork quilt of colors blanketed the earth in golds, rusts, and browns. I inhaled, and the purity of the untainted oxygen burned my lungs.

Gabe walked ahead toward the rental and called over his shoulder, "We need to drive. It's too far to walk and too cold."

The bridge creaked as Cali and I crossed it. I ran my hands along the railing and let my fingers slide over the smooth, cool iron. With the house behind me, I turned to get a good look at where we were staying.

The Stewart place could not have been described as a cottage or a house. It was a mansion. I'd never seen a home that large up close. The structure, made predominantly of stone and white siding, popped out of the pine trees sheltering it. Sunshine danced off the front windows of the three-story house, including one window that dominated a turret in the very center of the structure. The stone gave it a grander, older feel, though the house was a contemporary, open-concept party on the inside. A spring trickled beneath the bridge. Moving water might help protect us, like the moat at Leeds had. The Stewart's place made Stephen's Tudor-style manor house look like a shack.

"K, you coming?" Gabe stood at the car, half-in and half-out of the driver's seat. Cali had called shotgun and bounced up and down in her seat. She gestured animatedly for me to get in the car.

The writer in me wanted to take my time, to observe the area more. But that took a back seat to two hungry travelers. Okay, three.

Pushing my disappointment aside, I walked to the car and climbed in, cupping Cali's cheek lightly from behind before shutting my door.

"Okay, dudes. Breakfast is closer than you think. Hold tight, C." Gabe twisted the key in the ignition. Soon we were on our way.

As Gabe drove down the long lane, I began to orient myself. The house sat about a mile from the main road, and then the property ran right up against the bay. Once we reached Route 3 my eyes followed the endless sea of pines that framed the road on either side.

"This place is pretty isolated. Good choice, Gabe."

"Thanks. It's the start of the off-season, so there won't be too many people here." He grinned, tossing me a sideways glance and switching on his favorite streaming station. "We haven't had any trouble since Boston. Maybe we lost them."

Gabe began singing then, his somewhat out-of-tune baritone filling the car. Cali giggled as he added jazz hands to his one-handed choreography. But I couldn't bring myself to sing along. I couldn't shake the feeling that we weren't getting away with anything. That they knew exactly where we were.

CHAPTER 19

KELLEN

The quaint little shops and restaurants that made up downtown Bar Harbor lured in passersby with their curb appeal. Fall wreaths hung from storefronts along with signs promising free samples of hot apple cider and blueberry muffins. Small clusters of baby boomers wandered the sidewalks, whipping out their cameras every few seconds to capture the image of whatever curiosity had piqued their interest.

A group of people sat beneath a small circular pavilion with green and white trim, listening with rapt attention to a speaker. Part of a tour group or maybe a church service. There were already dozens of people out on that Sunday morning, but I could envision the potential for more in the summer. Hopefully our off-season arrival would work in our favor.

We passed by what looked like the busier side of town when Gabe spoke up. "I think those people are taking my picture." Gabe grinned and attempted to show his best side as he eased the rental into a spot on one of the side roads beside a restaurant with a blue striped awning.

I whipped around and spotted an elderly couple bundled in jackets and boots with matching scarves around their necks. They did indeed seem to be aiming their cameras in our direction. Though I'd lay odds the real target was the restaurant, we couldn't be too careful.

"Don't look at them. I'm not sure it's a good idea that we're being photographed."

"Right." Gabe nodded, averting his gaze. "I didn't think about that."

I'd picked up three ball caps last night and had left them in the back of the car—just in case. Now, I pulled them out, setting one atop Gabe's head. "Here." I set a plain, navy blue cap on Cali's head that read Softball Queen. "You push it down, like this." I shoved the final one onto my own head.

"Thanks." Cali beamed even as her ears poked out on the sides, reminding me of an elf. With care I arranged her hair over her ears, covering them from the cold.

Gabe adjusted his hat as a grin split his face. "That hat says you're a Bass Master, Kellen."

"What's a bass?" Cali's lips quirked.

"It's a type of fish. It means he's a rockin' fisherman." Gabe snorted.

I shook my head as I turned to Gabe. "At least mine doesn't say *Born to Ride a Hog*."

"Wha?" Gabe peered into the rearview, checking out his own cap.

"Come on." I patted his shoulder and climbed out of the car. Cali followed.

Gabe, on the other hand, stayed behind an extra handful of seconds, frowning as he tugged the bill down on his forehead. Finally he climbed out. "Nice, K. Touché."

"Hey, someday you'll thank me for adding to your wardrobe." I grinned and took Cali's hand.

We crossed the street to a restaurant and stepped inside

to find a haven of warmth and delicious smells. The restaurant was long and narrow with mostly booths on one side. We managed to snag the last free booth on the end.

The menus handed to us by a smiling waitress proclaimed the place as Jacob's. Their special was none other than Maine blueberry pancakes.

"What's a pancake?" Cali leaned close, squinting as she tried to interpret the menu.

"They're a slice of heaven, that's what they are." Gabe winked, but his face immediately fell as he recognized his mortal faux pas. "Oh, no pun intended, C."

She grinned at Gabe over the menu. "No worries for you, Gabriel."

I suppressed a snort at Cali's attempt at slang. It made me love her even more, the way she tried to fit into my world. *Our world*.

The waitress stopped at the end of our table, tablet at the ready. She was older, with curly white hair that rose up and around her head in one large puffball. She didn't make eye contact over her notepad, and the sound of her tapping foot on the linoleum reminded us she had a restaurant full of customers. "What'll it be?"

The three of us ordered rounds of coffee and the special. The waitress returned moments later with cups and a carafe of coffee. I waited until she was gone before I asked the question preying on my mind.

"Do you think we need to move on today?" Maybe the photographers had been legit tourists, but my time in Faerie, where nothing was ever as it seemed, had jaded me.

Gabe scoffed. "Kellen, this is a tiny town. They were just tourists. They probably weren't even trying to get us in frame."

I raised the coffee cup to my lips and sipped the overly strong brew. The waitress had skimped on the cream, and the blend hadn't reached my optimal coffee hue yet. I didn't bother signaling to her. She clearly didn't want to be there any more than I did. "I'm not sure we can write anything off."

"Kellen's right. We need to be less conspicuous." Cali frowned as she ran her fingertip along the tines of her fork. "I'm not saying that everyone's a threat, but it wouldn't hurt to be more aware of what's going on around us."

"Noted. Man, this is just like *Harry Potter and the Deathly Hallows: Part One.* You know, when they go on the run?"

Cali stopped fooling with her fork and stared at Gabe. "Should I know what you're talking about, Gabriel?"

I stifled a laugh, loving how she was already calling him on his bizarre tangents.

Gabe's expression turned serious. "Basically, C, it means I need to start treating everyone like the enemy and be less trusting."

Funny, but I'd never known Gabe to be trusting at all. When we'd been at Yale, he'd practically asked for a background check on everyone I had a study group with. At the very least he always asked to meet them.

After draining my cup, I found I'd almost returned to a half-human state. About twenty minutes later, our waitress set three ginormous plates of food in front of us. The meal could have fed us as well as about ten others. The pancakes steamed on my plate and I inhaled slowly, taking in the familiar smell of hot blueberries.

"Now, you have options here, C," Gabe said, using his fork as a pointer. "You can go with butter and syrup—either blueberry or maple."

"What do you use?" Cali asked me, her expression lit with curiosity.

I held out my hand and Gabe set a container of powdered sugar on my palm. "Thanks." I popped the top and sprinkled the sweet powder over my pancakes. "I highly recommend powdered sugar." I capped the jar and set it back on the table.

"Freak." Gabe grinned as he uncapped the blueberry syrup and dowsed his breakfast liberally. "Syrup's the only way to go."

"Or maybe," Cali reached out, collecting first the powdered sugar and then the syrup, "a compromise?" Without waiting for our responses, she added both powdered sugar and blueberry syrup to her pancakes.

"Huh." Gabe leaned forward, considering Cali's topping selection as though she were a scientific experiment.

Cali cut into the pancakes and took a bite. Her eyes widened to the size of the plates our food had been delivered on. "Delicious."

My own first bite was heaven. The blueberries burst open in my mouth, burning my tongue. It reminded me of the time Gran had made cookies and I'd taken one off the pan as soon as it came out of the oven. It had burnt my tongue so badly that it puffed up. It'd been worth it though. The cookie was awesome.

Gabe polished off half a pancake in one bite. He shoved it into his mouth and chewed for several seconds before swallowing. Syrup leaked from the corners of his mouth on either side. Cali burst into laughter. I'd never heard her laugh like that—with abandon, as though she didn't have a care in the world.

Gabe glanced up, a residual piece of pancake sticking to his pronounced chin like a goatee. "What?"

This only served to make the situation funnier, and I roared with laughter right along with Cali. I offered him my napkin. "Wipe off your face, man."

"Thanks." Gabe did so, then balled the napkin into a wad and tossed it onto his plate.

We ate like that, laughing as though we were on a normal

trip. I almost forgot for a moment that we were on the run. Gabe hadn't, though. The instant we finished our meals, he was all business.

"There's a grocery store around the corner. I can get milk and other stuff. Can you hit the hardware store across the street? We'll need extra flashlights. I've got oil lamps back at the house, but just in case. Sometimes the power goes out for a while when the wind picks up, and I don't know how long we'll be staying here. Or *if* we'll be staying."

"Extra napkins?" A petite blond waitress walked by and placed a pile of napkins in front of Gabe. Her wide smile parted her lips to reveal ultra-white teeth.

Gabe sat up straighter so that he was almost able to look her in the eye. "Thanks." He accepted the napkins with a warm smile, sending a faint blush creeping up the waitress's cheeks like a wine stain on a white rug.

She left our table, probably to gossip in the back about the nice, cute guy that had been a sloppy eater. Apparently Cali and I hadn't taken to our breakfast as ardently as Gabe had, because she didn't offer us any additional paper products.

The smile stayed stuck on Gabe's face until he opened the first napkin and blanched. He crumpled it up and reached for the second before dropping it on the table as well.

"Gabe, what's wrong?" I reached for the napkins, but he held up his fork with the tines pointed toward me. By the time he opened the third napkin, he let his fork fall onto the plate with a clatter. In silence, he inspected the other napkins and then quickly discarded them, returning to the first three.

"We need to leave. Now." He stood up and reached for his wallet.

"I've got it." I tossed a fifty on the table.

"Thanks." Gabe waited for Cali and me to stand, then

spread his arms, blocking us from view like security detail for a rock star as he ushered us out the side door.

I gripped Cali's hand tightly in mine, the same unease building inside of me as I glanced back at the restaurant.

The blond waitress was nowhere to be seen.

CHAPTER 20

Gabriel walked directly past us, beckoning for us to follow. Kellen held my hand in a bone-crushing grip.

"Gabe, what's going on?" Kellen asked the instant we'd distanced ourselves from the restaurant. Yet despite Gabriel and Kellen patching things up during our journey to Maine, the former did not stop, forcing us to do nothing but follow.

We trailed after Gabriel, away from the vehicle we'd ridden in and around a corner to the large gathering area that I'd noticed before. Gabriel kept going until he'd climbed up onto a raised covered platform and sat down on one of the benches. His breath came out in short bursts.

"What's wrong, Gabriel?" I moved to stand beside Kellen. A chill tore up my spine and I tugged my hand free from his to place it inside my pocket in a weak effort to shield it from the cold.

When Gabriel didn't immediately answer, Kellen knelt before him and spoke in low tones, as though comforting someone in shock. "What's up with the napkins?"

Gabriel stared at us, his mind seeming to wage a battle within itself. I recognized the signs. Kellen's best friend was deciding, like I'd had to on many occasions, how much information to withhold for a loved one's sake. A beat later he slowly withdrew the napkins from his pocket.

Silently, he opened the first one and held it out for us. Someone had written on the napkin with a fine-point black pen in a familiar spiny script.

Quit wasting time.

He rested the napkin on the floor of the bandstand and pulled out the second napkin, setting it down beside the first.

Protect yourselves.

We locked eyes for a moment. "There's one more," he said, his voice strained as though it were making him physically uncomfortable to sit there and share. With care, he unfolded the third napkin and lined it up with the other two.

They are coming.

The writing looked familiar, but I couldn't place it. It was as though its owner danced around in the fringes of my memory, teasing me. "Whose handwriting is that?"

But Kellen didn't hesitate. "It's Dillion's."

I turned to him, fascinated that a mortal could be so intelligent. "Your memory. I'd nearly forgotten."

"K's wicked smart." Gabe grinned, pride filling his face for a second before he seemed to remember the unfortunate circumstances we'd found ourselves in.

Crouching in front of the trio of messages, Kellen inspected the writing in more detail. "Dillion helped me translate something when Cali and I were in Faerie. His handwriting is . . . unique."

Gabriel's brow creased. "Dillion. That's the dude in the beret that blew everybody away, right?" He shot me a sideways glance. "Your badass uncle?"

I wasn't certain what the condition of my uncle's buttocks had to do with the situation, nor had I personally inspected them. Still, there were so many mortal expressions I found myself unfamiliar with that it seemed best to agree. "It is. He probably couldn't risk being here himself so he sent the message another way."

As if in response, the wind picked up and the napkins blew away from us. Gabriel rushed to catch them and scooped them up before they reached the steps.

Kellen's eyes roamed the square, yet there was no sign of Uncle. Besides, if Uncle Dillion had wanted to send us a message, he wouldn't have needed to be present to do so. That was the way of Faerie.

Gabriel began to pace, staring out at the water and the milling tourists. "Dillion's right. We haven't taken any of this as seriously as we need to. Me especially. We need a plan. Some way to protect us from their powers. Any ideas, Cali?"

I opened my mouth to answer, yet the responses that had landed on my tongue dissolved. Why? Was it possible that I couldn't remember how to repel the Children of Danu? Try as I might, I couldn't bring a single thing to mind. When Kellen and I had gone to Faerie, I'd protected him, cloaking him against enemies, pulling him from the clutches of the *Sluagh*, the souls of the unforgiven dead. Now, our roles had reversed.

"I don't know. I don't remember, and I don't have powers. I can't protect us. We're helpless."

Kellen squeezed my shoulder and warmth from his hand crept into me. "We're not helpless. There are things that we can do to protect ourselves. We don't need powers to repel them."

Suddenly an anger that surprised me rose up and I fisted my hands in my pockets. "I hate this!"

"Gabe, can you give us a minute?" Kellen stayed beside me, never moving. The heat from his stare burned my skin.

"Sure." Gabriel didn't sound all that certain, yet he didn't argue. "I'll handle the grocery store. If you can pick up anything you think we might need at the hardware store, I'll meet you at the car in twenty."

"Yep." Kellen's voice sounded close, the intensity of it urging me to meet his eye. A moment later, the crunch of frost-covered grass broke the silence as Gabriel left us alone.

"Do you hate being on the run? Hate being mortal? Or . . ." He hung his head, reducing the pressure enough so that I finally raised mine. Kellen tricked me by immediately raising his head, his green eyes locking onto mine. "Or do you hate being with me?"

His question dug into my soul and unearthed all the old fears that I'd once lived with on a day-to-day basis. *What if he doesn't want anything to do with me? What if he won't help us? What if I can't trust him?*

The last one left me frowning, because of course I could trust Kellen. I'd always been able to.

But my thoughts must have tied up my answer for too long, because Kellen let his hand drop from my shoulder. He moved to stand by the railing at the opposite end of the space from where I stood.

This time it was up to me to do the comforting. I placed my hands on his shoulders and rested my cheek against his back. "I don't hate being with you. What I despise is not being able to do anything to help. I'm nothing but a worthless mortal." Once I'd been able to fly Kellen from danger. Now I couldn't fly on anything but an air-o-plane. No, *airplane*. That was it.

My head began to pound, and an unfamiliar ache spread across my temples. I pressed my cool palm against it, but it did little to ease the pressure.

"You think mortals are worthless? That *I'm* worthless?" He spoke so softly that I almost didn't hear him.

An instant wave of remorse hit me. Oh no. "Kellen, I didn't mean—"

"But you said it, didn't you?" He whipped around. "As I recall, my mortal ass saved your family."

His anger surprised me. He'd never been angry with me. Not after I'd explained who I was and we'd found each other again. "I didn't mean it that way."

Though his expression didn't change, his shoulders relaxed. "Then choose your words carefully. They're the only things you can't take back." That sounded like something Kellen's gran would have said.

Tears burned the backs of my eyes and I bowed my head, letting them fall on the knees of my jean pants. "I never meant to say mortals are worthless—I don't believe that." The teardrops fell faster so that I no longer tried to search for him in my peripheral vision. "You don't understand, Kellen. I'm the one who doesn't have a purpose. You're smart, kind, caring, gifted at everything, handsome . . . You're everything, but I'm nothing without my powers."

Kellen rested his forehead against mine and for that moment in time everything melted away. "You can't say that. You've been the most incredible goddess, but you don't yet know who you'll become as a mortal. Give yourself time."

"But how can I do that when time is the one thing we don't have?"

Our wonderful little world had turned nightmarish with no apparent way out.

He leaned in and caught my lips in a quick kiss. Tingles ran over the entire map of my skin. As I leaned into him, our lips met one another's with a sweet hunger I ached to abate. The sounds of people and cars, and even of the wind in the trees dimmed as he touched me. As though we alone existed.

All too soon he drew back, leaving my head spinning. We needed time alone, just to be. My lips curved into a smile as I envisioned it. Yet when I raised my head, Kellen's expression had hardened.

"What is it? What's wrong?" I asked, already afraid of the answer.

Without a word Kellen raised a finger and pointed to a nearby tree. Someone had carved a message in the bark. *Kellen St. James,* it read, *they want you.*

CHAPTER 21

KELLEN

Cali seemed lost in thought as we did a quick scan of the hardware store's aisles. We picked up all the supplies we could think of, including flashlights and candles. The store was loaded with rock salt for the upcoming winter. Salt served as a purifier and a ward against evil. We could use it to protect the house. It repelled faeries, though whether it would be powerful enough in this instance, I didn't know. I purchased two bags and carried one on each shoulder as we made our way back to the car.

"You're not saying much." I thought back to the bandstand and our first fight. "Are we okay?" I tried not to look like I was holding my breath as I asked the question.

Cali frowned. "So far we seem to be okay. We haven't been attacked, though I suppose it's possible that they're watching us now."

"No." I smiled, despite myself. "I mean are you angry with me?" It was an overly kind question. After all, I'd been the one to lose my temper.

"Oh. I'm fine. If you are not angry with me?" The crease returned to her forehead, and she seemed farther away than she'd ever been. If I was honest with myself, I'd been feeling that way since the moment our wedding imploded. As if something unseen stood between us and I couldn't get to her.

"Yeah. I'm good." But I was far from it.

After Dillion's napkins and the impromptu tree carving, there seemed to be an urgency to everything. I kept glancing over my shoulder. The Girl Scouts standing at the corner could be selling cookies laced with poison. The fisherman behind the Maine Lobster Rolls to Go stand could have been a faerie. In my mind, everyone had converted to a potential enemy.

We met Gabe, and the three of us piled into the car and headed back to the house.

As we pulled onto the lane that led to the Stewart family's house, Cali craned her neck to take in the scenery. "This place is pretty," she said.

"Yeah. It's cool," Gabe admitted as he pulled into a parking spot, his enthusiasm forced.

"What don't you like about it? Is it just the cold?"

Gabe parked the car and glanced at me sideways before turning back to the road. "I don't do cold. I want the sun, the sand. The water doesn't even get warm enough to swim in here. The tourists try, but they're nuts. They run into the water and scream and stuff. It's crazy."

"So why'd you pick it?" I leaned forward, toward the still-idling car's heater.

Gabe stared through the windshield, as though pretending not to hear me. Then he muttered a response. "It's my mom's favorite place. It felt safe."

He killed the engine, and Cali and I climbed from the car and helped Gabe unload the bags. Together we crossed the short bridge to the front door and entered the house. The large kitchen island served as a temporary holding point for the groceries. Gabe took over the moment we set the bags down, storing our supplies in the fridge and within the host of surrounding cabinets.

He waited until he finished bundling up the remaining paper bags in the recycling bin before turning to us. "What do we need to do to protect the house?"

I slid onto one of the bar stools at the kitchen island and rested my elbows on the butcher block counter opposite Gabe. "What about saying that phrase again that you used on the plane? The one that Lugh gave you?"

Gabe stuffed his hands in his pockets.

"What's wrong?" My best friend was usually an easy read. Right then was no exception.

"I don't know what the words mean. What if it's something . . . *evil*?" He withdrew the piece of paper from his pocket and uncurled it, only to have the parchment bounce back again. "I mean, your family seems nice enough, Cali, but how do I know I can trust this?" He held up the paper and shook it for emphasis before returning it to the pocket of his jeans.

"I hear you. I had a pretty difficult time trusting Cali and her family at first."

"That's certainly an understatement." Cali slid onto the stool beside me. "I was convinced I'd have to use my magick on you just to get a word in." She winked when I turned to her, and some of the nerves I'd been carrying around dead-center in my gut eased.

"Nice." I shook my head at her teasing. "But seriously, Lugh would never tell you to say anything if it was evil."

Despite our reassurances, Gabe didn't seem any more certain. "I know. I just . . . I felt weird when I said it."

"Weird how?" Cali's voice barely concealed her curiosity.

"Like . . ." Gabe looked around the room, until his eyes finally met mine. "Like something is going to happen if I only let it. It freaks me out."

"Gabriel." Cali walked around the island and touched his arm. "All of us have some magick within us. I think you're just calling upon that when you say those words."

Air left him in a whoosh. "Really? Wow, that's good. Then maybe I'll try it again. But later," he added. "I need to call my parents. I know Cali sent them home safely, but I need to check. I also need to find out where the water shut-off valve is. I'd like a hot shower."

"Cali and I will have a look around. There has to be something we can do to increase security around here." Besides, I wanted to see the entire place in the daytime. We didn't have a ton of options for protecting ourselves against the C.O.D., but I'd sleep better that night knowing where all the entrances and exits were.

"Kellen, I don't have powers anymore." The crease returned to Cali's brow.

"But I'm sure you remember what we can do to repel them. You probably know more about that than I do." All I had to go on were Gran's stories. Sure, we'd had good luck, but I wasn't sure how comfortable I was solely relying on folklore.

An unexplained look of hesitation crossed her face. "Of course." But her answer came a tad too quickly and her head bobbed with too much enthusiasm for it to be legit.

"Good. I'll catch up with you guys." Gabe had already reached for his phone before we'd left the great room.

I grabbed one of the bags of rock salt that I'd left by the door. Once we were back outside, I tore open the corner of the bag and began sprinkling the stuff along the foundation. "There's no rule that we can only use table salt, right?"

"Not that I know of."

Cali took the bag from me and took over, mimicking my movements and sprinkling the salt along the perimeter. We weren't at it long though. Craggy rock bordered the house for a short span, only to end abruptly in a perilous drop-off above the bay. There wasn't any way to sprinkle salt completely around the building; nothing existed for it to cling to. That knowledge left me with an uneasy feeling of being exposed.

On the walk back to the house, I touched the cool metal of the bridge supports. "This is iron. I noticed it on the way out."

Cali touched the railing, testing. "Yes, it is."

Looking up at the house, I noticed even more of the black metal. There were iron lamps, decorative iron fixtures, and horseshoes above the doors and windows. I remembered that even the balcony in the back had iron rails. "At least they used a lot of iron here. I'm glad for that. There's not much more we can do."

Cali moved ahead of me. "We can place salt at the entrance to the house, and along the windowsills. We'll have to go back inside for that."

Movement in my periphery caught my attention. Gabe stood on one of the balconies, the piece of paper from Lugh clutched in his hand. His eyes were closed, and his brow was furrowed with concentration. But though his lips moved, I couldn't hear him.

Then Gabe seemed to brighten. At first I could have brushed it off as a trick of the light, but the longer he stood there, the lighter his skin became until he was somehow illuminated from within. If it had happened on the plane, I hadn't noticed, but at that moment he looked like a golden boy. Like Gabriel the Archangel. As he spoke the words, he took on an exultant expression.

Gabe's phone rang and the glow quickly faded to nothing. I forced myself to look away, only to discover that Cali had been watching too.

"I wish we knew what those words meant. It's old Gaelic, I think."

Her brow furrowed. "I should know what it means, but I just can't remember."

"It's okay."

But I only half paid attention as we walked back to the house. Thoughts of iron, the C.O.D., and a glowing Gabe kept turning over and over in my mind. So many questions and too few answers.

CHAPTER 22

CALI

By the time we'd sprinkled salt along each of the windowsills and the interior doors, my back ached. Gabriel's house was enormous, and the windows, which ran along one wall in many of the rooms, seemed endless. We were well into the afternoon by the time we finished, and we only had a little of the salt left.

It should have put me at ease, but I'd never been so afraid.

After Kellen had vanquished Arawn, he'd been turned into an immortal by my family's creator, Síl. Kellen would have stayed immortal too, if I hadn't noticed that something about the experience upset him. I could never get him to discuss it. I told Kellen that he didn't need to stay immortal, that I would change for him.

Then Kellen proposed and everything seemed set in motion. My parents hadn't been surprised that I'd agreed to give up my immortality. After all, it had been foreseen that Kellen and I would end up together. Since my brother and sister had married mortals, why wouldn't I?

They'd talked about the change at length with me, warning me what to expect. I'd been told I would forget things. It was a precaution the magick itself took. After all, my human brain couldn't handle all the knowledge I'd held as an immortal.

Yet I hadn't expected that I would lose so much of my memory.

Kellen waved his fingers in front of my eyes. "Where did you go?" His concerned smile slipped. "You're not worrying about not having powers again, are you?"

I didn't want to bring up my worries. I never wanted to do anything to upset this boy I loved.

One of the many doors shut with a snap as Gabriel walked back inside. His skin no longer carried the golden cast it had on the balcony. Now he seemed paler, and a bit shaken, as though he might vomit at any moment.

"Gabriel, did something happen when you said the protection spell?" I reached out to touch his arm, but he whirled around.

"I don't want to talk about it." He practically shouted his response, which was anything but normal for Gabriel. He ran his hands through his hair, causing it to stand on end on one side, and shook his head. "I'm sorry, C. I didn't mean to snap at you. I know you're just trying to help."

"I am. You're Kellen's friend, and mine too, I hope." I wanted that to be the case. I'd never had a friend other than Kellen. It would be nice to have one in Gabriel who was so essential to the most important person in my life.

"Of course I am." He patted my hands, but his were cold and clammy. He turned from me and began to search through the cabinets beside the stove. "Do you guys want some tea? My mom has a ton of it in here." He grinned as he found a small cannister and set it on the counter. "Here it is."

"Granola? Herbal tea? What is up with you?" Kellen asked, picking up the box and examining the writing on its exterior.

Gabriel pointed to his chest with two fingers. "Hey, this body is a temple, K. Someday you'll wish you were taking care of yours and I'll still look amazing at ninety."

"Whatever." Kellen laughed and rolled his eyes to the heavens. "D'you get ahold of your parents?"

"Yeah. They're good. They don't remember a thing about yesterday." He glanced at me over his shoulder. "Thanks for that, C."

"I'm pleased I could help." I toyed with the tea box Kellen had dropped onto the counter. A picture of a bear in a nightcap adorned the side. It made me smile.

"I tried to get to the water shut-off valve, but everything's locked up for when we rent this place out. I don't have a key. Mom's sending over the caretaker to turn on the water."

Gabriel opened three bottles of water, something that had seemed ludicrous to me at the time of purchase. He added the contents to a metal container—a *kettle*, that's what it was —before turning on a flame beneath it.

"That'll be good, even though I don't love the idea of a stranger coming in," Kellen said, his attention seeming to flit to the windows and then back to our conversation.

"I know, but this guy has been on Mom's payroll for years. We can trust him. Besides, we don't know how long we'll be staying."

"And *can* you stay?" Kellen leaned across the counter. "What about law school? You haven't been in classes very long."

Gabriel shrugged as though this news were inconsequential. "The drop/add date is tomorrow. I'm deferring."

Though I didn't understand half of what he'd said, it was clear from the way Kellen balled his hands into fists that he disagreed.

"Why would you do that? We'll hide out here. You can—"

Gabriel leaned toward Kellen so that the pair of them

were almost nose to nose. "I'm not leaving you guys to deal with this on your own." Slowly, he straightened. "You're my best friend, dude. This is where I need to be. Harvard Law will still be there when this is over, and if I need to reapply, then I will. They took me once, right?"

A clicking sounded and Gabriel turned toward the silver pot. He poured steamy water into one of the waiting mugs. "Tea?"

Kellen shook his head, but I accepted. Gabriel added a tiny bag to the mug and handed it to me before preparing his own drink. He picked up the mug from the kitchen counter and walked into the living room, then sat on the floor by the darkened fireplace.

My mind flashed back to a time when I'd used my magick to light a fire at Kellen's gran's house. That seemed ages ago. Now we had to sit and wait while Gabriel lit the fire manually. It didn't take all that long, by mortal standards. Soon, small flames sparked to life, and not long after that, the flames began augmenting the heat already in the room.

Gabriel sat down on a cushion beside the fire, the contents of his mug releasing little swirls of steam into the air. "Tell me more about these C.O.D."

Kellen was perfectly capable of answering, yet his eyes fell on me. I supposed it was my story to tell, as much as it pained me to do so.

"They were heroes, once. They fought alongside mortals, aiding them whenever asked, and often when they weren't." I swallowed hard, trying to think of what else to share.

Kellen squeezed my hand. He was picking up on emotions, just as he always did. He understood that I didn't want to tell the story alone. "They came to Earth to help the mortals of Ireland in a fierce battle, but they were set up. Arawn, the Lord of Faerie, forced them underground. It messed with them."

"They are not the same." The sadness in my own voice echoed back at me. I'd always wondered what my life would have been like with so many aunts, uncles, and cousins around. I'd never gotten the chance to find out.

"They're like fallen stars—or fallen Star Children, really," Kellen added, bringing me back from my thoughts. He relaxed more into the cushions, pulling me back against him.

"Fallen stars." I'd never thought of them that way. When they'd been immortal, they'd lit the stars in the sky too. That task had then been handed to me and the mortals had called me a Star Child. Would father remember to light the stars at night with me gone?

"Lugh couldn't save them, so they've been pissed at him and his family for eons. And now they're after me."

Kellen ran his hand idly up and down my side. He did that when he got nervous. The action made me want to laugh, though I couldn't say why. Another mortal quirk? I twined my fingers with his to stop the movement.

"I keep trying to go over everything in my mind, but it all happened so fast." Gabriel set his mug down on the hearth. The flames had taken hold and the fire licked happily at the logs.

"It isn't about revenge," Kellen said. "They had Lugh and Brigid captured. They could have killed them—and me, for that matter." He rubbed his eyes and a yawn escaped, slightly distorting the end of his sentence.

"Lugh said they think you have some sort of amulet. Any idea what they're talking about?" Gabriel frowned as he sipped his tea. He looked better than he had when he'd first come back inside.

"None." Kellen shook his head.

"That's because no one's seen that amulet in . . ." I should have remembered. I wracked my brain for facts about the stone, but they were slipping into the chasm in my mind, like grains of sand dragged under by the tide. It didn't matter that my parents had warned me. It still came as a shock. "A very long time."

All three of us yawned then in near unison. The events of yesterday—my almost-wedding to Kellen, the attack, our escape—had all taken a toll.

"We should rest now in the daylight. If they're going to come for us, it will be at night." I might not have remembered much, but that lesson had stayed with me.

"No argument here, C," Gabriel muttered, rolling over onto his side.

Kellen grabbed one of the blankets we'd used last night, and we moved to the couch to lie down. I snuggled up against him, and he spread the blanket over us. In no time at all, Kellen's breathing evened out and I could hear the steady rhythm of his heart as he rested in my arms.

Yet I couldn't sleep. They were out there somewhere, and if they didn't know where to find us, they would soon.

CHAPTER 23
KELLEN

I'd fallen into a warm and relaxed sleep, but the instant my surroundings changed, the muscles in my back shifted from being loose and relaxed to riddled with tension-induced knots. Somehow, impossibly, I was no longer on the couch with Cali. I was sitting in my father's study.

The scene was familiar. I stood in the same room we had when I'd said good-bye on my graduation day. During that visit he'd barely made eye contact with me. This time I blinked and met my father's eyes. His brown eyes, so much like Gran's that it pained me, locked onto my green ones.

"Kellen. I've been looking for you everywhere, Son. Where are you?" He lifted his hand as though to touch me and I jolted out of the dream.

"Come on in. I'm sorry, I wasn't sure when you'd be coming over." Gabe's voice sounded far away in my mind as I meandered back from a deep and dream-filled sleep. It had been one of those where I'd woken overly warm, almost unable to move afterward. I lingered longer in that pleasant purgatory that hovered between the sleep world and the real world.

Gabe's voice grew louder. "I can't remember when I needed a shower more."

A deep chuckle forced my eyes open. The room had grown dark. We must have slept our way into evening. I practically fell off the sofa as I realized someone stood directly above me.

Gabe switched on the lights and I blinked. The stranger was tall, easily six foot four, with pale skin and a jacket that dripped water onto the Stewart's hardwood floor. I'd expected a caretaker to be older, maybe around Alistair's age, but this guy wasn't much older than us. The guy smelled like dirt and rain as he regarded me with eyes that looked to be an odd shade of blue-gray. His neutral expression wasn't giving anything away. I couldn't tell whether he'd come on a mission of good or ill will.

"Sorry to wake you, guys," Gabe said as Cali moved against me and her eyes fluttered open. "This is William." Gabe stood beside the stranger. "He's the house caretaker."

"William." I gave a quick wave and a nod before disentangling myself from the blanket.

But William only seemed to notice one person. Cali. His eyes had locked onto her as though he'd been hunting something his entire life and had finally caught his target in his sights.

Cali must have noticed too, because she straightened, wrapping her arms around herself and leaning back into me. William's searching gaze went far beyond socially acceptable eye contact for a first meeting.

"Do you mind, sir?" Cali gritted her teeth, her eyes narrowing as she met William's stare head on. "I would prefer you ogle something else. Yourself in the mirror, perhaps?"

William reddened. "My apologies. I was daydreaming there for a moment." He immediately turned from Cali to

Gabe. "Sorry for coming over without calling first. I came at a bad time."

I would have sworn his voice held traces of an Irish accent. Or maybe I was trying to convince myself that everything was tied to home.

"No worries." Gabe's shoulders relaxed. "We really do need some hot water. Do you need me to show you where the water main is, or are you good?"

William shook his head and produced a key ring from his pocket. "No. I've got it. Won't be a minute." Holding the keys aloft, he walked through the living room and down the hall to the first door on the left.

"What's his problem?" I hissed the instant he'd gone.

"That's what I'd like to know." Cali straightened, and her head tilted in an almost regal expression. "His behavior was most unnerving."

Frowning, Gabe shrugged. "I don't know. He's strange. He probably lives alone."

"Did you see how he was staring at Cali? It was . . . inappropriate." God, I sounded like an eighty-year-old man.

Gabe rolled his eyes. "You sound like an eighty-year-old man, K."

I blinked as he mirrored my exact thought.

"Cali's beautiful," Gabe continued. "She isn't like most girls. She's something . . . special."

"Thank you, Gabriel." Cali said this on a yawn as she rose to a sitting position and stretched her arms above her head. "But you don't look at me like that."

"No. He probably just noticed something different about you." Gabe sat down on the pouf across from us. "I did."

Footsteps sounded and we all turned as William emerged into the great room. "You're all set. Water's turned on. You might need to run it for a moment or two, but it hasn't been off for more than a few weeks. The last renters were in at the end of September."

Gabe got to his feet. "Thanks, man."

William reached into the pocket of his tan barn jacket and withdrew a piece of paper. It looked like a check. "Gabe? If you talk to your mother, could you let her know that I found the check she sent me?" He held it up as if to emphasize his words. "Please give her my apologies for waiting so long to cash it."

Gabe stared at the check for a moment and then smiled, relief seeming to pour into him. Whatever he'd seen on the check had apparently convinced him William was the real deal. "No problem. I'll definitely do that. Hey, let me walk you to the door."

William glanced over his shoulder and then back at us. "Actually, this is going to sound odd, but would you all like to join me for dinner?"

The three of us stared at him. The clock on the wall read six o'clock. We'd all been sleeping and hadn't had time to make plans. Still, I wasn't sure a scintillating meal with William aligned with anyone's idea of a fun evening.

My brain kicked into gear. "Hey, man, that's nice of you, but I think we're all wiped from traveling. We're going to have to pass."

"Look, I know you're tired, uh . . ." he paused as he waited for our names.

My eyes landed on a coffee table book on the Kennedy family. "I'm Jack, this is . . . Kennedy." I gestured to Cali. "You know Gabe."

Though it put me more at ease knowing that William worked for Gabe's mom, I didn't want to let my guard down. There was nothing to stop the C.O.D. from manipulating mortals.

"Right. Nice to meet you." William's eyes rested on Cali again and he quickly averted them. "You wouldn't have to stay long. I've made a simple meal—it's nothing. I'm trying to start a side business. Gourmet meals for tourists. I need a test audience. You can eat and run for all I care."

It would have sounded like a generous offer if his neutral facial expression hadn't contradicted the message. And meals for tourists was an odd side hustle for a guy who acted like he hadn't been socialized much as a child.

Dillion's messages came back to haunt me. *No, we can't go.* I opened my mouth to decline, but Gabe spoke first.

"We can't stay long." Gabe's brow wrinkled, as though he'd surprised himself.

Turns out I didn't have the gift of telepathy. *Damn.*

"Great!" William answered with more enthusiasm this time. His attention flitted to Cali, and then he quickly turned and walked toward the door. "Follow me. You'll need your coats."

"Gabe?" I slid into the boots I'd abandoned when we took a nap. "Can you show us how to lock up? We couldn't get the latch shut all the way before."

Understanding dawned on Gabe's face. He nodded in triple time, wanting me to be sure he got the message. "Yep. We'll meet you outside, William."

William's weak smile had already flatlined. "No problem." He turned and walked out the front door, shutting it behind him with a snap.

As soon as he was gone, I faced Gabe. "I don't like it. This guy is weird. I'm not getting a good vibe from him."

Cali moved in beside me. Her eyes flickered to mine for a moment. "We need to make our apologies, Gabriel."

Gabe shook his head. "Look, he's legit. That was my mom's freakin' check in his hand. It was made out to

William . . . something. He has a key, and . . ." Gabe walked to the sink and twisted the knob on the faucet. Water poured from the spout until Gabe twisted it back to the off position. "We have water. I think William's legit."

"They can make things happen. Even if he is mortal, William could have been manipulated by the C.O.D. You know what Cali said. There are no coincidences."

Gabe shook his head. "But this isn't a question of coincidence. Look, man, I know you've been through some stuff, but things are simpler here. I think we can take this guy at face value. Besides," Gabe's stomach growled loudly and he glanced downward like he was harboring an alien creature, "I'm starving. Look, let's go, and if you or C really think we need to, we'll leave."

A squeaking sound broke into the moment. My eyes shot to the chalkboard on the wall behind Cali's head. It was one of those artsy things that people kept near the phone to take messages or write the menu of the day. A single piece of chalk had risen into the air by itself and begun to write a message.

Gabe and Cali spun around as the chalk formed letters on the faded black surface. When it was finished, the chalk dropped to the tray below as though all life had been drained from it.

We stared at the message written in familiar tight, spiny scrawl. *I trust him. Go.* Dillion's handwriting couldn't have been any more distinct.

The three of us stared at one another, locked in a silent discussion. Finally Cali straightened. "If my uncle trusts him, then I think we need to."

"Okay, but we leave at the slightest hint of anything . . ." I'd been about to say "weird," but I couldn't imagine an evening with William being anything but, ". . . funny."

"Agreed," Gabe and Cali said in unison, as though we'd

just sworn a pact like in one of those weird cult movies where they spit on one another's hands or exchange blood. Thankfully, this involved neither.

At least not yet.

The path took us directly to a small gatekeeper's house that I hadn't noticed before. How Hansel and Gretel-esque. Though I couldn't see much of the exterior in the dark, it definitely reminded me of something straight out of the Brothers Grimm fairy tale.

"This way," William muttered over his shoulder as he led us into his house.

As the last to cross the threshold, I couldn't have been more surprised at what greeted me. The cheerful cottage epitomized the phrase "neat and orderly." From the tidy blanket that covered the sofa to the colorful collection of books and music on the wall, it truly represented a home. Dried flowers and herbs hung artfully from the ceiling in various places, and a variety of plants rested on the windowsills, tabletops, and mantel.

A blazing hearth served as the focal point in the room flanked by two overstuffed chairs. The table overflowed with place settings for a formal dinner. Rich blue damask fabric covered its top and spilled to the floor where it pooled at the feet of the chairs.

William took our coats before removing his own over-sized outer gear. In the light of the cottage, I got a better read on his age. He was in his early twenties, perhaps in his late teens even. Longish brown hair framed his smooth-shaven face. His blue eyes were sharp, with an intensity that implied they saw everything and gave nothing away.

He froze in the act of hanging his jacket to stare at Cali, but this time she stared right back as though just as curious. Jealousy sparked to life inside of me.

I reached out for Cali's emotions, but all I got back was confusion, as though she wasn't sure what was happening. There wasn't the slightest hint of arousal or desire. Whatever passed between her and William was different.

Gabe stepped in. "Uh, William. Aren't you going to invite us to sit down? That's what paying customers would expect a host to do."

William blinked. "I'm sorry." He snapped into host mode, straightening and smiling widely. "Please, follow me."

The cottage wasn't big on square footage, so it took only a few steps to reach the table, which had been laid out for exactly four guests.

"I didn't know how many we'd have for dinner, but it looks like I guessed right!" He smiled, his hands outstretched as he indicated the table. "Take a seat. I have dinner to see to. I'll be back shortly."

Cali, Gabe, and I exchanged looks but took our seats, sinking into the comfortable cushions dotting each of the chairs.

"Maybe we shouldn't eat what he serves us?" I whispered to Cali. "You remember what you told me in Faerie. Eat or drink nothing."

"Wait." Gabe glanced back at the kitchen to make sure William was still there and then back to us. "You don't think he's one of them, do you?"

Cali shook her head. "Uncle Dillion would have warned us otherwise. Besides, wouldn't I feel something if he was one of them? A twinge?"

The word *no* lay on the tip of my tongue, threatening to come out, but I held it. In truth, I didn't know if Cali still had the ability to discern anything about Faerie, and that worried me more than I was ready to admit.

William returned, carrying a platter and four red ceramic dishes. He rested the platter on the table, then set one dish before each of us. Warm brown bread complemented the dish, along with a bottle of wine. "Nothing special, I'm afraid. Just a simple shepherd's pie."

The tantalizing smell of freshly baked bread wafted under my nose, teasing me. I hadn't eaten a meal like this since I'd found Dillion's farmhouse in the middle of Faerie—though I was just as suspicious of this new host as I had been of Dillion.

"Jack?" William held up the bottle, about to pour me a glass.

"No, thanks. I prefer to keep a clear head." *And you guys should too.* I widened my eyes, hoping Cali and Gabe would follow my lead. They both accepted the wine.

"Would you like something else?" he asked me. "Perhaps a glass of milk?" William's smile turned mocking.

Okay, this guy is a jerk. "Just water, thanks."

Gabe had already dug into his dinner with gusto.

Cali glanced at me and shrugged before she took her first forkful. My nerves rattled around inside me. I really was becoming suspicious of everyone. This guy was just a caretaker.

I took a bite and practically moaned. It far exceeded my low expectations. William had actually used ground lamb as opposed to the ground beef cheat many Americans used. The potatoes were perfectly mashed, with hardly a lump. He hadn't even overdone it on the garlic. It would never measure up to Gran's, but it was, without a doubt, an excellent meal.

"This is awesome, William. Restaurant quality, definitely," Gabe said before he returned to chewing with gusto.

"So, tell us a little bit about yourself, William." We needed more info on the only person besides Dillion who could pinpoint our location.

William's expression shuttered immediately. "What do you want to know?"

"Where are you from?" I tried to keep my voice light, not wanting it to sound like the interrogation it was.

"I was born near Dublin. I left Ireland as a boy." He quickly returned to eating his dinner as though the three of us weren't there. I didn't know what Cali and Gabe were thinking, but I wasn't holding out much hope for William's side business.

Gabe, who had never been able to stand silence, seemed compelled to break it. "Where's your family, man? Are they here?"

"Dead." William spoke in a flat voice.

Gabe flushed. He quickly returned to his meal.

Cali placed her hand on William's, then stared at it as though it had moved on its own. "I'm sorry to hear that," she said.

The jealousy monster leaped to life inside me once more. This caring Cali was completely at odds with the one who'd told William off back at the house.

William glanced up and met her eyes, looking into them as if he could see into her soul. "It's nothing."

Gabe leaned forward. "I'm sorry, dude. I totally didn't mean to—"

William turned to Gabe, breaking his connection with Cali, and she yanked her hand back as though she'd been burned. "It happened so long ago. A *lifetime* ago."

He stood and began clearing our plates. I hadn't even finished mine, and Gabe's spoon was still poised in midair. With no further comment, William left the room.

Before we could share any whispered thoughts in his absence, he returned with a tray laden with cheesecake, a pot of coffee, and several cups. "Dessert?"

"I never say no to dessert." Gabe grinned, his enthusiasm catching.

William dished out the tempting cake as though a supremely awkward moment hadn't passed between the four of us. Then he returned to his seat, digging into the cheesecake before any of us had a chance to pick up our forks.

He was about to scoop the second bite of his cheesecake when he paused and slowly lowered his fork to the plate. His eyes narrowed as he stared at me. No, not at me exactly. The pendant I'd received from my mother had somehow freed itself from beneath my sweater.

"That's a very interesting piece of jewelry. May I see it?" he asked, holding out his hand as though he expected me to give it to him.

The three of us froze. My pendant? How odd that he'd asked to see it. Could the pendant be what the C.O.D. were after? No, Lugh had said it only had sentimental value. He would have warned us otherwise. This guy was just weird, not a threat.

"It's a family heirloom." I tucked the pendant back beneath my sweater where it managed to feel warm against my skin. "It's important to me."

"I'll bet it is." William scowled as he returned to his dessert. What was this guy's problem?

"You a gardener?" Gabe asked, gesturing to the rows and rows of tiny potted plants positioned on racks in front of the window.

William smiled, making me wonder if his scowl hadn't been in my imagination. "A warlock, actually."

Cali's eyes darted to mine. This time her feelings of suspicion and fear slammed into me. She didn't believe for a second that any of it was a coincidence. Neither did I.

CHAPTER 25
CALI

William was a warlock and we'd wandered into his cabin in the woods. Swallowing hard, I forced myself to take another bite of my cake of cheese as the rushing in my ears subsided.

How was it that I hadn't sensed traces of magick in this house? Searching the space, I picked up on nothing out of the ordinary. My mortality had blinded me. I had no way to protect us.

"It sounds a lot more mysterious than it is. I use herbs to heal people and animals when they've been injured." William tipped his chair back, raising it off its front legs. His eyes latched on to mine and a weird buzzing sounded in my ears. It was as if I couldn't look away. "For example, Mr. Stonewall down the road has a bit of high blood pressure. I made him a concoction with hawthorn to help." He rubbed his fingers along his jaw as he spoke, his eyes never straying from mine.

I didn't like the way William made me feel, as though every inch of me fell under his inspection. He seemed to see straight through to the most vulnerable part of me. The part that I kept hidden.

Yet, no matter how much I disliked him, I couldn't force myself to break eye contact. Had Kellen seen me staring at William this way? What did he think of it?

"Do you have any other powers or gifts, William?"

"Yeah, like can you turn people into toads and stuff like that?" Gabriel drank the rest of his wine. He slouched in his chair as though the drink was getting to him, but his eyes were alert, his neck stiff. Regardless, I could have kissed him, because his question caused William to look away.

I turned to Kellen and found him watching me, suspicion on his face. I wasn't sure if it was directed at me or William, though I hoped the latter.

"Nothing like that, but . . ." William leaned toward me across the table, "I am good at picking up information from people."

"What, like, you can read minds?" Gabriel asked, his eyes widening into a mildly horrified expression.

William smiled at him, suddenly seeming more interested than he had been all night, if you didn't count the attention he'd paid to Kellen's pendant. "Sort of? I get impressions from people. Snippets of information here and there. Sometimes it's concrete and sometimes it isn't. It's often as unreliable as it is reliable."

Kellen leaned forward across the table, his elbow bumping mine. He looked William squarely in the eye. "Tell me, William, what impressions have you gotten from us?"

He didn't need to tell me how much he disliked William. Kellen's posture—rigid, leaning forward as though ready for a fight—told the story.

William sipped his wine. "Not much. Except that your name is Kellen, and this is Cali?" William raised an eyebrow, turning to me as he said my name.

I averted my gaze before William could trap me with

those eyes of his. Why would Dillion have us trust this man? How could a warlock mean anything but trouble?

"Interesting. How does that work exactly?" Kellen reached over and picked up my wine glass. Swirling the contents around for a moment, he studied it before drinking deeply, his throat bobbing as he swallowed. Kellen's eyes met William's over the brim momentarily before he offered it to me.

Our fingers brushed as the glass transferred and a current ran straight through me, the way it always did when we touched. Drinking from the same glass as Kellen seemed intimate somehow. I sipped my wine, wanting to turn any attention from my reddening cheeks.

"It's pretty simple actually." William sipped his wine. "A person's name is the easiest piece of information to read. When you introduced yourself, you gave me one set of names. I picked up on another."

Gabriel rested his glass on the table and leaned forward, mimicking Kellen's protective stance. "They're eloping. They're under eighteen and they don't want their parents to find out. Kellen's my cousin—I'm just trying to help them out."

William seemed to mull Gabriel's lie over for a moment before raising his glass. "Congratulations to both of you, then. Don't worry, your . . . secret is safe with me." Without warning, his eyes locked onto mine. I couldn't even blink. We might have been lying when we gave false names, but William had lied about his powers. He definitely had some—I just couldn't pinpoint how powerful he was.

"William, do you mind if I check out your collection?" Kellen gestured to the shelves of books.

I realized I'd been leaning in a little too close to William. I sat up abruptly.

William nodded, gesturing to the wall. "Be my guest."

The instant Kellen left the table, William turned back to me. There was something so unusual about him, yet strangely familiar. I didn't know this man, yet I knew him. I wanted to sit there forever, getting lost in his eyes.

Reassemble yourself, Cali. He has to be spelling you. True warlocks have that power.

"So, you're getting married, huh?" William said in a low voice, as though Gabriel no longer sat at the table with us. "My bad luck, then."

As if I you'd have any say in it. I tried to open my mouth to speak, but I could only stare. What was this trickery?

"Yes, they are *getting married*." Gabriel ground out each word. Thank goodness for Gabriel. "And they have a committed relationship. I wouldn't interfere if I were you."

"Pity." William took another drink, not breaking eye contact with me. He smiled as I squirmed in my seat.

"This is an interesting collection of jazz books you've got here, William. Or can I call you Bill?" Kellen asked from across the room.

I was ready for the evening to end. To put distance between myself and William. Out of the corner of my eye, Kellen perused each title, no doubt searching the contents of each book. It was most likely research. He'd only have to glance at the information once to recall it in perfect detail.

"William will be fine, thanks," our host said, never taking his eyes from me.

"When did you become a practicing warlock?" I raised my coffee cup to my lips. When I set it back on the table, William pushed the wine toward me. I reached behind the wine glass and took the coffee again, holding the steaming cup close, my eyebrows raised.

William laughed out loud, still watching me. "It was the family business, you could say. Now there's just me." Bitterness crept across his features.

"Man, I bet that's cool, though, being a warlock. Someone doesn't toe the line, you blast them away." Gabriel grinned, but his smile was still the guarded one that told me he was paying close attention.

William laughed again, breaking eye contact with me to look at Gabriel. Apparently the idea of blasting someone away—whatever that meant—held appeal for William. "It doesn't work that way, but you're right, that does sound cool."

Taking a slow, deep breath, I did my best not to show my relief at breaking my gaze away from his. I stared down into my cup, determined to look everywhere but at William for the rest of the night.

"You like Stanley Turrentine?" Kellen held up two small squares in different colors with pictures on the fronts. I couldn't remember what they were called but stopped myself before asking.

William stared at Kellen, his thin build growing still. "Yeah, he's great. I'm a big fan. Huge."

"Oh yeah? I always thought he was a fantastic trumpet player. He had this Bach Stradivarius trumpet that his parents bought him when he was a kid. He never played anything else," Kellen continued.

William's face lit, but it didn't reach his eyes. Forced enthusiasm. "I never knew that. Huh," William said, then just as quickly went back to sipping his wine.

"They just honored him in his hometown of Los Angeles too." Kellen replaced one of the square boxes on the shelf. "He gave that big concert afterward."

"I really wanted to go." William's voice held the false enthusiasm.

"Me too." Kellen moved toward the table as he talked, hooking his right thumb into the loop in the side of his pants. He rested his other hand on my shoulder.

I leaned toward Kellen and watched as William's eyes flashed. Good. Let him be angry.

"Tell me, William. How do you know Dillion?" Kellen asked, squeezing my shoulder.

Surprise crossed William's face, but it was forced. "Dillion?"

He was too late to deny it though. All night long, I'd been waiting for him to mention Uncle Dillion. After all, if Uncle Dillion trusted him, it made sense that they would know one another. But as my mind began to replay the scene with the chalkboard, I realized that the only people Uncle knew would be members of the Children of Danu, our enemies. Even if William's intentions were good—and I wasn't certain they were—he must have been one of them. He had to be.

His refusal to explain how he knew Dillion practically confirmed it.

I stood and pushed my chair back. "I think we'd better be going."

Gabriel mirrored my actions. His tall form beside Kellen's made for a pair of imposing guardians.

"Thank you for dinner." Kellen threaded his fingers through mine.

"Thank you for joining me." William stood and immediately tried to pin me with his gaze again. I avoided his eyes.

We walked toward the door. I couldn't wait to put this bizarre dinner behind us. The evening had been a mixture of compelling emotions, among them dread and a bizarre attraction that I still couldn't explain. I practically herded Gabriel to the exit with Kellen behind me.

"Kellen?" William's voice gave us pause.

"Yeah?" Kellen faced William once more. I gripped Kellen's arm and looked at the floor.

"Stay out of the woods." William's voice held either a note of warning or threat. I couldn't be sure which.

"Thanks for dinner *and* the PSA." Kellen turned and pulled me along, his hand gripping mine like a vice.

The door clicked shut behind us. I waited until we reached the end of William's yard and faced Kellen, but I didn't find his usual warm smile waiting, the one I was accustomed to. Instead, he'd gone pale, his eyes widened with fear.

"Cali. Gabe." His voice was hoarse with worry when he spoke. "Run."

He didn't have to ask twice.

CHAPTER 26

KELLEN

When we returned to the house, each of us was more than a little breathless. Though William's place couldn't have been that far, it'd seemed much farther on the return trip.

Gabe bolted the door behind us. He didn't ask why I'd wanted us to run, he just went about flicking on every light switch in the place until it was blazing.

For the first time since we'd arrived, I wished that the Stewarts had a wall of draperies instead of windows facing the bay. There were no streetlights to illuminate the exterior when the ocean bordered your home. At night the crash of waves against rock managed to sound threatening instead of soothing, and the darkness was unforgiving.

My heart pounded against my chest from our run, and my head swam with possibilities of where we could go next. None of them were good enough. We'd been in Maine a day and they'd already found us. Cali and I had no connections here. If they'd tracked us down in this location, there was nowhere we could go. I shrugged off my coat and laid it across the bench by the front door, then slumped atop it.

"What's going on, Kellen?" Cali primly took off her coat and hung it on a hook by the door, but concern was printed all over her face. "I wanted to leave too. I didn't care for William, but why ask us to run?"

She didn't care for William. That wasn't what it had looked like to me, but I wasn't ready to bring up the way her eyes had locked onto his. Not with Gabe standing by observing. Besides, the others needed to know what I'd found out in William's cottage.

"The guy's a fraud."

"You talking about the warlock thing?" Satisfied with the amount of wattage aglow in the room, Gabe tossed his coat on mine.

"There was more to it than that." I rubbed my hands together, trying to warm them. "That wasn't even his house."

Gabe's eyes narrowed. "Whaddaya mean?"

"He has this incredible music collection, and I know of one of the artists. Something told me to make up facts to see what he'd do. Stanley Turrentine wasn't a trumpet player from LA, he was a saxophonist from Pittsburgh. Plus, William said he'd wanted to go to his concert. For somebody who had such a big collection of one artist's music, you'd think he would have known Turrentine died over twenty years ago. William isn't who he claimed to be, and he knows even less about jazz than I do, if that's possible." I got to my feet and began to pace. We needed a plan. That had always been my strength, but this time I was coming up empty.

"He lied to us." Cali frowned as though she'd never expected him to lie.

Good. It was childish, but I wanted her illusions about him to be shattered. I didn't want her to have any illusions at all.

"Isn't it possible he likes what he likes and didn't research the facts, K? Not everyone has a bitchin' memory like you do." Gabe grinned and gave me a thumbs up.

"Thanks, but if the music thing isn't proof enough, there was a poncho for a guy about five times William's size hanging on the back of the closet door. I peeked." It had been easy enough to do. William had been so focused on staring at Cali, he hadn't even heard me turn the knob. "I'm wondering if William isn't the caretaker. Did your mom tell you the caretaker's name?"

"No, and I didn't ask. When he showed up, he knew right where to go. We even have hot water now."

Gabe meant well, but he wasn't getting it. He didn't understand Faerie, and that was why . . .

"You invited him in . . ." I let my voice trail off, not wanting it to sound like an accusation but knowing I was too late.

Gabe's eyes widened as he seemed to run through a mental checklist of his initial interaction with William. "But he had the keys. And that check from my mom. He has to be legit."

"You don't know them like we do. If William *is* one of them, he's got powers we can't even begin to understand. He can probably manifest fake checks and house keys without breaking a sweat.

Gabe paled considerably and slapped his hand against his forehead. "That was so stupid. I was expecting a caretaker to show up. William could have said any name and I wouldn't have questioned him."

"Don't beat yourself up." I held up my hands. "I totally get why you did it, man, but we have to face facts. If William's one of them, the invitation is binding. He can come back any time. He holds that power over us now."

"Lying bastard," Cali muttered, wrapping her arms around herself. I couldn't pinpoint whether she was angry or afraid.

"Clearly you have an issue with him." I reached out for her emotions, something I couldn't bring myself to do when I was at the table with William. But now Cali's fear and frustration flooded me and I kicked myself for not checking in sooner.

She looked at Gabe and me, then wrapped her arms tighter around herself. "I felt like he was doing something to me when we were there."

A million scenarios played out in my mind as the sensation of Cali's discomfort and fear broadened within my chest. "Like what?"

She frowned, that tell-tale crease above her brow returning. "It was like he was forcing me to look in his eyes, like he was trying to hold me in a trance. I couldn't look away. At one point I felt like I wanted to be closer to him, and then I caught myself and stopped leaning in."

"I'm sorry. I didn't realize William was such an unmitigated ass that he'd hit on your fiancée at dinner, K." Gabe growled. "That was way uncool. What a scumbag."

Cali turned to Gabe and her confusion mixed with fear. "But didn't you see what was happening between us? Didn't you pick up on what he was doing?"

Gabe stuffed his hands in his pockets. "What can I say, C? You're a lot older than K. He hasn't had much experience with girls, and I thought maybe—"

Oh, God. "That's enough, Gabe." I cut in on that cringe-worthy explanation, but it was too late. Embarrassment flooded every part of me.

Cali's expression turned pleading and her voice altered to match. "Kellen St. James, there never has been, and never could be, anyone for me but you. Go ahead. See for yourself."

"I don't understand." Gabe looked from Cali to me as though he'd missed part of the plot.

I took Cali's hands in mine and an incredible wave of love poured through me and over me. I closed my eyes against the force of Cali's feelings, absorbing them like the sun's rays. I'd never felt love like that before, and my throat tightened in response.

When the feeling subsided, I kept my eyes closed. "How do you feel about William?"

Dread and fear, the extreme opposite of the way she felt about me, rushed forward. I instantly relaxed.

I could have done this at any time, but I'd been afraid of what I'd see or sense. It had never occurred to me that Cali could love another—until tonight.

I'd been about to pull back when I sensed something else. Guilt. A nagging, persistent twinge that formed a bass beat to Cali's emotions. I focused on it. Nothing about that sensation was tied to William, but it did have everything to do with me. Regardless, Cali's secrets weren't mine and I had no business prying until she was ready to share. For now, it would have to be enough to know she was telling the truth about William.

"I can sense her emotions, Gabe. She wasn't lying about William." I released Cali's hands, though I didn't want to.

"Wow. That's boss." Gabe scratched his head, coming closer and staring at the space between us as though searching for physical evidence of the freak gift I'd picked up. "I wish I could do that with the women I date. That would be a big timesaver." Then he turned to Cali with a face full of apologies. "Sorry I didn't interrupt with William."

"There's no way you could have known. Uncle Dillion said we should trust him, and we didn't question it."

Guilt poured into me. Here I was, acting like Cali was still invincible, when in reality she needed someone to have her back more than ever.

"We should never have gone there tonight." My nerves grew taut with indecision. A stranger knew about us, knew our names. "Should we leave? Get in the car and go?"

"First thing in the morning. I'm not going to drive these roads at night. I think we're as safe as we can be for now. I'm going to call my mom and ask about the caretaker." Gabe picked up his phone from the counter. "I stuck your things in the bedroom at the end of the hall. Why don't you build a fire in there and try to relax. I'll see what I can find out and update you in the morning. I'm beat."

"Thanks," I said, but Gabe had already started down the hallway, leaving us on our own.

I wasn't sure relaxing in front of a fire was on the agenda until Cali shivered beside me. I turned to her and couldn't help noticing her stiffened shoulders and the way she worried her bottom lip. Moving closer, I trailed my fingers down her arm.

"Would you like a fire? You look cold."

"That would be nice."

I took her hand in mine, and together we walked down the hall to the last bedroom where I flicked the switch. Low lighting on the side tables illuminated the space, highlighting a massive four poster in the center of the room that was ladened with blankets.

Though there were large windows here too, these had curtains. I shut the door behind us then unhooked the drapes, pulling them across the windows until I'd shut out the outside world, leaving the two of us alone.

Cali didn't follow. Instead she toyed with her hair, wandering about the room as though she couldn't sit still. I understood. A restlessness had surged up inside of me too, but I realized it was twofold. It didn't just have to do with William and all we had learned. The two of us were alone, and it was one of the few times we'd ever truly been so.

My heart raced inside my chest, and for about the millionth time I wished we were anywhere but there. Somewhere where we could be together without the threat of anyone. Somewhere we could escape. That's what I needed, an escape from everything and everyone but Cali.

Crouching at the hearth, I pushed aside memories of Cali magically conjuring a fire and went through the steps Gran had taught me to start one. I checked to make sure the flue was open, added the wood, and lit a starter log with kindling. The flame took, and only then did I step back to examine my handiwork.

When I finally turned, I found Cali lying sideways across the bed and my throat ran dry. *God she's beautiful.* How was it that she'd fallen in love with me? She told me once that I was a good person, but I wasn't sure I'd ever done anything good enough in my life to deserve Cali.

I took a step toward her and swallowed. "We're in the middle of this mess and all I want to do is be close to you."

"That's all I want too." Her voice was soft, a step above a whisper, and she stretched her arms above her head in either temptation, restlessness, or a little bit of both.

I kicked off my boots and climbed onto the bed beside her, drawing down one of the pillows so we could prop up our heads. Cali wrapped her arms around me, snuggling close.

"What's wrong?" Her voice sounded insecure, so different from the voice of the goddess that I'd known.

Don't ask her. But before I could stop myself, I turned in Cali's embrace and met her eyes. "You really weren't flirting with him?"

Her cheeks turned red under my scrutiny. "No."

Guilt immediately flooded me. "I get it. I'm sorry. I was just—"

"Being a guy?" she finished for me, raising one eyebrow in an action that so closely mirrored the look I usually reserved for her that I laughed.

"What would you know about guys?"

She scowled in response and began pulling away, but I captured her hands in mine, wanting her to stay.

"I mean, you told me I was the first boyfriend you ever had."

"That's true. But remember, I once had the knowledge of the universe at my fingertips." She smiled saucily, but it didn't last. Her grin soon faded into nothing as she lay against me.

"You don't remember any of it now, do you." Interested, I waited for her answer, stroking her arm absentmindedly.

"As I said before, I gained knowledge, mostly what I needed to know to become a mortal, but almost everything about the history of our people is gone. A few trivial things stayed with me, but . . . I don't know how to live like this, Kellen. I'm trying, but I feel lost." Tear tracks ran down her cheeks and I ached to erase her pain. Her fears. The confession must have cost her.

I pulled a tissue from the box on the side table and offered it to her.

Cali accepted the tissue and stared at it for a moment. I took it back from her and balled it up, then showed her how to dab at her tears.

"Thanks." She smiled weakly and took over from there until her tears were nothing but a memory. "I would have been able to translate Gabe's protection spell easily before. I can remember being able to access centuries of information as a goddess, but not what any of it is."

The fire crackled. The room had warmed considerably, and Cali snuggled farther down into the pillows, yawning.

"It's going to take a little getting used to, Kellen. For both of us."

Cupping her cheek, I stared into her eyes, wanting her to understand how much she meant to me. "I could take a lifetime to get used to you."

Those were the last words I uttered before I kissed her. My lips met hers and the world around me disappeared. She was no longer immortal, yet the heat from her mouth seared mine. One kiss would never be enough. I deepened ours, encouraged as Cali's response told me she wanted this moment between us. This wasn't the first time we'd kissed, but it could hardly compare to the kisses that had come before.

Cali fought to get closer to me so that our bodies aligned with one another's. My world spun around me in wide disconcerting revolutions. I couldn't think. I could only kiss Calienta's lips raw as she sighed within my arms.

Her tongue swept over mine, tentative yet torturous, and I groaned aloud, kissing her back with everything I had. I didn't stop her when she wrapped her legs around me and we rolled across the bed, mouths fused. Cali was my muse, my greatest temptation, my everything, and I never wanted it to end.

After our last revolution she ended up beneath me.

"Cali—" Cutting off my own words, I kissed her even more deeply, our tongues in a dance that left us both breathless.

The drive to connect with her wreaked havoc with my self-control. I needed to be as close to her as possible, to feel the sensation of her skin against mine.

"Kellen . . ." Cali said my name on a sigh and closed her eyes against the contact.

Any sense of gravity I had went out the window as I touched her in a way I hadn't before. I grazed her neck with a kiss, inhaling the vanilla scent that was Cali. "I love you, Calienta."

"I love you, Kellen." She'd been pressing her lips against my hair, so her answer came back muffled. I didn't care.

I knew what we both wanted right then, but I hesitated. We'd never been this close, and things had never gotten so heated between us. As much as I desperately needed to take things further, I'd never had a physical relationship. Cali hadn't either. Whenever I'd envisioned making love to her, and God knew I'd envisioned it, we'd been married. But who knew how long we'd be on the run? Did I really want to die never having been close to her? That was a very possible outcome.

I pressed my lips to hers, closing my eyes against her soft kiss until I drew back and stared into her rounded blue ones. "Be with me tonight."

"I will. Goddess help me, I will."

This time, it was Cali who brought her lips to mine. It was slow and tantalizing and sent my head spinning and all logic into nothingness.

Then a knock at the door sounded its way into our private moment and I froze.

"Hey, guys? Got a moment?" Gabe's voice had the effect of dumping a gallon of cold water over my head.

With care, I sat back on my knees. Cali's eyes were still darkened with desire, her breathing erratic. I ached for more time alone with her.

Leaning down, I pressed a kiss to her forehead and helped her up. There was no way Gabe wouldn't know what had been going on, but that was on him for interrupting. Either way, whatever he had to say better have been good.

"Come in." I put every ounce of my frustration in my response.

For a moment nothing happened. Then the door swung open. Gabe's face fell when he glimpsed mine.

"Sorry, C, K. I didn't mean to interrupt anything." He backed up, as though considering closing the door again, which would have been even worse.

"It's fine." Though my answer made it sound anything but. Forcing myself to slide off the bed, I stood. "Did you get ahold of your mom?"

"I did, but that can wait. You were right, Kellen. I don't think William is the caretaker." Even in the room's low lighting I could make out the worry etched across his face.

Now he had my attention.

Cali sat up. "What are you talking about, Gabriel?"

"Come with me." Gabe turned and padded back down the hallway. His phone lay on top of the counter and he woke it, illuminating the dim room. He scrolled halfway down the page and handed it to me. "Look at this."

An older man's photo dominated the screen. He resembled a cartoon Santa Claus with the round belly to match. I didn't know the guy. I looked to Gabe for guidance.

"Trust me, dude. Keep scrolling."

I did as he asked and read the bio that followed out loud. "Thomas Jenkins, President. Thomas has had over thirty years' experience in gardening. An avid jazz enthusiast, Mr. Jenkins spends his days puttering about the rose gardens at Alastrom, a local summer vacation rental." I turned to Gabe. "What's Alastrom?"

"The name of this house. My dad picked it." Gabe swallowed, holding out his hand for his phone, which I returned. "This guy is our caretaker, not William."

Oh no. "But what about Dillion's note?"

"I don't know what the dealio is with that, but my mother never wrote a check to William, and that wasn't the dude's house." Gabe crossed his arms over his chest, as though ready to block William should he show up again.

There was little he'd be able to do to stop him. Gabe was mortal and William was . . . something.

"Do you want to leave in the morning or leave now?" I glanced at the impossibly darkened windows.

"I say we stick with tomorrow. They're out there right now. Leaving would put us directly in their path." Gabe polished off his water bottle before tossing it in an arc into the recycle bin.

I noted that Cali's lips were swollen from my kisses, her eyes hooded from the stolen moments we'd shared. I couldn't stand around and make small talk with Gabe after *that*. I needed a cold shower. Or some fresh air.

"I'm gonna go outside for a few minutes. I need to clear my head. I won't cross the bridge."

Cali nodded. "Do you want me to come with you?"

"It's okay. I need a minute." I moved toward the door. "I won't go anywhere, I promise."

I grabbed a light hoodie and shrugged into it. It wouldn't help much—the forecast had warned it would dip into the thirties tonight—but I wouldn't be gone long. I flicked the switch for the porch light.

A beat later, I stepped outside and shut the door. Leaning my elbows on the railing in front of me, I took a long, slow breath. The cold salt air blasted me and I could think again.

Inside, with Cali, I'd somehow managed to forget everything I'd wanted for us. I'd wanted a life in Gran's cottage by the sea. A simple existence that didn't involve our lives being threatened on a daily basis. No part of that game plan included me taking advantage of someone who hadn't been mortal for more than twenty-four hours. If we'd gotten married, tonight would have been different. Getting to know Cali even better now, as unbelievable as that sounded, would risk everything.

Touching my fingers to my lips, I let myself recall the sensation of her mouth on mine. We'd never kissed that way before. It had been all consuming. She made me feel different. Heck, she made me *feel*. It was like I'd never lived before she came into my life.

I picked up the flashlight beside the front door. I'd need it if I was going to take a walk. It was too dark.

Wait a minute. Why do you need a flashlight? You aren't going anywhere.

My feet disagreed. They were moving beneath me, and

before I realized it, I'd made it over the bridge and into the woods—the exact place I'd been warned not to go.

What are you doing? Seriously.

I did an about-face and began a light jog back to the house. I never should have left. I'd almost made it to the bridge when my feet took me in a wide arc and I found myself walking briskly in the opposite direction, the one leading from the house.

But I have to go back . . .

"No, you don't." A voice wandered into my ear, beckoning to me. At first I didn't recognize it, but it quickly morphed into one so familiar I ached to be close to it. "Just a little farther, Kellen, and we can be together."

I'd heard Cali's voice in my dreams all the time as a child, and later even in my waking hours, so hearing it now didn't surprise me.

"This is a bad idea, Cali. We need to go back."

But even as my internal nagging voice warned me that Cali no longer had the power to call to me, the need to continue overwhelmed all other emotions. I couldn't stop walking.

CHAPTER 28

CALI

When Gabriel interrupted us, I'd considered pleasantly murdering him.

Kellen. Dearest Danu, the way he touched me. His kisses were still on my mind, and I blushed as I remembered his hands on my body.

When Kellen went outside, Gabriel showed me a wonderful invention called a shower and helped me turn on the water. Already showers ranked among the things I enjoyed most as a mortal.

There were a variety of colored bottles. Kellen had labeled two of them in black ink. *Hair #1 and Hair #2—apply and rinse with water.* I smiled despite myself at his thoughtfulness, and I followed his instructions, cleaning my hair and body until the previous two days felt like nothing more than a dim nightmare.

Thoughts of Kellen came rushing back, however. I ached to be with him, and the hot water wasn't helping to cool my memories of our heated moments. I soon understood why Kellen had chosen the cold rather than stay indoors.

I washed the soap from my hair and body, turned off the

water, and exited the shower. After toweling off, I used the comb device to organize my hair and then wrapped the towel more securely around me. Of course, I wanted to be with Kellen, but that didn't mean I was without nerves.

But when I stepped into the bedroom, Kellen was nowhere to be found. Hurriedly I dried myself and dressed in clean clothing.

Gabriel was looking at his glowing communication device on the couch when I returned. He glanced up and smiled. "Feel better?"

"I do, thank you. I'm going to check on Kellen."

I didn't bother with a coat. After all, I had no plans to go outside, only to pull Kellen back in.

I only meant to open the door a crack, but it ended up swinging open all the way as I stood there in shock. I'd expected to find Kellen just outside, yet the space was empty.

"Kellen?" *Please let him answer. Please.*

There was no response. Dread coursed through me. *Oh no.* "Kellen!"

Gabriel raced over to join me. Panic flooded his features with tension. "K? Hold on, I'll call him." He held up his device and pressed the screen several times. Moments later a ringing sounded from somewhere deep in the house. "He doesn't have his phone."

"Kellen!" Fear edged into my voice as nothing but the emptiness of the cold night met me.

CHAPTER 29

KELLEN

Walking alone in the woods wasn't frightening, but peaceful. The moon acted as a natural spotlight on the path. With each step I caught glimpses of the ocean from between the trees.

The sea always had a quality about it that both terrified and intrigued me at the same time. Gran taught me from a young age to respect nature and never take it for granted. She wanted me to know that it could strike me down in an instant to keep me from doing anything stupid, and it had worked. Mostly.

I peered through the foliage in the direction of the water and sensed that familiar churning, sleeping power. One good storm could wake the giant at any moment. Wind whipped and whistled through the trees, howling like a specter.

That's it. Just a bit farther, Cali called to me in the dark.

Chills wracked me. My own voice screamed at me inside my head. *Go back. You know better than this.*

If only I'd thought to bring even a handful of salt with me. The natural ward to evil would have offered some protection.

I had nothing but my mother's pendant around my neck, and that didn't hold so much as a scrap of power.

I tried to turn around for the hundredth time, but my body moved of its own accord. It was as if I was attached to someone else's legs and they were in control. No matter how much I tried to go back, to run toward the relative safety of the house, the only thing I could do was move forward.

Tree roots poked from the ground in every direction. I couldn't focus, couldn't watch where I walked. The path forked up ahead. I could only move forward, though I had no idea what lay ahead.

Where am I going?

A sign, complete with an arrow, was staked into the ground ahead of me. It said Compass Harbor. I'd read about this path and these woods somewhere, but I couldn't remember anything about it. That didn't make sense. I always remembered way more than what was natural. My memory wasn't just photographic. I might have turned into a science experiment if Stephen had allowed it. It surprised me that he hadn't.

Quickly now, Kellen.

Cali's voice sounded farther away. I stumbled in my haste to keep up with her. The trail wound through the trees and ran alongside the ocean. It would be treacherous at best to continue.

"Kellen?"

The sound of my own name from a voice that wasn't Cali's shook me enough that I regained complete control over my legs. I could also now feel every knot of the howling wind through the light cotton of my hoodie and on my exposed head, neck, and hands in a way that I hadn't when I'd first been led into the woods.

Slowly, as if in a fog, I turned in the direction from which my name had been called. William stood there, his lantern raised high to illuminate his face.

He was absolutely the last person I wanted to see. He could have murdered the real caretaker or done something bad to him. The only good thing about William's being there was that he probably knew the way out of these woods.

"W-w-w-william-m-m. W-w-w-what're y-y-you—" My teeth chattered uncontrollably. There wasn't a time I ever remembered being this cold. Even in Faerie.

"I told you not to come out here. You're early." He grumbled this as he rifled through a duffle bag.

"E-e-early for w-w-what?"

But William didn't answer. Instead he pulled a flannel blanket from inside the bag and tossed it to me.

Begrudgingly, I opened the blanket and wrapped it around myself.

William continued to rifle through his bag and soon took out a thermos. He shoved it roughly in my direction. "Drink this."

There was no way I was drinking whatever it was, but curiosity got the better of me. The thermos top unscrewed with three turns, and I smelled its contents, cringing.

"What is this stuff?"

"It's a concoction I carry with me when I'm in the woods. Basil, ginger, turmeric, garlic, cayenne, and vegetable juice. It will prevent hypothermia."

"I don't have hypothermia." But a nagging voice warned me it was technically possible. I didn't know how long I'd been outside, and I hadn't dressed for a walk in the woods.

"No, but you'll get it, wandering out here in the night without so much as a scrap of protection against the elements." He zipped his bag and shouldered it again with something akin to disappointment on his face. "I'm trying to keep you alive. The least you can do is thank me."

Pivoting, he started off in the direction I'd come. At least I thought that was the direction. The urge to tell him to shove the drink up his lying warlock butt tempted me. Yet, I had no idea how to get home, and I'd left my phone at the house. Begrudgingly, I tightened the lid on the thermos and followed.

Up ahead lay a fork in the path. I needed to know where he was taking me.

"W-w-where d-does that o-o-other way g-g-go?" I could do nothing to stop my stuttering as the shivers overtook me again.

William stopped and gestured to the thermos. "The sea. Drink that or I'll make you drink it." He resumed his pace and left me to keep up.

No way was I drinking it. I'd dump the stuff when he wasn't paying attention.

"Your thoughts are loud, and you don't have much time. Drink it." William grabbed the thermos from me. Before I realized what he was planning to do, he'd uncapped it and forced some of the liquid into my mouth.

I tried to fight him off. The hot liquid scalded my hands in the process, but not before a decent quantity of the drink slid down my throat. I gagged at the foul taste. There was no doubt the crap was nasty, but it did send a path of heat through my body.

That didn't mean I appreciated having anything forced on me. I shoved the thermos back at William.

"Don't ever try that again." I didn't yell, but instead kept my voice even. I resisted the urge to rub my tongue on my sleeve. Anything to remove that indescribable taste from my mouth.

Unconcerned, William capped the thermos. "You ingested enough of it that you should be feeling better. Your speech sounds normal." He turned and continued on the path ahead.

Dammit, he was right. Though my stomach had battled an immediate wave of nausea with the first swallow, that had quickly passed. I could follow the thermos's contents through my body as it extended to my limbs. Tentatively, I wiggled my toes and moved each of my fingers. They seemed to be in working order. All the same, I took the opportunity to test them further by flipping William off while he had his back to me.

"What were you doing out here in the woods?" I did my best to make my voice sound casual—while taking a night-time walk with a warlock.

"Harvesting wintergreen. People are going to start getting sick this time of year and it's good for sore throats. I prefer to search for it at night."

"Huh." I didn't know what to think about that. It sounded plausible.

"My truck is just up here in the parking area." William gestured straight ahead.

"Parking area?"

"I'm not crazy enough to walk several miles in the dark like you."

William approached the lone vehicle in the parking lot, a black truck. I couldn't make out any more detail than that as our steps brought us closer.

"Miles? I didn't think I'd been gone that long."

William climbed in and opened the passenger door from the inside. A trickle of cool air shifted from the truck's vents as he started the engine. Reaching behind the seat, he grabbed another blanket and offered it to me.

"Thanks." I spread the fleece over me, tugging it up to my neck.

"They do that to you, you know. Take you away from space and time. The Good People do." He revved the engine, then put it in gear and drove us out of the parking area.

"What Good People?" It seemed better to play dumb.

The woods seemed to call to me again from beyond the truck. I turned from the window and wrapped the blanket tighter around me, impatient for the vehicle to heat up.

"Do you know anything about the legends and folklore of this place?" he asked. "Many locals in this area believe there are little people around these parts."

As he spoke, it felt like William's bizarre drink was trying to fight its way out of my stomach. I choked. Tears gathered in the corners of my eyes as I attempted to get my coughing under control.

"You know who I mean, right? The fey. Faerie folk."

The concept of faeries in Maine made me feel sick. "Faeries? Please."

"There are all kinds of spirits and beings that roam these woods. You'll want to be careful out here and not go wandering off." William cranked the heater as high as it would go and finally the cool air transitioned to a warm blast. "You're lucky I'm the one that found you first."

Neither of us spoke after that as we drove back to Gabe's. William's eyes stayed on the road and mine on the side window as I stared into the dark, moonless night, with barely a star to brighten it. Though I supposed there wouldn't be many stars, as Cali wasn't there to light them.

By the time we reached the Stewarts' house, I battled a strange mix of emotions—relief that I'd made it back to my temporary home, but also embarrassment at William having to haul me out of the woods. To my annoyance, William turned off the truck and got out with me. I'd been hoping that he would drop me off and go on his way. Together we walked toward the house.

Cali and Gabe ran to meet me as I stepped inside. Cali's emotions—worry, fear, and relief—rose up on me. She placed two palms on my chest, her panicked eyes locking onto mine. "What were you thinking? You could have been killed!"

Gabe looked like he'd been about to say the same. What kind of answer did they expect? It wasn't like I could speak truthfully with William beside me.

Staring at her hard, I tried to communicate without words that I'd been led into the woods. "I went for a walk. I'm sorry to worry you."

But Cali didn't seem to get that I'd lied for William's sake. "You know better than anyone what a bad idea that is. How could you?!" She put both palms up as if to perform magick, then must have remembered she was powerless in mid-move, because a frustrated-sounding "Oooh!" escaped her lips.

No one moved. In that moment I forgot about Gabe and William. I could only stare at Cali, hurt washing over me even as I fought not to show it. Cali had once used her powers on me to keep me from attacking her brother and getting myself killed, but then I'd asked her to trust me. Though we never talked about it afterward, I foolishly assumed that my reaction combined with her immediate apology meant she'd never try using her powers on me again.

Apparently not.

Forcing myself to smile, I turned to William. "Thanks, William."

"Don't mention it." That mocking smile of his had returned, and the level of gratitude I was feeling toward him shifted into a steady decline.

Cali's emotions pummeled me. Fear and anger mixed with worry so intense that she might as well have announced her feelings to the room.

Right then, I was tired of it. She didn't ask me how I felt. Maybe she assumed her own thoughts mattered more than mine. Annoyance sparked to life inside of me, but this wasn't from Cali. It was all me.

"I can show myself out. Good night, all." With a nod and one last lingering look at Cali, William turned away and headed for the door.

The anger in my gut began to build. It had been bad enough that William had looked at Cali that way all night, but to do it again was too much. I hated the direction of my thoughts. I wasn't a caveman, and I didn't own Cali. She had the right to look at whoever she wanted. Yet after the evening we'd had and her failed attempt to use magick on me . . .

"Good night, man, and thanks." Gabe shut the door after the phony caretaker and slid the deadbolt into place before whirling around. "What happened, K?"

"I just wanted to stand on the porch for a moment and the next thing I knew, I didn't have control over my body. I tried everything I could to turn around. I ran into William in the woods and he brought me home."

If they were looking for more of an explanation, I had none to give.

Cali reached for me, but I stepped out of her grasp. "I'm going to bed."

"Kellen, we need to talk." Cali's confusion and upset surrounded me as I left the room, but I was done.

"No." I shook my head, backing out of the room. "I can't deal with your world anymore tonight."

Before she or Gabe could reply, I whirled around and went to search for another bedroom. One that didn't remind me of Cali.

CHAPTER 30
CALI

The anger that had seethed inside me only a moment ago dissipated as Kellen walked away. I hadn't meant to try and use magick on him. Even if I still had my powers, I would have stopped myself. He had to know that.

"So . . . this has been fun." Gabriel ran his hand over his face. "I'm going to get some shut-eye. We'll get out of here at first light. Okay if I turn these off?" He hovered his finger over the panel on the wall.

I nodded, unsure of what to do next. "Good night, Gabriel."

"Good night, C." He pressed down on the switch, plunging the room into almost total darkness. Only a low light in the hallway illuminated Gabriel's retreating form.

Hugging myself, I stared at the room I'd been left alone in. It felt too large. Too exposed. The evening had been a whirlwind of emotions. I was too shaken to sleep.

Though it had grown colder outside, I wrapped one of the thick blankets from the great room around me and stepped out onto the balcony. I needed one more moment on my own before I found Kellen and apologized.

Shaking, I stared out at the sea and tried to imagine being back home and on the other side of the water. If Kellen and I had gotten married, we would have been on something called a honeymoon now. I didn't know what it involved other than that we would have been far from anyone we knew and there would be more moments like the one we shared earlier that night.

But I'd angered him and ended up alone.

An intense wind pummeled me. The cold stung my cheeks and sent my ears burning. Below me the sea tide churned, rocking back and forth. Unwelcome tears sprang up in my eyes. If I'd been home, I could have talked to my mother. She would have hugged me and taken me to one of my favorite stars. My parents and Uncle Dillion were all I had left.

Still, Father had promised someone would come for us and help us. Where were they? Perhaps my parents no longer cared about me now that I'd become mortal. Did they not understand that I needed them?

Wait. Cabhan was an angel, and angels were supposed to communicate with mortals, right? If Cabhan were here, perhaps he could get a message to my family.

It began to snow. Clusters of little white crystals drifted unthreateningly down from the sky. I gripped the cold iron railing and whispered my plea into the night. "Cab. Cabhan, can you hear me?"

My nerves jumped and danced inside my mortal body as I waited with my very breath on hold. Yet only the crash of wave against rock greeted me, leaving me feeling even more alone than I had when the last of my immortal powers floated away. The only thing my pleas to Cabhan had accomplished was that I'd almost frozen half to death. I was such a fool. I expected Cabhan to show up and solve my problems like he and the rest of my family had done for all of my existence. It wasn't until Kellen and I had gone to Faerie that I'd had the chance to solve a single problem for myself. Standing here shivering in my blanket wasn't going to resolve anything.

The snowflakes swirled through the air. They were beautiful. I'd so rarely seen snow. In the heavens, the weather was consistently sunny, but I would have loved the snowfall.

A snowflake landed on the center of my nose, directly below the bridge. Cross-eyed, I stared, waiting for it to melt. It didn't. Other snowflakes soon joined in until a small pile of them was perched there.

Laughter rose from the darkness and the sound made me jerk, causing the snowflakes to slide off.

"Calienta."

Cabhan's voice caught me off guard. Then relief burst inside my chest as I spotted him standing atop the rock below. My relief almost overwhelmed me.

"Cab!"

Cabhan didn't look much different from the last time I'd seen him—with the exception of his attire. He could have been any mortal with his jeans and fleece, at least from a distance. I'd never met an angel before, but I imagined part of him must glow with the intensity of that magickal star place that I'd wanted to visit back at the air-o-port. If only he'd come closer so I could see him properly.

But he didn't give me a chance to ask. "I don't have much time. You're in danger."

"They know we're here." Even as I spoke, I knew the truth. We should have been able to experience a quiet existence without magick, but it had followed us.

Cabhan's expression turned grave in the moonlight. "You are all in danger, but I can help. Open the door for me, Calienta, and invite me in!"

Spinning, I turned to the balcony door. I'd never gone to the bottom level, but I would find my way and open the latch to allow him inside.

I hadn't even opened the door when fear began to contort my insides. My hands grew numb upon the ice-cold handle. Cabhan wouldn't need an invitation to enter the house. That rule didn't apply to angels. I'd wanted this person to be my brother so badly that I'd been about to invite him in. The only protection we had left at our disposal was the house, and I would not relinquish it.

Slowly, I turned back, keeping my distance from the railing, yet remaining close enough that I could meet the fake Cabhan's eyes. "My brother would not need to make such a request."

"That's because I'm not Cabhan, you little witch!" Cabhan's form began to blur and shift in the moonlight. In moments, his healthy bronze skin transformed into an unearthly green. His blue eyes combined to form the single eye on the center of Cana's forehead. She drew back her hand as though to attack.

"Cali, get in the house!"

It wasn't Gabriel or Kellen behind me, but William who hissed the warning from inside the house. I tried to back up, but he drew me inside and slammed the door shut behind us.

The door vibrated with the force of something that sounded like waves crashing against the house. It shook as though it would blow from its hinges at any moment.

William wasted no time. Raising his hands, he ran them along the doorframe, mumbling a series of incoherent words. Quickly he moved to the windows, repeating himself. The entire process took a matter of moments, but when he finished, the house seemed calmer. The evil beyond it had been repelled.

"Are you okay?" I spoke loudly so that Kellen and Gabriel might hear me. "Were you injured in any way?"

Of course, no one came running. Kellen was fighting the effects of the cold from earlier, and Gabriel had gone to bed. I'd have to deal with William on my own.

Get control of yourself, Calienta. You are from a family of gods and goddesses that dates back to the beginning of time. You will not be weak.

William stuffed his hands into his pockets. "I am fine. Thank you for your concern."

"How did you get in?" My heart pounded, a slow, steady beat that I would have sworn he could hear. I had no powers, and William had definitely spelled me at dinner. I couldn't possibly be in a more vulnerable position. Well, unless I decided to open the door and invite Auntie in. The chill from outside clung to me and I suppressed a shiver.

William held up a shiny golden object. "Key. When I ran into Kellen in the woods, I thought it best to wait outside and watch the house. Much like a stakeout."

Frowning, I reached for my immortal catalog of knowledge, then remembered it was long gone. "I do not know this term."

William looked different in the moonlight. More relaxed. Still, I knew he wasn't who he claimed to be, and his proximity made me uncomfortable.

"It's when law enforcement sits outside a home and waits for any wrongdoing."

I stepped around him and tipped my chin. "Well, we don't need your protection. Please leave now." I made my words sound as formidable as possible.

William's easy smile faded. "No, I wouldn't imagine you do, but I was waiting for something to happen." He moved closer. "It did. Just not the way . . . never mind."

He was a frustrating sort of person, and my opinion of him hadn't changed since dinner. "What were you doing to me at dinner?"

A soft laugh escaped him. "Giving you a wonderful culinary experience, Cali. Did you not care for the meal?"

"It was more than that, and you know it." I spat out the accusation. "You were using magick on me." I was so close to that line I shouldn't cross. One where I admitted my involvement with magick. I had to tread carefully. "It was like you were trying to get me to want you instead of Kellen. It made me uncomfortable."

I anticipated anger from William, but it didn't come. His quiet answer followed instead. "I was using magick on you, and I'm sorry for it."

The last thing I ever expected was for him to apologize and admit his behavior outright. I took several moments to compose myself, to craft a cool retort, yet the only thing I could come up with was a single question.

"Why?"

He shrugged. "Because I wanted to win your affections. In my world, that's how we use magick."

"It's manipulative." Another shiver rippled through me, but I was too late to stop it. "And my affections have already been won. Kellen and I are to be wed." I wrung my hands together. I should walk away or ask him to leave again. I had a feeling he would listen if I asked him to go.

"I know. It won't happen again. You have my word." William placed his hands on my shoulders and a warmth seeped into me. The chill that had clung to me from outside faded away.

"Stop it." I stepped back and out of his grasp.

He held his hands up, palms out. "Listen to me, Cali. You aren't safe here."

"I don't know what you're talking about." The lie slipped

easily off my tongue and my cheeks burned. Part of me wanted to look away from William's eyes and part of me didn't.

"Don't pretend ignorance. I know who you are." His voice held wonder, as if he'd just puzzled out the secrets of the world. His eyes, an unusual shade of blue not unlike my own, bore into mine, holding me hostage.

Before I could respond, he leaned in and kissed me, his lips moving over mine in a soft, slow dance. William and his kiss mesmerized me, making me feel something down to my bones. Despite his magick and trickery at dinner, everything he'd done seemed to fade away in the face of his gentleness.

That's when I realized that he hadn't spelled me. William was kissing me, and I was letting him. I pressed my hands against his chest and pushed back hard.

William moved immediately, but he didn't seem to notice the wave of regret pounding through my soul.

"Come away with me," he whispered. "Come with me and be mine forever."

Before I finished running through my surging thoughts, he stepped closer, trailing his lips across my forehead, moving to find my mouth again. Why wasn't he stopping? Didn't he sense my hesitation?

He wouldn't, because William wasn't Kellen. No one was. Kellen was the one I wanted more than anything. The one whose kisses drove me to distraction. William might have desired me, but it was Kellen who truly understood me. He was my friend, and he would soon become my lover. He was the other half of my heart.

William could never replace him. We were relative strangers.

Then, cognizant once more of the missing caretaker and the lies William had told to gain entrance into our world, I placed my hands on William's shoulders and gently pushed him away.

"I'm sorry, William, but I chose Kellen a long time ago."

He brought his fingers to rest beneath his chin. "But your lips said something different."

I crossed my arms over my chest and backed up, putting distance between us. "No man will ever tell me what I feel. Kellen and I have a history that you cannot possibly understand. I love him." My mind drifted to earlier that night, when Kellen and I had clung to each other, kissing. My body had been on fire. Had that only been a few hours earlier? It seemed like days ago.

William looked like he was going to challenge me again, but then he lowered his hands to his sides. "If only you would choose me, I could protect you."

And that in and of itself was what broke the hold William had over me.

"I can protect myself." I jabbed my thumb at my own chest for emphasis. "Now give me your key and please leave."

He stared at me only a moment longer, though I took care not to meet his eyes directly. Finally, he reached into the front pocket of his oversized coat and extracted the key. When I didn't reach for it, he laid it on a nearby table.

"Good-bye, then. You will be in my dreams for the rest of my life."

The profession might have seemed romantic, but it was too close to what had actually happened with Kellen and me. My jaw set in a hard line as I watched William walk away, across the room and out the front door, shutting it softly behind him.

I'd have to wake up Gabriel and Kellen immediately. How long would it take William to leave? How quickly could we get in the automobile? Was there any way we could escape without William and the C.O.D. knowing?

Those last thoughts faded into nothing as Gabriel's shout woke me from my reverie. *Something's wrong.*

Unthinking, my feet carried me down the hall, toward the sound of his cries and the unmistakable smell . . . of salt water.

CHAPTER 31

KELLEN

Part of me had been convinced I'd never be able to sleep in the cold room without Cali. Within moments of hitting the pillow, however, exhaustion overtook me and I crashed right into a dream. In it, I walked along the same path I'd traveled earlier. Unlike earlier in the evening, I didn't feel as though anyone lured me anywhere. I was out for a walk on my own. It wasn't safe in the woods, but some part of me was acutely aware I was dreaming.

Voices caught my attention. The sound of people talking drifted in and out like a phone call with a poor signal.

"I do not like it . . ."

"We've never done this before and—"

As quickly as the voices rose, they disappeared, and I suddenly realized that I stood alone on the path. How had I ended up back in the woods again? It was dangerous. I had to get back to the house and fast.

Turning, I ran in the direction I'd come, but it wasn't easy going. Gnarled tree roots popped up from the ground like elderly hands, tripping me so that I fought to stay on my feet. I hadn't paid attention when I'd left the house. Had the path forked to the left or right? I veered right out of sheer desperation.

Too late I realized that the path I'd chosen led me down to the sea. I caught myself before the water could lap at my feet. I stood on tiptoe to remain on dry land.

The ocean seemed closer, bigger here. The tide was out but it quickly rolled in with plans to eat up the shore, like a beast waiting for a sacrifice.

Without warning, a monster wave shot toward me. It crashed over my head, pulling me under. The currents jerked me downward and upward, tossing me around like a rag doll. I broke through the surface and gasped for air, only to be plunged beneath as another wave rolled in. I wouldn't last long. I'd never been a strong swimmer, and the frigid water sank into my veins, freezing me down to my toes. My muscles stiffened, locked, and ached. I could barely move my arms to tread water.

Then the sea switched tactics. No longer did she toss me about, but she turned to slamming me against the rock. Stars broke out across my vision, and not the kind Cali used to light. I'd never even seen those. I should have asked Cali to light them for me. Why hadn't I? It had been important to her.

Slam! Pain radiated along my scalp, my back, and every limb as the tide knocked me against the rocks once more. I fought to stay afloat, searching blindly for the path that had led me to the sea. Again and again it tossed me against the unforgiving surface, its jagged edges slicing my skin like tiny knives.

I didn't think people were supposed to get hurt in dreams, but I felt everything as though it were actually happening. I tasted the salt and rust of my own blood in my mouth and a sinking feeling overtook me.

What if this isn't a dream?

For several seconds I stopped fighting the current and rode it out of pure shock. Fragments of memories swirled in my weary head, bouncing around inside my brain as I was tossed around in the sea. Calienta and the first moment that I saw her. Stephen when he'd told me my mother died. Seeing my mother in Faerie and holding her hand. Gran telling me that Calienta was a Star Child. All of those moments spun through my head in circles.

Wham! The water slammed me into the rock again. A searing pain shot up the center of my head as if it had been split in two. My arms flailed uselessly beside me. They might as well have been dead weights.

Then suddenly the swell of music rose above the roar of the waves, and the sea quieted. The water receded, and a blue light swung merrily along the shoreline. Scrambling to my feet, I staggered toward the water's edge, following the light as it led me back onto the path I'd come from.

The sounds of music, clinking champagne glasses, and laughter traveled to my ears. Someone was having a party.

Bobbing along, the blue light continued ahead of me, always out of reach. Its hypnotic movement kept me walking, gliding along the path in its wake. Then I rounded the bend and froze. A magnificent house loomed over me. Without exterior lighting, it was difficult to make out the details of the mansion in the woods. The party sounds were louder here, and lights winked merrily at me from every window. A set of wide stone steps led upward, and I began to climb, the music growing louder as I ascended. The style sounded like circa 1930s. Billie Holiday.

A dark-haired man stepped from the shadows. Though his clothing blended into the night, a lamp illuminated his face, swinging back and forth on a stick that he carried in his hand. The frame of the lamp gave the light a blue haze. "What are you doing here?"

"Sorry. I saw your light and heard the music." That answer wasn't right. I wasn't sure how I'd gotten there.

Yet he nodded, his expression not unfriendly. "I'm not on your side, but I'm not on theirs. You belong inside where it's warm." He turned and raced up the steps.

I followed, almost reaching him at the next-to-last step before the strange man halted.

"You must go back."

"But what about the party?" I gestured to the house. I was close enough now to make out the people dancing inside.

"The party's over."

As he said this, the lights winked out as if he'd flicked a light switch.

Then everything—the strange man, the house, the lights and party—all disappeared. The last vestiges of the Billie Holiday tune clung to the air like moisture on my skin on a high-humidity day.

My heart lodged itself in my throat as I found myself standing alone on the charred remains of a set of stone steps that now led . . . to nowhere.

"Kellen!" Cali's voice filled my head, sounding far away.

"Dude, wake up! Wake up!" Gabe sounded much closer.

Then warmth began to spread throughout my entire body, chasing away the chill and calming the sea. I was wrapped in something.

Gasping, I opened my eyes. Cali and Gabe stood over me. I sat up straighter, sucking in air as I looked wildly about, focusing on everything and nothing. The charred ruins, the empty stairs, the path, rocks, and ocean were gone.

I was back at the Stewarts' house. I'd been wrapped in a blanket and moved to a nearby sofa. I was inside, safe, and more importantly, *alive*. Blood rushed to my head as I tried to stand, and I fell back against the cushions from dizziness.

My teeth began to chatter, and I realized my sleep pants and T-shirt were soaking wet. Cali gripped my hand. Her concern for me snuck into my senses. It was a quiet emotion. Knowing Cali, she'd masked it to avoid upsetting me. Too late for that.

"You scared me. I was worried," she said.

"S-s-sorry." My teeth chattered too much to talk. I glanced over at the bed that I had lain down on. It appeared to be drenched, and the room smelled of salt water. It looked like I'd been swimming in the sea—in my bed.

None of it had been a dream.

Of course, this sort of thing had happened to me before, when I'd stepped right into Gran's backyard in Ireland from my graduation ceremony in Connecticut via a portal. At the time I assumed I'd been dreaming, until I returned to graduation and realized I had sand on my shoes and wore the same dinosaur socks I'd had when I was six. They'd been a little on the tight side.

"You're freezing," Gabe said as he and Cali took me by the arms and pulled me from the sofa. "You need to get into the shower and warm up ASAP, dude. This is so not cool."

I didn't argue as Cali's warm fingers closed over my arm and she guided me to the adjoining bathroom.

My teeth chattered as I let her lead me. I knew I should feel angry at Cali for what had happened before, but I didn't have the energy. Instead, I waited until she had turned on the hot spray and the steaming water poured into the stall before I moved toward it.

Cali touched my frigid arm. "Kellen, I'm sorry about before . . ."

Nodding, I met her eyes, anxiety-filled and so blue it almost hurt to look at them. Right then they were red and puffy in a way I hadn't seen before. I hated that I had played a part in making them look that way.

"S'okay." My words slurred as I spoke.

She seemed to want more from me, but the cold ate at me from the inside out. I removed my wet clothes, not caring that we hadn't had a chance to progress to that stage in our relationship yet, and stepped under the spray.

Thinking made my head hurt, so I closed my eyes. When I lifted my lids again, blood ran off me and onto the shower floor. My head throbbed and I touched my hand to it gingerly. More blood. As I surveyed the rest of my body, cuts and bruises slowly appeared before my eyes.

Moaning, I let the hot water rain down on my head, its warmth heating me. I stayed that way until I could move my fingers and toes again. Eventually my brain function began to return. I could at least process thoughts.

I'd been in the sea. But how had I gotten there, and who had wanted me there? Was it the C.O.D.? What purpose would my death serve if I had something they wanted?

After I cleaned up as best I could, I turned off the water and stepped from the shower. Cali had gone, so I positioned myself in front of the mirror. A large bruise covered the left side of my cheek. Blood trickled from my forehead and dripped onto the bathmat. I winced as a sharp pain lanced my side. I grabbed a washcloth from the shelf and ran cold water over the cloth. After ringing it out, I pressed the washcloth against the gash that had appeared, to stop the bleeding.

Gabe peeked his sandy blond head around the door. "Ew. When did you do—" The realization that this had all happened in my dream seemed to hit him like a freight train. "That's creepy, man. I don't understand. You didn't look like this when you woke up."

"Tell me about it. Do you have bandages and stuff?" I

scanned my legs, taking in the abundance of cuts, scratches, and bruises.

Gabe's eyes were impossibly wide, as though he'd gone into shock. He cleared his throat. "Yeah. Give me a minute." But he nodded way too many times.

By the time he returned with supplies, I'd managed to slide on some clean boxers and lower myself to a bench beside the shower. Together we patched me up in silence, applying bandages to any wounds that were bleeding freely. Though we covered the gash on my forehead and others on my chest and stomach, the bruises on my cheekbone, chin, and collarbone would be clearly visible even after I got dressed.

"I think that should do it." Gabe packed up the few remaining supplies into a small red and white box. I bet the Stewarts had never seen this much first-aid action in their vacation home.

"One more thing. I could use help getting dressed." When Gabe nodded, I added, "Do me a favor and turn those pajamas inside out first."

Gabe stared at me, sleep pants in hand. "Why?"

"It's supposed to repel faeries."

There were a million bits of lore about keeping faeries at bay. I'd try every last one of them if it meant I never ended up swimming in the sea again.

CHAPTER 32

CALI

My hands shook as I busied myself making tea. I took my time choosing the brew, filling the kettle with water, trying to think of anything other than what had almost happened—though my mind wasn't ready to let go of the image of the seaweed that had loosely clung to the sheets or the sand that had adhered itself to Kellen's pillow. Kellen had almost died in his sleep.

When Kellen came into the kitchen, I still hadn't calmed down enough to look at him. Instead, I remained at the kettle for one more moment, aligning the three mugs on the counter. Tiny white squares lassoed with thin twine hung over the sides of each cup, reminding me of white flags of surrender. The kettle flicked off and I poured the steaming liquid into Kellen's cup without spilling a drop.

Picking up the mugs, I carefully turned around. "I made you some tea. Gabriel taught me how."

I hadn't made it to the opposite counter when I took in Kellen's face and faltered. The hot liquid spilled onto my hand, scalding me, and I gasped in surprise.

But I couldn't move. I stared at his beautiful face covered

in bruises. A large bandage had been applied to his four-head —a ridiculous name because he only had one. Other cuts and scrapes must have covered his body, because he winced as he slid from the stool. I hastily set the tea on the counter and shook my hand, which had now taken to stinging.

"Let me see." He rounded the corner and reached for my hand, concern knitted across his brow.

"It's not important."

Though the sting was uncomfortable, the realization that I'd been injured was more troublesome. I'd never been hurt before. It had never been possible.

"It is important. You're hurt. Gabe, do you have something for burns?" he asked as Gabriel walked into the room, tugging on a sweatshirt that read Yalies Do It Right across the front.

Gabe immediately bobbed his head. "Sure, dude. Give me a sec."

Kellen held up my hand, examining it in the quiet. "It doesn't look like it's going to blister, but if Gabe has something we can put on, it will take the pain away."

I nodded, reaching up with my good hand to cup his battered face. "This is from your dream?"

"You tell me." His green eyes bored into mine as though I held answers to any question he might conjure. "How did they do this?"

I bit my lip, wishing I could answer differently. "You know I've been having a hard time remembering." I did my best not to grimace at my own frustration. "This stands out to me though, probably because I've appeared in your dreams so many times."

"Okay, so what do you remember?" He waited, without any sense of urgency in his expression, though he surely must have felt it.

"If they know where you are, they can't come in without

being invited. In dreams, however, they will have open access to your mind." I laced my fingers together, hoping the action would help me steady myself.

Gabriel returned to the kitchen with some supplies, looking more worried than I felt. As if such a thing were even possible.

Kellen applied the medicine and a bandage to the red area on my hand. Not soon after, the sting faded.

"That should take care of it." He yawned, suddenly seeming unsteady on his feet.

"Thank you." I turned him around. "Now please sit down and drink your tea."

"Not yet. This particular tea needs something stronger." Gabriel opened one of the doors and walked inside a large cupboard, only to return a moment later with a tall green bottle. "I think this tea needs to turn into a hot toddy."

Kellen shook his head. "I don't drink."

"You do tonight," Gabriel said, pouring a small amount into the cup. "At least if you want to avoid hypothermia for a second time."

Kellen frowned at the cup but seemed to think the better of it. "You have a point." He drank from the mug and grimaced. Yet after another moment, he returned to the brew, downing what looked like more than half.

Gabriel set the medical supplies on the countertop. I offered him a cup of tea and he accepted, pushing the green bottle to the side. "We should get in the car and drive some-where. Now." Panic crept into his eyes.

With Kellen settled, I picked up my own tea and sipped the hot liquid. "They'd get us the moment we stepped outside. For the time being, this is the only place we're truly safe." I didn't mention how I knew this. Would they question me?

Yet Gabriel only nodded and patted Kellen on the back.

"But what about William? He didn't try to hurt us before. Do you think he'll be back?"

Dearest Danu, I prayed William wouldn't return. I wanted him to go away and take his magick and his soft words with him.

"What's wrong?" Kellen's voice was rough and scratchy from the sea, and his eyes were narrowed. He picked up on my emotions so well.

What could I say? It didn't seem like the right time to mention my encounter with Cana. Not after what Kellen had had to deal with. Plus, if I told Kellen about Cana, then I'd feel compelled to tell him about William and the kiss. I purposely tamped down my emotions.

"Nothing." I swallowed hard. "If William had plans to harm us, he would have done it."

"Then we stay. We'd better get some sleep." Gabriel placed his empty mug in the sink. "It doesn't make sense for all of us to sleep at the same time. Not after K's dream. I'll take the first watch. K, C, you guys catch some Zs."

Neither one of us argued, even though I had no idea what Zs were or how I was supposed to catch them. We made our way back to the bedroom. After helping Kellen climb into bed, I lay down beside him and wrapped my arms around him. He smelled wonderful. Clean and fresh from the shower —not a normal guy smell, at least if Gabriel was any comparison. Relief at his safety and for the end to the fighting between us overwhelmed me.

Kellen opened his eyes, which were still puffy from his bout with the sea, and gave me a sleepy smile. "About before—"

"Rest. I'll be here." I kept my voice light as Gabriel entered the room and took up residence in a chair beside the door.

A satisfied smile raised the corners of Kellen's battered

face as I tugged the blankets up and over us, tucking them in around his neck and shoulders. Within seconds, Kellen's even breathing lulled me toward sleep.

One thought persisted as I fought my own weariness. Please let us all wake up.

The sun had come up, creeping in through the slats in the window coverings. I climbed from the otherwise empty bed and peered outside where light danced across the water, creating thousands of tiny diamonds on its surface.

Stretching, I moved to the bedroom door and opened it a crack. Kellen's and Gabriel's voices carried down the hallway. They were joking with one another and cooking something that smelled divine. Bacon? When I'd been immortal, I'd once conjured it magickally. Now I mourned the loss of that ability.

One more stretch and I went to collect fresh clothing, which included items Gabriel had referred to as "jeans" and a "rockin' sweatshirt." Both were heavenly, divine pieces of clothing designed with the wearer's comfort in mind. I added a pair of purple woolen "socks" to the pile, also exquisite.

Once I collected everything, I went into the bathroom. I jumped at the mess I presented in the mirror. After hundreds of years of looking gorgeous all the time with no effort, mortal mornings were something I'd have to get used to.

I applied tooth cleaner to a toothbrush and brushed my teeth thoroughly—twice.

Once I finished dressing, I opened the bathroom door and found Kellen sitting on a bench at the end of the bed, looking less battered than the night before. He raised his mug toward his lips but halted, his cup at a standstill in midair when I walked in. Despite the bruises he was still just as gorgeous.

He swallowed, his Adam's apple bobbing in his throat. "Good morning." His green eyes twinkled as I walked into the room.

"Good morning." For some reason, my face heated at the sight of him, as though I were a normal mortal girl.

"Gabe's cooking breakfast. I thought you might want coffee while we wait." He handed me a cup as I sat beside him.

"Thank you."

Kellen was enamored with coffee, and I was beginning to see why. The warm path the liquid left behind woke me up as it traveled through my body. My senses, dulled by sleep, seemed sharper.

"This is heavenly."

"Glad you like it." Kellen smiled, but the expression soon faded. When his expression vanished like this, I knew he was reaching out for my senses. I was anything but ready for him to practically read my mind and did my best to shut down my feelings.

Of course, he noticed. "I can't get a read on you. What's up?" He smiled that smile of his. The one that always captivated me.

"I'm worried. I didn't want to upset you." That was true. I had spent the night fretting over Kellen, but there were more things to be said and I didn't even know where to start.

"Don't worry about upsetting me. I'd rather you tell me the truth than try to hide how you're feeling." He smoothed back a lock of my hair. "You're beautiful. Even more than yesterday."

His words filled me with warmth, as though I were glowing inside. I'd never felt as loved as when I was with him.

"Thank you. Well, you're . . . *sexy*." Sitting up straighter, I smiled with pride at my use of this new word. I'd read it on the cover of a printed book in Walmart that Gabriel said they called a magazine. He said that it meant someone was super good-looking.

Kellen's eyes shot open. "I'm sexy? I've never been called that before." He sat up straighter. "Where did you learn that word?"

"Gabriel." My cheeks burned again.

He chuckled, the sound deep, warm, and wonderful. "Why am I not surprised." Kellen leaned in and caught my lips with his own then. The kiss was quick and gentle—he was most likely conscious of not doing damage to his injuries from the previous night.

"Breakfast is served, dudes!" Gabriel's voice traveled down the hall and we broke apart, chuckling.

Kellen scooped up our cups and followed me to the kitchen, where Gabriel stood, a fork in each hand, the twin tines piercing pieces of meat.

"I think I outdid myself this time. This is some awesome bacon."

"Sweet. Thanks, Gabe." Kellen gestured to the food in front of me. "These are hash browns—a kind of potato—eggs, and you already know about bacon." He winked as he offered me a plate. "Help yourself to as much as you want."

"It looks delicious, Gabriel." I scooped a portion of each onto the plate. "Thank you."

"You're super welcome, C." Gabriel grinned as he filled his own plate. "You know what they say: Breakfast is the most important meal of the day."

"How would she know that? She's been mortal for like two minutes." Kellen smirked as he added three strips of bacon to his plate.

"Oh yeah. Right. You seem so human sometimes. I keep forgetting that two days ago you transported my parents to another country with a wave of your hand." Gabriel shrugged and stabbed at a forkful of egg. "So, hands up if you think it was William that almost killed Kellen in his dream last night."

I'd been about to take my first bite of food but froze at the mention of William's name. The unbidden memory of our kiss rose up. I had to tell Kellen what had happened with William. He wouldn't like it, but I knew he'd listen and take my side.

Kellen continued to chew, raising his hand to cover his mouth. "He seems the likely choice—messed-up psycho in the woods and all."

"I'd place my money on him." Gabriel bit off a piece of bacon and chewed thoughtfully. "We need to get out of here, but this was the most remote place I could think of. If they found us here, I don't know where to go next."

"We'll figure something out." Kellen ate some more egg and bacon and I realized I'd been watching their exchange instead of eating my own breakfast. "It's too dangerous to stay here, and none of us can safely go to sleep. Not after last night."

A loud pounding broke into the moment and Gabriel paled. "Someone's at the front door."

They'd come for us.

CHAPTER 33

CALI

Gabriel, Kellen, and I froze, not wanting to move a muscle lest they sense we were inside. My mind reeled. There was nowhere we could go, no possible way we could sneak from the house without being seen.

A shout came from outside. "Open up. It's Uncle Dillion."

My heart hammered at the sound of the familiar voice. I so wanted it to be him. Growing up, I'd never known about my father's brother. After they'd been trapped by Arawn in Faerie, all of my father's family had turned and become our enemies. All except Uncle Dillion. Father told me once that Uncle Dillion had saved him when Father's attempt at a rescue mission had failed. He'd been the only one I could trust when Kellen and I were in Faerie.

Yet I couldn't trust him now. Last night I'd been about to let Cabhan inside, and he'd been an imposter.

"Kellen, open the door." Uncle Dillion's exasperated voice sounded from the other side.

"K, you don't seriously think it's him, do you?" Gabriel's eyes grew wide as he peered through the small round peep window on the door.

"I don't know. He did leave us messages, so it would make sense that he knew we were here." He turned to me. "What do you think?"

I tried to remember any trick at all that would tell us if Uncle Dillion was my true family. Yet that knowledge fluttered from my mind, gone as quickly as it surged up.

A sigh and shuffling followed from the other side of the door. "Oh, dearest Danu. Ask me something only I would know."

Kellen frowned, and then a smile spread across his face. "What advice did you give me before my almost-wedding day?"

A hearty chuckle followed from the other side of the door. "Whatever you do, don't make that one angry."

Kellen and Gabriel roared with laughter while my face burned with embarrassment. Old bastard.

"Enough of this." Unable to keep the scowl from my face, I marched over to the door, unlocked it, and then pulled it open.

All traces of my anger faded the moment I spotted Uncle Dillion waiting not-so-patiently on the other side of the door. He had switched out his red leather beret for a neat tartan flat cap. His kilt had been tailored from black and white plaid that made my eyeballs hurt. His bright yellow long-sleeve shirt read "*I went to Scranton and all I got was this lousy T-shirt.*" A bright orange vest that was so small it hugged his round belly completed the outfit. This creature could only be Uncle Dillion.

"Somebody had better call the fashion police," Gabriel muttered.

"Or maybe just the police." Kellen gripped the door and swung it open wide.

I crossed my arms over my chest. "Are you coming in,

Uncle? Or do you prefer to stand outside and make poor jokes at my expense?"

Uncle Dillion jogged across the threshold. He'd no sooner set foot inside when he whirled around. "Quickly, quickly, shut the door."

I pushed the door closed, sliding the impressive bolt across it the way I'd seen Gabriel do. It locked with a satisfying sound that gave me some measure of comfort.

"Uncle Dillion, it's good to see you again, as always," Kellen said, holding out his hand as Uncle removed his hat and vest, then let them both drop to the floor.

Uncle didn't need to dress for the cold, but he did so to blend in, in case he came across any mortals. Of course, he would stand out in any crowd in that ensemble. That was where the true irony lay. Well, perhaps not in the Walmart place where we'd purchased our clothing . . .

He seemed winded. That was unusual for Uncle Dillion as he was still immortal, even if Arawn's curse had changed his physical features, shrinking him and turning his once coal-black hair snow white.

Without his hat and vest, I got a better look at his haggard appearance. His long white hair and beard had thinned, and dark circles rimmed his bloodshot eyes. That didn't make any sense. Uncle Dillion wasn't mortal—he couldn't age or even change like the rest of us. Though immortals did age, the rate was so slow no one had ever taken the time to calculate it, and we'd seen him only a handful of days ago.

"Uncle Dillion, what happened to you?"

"Ah . . ." He waved off my question and walked farther into the house. "How about a bit of breakfast for this old man, eh? I've been traveling for a while now. I should at least get a bite of meat or toast out of the bargain."

"Since when do you need to eat?" Kellen asked, his brow

creasing. I had no doubt that he was also cataloguing the physical changes in my uncle.

"A man needs sustenance," Uncle Dillion declared, happily rolling back and forth on his feet as though there were a ball beneath them. "Gabriel, I'm certain you'll help me."

"Sure, man. We just ate. Come this way." Gabriel gestured to the kitchen where the heavenly smells of our leftover breakfast lingered.

Kellen busied himself, getting a plate with bacon, eggs, and those delicious potatoes for Uncle. It wasn't until Uncle had scrambled onto a tall stool—an awkward climb for someone three feet tall—and picked up a fork that I couldn't hold my tongue any longer.

"What's been happening, Uncle?" I rested my hand on his arm, but the instant my hand came in contact with him, I fought not to jerk it back. I'd expected to grip one of Uncle's generally plump arms, yet all I could feel were bones.

Uncle Dillion met my eyes and patted my hand. "This whole area has been locked down so that no one could get through."

"I'm surprised Cana let you pass after you attacked them in Ireland." Kellen set a coffee mug in front of Uncle and then immediately took a sip from his own.

Uncle Dillion forced a grim smile. "I was lucky. The local faeries don't know me, and they're the ones in charge of watching this place. I do not think they have much experience with this sort of thing. I used that to my advantage."

"How are they different from the C.O.D.?" Kellen asked.

"They were the original people, the indigenous beings who lived in Faerie before Arawn took it over and forced them above ground. They're a peaceful sort, unless you cross them. Most don't try." Uncle scooped egg and potato into his mouth and began to chew vigorously.

"Are they the reason Cana found us so fast?" I asked.

Uncle Dillion regarded Kellen in silence for several moments, then let out a carefully measured breath. "I am not sure, but there is magick at work here and most of it not good."

"What do you mean by 'not good'?" Gabriel asked, selecting one of the few remaining strips of bacon from the plate.

Uncle bit into his own slice of bacon, sighing happily as he enjoyed my new favorite food. "There are traces of magick out there that were designed to confuse or waylay someone. To tempt them into reckless behavior even."

Gabriel's expression darkened, despite the bright kitchen lights. "That sounds like what happened to Kellen last night."

"What do you mean?" Uncle Dillion picked up his coffee cup, sipped, and pulled a face. "Surely you weren't stupid enough to go outside alone—and at night no less?"

It was possible that Kellen, a brilliant mind in his own right, had never been called stupid before. He blinked at Uncle for several moments before answering.

"I didn't plan to. I went to stand on the porch for some fresh air. The next thing I knew, I was walking away from the house, even though I wanted to go back. Things got weird after we met William, even if he did help me." Kellen toyed with his collar and took another sip of coffee. "I know you told us to trust him, but the guy's weird."

"William?" Uncle Dillion stared at him, unblinking. "Who's William?"

Kellen slowly brought his cup down to the counter. He, Gabriel, and I looked at one another.

"You don't know him? He's a warlock. He lives nearby." My voice betrayed my dislike of William. Unbidden, I thought briefly of our kiss and I quickly blotted the image.

"What were you all doing keeping company with a

warlock?" Uncle Dillion sipped his coffee and cringed, this time pushing it away entirely.

"You left us that note telling us to trust him." But as Kellen gestured to the handwriting, I saw that the board had been wiped clean.

Gabriel walked toward the board, stared at it hard, and then turned back to us. "Dudes, this is sooo not good."

"So, you're saying you didn't leave us any notes?" I asked, the tone of my voice creeping skyward.

Uncle Dillion stared at me for a moment before speaking. "My dear, this entire area is so heavily barricaded that I was fortunate to even get to you."

"But the messages at the restaurant?" Kellen stared at Uncle as though trying to pluck the answer from his mind.

Gabriel went to retrieve the napkins from a kitchen drawer. He spread them out in a line before Uncle. "We received these when we went out to eat."

Kellen frowned, staring at the papers as though they would provide clues. "And then there was the carving on the tree."

"Tree? What tree?" Gabriel asked, scratching his head.

"It was a message for me. With everything going on, I forgot to tell you." Kellen frowned and held up the picture he'd taken on his phone for Gabe and Dillion to see.

Uncle Dillion examined the messages briefly before he finally shook his head. "Child, none of them came from me." He waved a hand in the direction of the chalkboard and the message from last night slowly materialized.

"Duuuude." Gabe stared in wonder. "I wish I could have done that the time I forgot to back up my Civil Law argument."

Uncle Dillion ignored the comment. "This isn't my writing, but it is extremely close." He opened his palm and revealed a tiny magnifying glass, which he used to inspect the script.

Kellen moved to stand alongside him. Together they regarded the board. "The S is different. You don't have a curl on yours."

Uncle finally lowered the glass. A slight smile appeared on the old faerie's face as he regarded Kellen. "You *are* intelligent —for a mortal."

"Thanks." Kellen didn't smile as he returned to the napkins Gabriel had spread across the counter.

"As helpful as this might have been, the last thing I would have been able to do is send you a message. They could have deciphered it and it would have given me away." Uncle Dillion waved his hand, and the napkins, as well as the message on the chalkboard, faded. "Tell me about this warlock. I've only known two others in my life, and they're both dead. I wish to know where this fellow came from."

A chill tore down my spine. I'd had my suspicions about William, especially at dinner. Now that Uncle Dillion had confirmed William was a stranger, a sliver of fear lodged its way into my soul.

My thoughts wandered everywhere and nowhere as Gabriel explained it all, including our dinner with William, his off behavior, and even Gabriel's discovery of Alastrom's real caretaker.

"I can't believe you ate dinner with a warlock!" Uncle Dillion sputtered, his eyebrows shooting up. He was most definitely unhappy with us. I couldn't say I blamed him. We'd thought we were being cautious, but we'd been anything but.

"To be fair, we thought we had your stamp of approval." Kellen frowned, probably chastising himself for our poor choices.

"We all decided to go, so we're all to blame." I had to chime in, lest Uncle think this was all Kellen's idea.

"And the dinner was just okay. I mean he's going to have to work a lot harder if he wants to work for tourists as a side hustle." Gabriel's smile faltered as the truth struck him. "I guess that was an act. Maybe I should have told him his bread was on the dry side?"

"What in Danu's name are you talking about?" Dillion demanded, thumping his fist on the counter and almost knocking his mug over.

"The facts. He invited us to dinner, he fed us, and let us leave. Then later, when I was lured into the woods—long story," Kellen added, in case Uncle Dillion or Gabriel felt compelled to interrupt, "—he forced me to drink this gross drink to stop hypothermia, and it didn't kill me, but now we know he's an imposter. None of it makes sense."

William had definitely been hiding so many things. He seemed to know about Cana—exactly who she was and what she wanted. Then, the way he'd acted when we'd been alone . . .

"What's wrong? What aren't you telling me?" Kellen asked, his voice soft yet intense, as though he could read everything I'd been thinking and not just my emotions.

I spun around to face Kellen, unaware that he'd been focusing on me. Gabriel and Uncle had ceased to be in the room with us. I only saw Kellen now, and the only thoughts and emotions that mattered to me were his. I could not put the time for honesty off any longer.

"There's more." I wrung my hands together as Kellen stood, silent and unreadable. "Last night after you both went to sleep, I went out on the balcony. Cabhan appeared." My attention wandered to the wall of glass out of instinct, as though Cabhan might return any moment. "He asked me to let him in and I refused. He turned out to be Cana in disguise."

Gabriel's expression turned cloudy. "C, that is way uncool. Glad you're okay."

"Glad you didn't agree to it," Uncle Dillion grumbled.

I nodded, knowing I was looking to the wrong person for a reaction. Swallowing hard, I met Kellen's eyes. "When I turned to come back into the house, William was there. He'd gotten in with his key." There was no easy way to say this but to plunge ahead. "William kissed me."

CHAPTER 34
KELLEN

William had kissed Cali. *My Cali*, who I'd sworn to love forever in a wedding ceremony that was never finished. I had no idea how I still stood. Surely my knees had buckled and I was on the floor. It felt like someone had sucker-punched me in the gut.

Cali paled and a wave of guilt and sadness eased into me from her direction. That almost made it worse.

"I didn't want him to, Kellen. I asked him to leave. I took his key back."

"Why didn't you tell me?" At first, I didn't recognize the voice as my own, but I had to ask.

"After I asked William to leave, you were attacked in your dream." She'd returned to wringing and unwringing her hands. That was the moment I realized her guilt now comingled with fear. It wasn't that she was about to tell me she and William were planning to run off together. She didn't want me to be angry with her.

"You were attacked? In your sleep?" Dillion asked, incredulity in his expression.

"Don't I look a little worse for wear, Dillion?" Though I felt better than the night before, my face was still puffy and my body was battered and bruised from its bout with the sea. Yet it was my heart that ached the most right now.

"That you do."

Dillion seemed to be puzzling it all out and coming up empty, same as me. If the C.O.D. wanted something from me, why try to kill me?

"Where did they take you?"

"A couple of miles along the path outside and into the ocean." I hadn't told Gabe and Cali much about my dream. There hadn't been time, what with all the revelations about traitor William coming to light.

"At least we know this William could not have been making you have your dream." Dillion spoke slowly, as though thinking through each word individually.

"How do you know?" I asked.

"Simple. It sounds like your dream and this, er, William's *experience* with Calienta happened simultaneously. Manipulating dreams is powerful magick. He would have needed total concentration for that." The little man shook his head as though he'd convinced himself. "The dream manipulation sounds like something Cana would have done."

"I thought she wanted to kidnap Kellen." Gabe gripped the counter as though it were a lifeline.

Dillion shook his head. "It's time we made plans to move the two of you. I don't know how we're going to get you past the barrier, but I'll think of something."

The little man's wrinkles deepened further. Dillion had always piqued my curiosity. He was a god who'd been banished underground and disfigured, yet his heart had remained pure. If you didn't count sarcasm.

"Another hideout?" We'd been on the run for two days,

but I hated the thought of moving again. There was nowhere we belonged.

Gabe sat up straighter. "We have another house. Down south. It would be a long drive, but if we leave now—"

"Gabriel. I appreciate what you're trying to do for Kellen, but right now you are in no condition to save him." Dillion patted his hand. "And don't you have someplace you're supposed to be now?"

Gabe had mention dropping his classes and asking for an extension. I'd never asked him if he'd followed through. "Did you fill out the deferral form?"

"Not yet, but it's no big deal, K. I was gonna call them tomorrow and tell them I needed to take personal time." Gabe's mouth flattened into a stubborn line.

So he was still enrolled. There was a chance Gabe could get out of this. I wanted him to have a normal life.

"Harvard Law has a waiting list a mile long. You could lose your spot in an instant."

Gabe crossed his arms and leaned back. "It's my fault the C.O.D. found us. I'm the one who made a mistake. I picked a bad location."

"You didn't. None of this is your fault. You can go back to your life and they'll leave you alone. It's me they want." Jealousy flared inside me. I would have given almost anything to be in his shoes, to have the freedom to walk away with Cali and live. I'd never had that freedom, though, even when I believed it existed.

Gabe shook his head. "I promised Lugh I wouldn't leave your side." He wrapped his arms around his torso, as though the thought of leaving physically pained him. "I can't go."

What was going on with Gabe? This new stubbornness went above and beyond.

"But you aren't my bodyguard. No one asked you to sign

up for that detail. Lugh won't be angry at you for leaving either."

"I'm pissed at me. I am, okay?" Gabe exclaimed, turning to Dillion who merely observed. "I've . . . failed."

Failed. What an odd choice of words. He made it sound like we were an assignment.

Dillion touched Gabe's arm. "Gabriel, you did not fail. There is another force at work here that none of us counted on." He climbed atop the chair next to Gabe's, putting himself nose to nose with him. "No, Gabriel, I think the best thing for you to do is to go back to school."

Dillion didn't have to say everything he was thinking for me to understand. If Gabe stayed, he wouldn't live. He knew little about the world Cali and I had been immersed in. He'd dipped two toes into this uncharted water over the past couple of days, but this all went so much deeper than he knew.

Gabe shoved his chair back, his anger focused on Dillion. "But they're my friends. Don't you understand? They need me."

Anger built in my gut and twisted knife-like inside me. I wanted to scream. To rage at our situation. Everything I'd hoped and planned for had fallen apart, and now Gabe thought he was ready to move to the front lines in a battle against the C.O.D.? "But you're mortal!"

"And so are you! You turned down immortality, remember?" Gabe's skin had gone blotchy, pink patches sprouting over pale flesh. "Cali's mortal too, so don't go pretending you guys aren't exactly like me!" His chest heaved, and his accusation hung in the air as he breathed in and out, his anger more out of control than I'd ever seen it.

Dillion must have sensed this, because he placed his hand on Gabe's forearm. "It's more important that you be safe right now. We're going to need you in the future. Your job isn't done, Gabe."

Uncle Dillion's use of Gabe's nickname seemed to calm him, but just as quickly I realized he wasn't trying to calm him down. Dillion was spelling Gabe, using magick to get my friend to leave.

Almost instantly the anger faded from Gabe's face. We stood in silence for several moments before he finally spoke. "What about the car?"

"Take it. Dillion will figure something out for us." It was true. Dillion could whisk us anywhere, though I couldn't fathom our next destination.

"You're right." Gabe wiped his eyes with the back of his sleeve. "I don't know why I'm so upset. It doesn't make any sense."

"My father gave you a job to do. You don't want to let him down." Cali patted Gabe's arm, a small frown forming at her lips. "Kellen and I will come and visit you when this has all died down."

As if reading my thoughts before they formed, Gabe looked to me. "What do you think, K? Do you think I should go?"

I swallowed hard, trying to imagine this journey without Gabe. I couldn't. But that didn't matter. Gabe had to go before he immersed himself in this world. I was the only one who could send him away. "You're my best friend. It's bad enough my fiancée is going to be in the middle of all of this . . . Please go, man."

He had to see right through me, though I did my best to act like I agreed with Cali and we'd see Gabe again when everything went back to normal. Yet there was no denying the scary truth. We might never see normal again.

CHAPTER 35

CALI

A sense of depressing finality settled over the house after Gabriel left. Despite the danger to Gabriel, we'd been a trio. It had seemed less ambitious, our fighting Faerie, with Kellen's best friend involved.

I turned to Uncle, finding his eyes resting on me and filling up with sadness, something I wasn't ready to investigate further.

"Uncle, why did Gabriel react that way? He's being sent away for his own safety." I could not say why I asked this of Uncle and not of Kellen. Maybe it was easier to believe Uncle Dillion had the answers to everything.

But before he could answer, a strange sort of thump made me whirl around. Kellen had slumped to the floor against the pillar at the entrance to the kitchen and the room for living. His eyes had glazed over, unseeing, and his body went rigid as his back arched.

I rushed to him, falling to my knees at his side. "Kellen." My voice sounded overly loud in the large room, jarring even me. "Kellen!"

"Boy! Boy!" Uncle Dillion shook Kellen's shoulder, gentle

at first, then harder. The intensity didn't change things. There was no response.

"Uncle Dillion, do something!" Panic constricted my chest and bound me up like a prisoner as I tried to stare past the glassiness of his eyes to where Kellen's light should have been.

Uncle Dillion closed his eyes as he clasped Kellen's bruised and battered hand. The place where their faerie and human hands joined began to glow a soft amber that quickly turned brilliant. Light ran up Kellen's arm and across his shoulders and chest before it split, rushing up to his head and down to his feet. Soon Kellen's entire body was encased in light. The scratches and bruises on his skin faded until they disappeared. It wasn't until the light dimmed that Uncle Dillion drew back. His eyes fluttered open, but they were less blue. Once more, Uncle Dillion looked as if he'd aged.

Kellen drew in several ragged breaths as though he couldn't take in enough air. He blinked repeatedly before finally meeting my eyes. What I read there spoke volumes. Fear.

"What's going on?" Kellen's familiar voice chased away my worries for Uncle.

"Kellen." I took him in my arms and pulled him close. I pressed a kiss to his cheek, taking in his familiar scent, which I could never describe, yet which somehow reminded me of my beloved Ireland. I released him and sat back on my knees. "You tell us. What happened?"

He pressed the heels of his hands against his eyes and rubbed them roughly. "I don't know. It's like I had a dream." He shook his head as though to blight it from his mind. His already unusually pale skin had grown whiter, and the green of his eyes stood out in stark contrast.

"The Children of Danu again? Tell us, boy." Uncle's voice bordered on patient but still held a trace of frustration.

Kellen slowly got to his feet. He swallowed hard as he

went to the refrigerator and pulled out one of the chocolate
bars he loved. "No. It wasn't the C.O.D. this time." After
biting off half the bar and chewing quickly, Kellen sat. "I keep
having these dreams about Stephen, my father." Kellen
pinched the bridge of his nose for a moment and met my
eyes. "He's not right in the dreams. There's something even
more messed up about him—and that's saying something.
Plus, I've never had a dream when I was awake."

After he finished the chocolate, he looked less pale, as
though the bar had revived him.

"In the first dream, Stephen talked about how he wanted
to find me and how worried he'd been about me. The second
dream was about how much he needs me . . ." Kellen hesitated. "In this dream . . . I think someone murdered him."
His eyes went wild from the memory. They wouldn't even
meet mine as he continued. "Someone in a cloak stood over
Stephen as he slept. They held a hand over him, and
Stephen was twitching, like he was in pain. And then the
person in the cloak looked up and all I saw was a pair of red
eyes."

"Red eyes. Like Arawn." Uncle Dillion shook his head. "It
couldn't be. Not yet."

Kellen paced as though tormented by a memory he was
unable to blight. "It's like I was there, watching it happen."

Uncle Dillion frowned and looked at me, his wizened eyes
narrowing. "Have you and Kellen talked about the second
part of the prophecy?"

For a moment I looked to my uncle as I once again fought
to remember. Before that moment, everything had been
blurry, the memories an unintelligible collage that had
papered themselves on the walls of my mind. Now, when
confronted with my greatest fear, the details came rushing
back.

"The second part of the prophecy?" Kellen's quiet voice

broke into my thoughts. "You told me that it had nothing to do with me, with *us*."

"You probably don't remember all the facts." Uncle Dillion touched my arm, his voice calm and understanding.

They were waiting for me to say something, to agree that I'd forgotten. I wouldn't give them that satisfaction. I was done lying.

Kellen stilled beside me. I wasn't the one that could sense emotion, yet I could've sworn his fear wrapped around me.

"He needs to know the truth, understand what he's up against," Uncle insisted. "You can't keep him safe by withholding something this important."

"What's he talking about, Cali?" Shock reverberated through Kellen's voice.

I wanted to take Uncle's hand and beg him to undo what he'd started, but there was no going back. Slowly I faced Kellen, the boy for whom the truth was crucial after a lifetime of lies.

Every part of me ached, but I pushed on. "The second part of the prophecy says you'll turn to the darkness. But you aren't evil. You never will be!"

He stared at me in shock for a moment before his face hardened like granite. Though I searched his green eyes for the love I'd come to expect, I found contempt, as though everything he'd felt for me had been erased, replaced by this cold new Kellen.

A sob escaped my lips. "You don't understand. I only remember patches of things, and when I do it's too late." It was a poor excuse. We both knew that I could have told him before. Should have told him before.

"I've had enough of people making decisions on my behalf. Enough lies and secrets. I can't handle any more, especially from you. You've . . . disappointed me."

Without another word, he stalked from the room.

My life crashed down around me. Why had I been so foolish? I could have told him about it in Faerie.

When? In the days before your wedding? Or after Kellen almost sacrificed his life in the Upside-Down Ocean? Shivers wracked me from the inside out as I remembered the sea filled with the unforgiven Celtic souls. The *Sluagh*.

Uncle Dillion stood next to me in an instant. "I'm sorry, my child, but if he is prepared, then he'll make the right choice when the time comes."

"And what choice is that, Uncle?" A tear slid down my cheek, dropping from my jaw. Despite any efforts to the contrary, my mind tried to process a life without Kellen St. James—or worse—one where Kellen was evil.

Uncle Dillion handed me a cloth to wipe my tears. "You."

Laughing wryly, I turned to Uncle Dillion. "What if I'm not the right choice for Kellen anymore?"

He waved me away. "Talk to him. I'm going to go outside and focus on dismantling the magick around this house. I'm sure I can reinforce the protection that was already in place too." He stopped partway to the door and turned around. "If I don't come back, it would be better if you acted like no one was at home."

Half listening, I nodded as Uncle left, abandoning me with my thoughts and fears. *Dearest Danu, help me.*

CHAPTER 36

KELLEN

I'd built walls around myself my entire life—for self-preservation, really. Despite those walls, I'd let Cali in. She was the only person I could count on. Gran had even told me to trust Cali.

Since we'd come to Maine, however, Cali had changed. She'd tried to use her powers on me. She'd kissed William, or he kissed her. That distinction didn't make it any less painful when my imagination went into overdrive.

And then this prophecy thing—she'd lied. That was the one thing I thought she'd never do. My trust in her was shattering, crumbling to the ground like the walls I'd spent years constructing.

My feet carried me down one hallway and then down another. Soon tall windows flanked my left side again and the sea came into view. The day had turned gray. The afternoon looked like early evening. Thick clouds hung over the house as the barrier Dillion mentioned hovered menacingly.

Eventually the hallway opened into a room in which the ceiling spanned all three stories. Three of the walls were made up of more windows, which ran from floor to ceiling.

The sea sat before me, churning, growing rougher by the second. The only section of solid wall space held floor-to-ceiling shelves stacked high with colorful books. Someone had attached a wall ladder to provide easy access for any bibliophiles who stumbled across it.

Under different circumstances, this would have been my favorite room in the house. It was the perfect place to write. Yet with Cali's secrets and Gabe's absence, the home had a depressed quality to it, as though it had dropped out of a Brontë novel in which they wandered the moors.

My heart hurt. Ached, as though someone had reached in and ripped it out. I fought the angry tears that wanted to come. I wiped at my eyes roughly with my sleeve, scratching my cheek with my watch.

Suddenly her emotions ambushed me. I fought the temptation to turn and take her in my arms and focused instead on the patterns in the old-school parquet flooring.

More of Cali's emotions assaulted me then, as though she'd chosen to project them. Sadness. Regret. Sorrow. If my own feelings were a small river of emotion, then hers were an endless sea, as if no one hurt more than Cali did.

But I'd always based my own beliefs on fact. The biggest one stared us both down. She'd lied. Worse, this lie could cost us, could get us killed.

Finally, I took in her red-rimmed eyes and blotchy face. "I asked you about the second part of the prophecy before, remember? In Faerie?"

She wrung her hands together. "I remember."

"But it sounds like it has *everything* to do with me. Why did you lie?"

Please say something to make me believe in you. Please fix this with words so we can go back to how we were before.

"When we first met again, at your gran's house, I said nothing because I thought it would be too much for you."

"What about later? After we saved your parents?"

"I was afraid. I didn't want it to come true like the other part of the prophecy did." Tears trailed down her cheeks. "How could I risk losing you like that, to *evil*?" She wrapped her arms around herself. I wished they were my arms holding her tight. I leaned forward, barely conquering the urge to touch her.

It began to rain then. Raindrops pelted the glass-walled room with sharp, unforgiving slaps.

Cali's intense regret washed over me as more of her emotions bridged the space between us. Her tears dropped to the floor, mimicking the scene outside. I shoved my hands into my pockets to keep from wiping them away.

"What else haven't you told me?" My words sounded harsh, but I needed them to. All my long-ago mortal insecurities about not being good enough for a goddess had vanished. We were no longer on uneven playing ground. We were both mortal now.

"You would know if there was something more." Cali regarded me as though looking at a stranger. "The prophecy claimed you would turn evil, would turn against me. Why would I want to talk about that? Even mention it?"

Anger burst to life in my chest. "Cali! God! To help me!" The shout rose, surprising us both. "Don't you want me to win? Don't you want me—*us*—to be able to walk away from this?"

"I do." Pink blotches spread across her cheeks as her eyes narrowed. "How could you even think otherwise?"

"Easy, because now I'm unprepared. You say I'm supposed to turn evil, but if I'd known about this, I could have done research, maybe found a way to stop it from happening." I was tired of being thrown in the middle of things, of being forced to play the role of underdog in every Faerie battle that came my way. "I don't even know what the damn second part of the prophecy says!"

"Neither do I!" she shouted, her words echoing in the large room. Her chest heaved even as she glared at me, daring me to question her again.

Doubt filtered in, deflating my anger. I could cast out for her emotions, but I wanted her to come clean, to confess what was really happening inside her. "What do you mean?"

Cali let her hands drop to her sides, her wringing forgotten. "I never wanted to know. The idea terrified me. And that's the truth."

She hung her head, her hair falling in a curtain on either side of her face. "I never meant to put you in danger. I was trying to do the opposite."

Tears stung my eyes and clogged my throat. I hated them, but a lifetime of repression made them hard to force back now, when my world sat on the precipice overlooking its beginning and end.

"Please, you have to believe me, Kellen." Cali raised both hands as if to touch me and then lowered them. "I did it because I love you."

"In my world, people haven't made choices on my behalf out of love. They did it to manipulate me."

Thoughts of Stephen crept in, closely followed by those of my dream from before, but I quickly pushed them to the back of my mind.

Cali cupped my cheek, her touch tender and so right that I leaned into it despite myself. "In my world, people protect the ones they love no matter what. That's what I was doing. Go ahead, you can read my emotions. You're the only one who can know for certain if I'm telling the truth."

This time I reached out with my senses, and it was as though a floodgate had opened. Her feelings weren't manipulative. Instead Cali's intense love washed over me, a tsunami that built in an instant, threatening to overwhelm me.

Cali had made a mistake. I'd certainly made enough of them to last a lifetime, and I could no sooner let her go than cut out my own heart.

"Will you forgive me?" She lowered her hand, taking the rightness with her.

The last of my reserves shattered and I took her in my arms, holding her close. "Of course." I whispered the words against her hair, drawing in her vanilla scent. Relief overwhelmed me. Finally, I held her. I'd come home.

Ever so carefully, I leaned in, trailing my lips first over her eyes, then her cheeks and nose, until finally I stopped an inch from her mouth. "Don't cry, love."

Her breath hitched. "Please kiss me. In the name of Danu, please—"

"It's not Danu I'm concerned with right at the moment." Leaning in, I caught her lips with mine in a slow exploration. We hadn't been apart, not really, and yet I took my time, reacquainting myself with her lips in a soft kiss while the rain blotted out the rest of the world.

She stood on tiptoe, her mouth opening over mine as she deepened our kiss.

I groaned as instinct took over and Cali's tongue met mine again and again. "Cali, my Cali." We clung to one another, and the need to be as close to her as possible overpowered me. There was nothing but us and the rain as we desperately fought to get closer. I felt for the divan one-handed and lowered us both to the cushions.

"Kellen." Cali slid her hands up into my hair, gripping it. The heat from her body as it melded into mine pitched me forward from a place of quiet relief to one from which I couldn't return.

I should slow things down, focus on setting the mood and

even get us to our shared bedroom, but my body screamed that we were done waiting. I could not stand to be apart from Cali another moment. I wanted to wipe away all the doubt that had happened between us.

"Kellen, please." Cali's request sounded breathless, beyond desperate, as her lips claimed mine again and again, searching for something she couldn't name.

"Where's Dillion?" I asked, my voice rough as I pressed my lips to her earlobe, the side of her neck, her collarbone . . . I didn't care where the old faerie had gone, apart from the fact that this time I wanted us to truly be alone.

"Outside." She wrapped her hand around mine, digging into my palm with her engagement ring, which had shifted on her finger.

Our mouths locked and our legs tangled as we rolled to our sides, entwined on the divan. Time had stopped, and only the two of us existed.

"Kellen, your bruises. What about your bruises?"

Though I hadn't given it much thought before, I no longer felt the aches and pains from my bout with the sea. "I'm fine. I think Dillion healed me when he pulled me from my dream." My mouth twisted with hers and I tasted the saltiness of her tears. "I don't care anyway. Cali . . ."

She looked up, breathless and beautiful. "Yes?"

Breathing was difficult and I had to coerce the words. "What I said was . . . out of line. I've always known I would marry you, from the moment we met."

"Me too." Cali shifted her position so that it was her pushing me into the cushions, unbuttoning the buttons on my shirt and pressing soft kisses onto my bared skin. Her fingers found my pendant where it lay against my chest. Slowly, she traced the outline of the symbol, her finger burning my skin where she touched me. When she repeated the same action I'd taken and kissed my neck, dizziness washed over me.

She had to be mine. I refused to die without ever having known what it was like to be with her. My hand slid ever so slowly from her stomach upwards . . .

"Kellen!"

Turning, I blinked, unable to comprehend the scene before me. William stood there, in the very room in which I'd been about to make love to Cali, again dripping water onto the hardwood. His expression could only be defined as one word: devastated.

CHAPTER 37

KELLEN

Tearing my hands from Cali's, I moved to block her from William's searching eyes. "What the hell are you doing here?"

"I'm sorry, I did ring the bell. It's Gabe. There's been an accident." Gone were all traces of the mocking tone that William usually clung to like a security blanket.

"We're done trusting you. Whatever way you got in here, use it to show yourself out." I scanned the room for any weapon, but this time I had no magickal sword with which to face down my enemy.

"No, you don't understand. I had a vision. I never have visions anymore." His eyes were wild, unfocused. "I saw his car go off the road. We need to find him."

Raindrops pounded on the glass all around us, dulling his voice. The space that had once seemed romantic had turned foreboding.

Cali paled as she met my eyes, a million questions evident in hers.

"Why should we believe anything you say? You've been playing with us. You sent us messages. You lured me out into the night and beat me up in my dreams. You lied to us, and then you kissed my fiancée. Tell me why I should listen to anything you have to say."

"Kellen, I did kiss Cali and I did tell more than a few untruths, but I never lured you outside or tried to beat you up. The local faeries are to blame for that. They're loyal to Cana."

Hearing William speak the evil hag's name had the effect of pulling everything that had happened to us together. It was no longer speculation. Despite the lies William had told and the games he'd played with Cali, we couldn't afford not to trust him now.

"Wait." I took out my phone and dialed Gabe. It rang and rang, but Gabe didn't pick up. He had never missed a call from me—not once in our entire friendship. Which, in hind-sight, seemed kind of remarkable.

Turning to Cali, I laid my cheek against her ear and whis-pered, "He's in trouble. Lock all the doors. Don't open them for anyone unless you know it's them. I'll be back." I pressed a swift kiss to her lips, knowing it would have to do.

"I have a bad feeling about this." Her whispered fears mirrored my thoughts. Then she stood on tiptoe and kissed me once more. Her emotions wrapped around me, and all her heartbreak and fear went into our intense meeting of lips. I knew it was as much for William's benefit as it was for mine.

"I'll come back for you. I promise." My words hung in the air like tangible things that followed me out the door as I left. I couldn't bring myself to meet Cali's eyes, though. Because I'd just made a promise I might not be able to keep.

William ran ahead as we made for the woods, the exact place William himself had told me to stay out of. The rain fell in torrents, creating a semitransparent curtain that separated us.

"Where is he, exactly?" I asked over the oppressive sound of the rain.

"Not too far," William cried over his shoulder. "Just off the main road. Stay close, okay?"

Though it was early afternoon, it was as if there'd been an eclipse and day had shifted into night. Not pitch black, but more like early evening.

"I'll do my best." Yet as fast as I ran, it was as if I couldn't quite catch up with him. All I could do was tail the warlock, keeping my eyes trained on his yellow parka. It reminded me of the bobbing blue light in my dream. The one that had been just out of reach.

"This way!" William shouted as we crossed Route 3 and headed into Acadia National Park. We'd barely reached the tree line when William's yellow coat disappeared from view.

"William!"

I stopped. The rain poured down on me and slowly soaked my coat, which the makers had claimed to be water-proof. I turned around. My phone beeped and I freed it from my pocket, waking the screen. No service. Great.

"William!"

But he didn't answer. *God, I'm an idiot.* This might have been part of William's plan. He had probably lied. Gabe could be in Portland by now.

Turning around had been a bad move. It eliminated any since of direction I'd had. There was zero chance of down-loading a compass app on my phone with no bars. Not that due north would help me much anyway. There was no compass designed to avoid faeries.

"I'm screwed." The rain beat down, pelting me with sharp, unforgiving pellets. "William, you bastard!"

"My, my, all this yelling! You are certain to wake . . . well, just about anybody." The deep voice resembled a bullfrog's and sounded out of place in the nightmare I'd fallen into.

Whipping around, I discovered a small man about three feet tall. He was dressed in a flannel that would have pegged him as a local townsperson if it weren't for his size. He only came to my hip, but the long knife in a sheath at his side told me I couldn't write him off. The shock of red hair on the little man's head matched the color of his hipster beard perfectly. Even stranger, the rain didn't fall on this creature, but around him, for he was encased in a bubble about the size of a compact car.

I blinked to rule out any hallucinations. *Nope, not so lucky*.

"Yeah, because my life can't be any weirder." I tugged my hood forward as far as it would go, but it didn't block the rain. I envied this creature in his bubble.

"What are you about, being out in this rain? And shouting? Some not-nice words, if I do say. Oh, yes, I *do* say."

Though it poured on the outside, sun shone on the inside of the bubble. The little man sat smiling, warm and dry and more than a little smug.

"Come with me, young one. We will get you dried off and give you something to eat."

Though I could hear him plainly, I found I needed to speak up to be heard over the rain. "I learned long ago not to trust the Children of Danu."

"Oh goodness, goodness." The little man jumped onto a nearby rock. The bubble expanded with him to include his new perch. "I'm not one of them, see. We're a different sort altogether."

William's caution about the local faeries came back to me. "William warned me about you." Though the moment I spoke, I questioned the validity of the information.

"William? Warned?" the little man sputtered.

The way I saw it, I had two options. I could hang out and see if I'd pissed this little man off, or I could run. I went with option two. Spinning on the spot, I took off as fast as I could through the thick maze of trees.

The faerie's voice rang out behind me. "Come back! Please!"

I ran, dodging trees that had grown too close together. They weren't like the trees of Faerie that had reached out to stroke my arms and shoulders as I passed. These trees were cold. Void of emotion.

Whipping out my phone once more, I checked the display. I had one small bar of coverage. Without hesitating I dialed 911. Even if I couldn't tell anyone where I was, I could get help for Gabe.

An operator picked up. "911 Emergency Dispatch," he answered in crisp, competent tones.

"Hi, I think my friend has been in a car accident on Route 3. He may have gone off the road. I'm lost. I tried to go through the woods to help him and I can't find my way out."

There was a great deal of typing as I waited, running in silence through the dark woods that never ended.

"What is your name, sir?"

"Kellen. Kellen St. James."

"Kellen let's start with your friend. What is his name?"

"Gabriel Stewart." My throat thickened. *Please let Gabe be okay.*

"Of the Stewart family at Alastrom?" the man asked.

"Yes, that's him." My breath heaved as I ran, but a glance behind me revealed that the faerie hadn't followed. I slowed so as to not run out of range of what little cell signal I had.

"I am dispatching an officer out to Route 3 now. Any idea where?" The operator's voice filled with concern, but it lacked sincerity. It was the kind people learned to convey with training.

"He was headed to Boston earlier."

There was a great deal of talking in the background. "Okay, let's try and pinpoint your location now, Kellen. Are you calling from a mobile phone with the GPS enabled?"

"Yes."

There was a long pause on the other end as the typing continued. Voices muffled as someone placed a hand over the receiver. Finally, after what felt like an eternity, the operator returned.

"Mr. St. James, I'm sorry to say that I don't think your GPS is working."

Dread pooled in my gut. "Why do you say that?"

"Because the location we're getting is in the middle of the Atlantic Ocean."

Before I could answer, my phone's screen went black.

The sound was the first to go—the pattering of heavy raindrops on the leaves of the trees faded away. It was as though I'd entered a soundproof room. I ran as hard as I could, but when I passed the same tree a third time—an old oak whose limbs crossed in front of it—I slowed to a halt. All I'd managed to do was run in circles. I crouched beside the tree and caught my breath, cursing myself for never making physical fitness a priority.

I drew a deep breath and scanned the clearing. Another little man stood a few feet away. His hair was shaved into a blond Mohawk, and several gold medallions hung from his chest. He looked like a very, *very* short Mr. T. He leaned against a pine tree, arms crossed, a smile stretching across his face. "Why hello there, Mr. St. James."

I jumped to my feet and turned to run, but I suddenly

couldn't move my legs. "Stop it. Whatever this is, I need to look for my friend."

"It's a pleasure to finally meet the one everyone's been making such a fuss over." The little man circled me until only a few feet separated us. "I'm sorry about your friend. I had to get him out of the picture, you see. It was a shame to do it."

Anger and fear thrummed together in my veins. "What do you mean, get him out of the picture?"

He stopped and looked at his nails as though contemplating filing them. They were about an inch longer than normal nails might have been, even on a woman. "Cana wanted you pretty badly, and none of us could enter that blasted house of iron to get you. You had to be flushed out, and we don't have time for a battle."

"What did you do with my friend? He was leaving. I sent him away to be safe."

The little man's bushy eyebrows resembled twin caterpillars as they rose up and down with his sigh. "I dare say that wasn't a very good idea. I ran your friend's car off the road."

Some part of me screamed on the inside. That couldn't be right. There was no way Gabe could be gone. "He's—"

"Dead? Oh, yes. I don't imagine how he couldn't be. I'd say that rental flipped five revolutions over the cliff at the least." The little man's Mohawk quivered as he laughed.

My heart stopped working and my body slipped into a wicked paralysis, but it was temporary. Before I realized it, my feet had carried me across the clearing. "You bastard! You killed him! You killed my best friend!"

Yet no sooner had I lunged across the space when I slammed into an invisible wall. I fell backward onto the hard ground with a thud. In seconds, I was back on my feet, pushing against the barrier that separated us, yet nothing I did made any difference. He'd encased me in a large bubble. I was trapped.

"Why did you kill him? He meant nothing to you." I gritted my teeth on the last word as rain streaked against the outside of my bubble.

The little man smiled, but it didn't last. "Cana wanted you, and I swore allegiance to her. There's too much at risk, too much at stake to go against her."

"Why does she want me?" I felt like an idiot having the conversation from the center of a huge bubble. I sat down roughly. At least the ground was no longer cold.

When I'd been trapped in Faerie, I'd used a black-handled knife Cali had given me to escape a whole crew of Trooping Faeries and even travel through time. That knife was back at Gran's cottage in Ireland. I didn't even have my Swiss Army knife on me this time.

"Don't pretend you don't know, boy. You will have to turn it over. When you do, we'll keep our freedom and Cana will gain hers."

"But I don't know what she thinks I have."

The first faerie burst through the clearing then, his arms thrown out to both sides as if to separate us. "Why are you involving us in this, Walter? It is foolish. We should not believe anything that Cana promises. More stories are surfacing. I heard tell that this young one didn't side with the mighty Arawn, he *stopped* him."

The faerie named Walter shook his head. "It does not matter, Bob. We can't walk away now. We're in trouble. You're the one who almost gave him hypothermia. How could he have told us where it's hidden if he'd died?" He scowled, crossing his arms over his small chest.

"Me?! You're the one who almost drowned him," Bob spat, curling his fingers into tiny claws as though he meant to attack Walter.

"He was supposed to sleepwalk, not almost drown!" Walter leaned in, his posture mimicking Bob's.

"Wait . . . you two led me out to Compass Harbor? You messed with my dreams?" William had been telling the truth.

They both swiveled around, their eyes wide as though they'd forgotten I was there.

"We made you think that you wanted to go outside." Bob grinned with something resembling pride.

"You should have at least convinced the mortal to put on a coat first. They're fragile. I don't know what you could have been thinking." Walter shook his head. "At least the warlock showed up and saved him, else we would have been imprisoned, or worse."

William. They were talking about William.

Walter leaned in until he and Bob were nose to nose. "Who are you to cast suspicion? I didn't almost drown him in the sea! Poor dreamwork indeed! Thank goodness the ghosts stopped him from being drowned."

Ghosts. Memories of the blue light and the vanishing party came back to me.

"If they hadn't intervened, Mistress Cana would have had our heads." Bob threw up his hands, glaring at Walter.

Cana. My blood grew cold even as the little men stood nose to nose, their voices rising.

Walter finally drew back and jerked his thumb at me. "Let us kill him now and be done with it. We can run away, north to our Canadian brothers. They can hide us."

My opinion of Walter continued on a downhill slide.

Bob glanced at me. "We're supposed to leave him alive. Since when has our kind ever taken a life on purpose?"

"But they will kill us. I don't think anything good can come from this, no matter what Cana promised." Walter's threatening demeanor crumbled before my eyes. "They will kill our families." He met my eye with his last revelation.

The rain poured down around us, the water blurring the little man slightly.

"I understand how you feel about wanting to protect your family."

Walter's expression changed in an instant and he scowled at me. "Mortal." He spat on the ground. "How could you ever comprehend my plight?"

"Look, punk ass, being mortal doesn't mean I don't have feelings. Nearly all my family is dead, and now so is my best friend." I swallowed hard, not allowing myself to think about Gabe. "And if you don't let me out of this bubble, I'm pretty sure Cana will kill me and the girl I love." It didn't matter to them, but I had to try.

A strange sound trumpeted in the night. The sky remained dark, and there wasn't much to see from within the thicket of the trees, until I spotted it. The enormous bird gave a second trumpeting cry and then dive-bombed the clearing.

"It's him. Take cover!" Walter flung his hands over his head.

The great bird swooped down and pierced the bubble. It latched onto the collar of my coat and lifted me off the ground. I flapped my arms and legs, acting on instinct. The bird's rough beak cut into the skin on the back of my neck, but I didn't get the impression it had been on purpose.

Gagging, I shoved my fingers between my neck and collar. The last thing I needed was to suffocate or end up with a crushed windpipe. The bird didn't appear to notice. It flew even faster despite its size. I lifted my feet as we skimmed the treetops.

"You aren't going to drop me in the ocean, are you?" I choked out. "That would be bad."

The bird chuckled at my words, reminding me of another time I'd been rescued by its kind. That bird's name had been Ghárda and he'd been a pelican in Faerie. Thanks to him I hadn't been captured by the Hounds of the Hill and deposited on Arawn's doorstep.

"Are you one of Ghárda's clan? Are you a Protector?"

The bird grunted in answer. Since I didn't want it to drop me, that would have to do.

As the pair of us soared over the water, my coat began to tear. I swallowed hard, turning my attention to holding the fabric together. The ocean raged beneath us. We'd gone ten feet out when the air ahead rippled and bunched.

The bird lowered its head and aimed for the shimmering wall.

Riiiiip. My coat tore again, and I jerked an inch closer to the sea.

"Are you going to set me down soon? Because this coat isn't holding."

My rescuer didn't speak. Instead we blasted directly into the shimmering air. The moment we did, the salty ocean air tweaked my nose, the wind chilled me, and the sound of the rain surrounded us as we flew.

Slowly the bird guided us toward a rock that jutted out over the water. We were about a foot from land when my coat finally gave out. The next thing I knew, I'd landed on my butt on the hard stone.

"Ouch."

I glanced up as the bird glided to the ground in front of me. It didn't attack. There was something oddly familiar about it. It had Ghárda's calm blue eyes. That was it.

Now that we weren't airborne, I was able to identify it courtesy of that book in Walmart. This was a sandhill crane, but it was five times the size of any of the ones I'd read about. Cranes were supposed to signify long life and immortality. Whether that meant the crane's or mine, I had no idea. Right then I was hoping for both.

Slowly, I got to my feet. "Thanks for saving me."

The bird let out another trumpeting call. Unlike Ghárda, this bird didn't seem to speak. It nodded, inclining its head in my direction.

The bird regarded me for a moment before turning and shooting in an arc into the air where it disappeared.

Sighing, I looked across the water. Alastrom sat on its perch above the sea no more than a quarter of a mile's walk from I stood. Yet I couldn't go back. Not yet.

I had to find Gabe's body.

CHAPTER 38

CALI

Clouds shifted into position above us, forming a ceiling. It grew dark early in Maine, yet this was something more. Only the Children of Danu could create such a barrier, which meant the clouds could only be the amalgamation of their twisted power.

I'd been pacing for what felt like hours, waiting for Kellen to come back with Gabriel or even for Uncle Dillion to return. Neither had happened and the silence grated on my nerves. If I'd been immortal, I would have been out there with Kellen. I could have transported us to Gabriel's side.

But I was no longer immortal.

My stomach twisted into knots, clenching and bunching inside me as I lifted the window covering to peer outside. Kellen gone, Gabriel injured, and I couldn't do anything about any of it. If only I'd stayed immortal and had my powers. This exercise—hiding in Maine—hadn't done us any good at all.

I dropped the covering and moved from the window. Uncle Dillion said it would be best to act like no one was at home. I didn't see the point. Our enemies knew where we were. Sitting in the house served little purpose.

I went to the fireplace and used the flame of aim to light one of the many candles placed in an artful arrangement at the base of the hearth. I picked up the fat pillar and held it in my hands, soaking up the warmth and light from its flame. "Calm yourself, Calienta. You were a goddess once. Be strong."

My hands began to shake so violently that I quickly replaced the candle in its holder. My usually nimble fingers could've dropped it. I didn't have much experience with this mortal life, but setting the house on fire would have been a poor choice indeed.

Finally the front door opened and Uncle Dillion walked in. I got to my feet and rushed to meet him, slowing to a stop when I was only a little way away. More lines had appeared beneath Uncle's eyes, altering the landscape of his skin.

He moved into the living room and sank onto the sofa. "I've done all I can to protect this place."

"Uncle Dillion, I had no idea where you were. Gabriel has been injured—William came to the house to tell us and Kellen went with him. Neither of them has come back."

"Kellen went outside?" Uncle's eyebrows shot up and he shook his head. "That won't do. This William character concerns me."

"I think we need to look for them."

Uncle Dillion shook his head. "The last thing we need is for you to go out there as a mortal and get into trouble."

The sound of the door opening and closing put us both on alert. I leaped to my feet and gasped as Gabriel walked in. His clothes were torn and both of his eyes were blackened. Blood stained his pants, both of his hands, and even the fringes of his sandy brown hair. He looked from Uncle Dillion to me.

"Sorry, C. I wrecked the car."

Gabriel appeared more weakened than I'd ever seen him, as though a part of him had shattered inside. I moved to give him aid, but Uncle Dillion waved his had in an arc, pinning Gabriel to the wall.

Uncle muttered something as he magickally gripped Gabriel by the neck, raising him a foot off the ground without touching him. "He's not Gabriel. He's an imposter."

Holding my ground, I stayed behind Uncle Dillion, out of reach of the prisoner. If anyone would have the power to discern an imposter, it was Uncle. He was used to telling friend from foe in Faerie—he'd risked his humanity there every single day for eons.

I narrowed my eyes. "How dare you impersonate my friend. Who are you, stranger?"

Uncle Dillion waved a hand in front of the fake Gabriel and he instantly began to transform. The black eyes faded away, along with the blood and bruises. His short sandy brown hair grew longer and darkened to a deeper brown.

"William." I sputtered the last name I'd ever expected. "Where's Kellen?" I demanded, wishing I had my powers so I could do more than glare at him. "Did you turn him over to Cana?"

"No." His expression shifted. "The others snatched him as we ran. He's in the Cusp of Faerie, so I guess he's losing his mind about now."

But William's words only brought forward fuzzy thoughts that I was incapable of forming on my own. "Damn my memories!" I bit back a frustrated scream. "What is the Cusp?"

Uncle Dillion drew a breath. "It is a place neither of Faerie nor of Earth. It exists as a purgatory, where you can see both sides but never belong anywhere. Many call it the In-Between."

A chill swept across my skin. I couldn't believe I'd

forgotten that piece of information, though part of me wished it had stayed forgotten.

They had Kellen. *My Kellen.*

Uncle Dillion peered intently into William's eyes. "Dearest Danu." He blanched, then ever-so-slowly lowered William to his feet. "So *you're* the warlock they've been talking about."

"The one and only." William's face stretched into a wide, welcoming smile. "Hello, Father. It's been an age."

The two men stared at one another. To them, no one else existed. William's smile had turned mocking and cruel, while Uncle looked . . . devastated.

"Father? Uncle Dillion, you never told me you had a son." There hadn't been time to keep my words from sounding like an accusation.

"You knew it once, child." He cupped William's cheek in his hands, staring as if memorizing every feature, every mannerism. Tears trailed down his wrinkled face. "I cannot believe it is you, Son. I thought—"

"I know. You thought you'd gotten rid of me for good." William jerked free of Uncle's grasp and walked toward the kitchen counter, breaking the hold Uncle Dillion had had on him. "Surprise!"

Uncle Dillion sagged, his expression worsening. "You're one of them. You've turned."

"What did you expect?" William's face contorted in rage. His composure, which had always remained tightly in check, was gone.

Uncle Dillion took a half step forward. "I thought you'd died. Your mother—"

"Do not speak of her to me." William backed up as he choked out his words. It was the first time I'd seen him display any real emotion, outside of our single shared moment. It confused me even more.

"I'm sorry, Willock." Uncle finally turned to me. "This is my son, Calienta. Willock's his name, or Wil'k as we called him."

"And this is the William that we told you about. I apologize for missing the family resemblance." Inclining my head to William—*Willock*—I hinted at the obvious difference in size and looks between father and son.

"Why are you here?" Uncle Dillion kept his voice neutral, but his expression grew guarded.

"Why else? The boy." He glanced in my direction, looking at me with such longing it made me want to wrap a thick blanket around myself.

Dillion's rigid expression, however, gave little away. "How did you find them?"

"A simple location spell. I figured out which plane they'd boarded, so I knew they'd gone to the States. I lost them for a bit in the air, but they resurfaced in Boston. Then I hacked into the rental car records, and tailed them the entire way here, 'old school,' as the mortals say." Willock's eyes met mine and a sad smile filled his face. "It was too easy. Sorry."

"Location spells aren't simple, Willock. What did you have to trade to get that power?" Uncle Dillion rubbed his fingers on his chin as he awaited his son's response.

Willock's smile slipped. "I don't answer to you anymore, Father."

I glared at him, resting my hands on my hips. "Then how about answering to me? I think you owe me that much. Where is Gabriel? You had Kellen go out there with you to look for him." The thin line separating me from rational and nonrational behavior could thin more, depending upon his response.

Willock rolled his eyes. "One of the local faeries sent Gabe's car over a cliff. I don't know if he's alive, but he would have only been in the way."

My temper, having previously been dampened by fear and my own mortal state, came back with a vengeance. Willock had come here, manipulated all of us. And Gabriel . . . Gabriel was . . .

"You bastard!" I shrieked. I drew back my foot and kicked Willock in a very crucial area of his anatomy. Gabriel had assured me that, should I ever need to keep Kellen in line, this would work well, and his guidance proved accurate. Willock doubled over in pain, wrapping his arms around himself and moaning.

I clapped my hands together. "My, that is quite effective!"

Uncle Dillion coughed before turning from me and waving a hand over Willock's bent form. A thousand tiny ropes slithered from thin air. They bound Willock, twisting themselves around his limbs like little snakes. In no time at all, Willock was able to breathe, but his movement and ability to speak was restricted. Uncle Dillion lowered Willock to the floor and waved his hand over him. The younger man's head fell to the side, his eyes rolling back.

"This should hold him for several hours." Dillion rubbed his hands together, looking even more exhausted than when he arrived. "After that time, he will be able to break free. We need to figure out what to do with him. I'm sorry about Kellen, my dear."

"There's no need to be sorry. We're going out there to find him."

Uncle Dillion sighed. "Calienta, you do realize what a lost cause that could be? Kellen could be out there somewhere, just out of reach. Perhaps he's standing on the other side of the window looking in, but you just can't see him. That's how the Cusp works. You are neither here nor there."

"Stop!" I held out my hand to him, threatening him with powers I no longer had. Frustrated, I dropped my hand, hating the tears that wanted to follow. "We will not accept any other outcome. We will find both Kellen and Gabriel. Alive."

Uncle's eyebrows rose. "Calienta—"

"You'll help me, or I will do the same to you." I gestured to the crumpled Willock. "What do we do with him? We can't leave him on the floor."

Uncle Dillion looked at Willock with sadness as he passed his hand over him. The younger man levitated, hovering through the air to stop above the couch. He closed his fist and Willock dropped roughly to the cushions.

"As for Kellen, there might be a way."

Uncle reached into his pocket and pulled out a small ball. He drew an invisible line across it with his finger. Initially it seemed as if nothing would happen, but then the ball's surface split open and light burst forth. Uncle set the ball on the ground and stood back. A small circle of light trickled out from inside the ball. It began to rise higher and higher until it was even with Dillion's nose. The glowing ball rose and then slowly lowered to the ground outside of its original casing.

Then *poof!* One moment there was a small glowing orb and the next a dog stood there—a beast of large proportions that I hadn't seen since Faerie. The hell hound regarded me through red eyes that sent a chill skating down my spine. Then it leaned over and licked my hand before sitting on its haunches at my side with a huff.

Uncle rubbed his hands together. "This is Skyler. She can travel between the Cusp and our world. Not your average dog, as it were. And she's friendly. She chose to come with me."

Memories of another time and another dog flooded my mind. Kellen had once accused me of being an animal hater. Little had he known that the dog in question had been my father in disguise. I wrapped my arms around Skyler and placed a kiss on her head. "Good girl."

"Do you have anything of Kellen's and Gabriel's that she can smell so that she can learn their scents?"

I rushed down the hall toward our bedroom. My heart ached when I found Kellen's sweatshirt neatly folded and placed on one of the chairs. Then I headed to Gabriel's room and retrieved one of the blankets I'd seen him use. When I returned to the great room, Skyler was whining, anxious to begin her search. Crouching down, I allowed the animal to smell first the sweatshirt and then the blanket.

After Skyler had learned the scents, Uncle Dillion patted the huge animal, his small hand barely reaching the beast's throat. "Be careful now, old friend. This is going to be a difficult journey, I'm afraid. Make sure you report back."

The dog extended her pink tongue to lick Uncle on the cheek.

Uncle Dillion walked to the door and opened it. Skyler shot out into the night. I rushed to the window and peered out into the blackness.

"Please come back to me, Kellen. Please keep your promise."

CHAPTER 39

KELLEN

Gabe was dead—at least that's what that Walter guy had told me. It was inconceivable that Gabe was gone. He had been young, so full of life.

But I couldn't let myself think about him. When all of this was over, I could grieve properly. In the meantime, I had to find my best friend's body and see him one last time. And I needed to find a way to get him home to his family. Then I'd go home to Cali. I had to make that happen. I had to keep my promise.

My muscles ached, a combination of running through the woods and riding in the cold air with the crane. I felt like I'd aged a hundred years since I left the house with William.

William. I seethed internally.

The sound of a passing car clued me in to the location of the road and I found my way back. My mind ran round and round in circles, trying to figure it out. I decided to search the stretch of road leading back to the house. If I didn't find anything there, I'd ask Uncle Dillion.

My mental musings helped me forget my frozen fingers and toes. At least I'd had the foresight to put on a coat, but that didn't mean that the results were much better. I rounded a bend in the road and a low-pitched growl sounded. I froze in place.

Two bright red eyes glared at me from the dark road ahead. I knew only one type of beast that had red eyes and that growl. It was a hell hound, one of Arawn's dogs from Faerie.

Oh crap, I'm screwed.

I had no idea what to do. These beasts were deadly. In Faerie they were the dogs that Arawn used when he had to *collect someone.* I'd had several close calls with them until Calienta had destroyed them all.

No, not all. There was one that had faded away when I'd ended Arawn. Was this the creature? Had I displaced the beast when I'd killed its master?

I knew I couldn't outrun it or pass by it. My only hope was to make friends with it. With its master gone, it might be possible. Keeping my head down, I avoided eye contact. It was difficult. The red eyes drew me in.

Memories of a book I'd once read on dogs as a child came back to me. I had hoped Stephen would let me have a pet. That wasn't long before I'd been sent away to boarding school.

I'd been too afraid to actually ask for a dog, but I still had the memories of the text. I had to stay relaxed and let it come to me.

"It's okay, boy."

The beast let out a growl that sent every potential goose-bump on my body into action.

Whoops. "Sorry. I meant girl."

She let out a low whine and after a few tentative steps walked toward me and began to nuzzle my hand. When she stood to her full height, I was nearly eye to eye with one of the largest dogs I'd ever seen.

Pushing my fears aside, I pet the animal, gently stroking the side of her head. Maybe when I had taken out Arawn, she had turned good.

"I have to find my friend. Do you want to come with me?" To illustrate my point, I started walking, but the dog didn't follow and continued to whine.

When I turned around, she walked toward me and sat. Then she leaned into me, pushing against my leg with her behind as though to communicate something. She let out another low whine.

"Look, I'm sure you're a nice dog and all, but my friend, Gabe, needs me. So does Cali."

At the mention of Cali's name, the dog let out a low whine and began to prance around in circles.

"What? Do you know Cali?"

The animal's whines grew louder, her eyes pleading.

"Look, it's nothing personal. You seem like a nice dog. It's just that I don't know if I can trust you. I've been through some . . . stuff." *That was putting it mildly.*

In response, the dog lay down on the ground and buried her face beneath one paw as though ashamed. Then her large, fluffy tail began to wag in a very un-hell-hound–like way."

"Are you playing with me?" I half laughed as she leaped to her feet and barked once, as if it to say "Right answer!" She whined again, this time nudging my hip with her body, her tail swinging back and forth behind her like a swift pendulum.

"Do you want me to climb on your back?" It was a bad idea. This was a hell hound, after all. She looked *exactly* like those extreme beasts that terrorized the inhabitants or Faerie. Then again, I'd learned firsthand that looks could be deceiving.

She whined again and slid her head beneath my hand as though begging for pets. This was exactly what another dog I'd known had done. Of course, that dog had turned out to be

Cali's father in disguise, but he didn't hurt me. He'd been protecting me.

Was it possible this beast was doing the same?

I scratched behind her right ear and she began to beat one of her back paws against the ground in response. Just like a normal dog. Then she nudged my hip again.

"Oh man. I will probably regret this sometime in the future, but . . ." Slowly, I lifted one leg over the dog's back and leaned against her, gripping the coarse fur of her neck. As if on cue, she stood to her full height.

"Wow. Please tell me that you're not one of the bad guys."

She tilted her head back and swiped her long, sticky tongue against my cheek.

"I'll take that as a no. Can you show me where Gabe is?"

The animal leaped into action, carting me straight into the woods, running as though she knew exactly where to go. Several low-hanging tree branches threatened to unseat me. I brought my head close to hers and kept my eyes partially shut.

The dog galloped full-out through the woods, her heavy paws thudding on the ground. *Thump-thump. Thump-thump.* She howled as she ran, the sound mesmerizing me.

Keeping my head down, I closed my eyes. I couldn't let myself think about Gabe, so I focused on Cali. *Please let me see her again.* The thought repeated inside my head, almost in time with the pounding of the beast's feet.

The dog howled as she ran down a steep embankment. I clung on, gripping her fur tightly and pushing my knees into her flanks. Down and down she ran. The instant she reached the bottom, she skidded to a stop and sat, forcing me to roll off and end up on my backside.

My breath rushed from my chest and I glared at her. "You could have given me warning."

She turned and licked my cheek once more. Her tongue

left a slobbery path on my skin. Whining, she took a handful of steps forward and stopped at the base of a massive oak tree. Its branches were so wide that they shielded me from the rain when I stepped beneath them.

Swallowing hard, I looked up and almost sat back down again. The tree had impaled Gabe's rental car. A large branch ran through the front windshield and jutted out the rear window.

"Gabe!" Slamming one foot in front of the other, I rushed to the tree and circled its monster base. There had to be a way up.

A low-lying branch provided the foothold I needed. My stomach heaved as I began to climb, trying not to imagine what I would find when I reached the car. Gabe at the wheel with dead, lifeless eyes . . .

The bark bit into my hands as I scaled the tree, dreading my destination all the more the higher I got. I only needed to make it halfway up, then it would be a short climb until I reached the branch overlooking the car. All too soon I made it to the one that would give me a prime view.

I crouched on the hard surface and peered into the car. It was . . . "Empty? How can it be empty?"

Though I did my best to search both the front and back seats from my tree branch, there was no one inside. Which meant one thing.

I looked to my companion. "Gabe's alive."

CHAPTER 40
CALI

Waiting for Skyler to return with Kellen was intolerable. I couldn't sit. Couldn't think. I could do little else besides pace, checking the blackened windows with every pass.

"Calienta, come and sit with me. You're shivering." Uncle Dillion stopped in front of the fireplace and waved his hand in an arc, sending flames licking cheerfully at a pile of logs that hadn't been in the grate a moment before.

I didn't want to abandon my post at the window, but I looked like a fool for having stationed myself there. Whether I stood at the door or across the room had no bearing on whether Kellen returned. Forcing myself to leave the glass, I walked to the fireplace. My head throbbed. I wanted to sleep, but I couldn't, *wouldn't* sleep until Kellen returned.

"As I was saying," Uncle began, but then he stopped. He rolled his eyes and whirled around. "How did you free yourself from my binding?"

"It's not like I've forgotten everything you taught me, Father." Willock rose, but this time his smile contained less mockery and more boyishness.

"That's a surprise." Dillion replied, but a slight smile crossed his face as something resembling pride lit Uncle's eyes.

"Your bindings were quite a bit tighter than before." Willock rubbed his reddened wrists, grimacing.

Uncle Dillion cocked an eyebrow. "I've gotten stronger with age."

"Oh, is that how you're explaining it?" Willock smirked.

"Plus, you are fully grown. I no longer need to let you win." Dillion winked as though he were speaking to Willock the child and not Willock the man. "Now, how about you explain what's going on. Indulge us."

Willock walked toward his father. "I heard rumors from Cana about how you showed up at Calienta and Kellen's wedding, so I knew you'd come for them eventually. I've simply been waiting for you to show."

Panic seized me and I threw myself between Uncle Dillion and Willock. "You will not harm him."

Willock stared at me for a long, silent series of seconds until he burst into laughter. "You think you could stop me if I wished to? You're mortal!" His laughter rose up, grating on my nerves.

The puzzle of Willock I thought I'd been close to solving broke apart once more. How had the boy Uncle Dillion loved turned into this cold man? A man who'd been manipulating all of us.

"I hate you." The words sounded impossibly cold and callous on my tongue. They were words I had never spoken to anyone, for my father had told me once that hating something was the worst kind of evil—that the true blackness could begin within ourselves if we let it.

"Hate. That's not what he told me you would feel." Willock frowned, something akin to disappointment filtering into his expression.

"What do you mean, Willock?" Uncle leaned forward, as though inspecting his son for something, some tarnish on his soul.

"It's nothing." A ding came from somewhere in the room and Willock pulled a phone from his pocket. He rolled his eyes. "Dearest Danu. Why can't anyone follow instructions?"

"Problems at the Camp of Evil?" I cocked an eyebrow, doing my best to sound exactly like Kellen would if he'd been there.

Willock smirked. "It's these local faeries. Cana recruited them and they keep making mistakes. Like leading Kellen out into the woods and interfering with his dreams."

"You didn't do that?" I asked, puzzled.

"Of course not. I wanted them to track you all, not kill you. I was the one who put Cana onto your trail in the first place. I told her Kellen was keeping the curse that deformed her alive. That it was Kellen's magick that trapped her. Not many of our kind would help. She recruited the local faeries and I've been using them as a back-up plan ever since. If I lost sight of you, then I knew that the Children of Danu would find you."

In an odd way that made sense. At least it didn't surprise me. Yet that couldn't be all to the story. "There's more, isn't there? You wouldn't align yourself with amateurs unless you wanted something for yourself." I narrowed my eyes, inspecting him, trying to see past the mask to the little boy, or to the quiet man who'd kissed me. Yet Willock shuttered his expression, locking away his vulnerability, and I was only left with assumptions. "So that means you either have your own plan, or you're working for someone else—maybe both?"

Willock's eyes widened and for a moment there was something more there. "I *am* impressed. You're right. I am working for someone who has a vested interest in your Mr. St. James."

Uncle Dillion paled. He gripped the back of a chair for support. "He's alive then?"

"Of course he's alive!" Willock edged closer to me. "He's a bit ticked off at Kellen. I'd be furious too if someone tried to destroy me with the Sword of Light."

Arawn. My heart slammed into my chest. Not only was he alive, but the Lord of Faerie wanted Kellen. Dearest Danu. When would it end?!

CHAPTER 41

CALI

My head throbbed. The dull ache that had clung to it from the moment Kellen left hadn't gotten any better. Things weren't likely to improve now that I'd learned the truth: Arawn was alive and he was extremely angry with Kellen.

"Kellen didn't want to fight Arawn. He was trying to protect this world."

"Arawn understands. He's willing to overlook it if Kellen comes with me." Willock smiled as though he'd given me an award. "It's a great honor."

"Great honor, my ass." I blurted out the words without thinking, but given how Uncle reddened, I was quite certain I'd said an improper word. "What does he want with Kellen?"

"Kellen is the key to Danu's amulet." Willock clapped his hands together as though he'd made the very best of announcements.

"But Kellen doesn't have the amulet."

All he had was his mother's pendant, and Father had admitted it had little more than sentimental value.

Willock dropped his hands. "He doesn't, but I know who

does." He turned then, his eyes scanning Uncle Dillion with interest.

"What is he talking about, Uncle?" My voice shook. I didn't want to ask the question. The chances were too great that I would not like what I heard.

"I'm talking about a secret he's been keeping from you." Willock scowled, flicking his wrist and sending Uncle Dillion into the air where he hung, suspended, his short legs kicking about uselessly. My stomach turned at the gross abuse of magick.

Yet in the next instant Uncle Dillion flipped down to his feet, and Willock flew backward across the room. He slammed through the front door with enough force to leave a Willock-like hole in the wooden structure.

But he wasn't gone. Willock returned with a popping sound, and with a flick of his wrist, suspended his father upside down by his feet once more.

Uncle Dillion hung there only a second before he reversed their roles, suspending Willock and binding his arms. Then Willock was free and Dillion bound. This went on for several more rounds before Uncle Dillion threw his arms out.

"Enough!"

A terrible rumbling began and the ground beneath us trembled. A mighty series of crashes followed as the Stewart's house began to collapse. The floor vibrated, ceiling beams buckled, and windowpanes shattered. Uncle Dillion threw his hands down at his sides and in one swift motion the entire house crashed down in a deafening roar until only dust and rubble remained, clogging the air.

Uncle Dillion had spared nothing, save the small circle in which we remained, dust-covered but otherwise free from harm. Darkness formed a halo around us as the moon made an appearance, its bright rays illuminating the incredible scene before us. There was nothing left of Alastrom but an immense pile of debris.

Before I could point out how unhappy Gabriel would be when he discovered this, Uncle Dillion raised his arms slowly. The magick began to reverse. Beams repaired themselves, shattered glass heated and melted together, and the dust faded away. One second, we stood in the middle of the inglorious wreckage of Gabriel's house and the next we stood within the house exactly as it had been. He'd even repaired the Willock-like shape in the front door.

Dillion's magick had been restrained when Arawn bound him. The display we'd witnessed was something he *shouldn't* have been able to do. Even I knew that.

"Very good, Father! Impressive magick!" Willock applauded, the harsh sound echoing in the lonely house. "I had my suspicions, but you've given me the proof. Give me the amulet."

Horror washed over me. So, it was true. "Uncle."

All of Uncle's energy seemed to drain from him. "You know she wouldn't have wanted this. You believed in her cause once, you knew what we signed up for."

"That was before my father gave up on me." All the mockery left Willock's voice.

Uncle reached for Willock's hand and, to my surprise, the younger man let him take it. "That's what Arawn wanted you to believe. He specializes in crafting worlds for those he entraps, but none of it is real. It is trickery!" Uncle Dillion then turned to me. "I'm sorry you've lost your memories, my dear. Having spent my time in Faerie absorbed in them, I understand how tragic losing them must be." Then he took my hand in his. "Let me give you both some of mine."

The instant our hands connected, it was as if we were no longer in the room. We were in the Green Lands—my home. The heady scent of grass filled my nostrils, the warmth of the untainted air rushed over my skin. Home. I never thought I'd see it again.

"My wife was called Mairin, and she was the kindest, bravest soul I'd ever hoped to meet. Danu herself created her for me, you see. Mairin had been a mortal once—a witch, in fact."

In Uncle's memory, a beautiful woman with long dark hair ran through the fields.

"Our son, our Willock, was everything to us."

A small boy ran beside Mairin. The pair laughed and danced across the grasses. Soon a tall, dark-haired, beautiful man joined them. He seemed achingly familiar and I realized this was Uncle Dillion as he had been before Arawn's entrapment. He'd been as muscular and imposing as my father, but with a quieter persona. Dillion would have been the scholar. The bookworm who chose words over violence.

"By the time the first of the Great Wars arrived, Willock was the immortal equivalent of a teenager. He was the youngest of all of us after Lugh." Uncle Dillion cleared his throat, but I wasn't seeing him, only image after image of a battlefield and a young boy dressed in armor. "Mairin and I had always agreed that we would let Willock choose for himself how he would live, so we allowed it. The three of us went into the fight together."

Mortals with crude spears and heavy armor raced through bitter rain in hand-to-hand combat in Uncle's memory world. Bloodshed, death, and decay reigned.

When he released our hands and the three of us broke apart, the memories faded from view, but not from my mind.

"We did not know that Arawn had partnered with the opposing army. His magick was so strong. At the time, I didn't understand how he could have so much power. The immortals were captured and forced below ground. My wife was . . . beheaded by the mortals." Uncle's face crinkled up like paper, and tears streamed down his cheeks. "I never knew where they took her body. Willock had been fighting across the field when he saw . . . what happened. He was running toward me when Arawn himself appeared between us. Arawn just . . . took Willock." His tears fell faster and harder now. It unsettled me to see him cry, but then, so much of my world disquieted me these days.

"I tried to find you, Willock. Look at this." Uncle reached into his pocket and withdrew a battered bit of parchment. It was a hand-drawn map faded with time and tears. "I searched every inch of Faerie, marking it on the map. I even searched for you in the mortal world. Yet every morning The Call would come, and I was forced to return underground."

"What's The Call?" The sensation of being watched weighed on me, and I turned to find Willock, his eyes wide, pain etched across his face.

Uncle wiped his eyes on the back of his sleeve. It was such a mortal action that I smiled. "Arawn's call. We were trapped, though we had the illusion of freedom. We could come and go from Faerie in the mortal nighttime, but when the first rays of dawn touched the sky, we had to return, otherwise we'd hear The Call."

"Couldn't you just ignore it?" I instantly regretted my question. As if I had any idea what he'd been through.

Uncle's eyes rounded in horror. "Ignoring The Call meant that you'd hear and see your loved ones being tortured. It would replay inside your mind. For most of us, it was enough—"

"To make you completely lose your mind." This came from Willock, his voice breaking.

"Yes. I only witnessed it once, you see, and I would never risk it again." Another tear streaked a trail down Uncle's face. "The others, though, their need for freedom was too strong. They kept trying again and again and it changed them. We all changed physically as a result of being forced into Faerie and away from the heavens, but The Call altered their minds. Searching for Willock was what saved me. I never stopped." The little man shook his head, his attention flickering to the fire. "After a long while, I assumed that Arawn had killed him. Now I know Arawn took him under his wing."

"How do you know, Uncle?" Did he sense the evil lying in Willock? Perhaps pick up on Arawn's influence just by standing near his son?

"Because he's . . . *beautiful*." He gestured to Willock without looking at him, as though he couldn't bear it. "Only someone close to Arawn, someone who'd sworn complete allegiance, could have kept their looks. He's *so* like Mairin."

Tears trailed down Willock's face. "My new father warned me that I shouldn't waste sadness on you. That you would never come for me. He swore an oath on Danu that my mother was the only one you ever loved."

"I never gave up on you, Willock. Not once." Uncle Dillion stepped forward, gripping his son's arms. "I imagine that Arawn treated you in much the same way that a normal father would treat a son. The way I treated you?"

Willock shuddered. His eyes seemed empty, haunted by the ghosts of a million memories. "At first . . . but then he found another favorite. I became nothing more than a servant to him."

A chill swept over me. I couldn't imagine the nightmare of a life with Arawn.

Uncle placed his hand over Willock's head. "Ah, how he's twisted your mind. Manipulated you into doing his bidding." Closing his eyes, the older man continued. "Let go of the hate inside of you, Willock. You were not made of hate, you were made of light. Our job was always to protect the Crown." With his other hand he cupped Willock's cheek. "*Remember*."

As Willock stared at Uncle, all traces of bitterness and

mockery faded away and his eyes glistened with more tears. Golden light shot from Dillion's fingertips, encircling them both and shading each of them in turn so that their skin took on a glow.

"Let go now, Son."

Willock's back arched and then he slumped against Dillion, his eyes closed, his head resting on his father's shoulder. What had Uncle done to him?

CHAPTER 42

KELLEN

T hough I searched all around the tree where Gabe's accident had taken place, there was no sign of him. Perhaps that should have filled me with fear, but I was oddly calm. I felt like I would know if something had happened to him. The how's and why's around that evaded me, but a certainty filled me. Wherever Gabe was, he was okay. For now.

The dog whined impatiently. She stamped her paw on the ground as though she was past ready to go.

"Thanks for waiting. Mind giving me a lift home?" I was talking to this hell hound like it was a taxi service. How would she even know where to take me? Yet she hadn't had any problem finding Gabe's car, and she was a magickal being.

She sat, allowing me to mount her back and I gripped her fur once more. She stood and paced for several moments as though unsure. Then, with a huff she bolted forward, tearing through the woods. Her paw-falls thundered in the quiet, and the beast let out an unearthly howl.

The main road lay to the right. Intermittent headlights from passing cars brightened the night. The dog changed course, whining as she headed for the main road. We dashed from the woods and had almost crossed the road when she suddenly disappeared from under me. I landed in the middle of the darkened asphalt with a speeding car headed straight for me.

"Get out of the way, *eejit*!"

The gruff male voice jolted me along with the shove that forced me out of the road and into the woods that banked it. Large hands gripped my shoulders, and we hit the ground hard, rolling through the damp woods in the dark. I couldn't see my rescuer's face. My eyes fought to adjust after being plunged into the darkness of the still woods.

Before I could stand, the stranger scooped me up and began to run with me through the woods as though I were a small child. The distinct smells of fish and pine tickled my nose.

"Put me down. I can run on my own."

"Sure, and we'd be waitin' all night. My way's faster, and we're almost there." Once more, a shimmering wall appeared. Before I could fight my way free or even protest, we passed through it.

A small cheerfully lit cottage lay up ahead. The last time I'd been in a cottage, a dubious warlock with no social skills had taken up residence as a squatter. Hopefully this experience would be better, otherwise I'd be giving Faerie a customer-service rating of zero.

Lights twinkled at each of the windows. Flowers sat along the porch in pots illuminated by the inside lights. This place wasn't a hideout, but a home.

When we reached the bottom of the two steps leading into the house, my savior lowered me to the ground. I followed him up the steps and nearly bumped into him when he stopped abruptly.

"Sorry we had to leave your pet behind, but hell hounds

aren't welcome here." The stranger pointed to a mat. "Wipe your feet. Then come in. Or don't, I suppose. Your choice."

Squinting, I made out the word *Welcome written across the doormat*. The man turned and went inside, leaving the front door open as though his departure wasn't explicit enough.

He didn't seem particularly interested in holding me prisoner.

Short on options, I wiped my feet three times on the mat and went inside. The interior of the one-room cottage was modest but tidy. A small kitchen with a sink, stove, and a round table with two chairs occupied one side while a twin bed draped in a colorful quilt took up the other. Fishing nets and poles leaned in a neat stack by the front door. A vase of spring-like yellow flowers, the kind Gran used to pick, was set on the table. They were an odd sight for October. A large stone fireplace filled the wall space in between the bed and table, and a fire blazed there, reminding me of the one back at Gabe's.

The home had a good feeling to it, like I'd be safe here— at least until I came up with an alternative plan to get back to Cali and make our escape.

The odor of fish reached me again. Either this unusual man had eaten it for dinner, or he worked as a fisherman. Judging by the gear, I assumed the latter.

In the light of the cabin, I could see the man clearly. His dishwater-blond hair was cropped short, probably for ease of management. He looked younger than I'd first thought. He was perhaps in his late thirties, but beyond that there was something familiar about him that I couldn't place.

"Tea?" the stranger asked with a smile.

Gran had warned me about eating or drinking anything the Good People served, but now that we were inside, I was fairly certain this man wasn't one of them. For starters, he didn't *look* like one of them.

Just in case, I concentrated hard on him the way I had when I'd been invited to dinner with a group of bloodthirsty Trooping Faeries. That group had used magick called a glamour to make plates of rocks and peat moss resemble real food. Fortunately I'd been able to see through it before I ingested any. Still, this man didn't change. He wasn't using a glamour to hide his real persona.

Whatever this man was, he wasn't one of the C.O.D.

What the hell. "Yes, please. Black."

"Right-o." He smiled and went back to his preparations.

I hung my coat beside my host's near the front door and moved toward the heat of the fire, taking a seat on the over-stuffed sofa positioned in front of its flames. The warmth teased my frozen digits.

"Here you go." My host held a steaming blue mug filled with tea under my nose.

"Thanks." I accepted the mug and sipped the brew, not caring when it scalded my tongue. The spicy concoction slid down my throat in a slow burn.

The man lifted the lid on a chest next to the fire and pulled out a quilt with a pattern of wildflowers spilling across it. He dropped it over my shoulders and warmth instantly spread across my back.

The stranger wore denim overalls with patched knees. White long underwear peeked out from the sides as he bent to stoke the fire. When he righted himself, I realized the top of his head wasn't very far from the ceiling. His wiry frame was either much taller than it'd seemed outside or the cabin was smaller.

After fussing with the fire, he went to the kitchen and returned a moment later with his own cup of tea. He took a seat beside me on the sofa.

"What's your name, lad?" He regarded me through kind hazel eyes.

Though I was convinced he wasn't one of the C.O.D., I didn't think he was ignorant of my situation either. I didn't see any point in dancing around the truth. "What's *your* name? I know that you know mine, so why pretend?" I lifted the cup to my lips and took another sip.

Chuckling, he smiled. "Taiclaigh. Call me Tai."

Now that I'd warmed up and had a cup of tea to sustain me, I picked up on Tai's Irish accent. "Oh, like a Thai restaurant."

"They have named a restaurant after me? I'm famous." His eyes crinkled as he smiled.

I couldn't help laughing. "Nice to meet you, Tai."

"Pleased to meet ya, Kellen." Tai clasped my hand and shook it heartily. "Glad to be of service. That loony on the road nearly took you out."

"That's what it looked like."

"What were you doing out in the middle of the night, anyway?"

Hmm. Should I tell him how I'd come to be riding on the back of a hell hound? I vote no.

"I got lost. What were you up to?"

Tai sipped his tea and nodded in agreement. "Fishing for sea bass. You get some good ones at night."

"So, you're a fisherman, then?" I moved to drink more of the tea but halted when I realized I'd already drained my cup.

"Yes. Ten generations." Tai stood and went to the kitchen, returning with a small pot and wooden board filled with cheese, crackers, sliced apple, summer sausage, and grapes. He set the food on the low table in front of us and refilled my mug. "Thought you might be hungry."

When had I last eaten? Breakfast. It wasn't all that long ago, but for some reason I was famished. "Thank you. I'm starving."

Outside the wind howled, reminding me of the dark night

this man could have left me out in. Shivering, I drank more tea, then bit into a piece of the sausage.

"You know, my granda was a fisherman." I piled cheese and more sausage on top of one of the crackers, catching the crumbs in my opposite hand and dashing them into my mouth.

"That so?" He built himself a cracker stacked with everything but the grapes, then bit into the concoction. He polished it off with his tea, which he held on to as he sat back against the sofa. He regarded me in silence for several moments before he finally spoke. "How long are you going to run from the second part of the prophecy, Kellen?"

My heart leaped inside my chest. "Interesting. You aren't one of them."

He grinned as though I'd pleased him. "No, I am not."

"So how do you know about the prophecy? About me? Where do you fit in?"

Tai tipped the remaining contents of his mug into his mouth. "Get some rest." He opened the chest again and pulled out a pillow and a stack of blankets that he placed on one end of the sofa. "You'll need your strength, Kellen."

"For what?" But I'd no sooner asked the question when my eyes grew heavy. I blinked to clear them, but it didn't do any good. I couldn't keep my eyelids propped open another moment.

I slid off my shoes and nestled under the blankets. The instant my head hit the pillow, I fell into a deep sleep and the dreams began, *again*.

CHAPTER 43

CALI

Together Uncle and I helped Willock lie down on a nearby sofa. Once there, Willock collapsed atop the cushions, his eyes already closed and his breathing slowed as though he'd already slipped into a deep sleep.

Uncle, too, seemed drained. He slowly sank to the floor, as though he could no longer bear to stand. When he arranged himself in a sitting position against the end of the sofa, he drew a ragged breath.

"Are you all right, Uncle?" I asked, knowing he wasn't.

He shook his head, seeming even older than he had before. "Healing magick is draining. There were so many locks buried deep within his mind. Magickal trappings to keep him from remembering who he is." He reached inside his pocket and withdrew a green stone that pulsed a golden hue and glowed where it rested on his palm.

"Danu's amulet—you do have it!" Awe mingled with fear and excitement as the knowledge I'd once held about the amulet came crashing down around me. "How did it come to be in your possession? Why do you have it?"

Without taking his eyes from Willock, Uncle Dillion positioned the amulet over Willock's head. He muttered a series of words my mortal ears couldn't hear. Slowly, Willock's body seemed to sink against the cushions as the glow from the amulet brightened.

"When Kellen slew Arawn, the Children of Danu found themselves free after centuries of imprisonment." Uncle Dillion coughed, the action wracking his body for several moments before he could speak again. "Can you imagine what would have happened if any of our family claimed this stone as their own?"

After several moments, Uncle Dillion returned the amulet to his pocket. All the color had faded from his skin and his cheeks had grown sunken.

"Yet, they soon discovered that Arawn's death wasn't enough to end their entrapment. They needed to be freed by the amulet. They planned to run rampant in the mortal world. In truth, Faerie itself needs to be healed."

I couldn't imagine the Children of Danu with free reign in the mortal world. "Why haven't you healed them all and ended this?"

"Because . . ." Uncle Dillion burst into a coughing fit, ". . . it was never meant for me to control. It's too . . . much."

Immortals didn't age. They didn't get coughs. Acid rose in my throat so that I could barely speak my fears, but I had to. "It's killing you."

"It is fine. I will be with my lovely wife again. I regret nothing."

"I wish I could say the same." As far as regrets went, I had more than I could count.

"But I can't help noticing that Kellen hasn't come back with Skyler." Uncle frowned, his eyes flickering to the door.

I'd been acutely aware of Kellen's absence. Uncle's mention of if made me worry even more.

"It's coming true, isn't it? The second part of the prophecy."

Uncle Dillion's eyes held all the same pain and anguish that lived within me. "The one who refuses immortality in light will receive it in darkness."

"I never read the words. I didn't want to have to remember them." I could see now how foolish I'd been. By hiding from the future, I had kept Kellen from preparing. His anger in me had been justified. "Uncle, Kellen would never turn—"

"You do not know what choice he will have to make." Uncle's voice grew breathless. "Arawn will likely offer him something that he desperately wants, something he has always yearned for. Or it may happen, but not the way you think."

Slowly, Willock began to stir on the couch. He blinked once, twice, three times before moving to a sitting position beside his father. He looked different somehow. My heart ached for the boy who'd lost his childhood. Willock had more in common with Kellen than he knew.

Uncle Dillion reached back to hold his son's hand. "How are you feeling?"

Willock shook his head, tears pooling in his eyes as he slid to the floor beside his father. "All those years. All this time, he lied."

Uncle's sympathetic expression changed to a knowing one, his smile grim. "That's what he does. He's a brilliant liar, which is why Danu herself never trusted him."

"A wise decision." I couldn't pinpoint how erasing Arawn's influence had changed him, but Willock seemed lighter somehow. He resembled a man who no longer had any decisions, one that simply needed to follow the path charted for him.

"And you know what you need to do now?" Uncle Dillion patted Willock's hand, waiting.

"I do." Willock wrapped his arms around Dillion and clung to him. "Father. Give me the amulet," he whispered.

Tears pooled in Uncle's eyes. He shook his head violently, shrinking back from Willock as though he didn't have the power to stand.

"Father, *please*." Willock's voice turned pleading.

"I cannot do that. I *will* not."

"It's not up to you." Willock stared at his father and knelt before him, gripping his forearms. "You wanted me to remember the oath that I took, and I have. You need to as well. When we swore to help Danu, we promised to get the amulet to the one who was supposed to bear the power."

Panic built in my chest. "And who is that?"

Yet it was as if neither of them heard me. All I could do was bear witness to the drama playing out.

"But he's not here and you won't be able to bear it. Just like I can't." Uncle Dillion went into another coughing fit, fierce and long. When he lowered his hand from his mouth, his skin was covered in speckles of blood.

"Then I view it as my penance for the mistake that I made with you." Willock squeezed his eyes shut.

"But you aren't to blame!" Uncle Dillion insisted, and another coughing spell wracked his little body. More blood splattered across his hands, dark spots staining his aged skin in the dim light. Uncle Dillion clutched his hand to his chest, staining parts of his shirt with blood. He crossed his other arm over that one. "Please let me finish this."

"You won't make it." His voice broke. Willock slowly tapped his finger against his head. "I've seen it." Willock closed his eyes against the scene, yet tears slipped from his closed eyelids as he concentrated.

Before Uncle Dillion could protest again, Willock waved his hand over his father's chest. The older man's eyes widened, and he frantically began shaking his head as his hands glowed a bright green.

The large green stone slipped from Uncle's fingers. He reached for it but wasn't quick enough. The instant it left his grasp, he gasped, his eyes closed, and he slumped against the sofa.

Dillion was gone.

Willock quickly pocketed the amulet. He'd no sooner done so, when a rush of golden light passed over him in a wave. When it faded, he was still the same Willock—beautiful in his own way—but there was more definition to his jaw and cheekbones. Minute gray hairs threaded their way through the dark ones on his head. Had I been immortal, I would have seen more, perhaps the slow deterioration of muscle tone or lines within his skin that hadn't quite reached the surface.

Sinking to his knees, Willock cradled his father's head in his hands. Tears fell from his eyes like the raindrops that had fallen from the sky earlier. "I'm so sorry, Father."

We stayed like that, silent in our separate spaces, while Willock mentally said whatever good-bye he needed to. Eventually, Willock stood and faced me, a pained expression on his face. Gone was the confused man who couldn't decide if he wished to be friend or foe. This new Willock wore an open expression that let me see all the way into his soul.

"I'm sorry, Calienta. For everything." Then he turned as though he meant to leave without another word.

I couldn't let that happen. Not yet.

"Does Arawn have Kellen?"

Willock froze, his shoulders stiffening. He hung his head as though debating whether he should answer. After what felt to me like far too many moments of indecision, he finally faced me.

"I think so. If he doesn't, he will soon, now that Kellen no longer has the protection of the house."

It was such a poor explanation to accompany all of my worst fears coming true. "He's not going to let Kellen go, is he?"

More tears trailed down Willock's face. "Never."

"So that's it. He's just gone." My voice broke on that last impossible word as my own desperation increased. I couldn't lose Kellen. "And you're not going to help me. I thought I meant something to you?"

Before I realized what I was doing, I stood on tiptoe and claimed Willock's mouth with my own. His lips were rough and demanding in a way that was different from Kellen's. Willock's kiss was built on sorrow and shattered dreams. On loneliness and good-byes. His kiss was a demand and an accusation all at the same time, as though he wanted to reach into my soul and pull out an answer I didn't have. Some solution that could never come to fruition.

Guilt pressed in on me. It was wrong of me to manipulate Willock this way, but I was desperate for something—anything I could do to help Kellen.

Slowly, a vision of Willock and myself stirred to life in my mind. The pair of us were together and desperately in love. It was an illustration of the life we might have had in the Green Lands if Arawn hadn't imprisoned my family. If there had never been a Great War, a prophecy . . . if there had never been Kellen. Another world, another life.

His lips pleaded with mine to be his as he tried to coax an impossible allegiance from me. A tiny part of my heart broke then, because Willock's dream would never be realized. For even as Willock stirred something within me, it was just a spark compared to what I felt for Kellen. I felt everything for Kellen.

Willock must have read my mind, for he broke away,

putting distance between us. His breathing hitched. "There's no future for you with either of us. Surely you must know that."

I pressed the heels of my hands against my eyes, hating his words and the possible truth that might lie in them. "It's not too late for you to choose the right side. Please help him, Willock."

But when I lowered my hands, Willock had disappeared and so had Uncle Dillion.

CHAPTER 44
KELLEN

Stephen stood and walked around the desk, holding out his hands. "Kellen!" A smile brighter than the sun lit his skin as he clasped my hands in his.

We were in his study. The last time I'd been in this room, I'd told him that I wanted nothing more to do with him and that his own mother had willed the money he'd given her over the years to me. He shouldn't be this happy to see me.

This had to be a dream. I couldn't even remember the last time he'd touched me, or even if he ever had.

He frowned, concern sneaking into his features. "Are you all right?"

Clearing my throat, I found my voice. "You don't usually seem so happy to see me."

Stephen's face fell. "About that. Here, come and sit with me."

He led me to the couch—no longer the stiff brown leather version of my youth, but a blue-and-white-checked fabric. The cushions squished underneath me when I sat.

He took a seat across from me, a sad frown weaving its way onto his face. "I owe you an apology."

My mouth must have fallen open, because he nudged the bottom of my chin with his thumb.

"You look like one of the fishes we used to see when I took you out on the water as a boy." He laughed at the fabricated memory he was recalling.

"You never took me fishing as a boy. You didn't speak to me unless I did something wrong." Memories of the lonely days in this house crept up on me as though I'd never left and my time with Cali had been the dream.

Stephen patted my hand, not commenting when I pulled mine away. "I've been a terrible father to you, Kellen. I do love you, but when your mother died—well, I've never been good at showing emotion."

"Showing emotion isn't even the beginning of your issues." My anger kicked in and snapped me from my daze. "You had her committed when she was fully mentally competent!"

"I thought she would receive the best care there. I believed I was putting her into a cancer treatment center. How was I to know? I'm not a doctor of internal medicine, though I wish I had been. I might have been able to save her." A tear formed in the corner of his eye.

"You told me she was dead." I didn't bother to ease my steel-coated tone.

"It was her doctor, see? He said she wasn't going to make it. He suggested that I tell you she'd passed. Get the pain over with."

"You're a child psychologist. Was that really the best you could do?"

Stephen shrugged. "I was lost in my grief. There's no manual for this. Every parent does what he or she thinks is right."

"You had a funeral for her!"

Stephen brought his hand to his heart. "The better to help you and your brother through the grieving process, Son.

I only ever wanted to take care of you and Roger. Sure, I've made mistakes—quite a few—but I want to start again."

"No." I had no other words. I didn't want this man around me. My memories of Orkney Hospital and my mother's room, of her journal, were still fresh in my mind.

"I love you, Kellen. Please forgive me." More tears glistened in his eyes.

Swallowing hard, I shook my head. "No."

Before he could answer, I jerked awake on Tai's sofa, sweating from the heat of the roaring fire and pile of blankets. I'd wanted an apology from my father for most of my life, and now, after he'd done unspeakable things, unforgivable things, he'd asked for my forgiveness. I'd never expected that —even in my dreams.

Yet it was all wrong. He'd said the words, but they'd come too late.

"So it's started then."

I jumped at the sound of Tai's kind voice. I spotted him sitting with two mugs and a teapot at the small table.

"What has?" I asked, freeing myself from the blankets.

He shrugged. "Why, the offer you can't refuse."

If Gabe were here, he'd absolutely move on to Mafia movie references. Historic movie quotes aside, I swallowed hard as I processed his words. Maybe the wheels of the second part of the prophecy had already been set into motion.

CHAPTER 45

CALI

In a matter of moments, I'd ended up alone. Uncle Dillion and Willock were gone. Willock off to Danu knew where, and Uncle Dillion to wherever immortals go when they die. I didn't know. We weren't supposed to die, so I'd never been told.

All I knew was that there was only one option for me now. I had to go after Kellen. Uncle's warnings mattered little if he wasn't here to deliver them.

I tossed a cup of water on the fire and shut the lights off with the switch the way I'd seen Gabriel do. Donning my poufy coat and boots, I stepped outside.

A low growl sounded from somewhere behind me and I spun around to meet a pair of menacing red eyes in the dark.

"Skyler. I'm here, girl."

The dog whined as she made her way out of the shadows. She turned and sat, offering her back to me to ride on. I climbed on awkwardly and wrapped my arms around her neck.

"Is it Kellen? Can you take me to him?"

The beast whined again, then turned and took off,

charging up a hill and into the woods. The rain continued, persistent and chilling, and I was glad I had a coat with a hood to keep me warm.

Skyler huffed as we ran for what felt like days through the rain and darkness. I knew that wasn't right though. My mortal sense of time was as confused as my immortal one had been. On and on through the forest we ran, through trees and up hillsides. Skyler had a destination in mind, but I'd have to wait to discover it.

Finally, we rounded a bend and she slowed, her tongue lolling as she panted.

"Are you okay, girl?" I petted the smooth fur on her head.

She whined as she sat down on the ground and waited.

"You can't find him, can you."

She whined again and licked the back of my hand.

"That's a yes, then. What do we do now? Where do we go?"

As if in answer, Skyler lowered herself down to the ground and crossed one paw over the other before she rested her head atop both. She let out one more loud, plaintive whine and then faded away to nothing.

It made sense in the twisted way of the universe. Uncle Dillion had been Skyler's master. Perhaps the beast couldn't exist outside Faerie without his magick to sustain her.

The reason didn't matter.

I swiveled in place as voices reached me from the darkness.

"She's betrothed to the one the mistress wants. Surely the mistress would appreciate her in his place."

"But she didn't ask for *her*. She asked for the other one, Kellen St. James."

My heart lodged in my throat at the sound of Kellen's name. As my thoughts consumed me, the voices continued, their argument growing louder.

"We should take her!"

"Shouldn't!"

"Should!"

"Shouldn't!"

"What is wrong with you?"

My breath caught. "Oh no." I spun around in a circle, searching for a way out of the woods. Skyler had been running forever, and now I had no idea of my whereabouts.

Finally I took a deep breath and ran. Running used to be one of my greatest pleasures. Back home, I would tear across the lands of the stars, for stars weren't the gaseous bodies mortal science taught, but unique worlds all their own. When I ran across their beaches and forests, I could block out the immortal responsibilities that weighed on me as I flew, inches above the ground.

Though I tried to recreate my past in my mind, running as a mortal dimmed in comparison. The ground was hard and uneven with tree roots that tripped me more than a few times. It was as if I were running through an obstacle course.

Gabriel had told me about a movie on Netflix where a traveler got lost in the woods. His family had tracked him down and he'd been saved after surviving weeks alone in the wilderness. Yet, no one knew where I was. If I managed to lose myself, no one would come for me. I'd never make it back.

Doubt whipped around me, creating a vortex that threatened to pull me in with each step. The burden fell solely on my mortal shoulders.

If only my father had told me what special power I'd been granted. This whole business about a gift that would reveal itself in my moment of need was entirely too vague. Surely *this* classified as such an instance. It would have been immensely helpful now to have been given a gift from Air—to be able to fly.

As if, as Gabriel would have said.

Maybe I should try testing out the possibilities and see if one would make itself known.

As I ran, I closed my eyes and focused on flying. I raised my arms and leaped into the air, but instead of soaring upward, I slammed down onto the muddy earth. Air wasn't the gift.

"Ugh." I spat mud from my mouth and brushed at my clothes as I stood.

I closed my eyes and whispered, "Water, I call upon you."

I waited for the rain to increase and the thunder to rumble, yet there was no change.

The further I ran, the wearier I became. Darkness had fallen over the wood in a thick blanket. The trees seemed to close in on me, still yet calculating, while storm clouds brewed overhead.

My nerves ratcheted up several notches. "Earth, I call upon you."

Surely Earth would answer my call. She would send some sign that she was there for me. Yet no scents, smells, or sounds came to me.

"Fire—"

"She came this way." Voices slithered through the woods. The same ones from before. The pair who'd debated taking me prisoner had arrived.

My heart pounded in my chest. I could never outrun them, never hope to hide if they wanted to find me. "You're a fool, Cali. You need a plan and you're running away like a scared little girl."

I needed to go about things differently. They were looking for me in the woods, which meant they expected me to be on foot. I had to find a different hiding spot, at least until they passed by.

I rested my hand against the rough bark of a massive oak

tree. It reminded me of the willow that had sheltered Kellen and me in Faerie. Trees had helped me once. Could they work twice?

I hoisted myself onto the lowest branch and found my footing as I stretched to the one above it. The climb was slow and wet. Though it wasn't even close to what I'd been capable of as an immortal, I could do it. I quickly put distance between myself and the ground, climbing higher and higher until I could go no farther.

Winter hadn't arrived, which meant there were enough leaves remaining on the trees to conceal me. I slid onto the highest stable branch and took shelter amid the leaves, waiting.

"This way! Do not let her get to the mountain!"

"She's close. I can smell her filthy mortal flesh." Another voice—the greedy voice of Cana—pierced the night air.

"See, I told you we should have captured her when we had the chance!"

"You're right, Walter. I want her. She'll lead me straight to Kellen St. James." Cana's voice sent my skin crawling. "Plus, there is the added benefit that once she has been killed, my brother will *finally* suffer for all the pain his failure caused."

"But, Mistress Cana, you did not ask us for her. How were we to know?"

"Bob, must you always be so dramatic? The point is, I want her *now*." Cana's voice radiated anger. This Bob would do well to take note.

"I did not agree to capture the goddess."

I was beginning to like Bob.

"But she is a goddess no longer. She has no powers. She will be ours for the taking."

Even in the darkness, I could envision Cana's evil grin. And this was my aunt.

"Should we spread out?"

"We could . . ." Cana's sly voice caused my heart rate to jump a couple of notches.

I had tried to pick the sturdiest branch at this height. Any shift in weight on the top of the tall, thin tree, however, could throw it off-balance. My legs shook from the effort of crouching.

"Or we could . . . look up." Then Cana did just that, meeting my eyes through the branches from the ground below. Her smile widened. "Hi, sweetie! It's Auntie!"

Pure evil.

The rain had picked up again, sending ice-cold pellets of water down the back of my neck. My frigid hands cramped from the effort of holding on to the tree.

"You should come down from there. You have no one. We've made it impossible for even your parents to assist you." A sly grin filled Cana's face. "Why don't you come down here and lead us to Kellen St. James?"

I had nowhere to go, but that didn't mean I had plans to cooperate. "I don't know where Kellen is, and he doesn't have the amulet."

"This conversation bores me." Cana raised her hand in an arc and magickally dragged me downward. My bottom rapped smartly on each branch as I descended. I bit back a cry as the rough wood beat my mortal flesh through my clothing.

Relief rushed through me as I cleared the last branch, until I plummeted several feet to the wet ground and landed in the mud on my backside. Wincing, I stood and found myself face to face with Cana's hideous single eye.

Two faeries stood at her side, both incased in bubbles that shielded them from the rain. One wore a worried expression that clashed with his involvement with Cana. The other had hair that stood up on his head and came to a point in the center, giving the impression that his hair itself was a weapon.

"I'm here. Are you happy now?" I tipped my chin, letting out my breath nice and slow to keep Cana from realizing how shaken I was.

"Enough of your lies," Cana hissed—fitting, as her green skin made her appear snake-like. "Your father was a liar as well, but no matter. You'll lead us to St. James."

The other two faeries quickly averted their eyes, but Cana didn't seem to notice. "After we get Danu's amulet and win our freedom, we'll kill you and have the ultimate revenge on Lugh. Don't even think about calling the Old Ones again for help."

A collective gasp rose from the other faeries.

Old Ones? Why couldn't I remember what that meant? "How can I call someone if I don't know who they are?"

Her green lips curled back in a sneer. "Nice try, little liar."

The truth wasn't working. I had to try a different tactic: stalling. "Kellen never had it. Willock used you to get information and steal the amulet. He's been siphoning it to Arawn, who's alive, you foolish woman."

"Lies. All lies!" Cana fisted her plump green hands. "Willock has been part of our plan from the beginning. He's not on your side."

The concerned-looking faerie waved his hands wildly. "But, Cana, Walter and I don't want—"

But he didn't get the chance to answer. The little man, who must be Bob, had barely spoken when the ground beneath his feet exploded and he was tossed into the air. Up, up and away he went until he'd been thrown higher than the trees and out of sight.

"Don't worry, he'll be back." Cana's voice sounded almost apologetic as she looked at Walter, who'd extended both hands ineffectually as if to catch Bob, a horrified expression upon his face.

Then, as quickly as he'd shot up, Bob came down. Walter raised his hand in an arc, and Bob's progress slowed. A moment later the little man landed unscathed on the wet ground.

Bob threw Cana a murderous look. "You would try and repel me from Earth for speaking my mind?" He turned to the other man, Walter. "I warned you we couldn't trust her."

Cana leaned forward and cupped his tiny chin in her hand. "Why, Bob! Of course you can trust me."

She released him, and Bob wiped his chin on his sleeve as though something filthy had touched him.

Cana either didn't see or didn't care, for she turned back to me and leaned in close, her already-wide smile broadening. "Goodness, but I can't wait to kill you. To peel your skin from your bony little body."

"Go to hell."

"Ha! I've been there! Once you've done Hell in the spring, Niece, it's passé." With a wave of her hand, Cana propelled me backward into the trunk of the very tree she'd ripped me from before.

White-hot pain tore up my back. I bit my lip to keep from reacting. I wouldn't give Cana the satisfaction of seeing me hurt. I held my head high.

Cana stood there simpering. "The younger generation is such a disappointment. You need to learn to respect your elders. As for you two," she faced Bob and Walter once more, "once we have the young St. James, my kind will be free for good and your people will reap the rewards. So, stop questioning me."

The very idea made me cringe. "You don't deserve freedom. Any of you. This hateful vendetta needs to stop."

I anticipated her anger with clenched muscles, but she

didn't lash out. She stared at me, curiosity in her expression.

I continued. "My father came for you more than once to save you. He loves you." I made sure to put emphasis on the word love. When Cana didn't interrupt, I continued. "It's true. He even pleaded with Danu and Bilé for help, and then Arawn murdered them. The only thing that made my father give up was when you all tried to imprison him. He knew he could no longer help you."

Shock registered briefly across Cana's face. The rain pelted the ground around us, yet her green hair and skin remained untouched while the wet seeped through my clothes, sending shivers through my body.

"Perhaps we're acting hastily." Bob held up his hands as though to calm a wounded animal.

Whatever spell my words had cast over Cana was broken. "No." She narrowed her eyes, approaching slowly. "You know nothing, child. Nothing! Look at what I once was!" She squeezed the large eye in the center of her green forehead closed. Her body trembled as though it took every ounce of her strength.

One moment she was hideous and green, the next, Cana faded into a vision of her former self. Thick blond hair flowed down her back. Her unblemished porcelain skin glowed in its radiance. We even shared the same blue eyes—a family trait. She was easily the most beautiful woman I'd ever seen.

Yet the vision only lasted seconds. When Cana opened her eye, which had grown red-rimmed, the glamour evaporated. She couldn't keep it up. A disfigurement this severe would have been woven into Arawn's magick. Insurance that Cana would lose the one thing she wanted above all else.

Sharing had cost her, for her shoulders slumped. I felt sorry for her—sorry that she'd needed me to know the beauty she once possessed. Still, I'd have been a fool if I didn't use her vanity to my advantage.

"You were beautiful once. If you help me, you could have your beauty again."

Cana stared hard at me for several silent moments. Part of me even imagined I'd swayed her, but soon her evil smile returned. She would never be on my side. She'd lived too long with her own twisted perceptions to believe anything I said.

"Kill her, Bob. I'll find a way to get Kellen St. James—without her. If I have to chase her down later, then I'll know where your true allegiance lies."

Cana turned and vanished, leaving Bob, Walter, and me standing alone in the clearing.

Bob began to tremble. "You do it, Walter. I can't kill her. I've never killed anyone."

Walter shook his head. "But it's *your* assignment. She'll know if you don't do what she asks." And in the fastest of winks he was gone, leaving me with Bob to decide my fate.

Bob appeared to be the more logical of the two. Perhaps I could reason with him. "Bob, listen to me. Cana's wrong. You know that."

"But I have to protect my own. I have children . . ." He broke off as he stared at me.

"I understand, but Kellen St. James is my fiancé. I speak the truth when I tell you he never had the amulet. If you kill me now, you would be doing it for no reason." I stood taller, drawing on my dim memories of being a goddess and inspiring others to follow me. "But if you let me live, I will remember your kindness, and my father, the God Lugh, will reward you with protection and anything else you desire."

Bob's face clouded over as his own thoughts warred within him. He stared at me for a long moment before he nodded slowly and spoke. "Young lady, I do believe you are telling the truth. Your Mr. St. James was here already and escaped."

I gasped, hope flooding every part of my body. "Kellen's alive? You saw him."

"He is, but I don't know for how much longer if Cana catches up with him. Get to the top of Cadillac Mountain. There is a portal there that will take you anywhere if you wish it hard enough."

I frowned. "But I thought this area was protected by your people. That no one could get through."

"It should only be blocked in one direction. Approach the portal at a run and jump into it."

Though I hated the idea of jumping into anything blindly, I had no choice. It might be my only chance at salvation. For Kellen, myself, and now Bob.

"How do I reach it?"

"A vehicle would be fastest for a mortal." He pointed to a worn path ahead. "A carpenter lives through those trees. He has a car and he always leaves the key inside. Take a piece of paper from the dashboard and write him a note letting him know that you borrowed the car. He lends it to people all the time."

"Thank you."

"You have everyone's skepticism on your side. No one is expecting you to be successful, therefore, you will be. Now, go!" With that he aimed his own hands at himself and whispered a series of words. Green light shot from his hands popping his bubble. He collapsed in a heap on the ground. For a few seconds I stared, waiting. When his chest rose and fell, I realized what he'd done. Bob had knocked himself unconscious to give me time.

I wasn't going to get any more of an opportunity than this. I turned and fled in the direction of the path. I would leave a note, drive to the mountaintop, and take the portal to get help. I didn't stop running until an old, rusty truck came into view and I froze.

"Oh my goodness. I don't even know how to make it go."

CHAPTER 46
KELLEN

Sunlight streamed through the curtains, but I had no idea if it was truly morning. This place seemed to be running on its own schedule. A rushing sound filled my ears as I sat frozen on the couch, staring hard at Tai. "Are you one of them?" One night of sleep and I was right back to where I'd started—questioning his loyalty.

Again he waved me off, taking a long sip of his tea. "No. You want a cuppa?" He raised his mug in a half salute.

"Yeah."

I would've preferred coffee, but I had sadly not ended up at a Holiday Inn. Tea would have to do. I got up and joined Tai at the table. I froze as I took in the green shamrock design that bordered the top and encircled the middle of the teapot. It was identical to the one Gran used to have. Tai filled my empty mug then offered me the steaming brew.

I waited until I downed my first sip before forcing the question from my lips. "What did you mean about an offer I can't refuse?"

Tai arched one bushy eyebrow. "You're gonna be challenged, Kellen."

Some would argue that I'd already been challenged, but this was not the time to give up whatever pitiful poker face I had going on. "What role do you play in that?"

"I'm here to help." Tai cradled his mug in his hands as the steam rose up before him. Again, he seemed so familiar to me.

"And you get what out of that exactly?" I mirrored his position with the tea, letting the heat seep into my skin.

Chuckling, he smiled, eyes twinkling and filled with more secrets than I had any hope of deciphering. "Eternal salvation. It's what I do, you see." He patted his own knee with one hand. "I save lost souls."

"I didn't know my soul was lost."

"But it *could* be." He said this so matter-of-factly that my stomach lurched.

Restless, I stared into the depths of the fire. The wood glowed orange from the flame while little pieces of ash drifted below the grate. Perhaps this was the direction I was headed—straight into the flames.

"I need to know everything you can tell me about the second part of the prophecy."

"I thought you might ask me that."

Tai stood and walked to a small bookshelf. Though it was one of those corner deals that came to my waist, it was crammed with books, the colors on their fat spines forming a dark rainbow. Tai surveyed the titles for several moments before he selected a hardbound, rust-colored volume. He returned to the table and offered it to me.

Never able to refuse a book, I accepted it. Its pages were lightly stained on the outside. The musty smell screamed water damage. I scanned the title.

"*On the Immortals and the Great Prophecy*. Someone's written a book about this?"

"Many people. This is one of the more accurate accounts."
Tai raised an eyebrow. "Go on."

I set down my tea and slowly opened the book. As I
skimmed the aged pages, I passed chapters outlining the
history of the Children of Danu. The author had painstak-
ingly plotted biographies for every one of Cali's family
members, including Cali herself. I ached as I read her name:
Calienta of the Stars.

The volume was too long to consume at once. I skimmed
faster, knowing what I would find if I kept searching. When I
finally reached the passage on the prophecies, I held my
breath and read on.

*As to the topic of the Great Prophecy, drawings depicting it
appeared in a sea cave on the coast of western Ireland. Before we
dissect the prophecy in detail, let us review the information the art
tells us.*

*Cabhan, god and Star Child, will turn against his father, Lugh,
only to be stopped by a young, unknown boy. Many scholars who've
interpreted these creations also believe the boy will wed Calienta of
the Stars.*

Recreations of the sketches Calienta had shown me in the
cave near Gran's house were splashed across the pages. It had
been those sketches, along with my uncanny ability to sense
Cali's emotions, that had convinced me she was telling the
truth in the first place.

*Not much is known about this young boy, with the exception that
he will be born in the twenty-first century, on the eighteenth day
of May.*

My birthday was May eighteenth. I'd been told the
prophecy was about me. That information wasn't new.
Reading it in a book—finding my birthday printed in
conjunction with the prophecy—made it all the more real.

I swallowed and looked to Tai for a moment. "It's strange

reading about yourself in a book, not to mention in the third person." My life and Cali's documented in a textbook as though it were a historical event.

"Keep going." Tai gestured to the book again.

Sighing, I returned to the page once more.

In 1920, during an expedition to discover western Ireland's history as it relates to the Mesolithic period, explorers from the Department of Archaeology, National University of Ireland, found a cliff cave. Inside, they came upon a large, cavernous room lit from the inside. When the group entered the cavern, they found writing on the wall. "Born of lost man and lost woman, the forgotten boy will return to Ériu. He will claim the Star Child as his own and ascend to the crown, else night will cover the Earth, and all will be lost."

This supported the original prophecy. Yet there were other words written beneath the first. "The one who refuses immortality in light will receive it in darkness." These last words were far more chilling than the other, for tests revealed they'd been written in blood.

The author seemed incredibly well informed for a mortal —if he or she *was* mortal. I partially closed the book to check, but no author's name was imprinted on the cover, and the spine was blank.

Curious, I flipped to the front of the book. Still no author, but there, on the title page, was a single line in tidy print: *Property of Stephen St. James.*

My fingers stiffened and my whole body numbed. Tai was speaking—saying something—but I couldn't hear anything over the volume of my own thoughts.

"How did you get this book? It belongs to my father, Stephen St. James." I set the volume down on the table. "Do you know him?"

"Never mind that." Tai's voice turned gruff.

"Tai—"

"Forget about it!" His voice had taken on a steel edge.

Many would have viewed it as a warning, but he had information. I couldn't afford to stand down. "Do you know about *your* father's past?"

Considering this, Tai smiled. "Da was a character."

"Yeah, well they say my father was great as a boy and then he just went bad, like something happened to him to turn him the wrong way. If you were me, wouldn't you want to know?"

Tai poured more of the brew into my cup. "I suppose I would, but this is not my purpose. I'm here to warn you about *that* business." Tai indicated the book as he set the teapot on the table.

"But you're going to tell me anyway, aren't you?" I asked, not bothering to hide the hope from my voice.

And just like that, the twinkle returned to Tai's eye. "We were from the same village, your da and me." He settled a black-and-red rooster cozy over the pot and sat across from me. "We didn't have the same friends, but we knew each other well. We sometimes went at one another's throats."

"You knew my gran? My granda?" The tea scalded my tongue as I drank.

"I knew your granda better, but your gran—ah, she was a looker." His expression grew wistful for a moment before I cleared my throat. "When Stephen was about eight years on, he disappeared."

I'd never heard this version before. I leaned toward Tai despite myself. "Someone kidnapped him?"

But Tai, like every Irish man or woman I'd ever met, would not be deterred from a story in the making. "I'd told him about the wee folk that I'd heard the night before. It'd been a full moon and I could hear their flutes from my window." He shook his head, a sad smile across his face. "Your da, though, he kept telling me he didn't believe. That he wasn't sure they were real."

That struck me as odd. Especially considering that Gran had been the one to teach me about faeries. Calienta hadn't taken up the mantle until after Gran's death. "And you disagreed."

"I'd been raised on the folklore, so I knew not to question it."

"He would have been too."

Tai's eyebrows shot up as though he'd asked himself that question a million times. "Young Stephen was skeptical, yet bold and full of adventure and spirit at the same time."

"He sounds like your average kid."

"He was that, but he was also a nice lad. Always helping others out. Very kind. Oh, and his mother—he would have done anything for her. He adored her."

The idea that my father had been nice at one time blew my mind. How did someone go from a kind boy to the creature that had imprisoned my mother?

"Stephen was too adventurous for his own good. He bragged that he was going out to climb into a *rath* that night."

I was more than familiar with *raths* myself. The forts acted as a gateway to Faerie. They were supposedly all over Ireland. Everyone knew you didn't go looking for them unless you wanted trouble.

The plot was utterly predictable, but I had to know. "What happened?"

"He wanted me to walk up to the thing with him. He'd found it when he was out exploring with his friends. I could feel the evil from the thing. The badness of it. I wouldn't go near it, and I told him not to either. The next day he was missing. His parents were mad with worry."

As Tai spoke, his face transformed with barely disguised grief, as though he himself were reliving the loss of a child to Faerie.

"But he got out, right? He's here now and alive so . . ."

"That's where you're wrong, boy. Something did make it out, but it wasn't young Stephen. You can be sure of that."

A feeling of dread settled in the pit of my stomach.

CHAPTER 47

CALI

B ob had been right about the notepad and pen. I took care to leave a note on the outside table, directly next to the door of the small house. Then I ran to the truck and climbed inside. The interior was cold and unwelcoming. A round steering device protruded from the front, along with a series of levers and knobs.

The rain picked up outside and a gust of wind rattled the vehicle. The frigid interior did little to protect me from the cold. I shook violently. Cana might appear beside me at any moment and what would I do then? None of the elements had worked for me.

I hadn't tried Fire, but she was capricious with her gifts at best, and I'd never had an affinity with the element. It seemed more likely that I hadn't been given any powers. I'd have to get through this on my own.

"You were a goddess for years, Cali. You can figure out how to run a steel beast."

Suddenly I remembered Kellen telling me to look for instructions in the airplane bathroom. Did this thing come equipped with guidance? But though I searched every compartment and possible niche, there was nothing.

Ridiculous. Surely, people forgot how to drive from time to time and needed to be reminded? I put my head down on the steering ring and a loud beep sounded in the night, sending me jerking back in my seat.

Just days ago I'd maneuvered a taxi through central London without a thought. Now I could not even call upon my magick to make a simple truck go.

Closing my eyes, I imagined holding Kellen, breathing in his scent and feeling the soft wool sweater he'd worn that day. I wrapped my arms around myself. I couldn't fall apart. Not yet. Not until Kellen was safe.

A rapping sounded at the window and I screamed, jumping in the seat as I twisted around, expecting to find Cana. Instead a man stood there, gesturing in an odd downward motion.

My brow furrowed, but the man continued to point.

Resigned, I tried to exit the beast, but found I didn't know how to open the door. I rested my head on the round thing, hoping he would go away.

A moment later, the click of the door alerted me that the gentleman was coming in. Lifting my head, I did my best to meet his eye.

"Are you going to kill me?"

He was impossibly tall, even more so than Gabriel. He crouched down beside the car. The light of the full moon illuminated his kind face. The whites of his eyes stood in sharp relief against the darkness.

"Um . . . no. It's just that you seem a little confused."

I stared hard at this man, trying to affix him with a mean glare in the event that he'd lied about wanting to kill me. "Who are you?"

He shrank back as though afraid, yet still had the presence of mind to give a little wave. "I'm, uh, I'm Fred. I live in this house and this is my truck that you're trying to borrow." Swallowing, he stepped back a bit more.

"I left a note." My voice took on an accusatory tone.

"Thanks for that." He spoke quickly. "It was nice. I've never seen handwriting that pretty before."

My temper interfered with my brain, causing it not to function. Kellen was in danger and this man, no matter how polite, blocked my way. At least he would have if I had any idea about how to run the car—truck—*whatever*.

"Bob told me you wouldn't mind."

"Bob." His eyes widened. "Oh, you're one of them . . ."

"You refer to the faeries?" I asked.

He bounced uneasily, rolling on the balls of his feet as though contemplating running. "I don't want to be involved."

It would have been kinder to put him at ease, but I had a feeling I'd get better results from leaning on the "one of them" conclusion he'd drawn. "Yes, I am one of them."

His emotions seemed to war with one another—his need to protect his car versus his need to protect himself. "Would you like me to help you?"

If I had my powers, I wouldn't need his help. I wouldn't even be here, sitting and freezing inside the old truck, worry for Kellen eating me inside. "I need to drive this contraption."

Again, his eyes widened as though the idea terrified him. "Uh, I could drive you."

I could let this man take over and get me to where I needed to go, yet danger followed me at every turn. "What you must do is sprinkle as much salt as you can find around the perimeter of your house, then go inside, shut the door, and stay inside until first light."

The fact that he didn't question my directive spoke volumes. He'd received that advice before. "I have salt. Let me show you how to get Cindy started first though."

"Cindy?" I asked, turning and peering into the back seat for the invisible woman who would drive the car.

"It's the truck's name. My daughter picked it." He smiled, almost in apology. "It doesn't matter. Let's get you on the road."

My first driving lesson followed. Fred explained in patient tones about the "shifter," "brake," and "gas." He showed me how to turn on the truck's heater and soon glorious warm air poured out of Cindy's "vents," sending my mortal body into what could only be described as bliss.

Once I'd gotten the hang of it, he waved me on. I left him standing in front of his house as I drove—albeit with some inconsistency—off his property.

The truck vibrated beneath me as I barreled forward at a great speed. I stomped my foot on the pedal on the left, the brake, and lurched to a stop.

"Take a deep breath. You can do this."

I let out a slow breath and carefully eased the other pedal down again. The truck began to move, and I took care not to press it too hard.

Worry nagged me. I'd taken too much time with the car. Bob would have been found out by now, wouldn't he? The clock on the dashboard read four thirty, but although I could tell time—one of the basic functions that came with my mortality—I didn't have a sense of what that meant. It didn't help that the bizarre darkness that shouldn't be allowed had lingered.

The road wound its way up the mountain on a curving course through the woods. When I approached a small building with a guard inside reading, he barely glanced at the truck before he waved me on and returned to his book.

Fred had warned that I would need to keep pressure on the gas or Cindy might get stalled. Yet as I continued up the mountain, the truck sailed right on up without a problem. I patted the part of the truck that Fred had called the "wheel."

"You're doing so well, Cindy!"

The truck continued upward, and my confidence increased.

"Good girl, Cindy!" I could do this after all. I'd find my parents and get them to help me reach Kellen. Mile after mile we crept along in the dark. A bit farther and I'd make it to the top of the mountain.

But Cindy sputtered. Her wheel jerked beneath me. I fought to keep her under control and on the road. The higher we ascended, the worse the truck shook.

Fred had told me I'd need to drive seven miles before I reached the top. What if Cindy quit before then? Though my foot now pressed the gas pedal nearly to the floor, she began to slow. We'd barely rounded the next corner when Cindy rolled to a stop in the center of the road. No matter how much I stomped on the gas, she wouldn't budge.

Truthfully, I no longer cared for Cindy.

I had no choice but to continue up the mountain on foot. I'd have to be as careful as possible. Cana most certainly would have discovered my escape by now, and they would be looking for me. I switched Cindy off and exited as Fred had shown me. He would have to collect his truck later.

I broke into a run, shivering despite myself. My coat and clothing weren't enough to keep away the chill. I plunged my hands in my pockets, moving as fast as my mortal body would allow. My breath heaved in and out of my chest as I rounded another corner and another. But when I rounded the next and possibly last curve, I froze. Cana herself stood ahead of me, with her army drawing up the rear. Dozens and dozens of winged faeries awaited me. Some of the C.O.D. hovered in midair, others stood tall behind groups of local faeries. Regardless of their origin, their arrows were all pointed in one unified direction: mine.

CHAPTER 48

KELLEN

Slowly, I lowered my tea to the table, unable to do more than stare at Tai, who'd taken to pacing the room. As much as I wanted to know the truth about my father, I feared the worst. Of course, I shouldn't have wasted my energies on fear. I already knew Stephen's story didn't end well.

"Your granda went out looking for Stephen every night. It tore him up inside. He blamed himself, you see."

I stopped waiting for more words and mentally replayed the ones he'd spoken.

"He told you all this?" It didn't seem like the sort of thing that an adult would confide in a child.

Tai met my eyes, his sharp ones narrowing as he regarded me. "You always were smart as a whip, boy."

"How do you know how I was?" I narrowed my eyes, staring hard at him. "What aren't you telling me?"

In answer, he blurred before me. In the time it took me to blink, he'd aged. Tai's youthful skin gained lines and coloration from sun damage. He gained weight around his middle, so that it was fuller and softer looking than before. His eyes never left my face, their deep honey-tinged brown color reminding me of someone. Reminding me because this man was that same someone.

Tai had been right. He wasn't one of the C.O.D. He was family.

"How did you come to be here, Granda?" I'd never known his first name. He'd always been "Granda." "Why didn't you tell me who you were?"

A warm smile lit his face, and the skin around his eyes crinkled as he grinned. "You've been through too much. I didn't want you to go into shock." His smile suddenly faded to portray enough worry to encompass my lifetime.

A bitter laugh slipped out before I could stop it. "I'm past the point of shock. I should be in therapy." I shook my head. "Are you . . . *alive?*"

"I'm what they call a ghost. A spirit. A lost soul in my own right, you might say." He winked, the smile never leaving his face.

"But why? You had a good life. Why would you be lost?" I'd never studied much of the supernatural, but there were guidelines weren't there? Rules explaining why some people became ghosts and others moved on.

He shrugged. "I made a deal, you see. A deal to get my son back. In exchange, I have to stay here in the Cusp instead of with my beloved wife." He reached into his pocket and withdrew a small framed photograph about the size of a business card. He held it out for me to see. "Isn't she beautiful?"

Gran beamed back at me from the worn photo. I'd seen it before. It had been taken on their wedding day.

"She *was* beautiful." My heart gave a squeeze and I quickly handed the picture back. "If I'm here with you, does that mean I'm dead?"

He patted the picture and returned it to his pocket. The twinkle in his eyes was more than a little faded now. "This is an interlude, as they say. As soon as you leave, the threats will be real and you will no longer be safe."

I took another sip of my tea as I processed this information. The worry hung in my mind with all the finality of a promise, but I pushed it aside, too curious to know how the story ended. "What happened with Stephen?"

"When he went missing, I knew exactly where he'd gone. Every night I left an offering at the *rath*. A bit of leather, bread, anything that I supposed they might like. But *raths* move, you see. When it moved, I had to locate it again. Nothing happened for weeks, then months. I began to fear that I would never find him.

"Then on the ninetieth night, a little man waited for me. I remember his white beard ran to his boots and there was a tiny yellow bird living inside it, just a little thing. At first I found it fascinating, but that didn't last when I realized he'd trapped it there. The bird kept fighting to escape into the fresh air, until the man made a fist and squashed it. The little body fell on the ground between us. I kept thinking, 'these are the people who have my boy.'" For a moment Granda choked up, but he cleared his throat and quickly proceeded.

"He thanked me for my gifts and told me that I would be granted a boon of my choosing. He made a few suggestions— livestock, property, and more. I told him all I wanted was for my son to come home. Too late I remembered I should have set stipulations. I should have asked him to be returned *exactly* as he'd been."

Granda shook his head. "The next morning, he was in his bed when we woke, but the Stephen that came back wasn't right. He hated us, for one thing. The worst part was how he treated his mother. He was cold, and she was devastated. I don't know if she ever got over that in her whole life.

"Night after night I returned to the *rath*. I wanted my real son back, not a changeling. Imagine knowing your real son is trapped while an impostor stays with you." Granda looked down at his tea.

"What did the changeling do that was so horrible?"

"That's just it. You never caught him doing anything, but you felt like it was a matter of time before he did. There was something in the way he looked at you. Like he knew all the secrets of the world, and you were in the way. He was cold. After the closeness our real Stephen had shared with your gran, she couldn't handle it.

"When Alistair found us and offered to take Stephen with him to get to know his half brothers, we agreed. I hate to say it, but it was a relief getting him out of the house."

That sounded like the version of Stephen that I had grown up with. Yet it was the first Stephen's story that worried me more.

"Did you ever meet any of the faeries again?"

"I kept trying to find a way to reach anyone in Faerie who would help me. But no matter how many visits I paid, I never saw the little man again. I kept up the visits for over twenty years."

"Why did you stop?"

He rubbed at his beard. "I had to keep my part of the bargain. In exchange for getting my son back, I had to give up my soul—to Arawn."

A wave of dizziness hit me, and it felt as if all the blood had drained from my body.

"By that time you'd been born, and you were a smart little tyke even then." A smile lit his face, making him almost boyish for a second until the memories flooded back to him. "Our boat went down off the coast. There were no survivors. He came for me then—Arawn did—and he took the rest. They hadn't done anything wrong. He called them spares."

I grabbed the book and waved it at him. "But what does either Stephen or the changeling have to do with the second part of the prophecy? They aren't in the book. There's nothing mentioned about them at all."

"There are some things even I can't tell you, boy. You'll have to find those out for yourself. See the prophecy out. I only told you this because . . ." he swallowed hard.

"Because you don't want to see me go into this as one person and come out another."

After the horror of finding Gabe's car, being ripped from Cali's side, and nearly run over, being with Granda filled me with emotion. The polar opposite compared to the crushing numbness that had kept me moving forward before.

He grinned. "*Jaysus,* you're quick."

"You could come with me."

Suddenly, the idea of having someone at my side, an adult I could trust, appealed. It would be a new experience, not having to be the one in charge all the time. But Granda quickly put that idea to rest.

"I can't leave the Cusp. I'm forever trapped here."

"If I get out of this, Cali and I will go and look for your real son." A small smile escaped me as I imagined seeing Cali again. Holding her. Loving her. Still, I couldn't sustain it. I had no idea if she'd been captured or how I'd find her again. My own fears haunted me like the dreams Cali used to plant inside my mind each night.

Granda frowned, his expression turning more wistful than grateful. "You two are going to have a rough time of it."

"Let's state the obvious. I think we're already having a rough time." I looked at my shoes. Tears filled my eyes because I would have to leave soon and because Granda had saved me. "I'm sorry."

"But you did nothing, my boy. You didn't bring any of this upon yourself." He reached out as though to take my hand but let his own drop.

"Yes, but I'm sorry for what you had to go through." My words sat in the room like a third person.

Granda shook his head as though warring with something internally. He wrapped his arms around me. For the briefest of moments, warmth and hope filled me to the brim. Everything would be all right. Cali and I would get through this.

"I love you, boy. Never forget how much you are loved, even now." As he stepped away, he appeared almost blurry around the edges, as though he were a TV with bad reception or a pixelated image stretched beyond its resolution.

"I have to go now, don't I." My knees grew weak at the prospect of stepping outside. Of facing what awaited me.

"I'm afraid it's time." Granda walked to the door and opened it. As he stood by the exit that would take me away, his expression mirrored the one he'd worn when he'd talked about losing Stephen.

I stood and walked to the door, pausing just in front of Granda. "Thank you. For everything. I'm so glad I got to meet you again."

He patted my shoulder. "And I you, boy."

I stepped over the threshold of the little house, then turned back to Granda. In an instant, both the cottage and the man began to fade away.

"Don't ever forget who you are, Kellen. Each of us lives our own life. Our past is one part of it. Never forget you have a choice about who you want to be." He raised his hand as if to wave, but he was gone before he got the chance, along with the little cottage in the woods.

I was on my own.

Turning, I took my next step and found myself on the front porch of my father's Tudor mansion in upstate New York.

CHAPTER 49
CALI

Part of me wanted to close my eyes, to pretend this wasn't happening. Yet the faeries didn't immediately attack as I'd expected. Instead, they all stood staring, hundreds of them, transfixed by the goddess-turned-mortal, waiting for their next command.

How was it possible I had been a goddess a few days ago? I'd stood in my wedding dress, waiting to marry Kellen, with no idea what lay ahead. Now I stood in the middle of the road near a mountaintop—alone. No one would come to help me. Uncle Dillion was dead. Skyler had disappeared. Willock had fled. Gabriel was injured—or worse. Then there was Kellen, dear Kellen, who felt farther away than he ever had.

My body served as a weak and weary shell for my battered soul. I could see no way out—not if I had to fight an army of immortals.

I had to find the gift I'd been given—the dormant element within me that needed to be reawakened. There was only one element I hadn't tried, the most unlikely of them all.

"Surround her!" Cana cried, pointing a plump, green finger in my direction. In the time it took me to blink, the faerie army had formed a circle around me. Their weapons were all pointed in my direction, though that was just a formality. They could kill me with magick if they wished. I only had one chance at freedom.

"Fire. Come to me." I whispered the words to myself, hoping no one heard, praying it would work. Yet, there wasn't so much as a single spark between my fingertips.

Of course, fire wasn't an element for the timid. Was she holding back, waiting for me to be brave, waiting for me to show courage? Drawing a deep breath, I yelled, "Fire. Come to me."

But as bold as I'd wanted to sound, my words came across muffled and weak in the damp, and worse—nothing happened.

Cana burst into laughter from her position before the army. "Fire! You, a mortal, dare to call upon the elements?" The rest of the would-be warriors chuckled nervously along with her, as though they weren't sure what was happening.

Doubt crept into my soul. Perhaps Cana was right. There wasn't even the slightest warmth rising across my skin. What if none of the elements deigned to give me a gift. Was this the end?

"You waste your time, mortal!" Cana croaked between fits of laughter. "You have no more power."

Gritting my teeth, I stood tall and forced as much animosity into my voice as I could muster. "I am the daughter of Lugh and Brigid. I will *always* have power."

Something remarkable happened then. My fingers, once frigid with the cold, began to warm. Quickly the warmth grew and spread, as if my entire body were defrosting. My temperature wasn't the only thing building. So was my strength. Fire had come to me and I knew I had only to call upon her to do my bidding. As a test, I called Fire with my mind, asking her to warm my hands. In answer, they warmed as though I sat before a roaring fire.

I forced back the triumphant smile that wanted desperately to fill my face. Instead, I let my shoulders slump, I needed to appear weaker, as though I was no longer a threat.

Cana pulled a face. "A lovely sentiment. I've never had patience for those." She waved her hand, and something dropped from the sky and landed on the ground before me. "It's a pity what happened to dear Bob, but it's your fault. You shouldn't have asked him to help you."

The charred husk of the small faerie lay, still smoking, on the ground. His clothing had burnt away to nothing. Though I could make out no discernable shape to his body, save for the occasional spot of bone peeking from skin, the acrid odor of burnt flowers and lemons combined with ash identified him as a faerie. Bob resembled a charred piece of meat. I steeled myself to keep from vomiting, but it didn't ease my heartache. Bob, who'd been so worried for his family and so concerned for my welfare.

"You're a disgusting disgrace to our race, Cana." My voice rose as I spoke.

"Our race? I am no longer one of you. I am something much more." Cana walked closer, her sly smile dripping like melted wax across her face.

I stepped forward to meet her and spat, "You are nothing."

Cana's singular eye widened in surprise before reverting to cold blankness. "Slit her throat. This time, get it right."

A large faerie with an even larger knife advanced, a sinister smile filling his face as though he couldn't wait to spill my blood.

I had one chance. It went against everything I believed in, but I wouldn't get a second opportunity. I had to catch her by surprise.

"I'm sorry, Cana." I raised my hands, palms out. "Fire. *Destroy*."

Her eyes registered shock, then horror as flames shot from my hands, enveloping her in an inferno of fire. Heat surged out of me with all the power of a gift that had been restrained entirely too long.

I didn't look. I couldn't. Only when the smells intensified —flowers, chocolate, ash—did I lower my hands and draw back my flames. Cana's charred husk of a body clattered to the ground before me. I'd done the same to her as she had to dear Bob.

Tears and soot clouded my vision. I'd never taken a life before. I had injured others, but I'd never seen a battle, never caused someone to draw their last breath. Forcing myself to look up, I faced the army, expecting an attack.

For a heartbeat, we stared at one another. They examined me and Cana's remains. I focused on them and their mortal-wounding weapons. Neither side moved. Then they began to back away. Some fell sideways, stumbling into one another in an effort to avoid me.

Then, all at once, over half of them turned and fled into the woods. They, like Bob, had probably been coerced into joining Cana. I scanned the group that remained, searching for a second-in-command, but no one stepped forward.

Walter shook where he stood, his eyes bloodshot as he came forward and knelt beside his fallen friend. Silently, he waved a hand over Bob's body and the dead faerie disappeared.

When Walter stood, he faced me. "The Children of Danu no longer have a leader. If you take charge now, you can command them. They will listen to you." He nodded once, then turned and went back to the others.

I cleared my throat and addressed them. "Children of Danu!" I hadn't much experience speaking to large groups, but I had to try. "You have been misled! Kellen St. James is not the one responsible for trapping you. Arawn is. He's the one that imprisoned you, with the power of an amulet. Danu's amulet."

There were whispers from the group, but I continued.

"You've been told that Kellen has the amulet. This is a lie. Willock has it, and he is going to give it to Arawn, who lives —unless you help me!"

There was a collective gasp across the group as many took this in.

"With the amulet in his possession, Arawn's power will be restored. You will become his prisoners once more."

Several outraged cries arose from the group.

"Why should we believe you?" This came from a faerie that stood behind Walter. He was short and squat, but that was the most that I could make out. He jumped up, peering at me from around Walter's pointed hair.

My heart banged an out-of-control rhythm in my chest. If a fight broke out, there was no one to help—only me in the middle of the empty road, woods on either side and the salt smell of the ocean tickling my nose.

"You should believe me because I'm telling the truth." That was probably what a liar would have said, but I could think of no better argument.

A small faerie with blue-white wings and blue-tinted skin, stepped forward. I'd never seen him before as he was probably a member of the local order. The little man began to dance on the spot as though he couldn't help himself. His voice squeaked when he spoke. "There are many of us who lived in Faerie before the Children of Danu were exiled there. When Arawn sent your kind below the earth, we fled. We've been living in hiding aboveground these many years." He finished his dance and bowed. "My family couldn't help you then, but we will stand by you now."

"Thank you. I accept your help most gratefully."

There were murmurs from the group and more head bobbing. A taller faerie—at least four feet in height and a giant compared to the rest of them—moved from the group to stand before me.

"I don't hold with the beliefs of the Children of Danu. We've been free on Mortal Earth for as long as I can remember. Cana threatened us. That's the only reason any of us are here."

I nodded my approval. "Then stand with me and fight Arawn. I am trying to protect my family. If you align with me, I can help keep you and yours safe. Against me, and you're on your own. I'm your only chance to get your homes back."

Several other faeries began to move toward me, coming not to attack, but to stand by my side. My heart soared.

"Welcome, friends."

Yet for all the faeries who came to join me, there were still many who faced me in opposition. I prepared for another speech when a tall man, about Gabriel's height, stepped out from behind them. I hadn't noticed him before. It was as if he'd popped into place. He had long snow-white hair, much like Uncle Dillion's, and was dressed in a white robe.

"Princess." When he spoke, his voice was smooth, almost elegant. "That was a wonderful speech. Brava!" He clapped for several seconds before he let his hands drop. "You saved me quite a bit of time in weeding out this army. Now that the weak have chosen sides, I know who my allies are."

Suddenly I couldn't move a single muscle. I tried to break free of whatever magick had taken hold of me, but I was paralyzed. It reminded me of the time Kellen and I had been trapped by a Soul Snatcher in Faerie. The invisible creature had frozen us with depression and urged us to end our own lives. It would have taken our souls if we'd died.

The power that bound me now seemed similar. This was a

spell. It was only a spell. Maybe I would be able to break it the same way.

Come on, Cali.

Forcing my eyes shut, I tried to move the muscles in my jaw, to flex my fingers, to do something—anything—that would help us. Not a single muscle responded to my mental commands.

The man in white paced, inspecting us. Pushing the increasing tempo of his footsteps aside, I focused on the paralysis that held me. *I am not trapped, I am free.* Over and over I repeated this mantra in my head. It wasn't a matter of thinking it. I had to believe.

Letting go of my fears, I focused on the words. As my worries began to fade, the paralysis lessened. Soon I could feel my fingers and toes. In rapid succession, my limbs and torso followed until I'd regained control of my body.

The entire time I was working through my bindings, the footsteps of the man in white were a constant. He paced before our group as though assessing us all. Finally, with full control of my body in place, I opened my eyes. The man nodded to me. His eyes glinted with something that looked like greed or desire. I forced back a shudder.

"Now that we have our little rebellion under control, it is time that we put an end to this. It will be most entertaining for me to execute each of you—individually."

He came to a stop in front of me. "Except for you, Princess. You will bear witness." Wearily, as though he'd aged a hundred years in the span of that conversation, he rested his hand on my shoulder.

Throwing up my hands, I called to Fire. Flames knocked the man from his feet and propelled him several hundred yards away where he landed beside the road in a clump of pine trees. A moment later he stirred, clearly not dead. Still, my diversion was enough to break his hold on the rest of the group.

Sparks flew all around us as a battle began. Someone tugged on the leg of my pants and I looked down to find Walter, his pointy hair quivering.

"We need your father's help, young goddess. You must get to the portal at the top of the mountain. Go now!"

"Thank you." Without hesitating I made for the tree line and ran beneath the branches. Hopefully no one had noticed my departure.

CHAPTER 50

KELLEN

Maine had ceased to exist, at least for me. Granda's cottage had been a respite. Now my legs went numb with remembered fear as I stood on the porch outside my childhood home. Try as I might, I couldn't shake the all-encompassing anxiety.

The last time my father and I had met, I hadn't known about my mother. On that day—incidentally, the day of my college graduation—I'd thought of him as a self-indulgent ass. A *harmless* self-indulgent ass.

Now he'd graduated to murderer.

Being here and knowing how my mother had died ripped open that wound. I touched my mother's pendant where it rested against my chest. It comforted me if only for a moment. Letting go, I reached for the door.

But my body shook so badly I could barely move. I didn't want to go in there and face him. Yet Stephen's house was in the suburbs. There was nowhere I could walk on foot. I needed a car.

Turning from the house, I jogged toward the large garage.

Cali's name pounded inside my head with each step. *Cali. Cali. Cali. Cali.* The farther I got from the main house, the more my fear lessened, as if the house itself drew energy from me. When I reached the garage, I opened the box that hung next to the door and took out the spare key that Stephen's driver left there. Stephen had no idea. Otherwise he'd have had the man fired long ago for posing a security risk. I unlocked the door and let myself in.

A low utility light kicked on in one corner, illuminating various sets of keys hanging in orderly rows on the wall. Stephen had several cars, though I couldn't say that he loved them. He never loved anything.

I had to get out of there before someone found me. I searched for the least conspicuous vehicle and settled on a gray Lexus.

Cali. Cali. Cali. Cali. My weary mind repeated her name.

Repressing my thoughts again, I slid behind the wheel, cringing as the garage door opened too loudly for my taste. I started the car and floored it, memory guiding me toward the open gate and down the twisting, turning drive that would take me from Stephen's house. With every second I drove, the unease that had attacked me on the front steps evaporated.

One final turn and then I'm out. Then I'll be home free and can get on the highway.

But where am I going?

Oh right, Cali.

My heart pounded. For a moment I'd been on the verge of forgetting.

But who's Cali?

The question flew into my mind as I turned the last bend and a figure appeared before the exit, his arms thrust out in front of him. Stephen. We locked eyes as the second set of gates closed behind him. I slammed on the brakes, my tires squealing as I fought to control the car. Stephen jumped aside just as I crashed into the locked gates.

CHAPTER 51
KELLEN

"Kellen! Wake up! Please!"

Though the voice sounded distant, as if it was floating away, it still annoyed me. I wanted sleep. It had been a too long since I'd slept. It had been wonderful to give myself over to unconsciousness without worrying about being attacked.

My arm was numb, and my inability to move made me want to sleep longer. Moving took too much effort. The heavy weight of weariness had me snuggling in deeper.

"Kellen!" Someone shook me, then pressed something cold to my forehead. "What do you think is wrong with him?"

"He's in shock, I think." A second vaguely familiar voice advised. Something about it tempted me to open my eyes, to see its owner.

"Should I make him some tea?" The first voice asked, muffled.

"That would probably be a good idea."

More shuffling about as the first person went to get tea, I guessed. Shifting my arm, I realized that I wasn't numb. I'd been wrapped in a blanket burrito, the way my mother used to tuck us in when we were children.

My mind began shifting into gear as the memories flooded it.

Stephen, the car, my escape . . .

My eyes shot open and their focus landed on the unusually concerned face of Stephen St. James, my father.

He drew a large breath and let it out slowly. "Kellen, thank goodness you're all right. We've been worried about you."

I gaped at him. Stephen had never worried about me once in my entire life. He'd shuffled me from boarding school to college without so much as a visit in all the years in between.

Stephen knelt beside the sofa where I'd apparently been napping. "You must be starving. Can I get you something to eat?"

Sarah, the cook, walked in with a tea tray and freshly baked cookies. "Ah, Master Kellen, you're awake!" She beamed in greeting.

I'd never seen her smile around my father. She had always saved her smiles for when I was alone, often sneaking me a piece of candy when we passed in the hall. "It's not right to treat a child so. And his poor mum dead and in the ground," she'd mutter as she walked away before Stephen could catch us.

Which was why I had zero words for this moment. I gaped at them. *What is going on here? Stephen sounds friendly, Sarah's cheerful . . . What alternate universe have I landed in?*

"If you were of age, I'd make you a hot toddy." Stephen's voice sounded serious. "But maybe that's what you need. Sarah?"

Hot toddy. Someone else had made me one. Who had that been?

The cook nodded. "Right away, Master Stephen." Sarah bustled out of the room and into the hall.

Stephen placed his hand on my own. "Son, I'm sorry I scared you. I didn't want you to leave yet. I have a few things to tell you before you go back to school."

Back to school? I didn't trust myself to speak. Swallowing, I sat up straighter and surveyed my surroundings. We were in the study, which doubled as Stephen's office.

I hated the study. It was where I'd been sent for the delivery of punishments or bad news. I'd be brought in so that Stephen could share, often with undisguised enthusiasm, that I was being sent to a camp, a class, or boarding school. He sent me away as often as possible.

Now I'd returned to the room, but it wasn't anywhere close to the cold leather-and-mahogany nightmare I remembered. The physical location was the same, but the decor was so wholly different that it perplexed me even more than Stephen. The place had gone through a makeover. Gone were the maroon-and-gold brocade curtains and plush furnishings that radiated wealth. Gone were the diplomas and honors. Gone were the walls of psychology books and the massive desk and wingback chair Stephen always sat in when he doled out his punishments.

Someone had repainted this room in tones of yellow and blue, my mother's favorite colors. Where once there were no reminders of my mother in the house, now her framed likeness graced every surface, along with pictures of Roger and me as kids.

Behind Stephen's desk, a wooden plaque hung that read Addison and Stephen—A Forever Love. Below it was a painting of Stephen, Roger, and myself that looked to have been done recently, even though I hadn't spent time with either of them since before the age of ten. Even stranger, the three of us were smiling, as though we wanted to be in each other's company.

The space reminded me of one of the magazine clippings I'd saved as a kid. After my mother died, I would look through magazines that Sarah, the cook, had in the kitchen. With her permission, I would cut out images of places that looked like real homes. Homes where they had both a mother and a loving father. I kept them, first in an envelope and then later in one of my Calienta journals, the pictures clumsily pasted onto the pages. I would write in my journal or look at the pictures and pretend that I lived in one of those houses with the happy people.

Strange that my familial home was now an exact replica of those images from my journal. As if the design had been plucked from the version in my childhood memory.

I struggled to free myself from the rest of the blankets and sat up straighter. "What the hell is going on?"

Stephen reached up as though to place a hand on my forehead. I instinctively blocked him.

"Kellen, are you sure you're all right?" Cocking his head to one side, he stared hard at me. "I'm only trying to feel your forehead. We need to make sure you don't have a fever."

Sarah returned with the hot toddy. "Here you go, Master Kellen."

"Thank you." I accepted the drink. The smell of whiskey burned my nostrils. No way was I drinking that. Alcohol in my system wasn't going to make this freak fest any less bizarre.

"That'll be all, Sarah. You may leave us." My father turned back to me with that same worried expression on his face.

"Yes, Master Stephen." Sarah curtsied and left the room, passing, of all people, my brother, who gave her a high five.

"Hey, Sarah!" Roger walked into the room and then plopped down on the couch beside me, giving me a playful punch on the arm. "If it isn't my little bro, back from college already. Hey, Kell, wassup?"

What in the hell? Roger had spent my entire childhood bullying me. He didn't even like me. The last time I'd seen him, we didn't even speak. He'd given me the finger.

"Your brother has had a bit of a shock. He almost hit me with the car." Stephen patted my knee above the multiple layers of blankets I still hadn't discarded.

"Cool! Too bad you didn't take him out. We could have done damage to those trust funds, eh, bro?" Roger winked, and he and Stephen chuckled. Yet just as quickly all traces of Roger's humor faded. He rested one of his meaty hands on my shoulder. "Seriously, though. You okay?"

There were no words.

"I think he's all right now." Stephen touched my forehead, his hand cool but certain.

My mind spun and a wave of exhaustion hit me. None of this made sense. Minutes ago, I'd been on Granda's porch, and now here I was in Stephen's house, and he and Roger were acting like normal people.

Plus, there was something that I had to remember. What was that?

Oh, right. *Cali. The prophecy.*

"What's wrong with the two of you? Acting like we're a family? Acting like you care?" I turned on Stephen. "You murdered our mother!"

Stephen's eyes widened, but he drew back from me. "What a weird sense of humor you have, Kellen!" Both he and Roger burst into awkward laughter.

Before I could demand answers, I heard the sound of the front door opening and closing accompanied by the jingle of keys as someone hung them on the hook. That sound. I remembered it as if it had been seconds since I'd last heard it and not years.

Footsteps crossed the foyer and a voice called out, "Boys, are you home?"

My breath stuck in my chest. I gripped the couch cushions, waiting.

"In here, love." His smile transformed Stephen into a version of him I'd never seen—that of a man in love.

Then my mother entered the room, plucking at the sides of her exercise pants as she walked. When she looked up, a wide smile broke across her face like the dawn on the sunniest day of the year. "There are my guys!"

Stephen walked to her and pulled her into his arms. "Don't you look adorable? How was yoga?" Without waiting for an answer, he kissed her firmly on the lips.

This time, when the blackness came, I didn't feel my head hit the pillows.

CHAPTER 52
CALI

My breath came in quick gasps as I ran with as much speed as my mortal body would allow. Up and up, around curve after curve. I had to get to the portal and ask for help.

It had grown colder. The chill air set my lungs on fire with every breath. This could not be a good sign for my mortal body. My stomach growled, begging for food, but food would be a long time in coming. Every tree looked the same, every curve a replica of the one before. The only way for me to go was up.

"One step at a time, girl." My own voice surprised me, as I'd been running alone for so long. I stumbled on a pile of rocks and my right foot seized up. I bit back a howl of pain, but I had to keep running if I wanted to reach the portal and get help.

Hope flared in my heart as I imagined seeing my mother and father again. They would be on the other side of the portal waiting for me, and everything would be all right. They would fix this.

You are a fool, Cali. If there was one thing that I'd learned in my time as a mortal, it was that I'd been nothing more than a pampered princess before. Everything I'd ever wanted, I'd received. If I made a mistake, my father always fixed it. But some things couldn't be repaired, even by my father. Some things—

A cry escaped my throat as the ground beneath me gave way. I was falling, flailing my arms and legs as I plunged into darkness. With a thud, I landed on my backside on something soft and wet.

Cringing, I rested my hands at my sides, unable to make out anything. I'd fallen into some sort of pit or possibly even a ravine. I missed my night vision. The dark was ever so much scarier when I couldn't see through it.

The moon peeked out from behind the clouds to illuminate the muddy hollow I'd fallen into.

I stood up and searched along the edges of the small space for any outcroppings that might be substantial enough to climb. It was slow going. My boots sank into the mire, and with each step I had to unglue myself from the previous one. After endless minutes of feeling along the middle of the wall I located a series of rocks lodged into the side of the pit. It would provide the perfect foothold.

I launched myself onto the rocks. Dirt embedded itself under my fingernails as I reached for any possible handhold, but there was nothing to grip but wet earth. Soon the rocks on which I stood dislodged from the dirt. I slammed into the wall, mud covering my front as I slid back to the ground.

Panic seized me. That had been my best chance of getting out of here and it hadn't worked.

"Somebody help me!" The cry escaped me before I could stop it. I had to get myself under control. A battle waged on that I had initiated. If I wasn't careful, I'd alert them to my whereabouts.

Without anything better to do, I sat down on the driest

part of the pit, which wasn't saying much. Mud oozed through the fabric of my jeans. The big book about Gabriel's house had contained a paper advertising mud baths for mortals. Why anyone would choose this for relaxation went beyond my reasoning.

A cry echoed above me and I looked to the sky as a large bird began circling the pit. It called out in soft tones, as though it, too, was conscious of the nearby battle.

When it began to lower itself into the pit, my breath caught. This wasn't any bird, it was an immense crane, close to the size of the vehicle in which we'd traveled to Maine. It seemed to be approaching slowly with intention, as though it didn't want to frighten me. It wasn't until it landed in the mud that it cocked its head and regarded me with kind, patient eyes.

I examined my company closely in the confined space. This was not what I'd had in mind when I asked for help. Inching forward, I leaned toward the bird's face. "Hello, gentle bird. Have you come to free me?"

As if in answer, the bird turned and lowered its back. When I didn't immediately climb on, it faced me. I would have sworn it was laughing at me.

No matter. My decision was a simple one. I couldn't get out of the pit without the bird's help. I needed him. That meant I had to put my fears aside and climb atop this beast.

I clambered awkwardly onto its back. I quickly dug my knees into its sides and wrapped my arms around its neck. As it shot out of the pit and into the air, my lungs expanded, and relief filled me up as though I were a balloon.

Snuggling close to the bird, I let its warmth seep into me. "Can you take me to Kellen St. James?"

"Kellen is on his own journey." The deep rumbling of the bird's voice startled me, nearly unseating me in the air. "You and I both know about the second part of the prophecy. We cannot interfere. It has been set into motion."

Fear settled around my neck like a noose. I shook my head vehemently, though my feathered friend couldn't see. "Kellen would never—"

"We have yet to see what path Kellen will choose." The bird's voice held a note of despair. Yet something was familiar about it. Something I couldn't place. I searched my memories for a match, but they were such fragile things that I had no hope of one.

"Father?"

The bird's chuckle calmed me. "You honor me, but no."

Tears choked me as my frustration mounted. "Is there nothing we can do to save my love?"

The bird expelled a large breath, almost the way a mortal would sigh. "For now, we wait. I will do all I can to protect him. Your job, however, is to open the portal for your family. We all have a job to do. You must do yours."

After what seemed an eternity but lasted only a moment, the bird touched down on the top of Cadillac Mountain. Little could be seen from the rocky peak in the dark, but I needed only to reach the portal. The wind whipped fiercely here, as though a storm brewed.

Reaching up, I patted the bird's neck. "Thank you for saving me."

"You are most welcome, my lady." The bird bowed, its aristocratic head nearly touching the ground.

Letting my fingers drop, I wrapped my arms around myself. "What is your name?"

"I am told they call me many things, but most commonly *An Cosantóir*." Then my rescuer turned and shot once more into the sky, leaving me alone in the darkness.

My mind worked to translate the Gaelic term until finally

my memory found the words: The Protector. When I looked to the sky again, my friend had gone.

CHAPTER 53
KELLEN

There was no way I could ever allow myself to wake up. I'd had the most wonderful dream. It had been beyond anything that I could ever hope for.

My mother lived, my parents were together, and they loved me. They even loved one another. And Roger had been nice to me. I wanted to soak up every bit of it for all it was worth.

But then I remembered where I'd been before the dream. Trying to get back to Cali . . .

"Kellen? Sweetie, wake up." My mother's voice broke into my thoughts.

My eyes shot open. Both my parents were standing above me, concern evident on their faces. I fought a wave of my own emotion. This was happening, yet it wasn't real.

I scooted back against the arm of the sofa, away from them, and used my pillow as a barrier between us. "Who are you, and what is this?"

My parents looked to one another. Slowly Stephen got to his feet.

"Addison, I'm going to call the doctor."

My mother nodded her consent before facing me. "Sweetie, you're not feeling well right now." She placed a hand on either side of my face. "We'll find a way to make you feel better."

All the tension that wracked my body melted away. My mother was here. Everything was wonderful. Perfect. There was nothing missing. My family was all I'd ever need.

I swallowed hard, trying to remember the urgency, the tension from a moment ago. I fought to recall why I'd panicked, but I couldn't. After several moments of searching, I remembered.

"Mom, can you help me with my resumé later?" That was it. It felt so much better to ask for her help. I'd been struggling with it for weeks.

"Sweetie, I can't believe you're even old enough to ask that question or that we're going to visit medical schools next month." She beamed, patting my hand. "You're going to be a wonderful doctor, Kellen."

I hugged my mother. Her praise was the greatest gift. "It's all I've ever wanted." Carefully, I released her, feeling better.

"Come on, you. Let's go have breakfast before Roger finishes it all." She laughed, extending her hand to me. I took it and together we walked to the kitchen, the sound of our footsteps evaporating on the rich, gold plush carpeting.

"Mom, did you have the carpet changed in here?"

She turned to me, a surprised smile on her face. "The place was so depressing and intimidating. It's much homier with these lighter colors, don't you think?"

"Yeah." Something nagged at my brain, forgotten thoughts knocking at the door to my mind. I ignored them. "What's for breakfast?"

We walked into the kitchen and as I looked out through the windows, I couldn't help but stop and stare at the glorious fall day outside. As I sat down at the table, Roger walked in, a towel around his neck, his wet swim trunks dripping on the stone floor.

Someone else had dripped water onto the floor. Where had that been?

"Go up and change, right now." My mother spoke in a stern voice. "You're getting water all over the floor."

Roger shrugged. "Sorry, Mom." With a wink and a small smile for me, he turned and walked back in the direction he'd come.

"Here we are, Master Kellen."

My stomach growled as Sarah brought over an enormous stack of pancakes, a plate of fruit, and a pot of coffee. When had I last had pancakes? Visions of powdered sugar and syrup on a wide table filled my mind. I shook it off and poured the coffee into a cup, then took a huge, calming drink. Did they have any Snickers bars around this place?

Stephen walked in then, concern etched onto his face. "Got off the phone with Dr. Evans. He'll be here in a few minutes." He patted my shoulder then walked to the fridge and extracted a bottled water. "Thanks, Sarah. Breakfast looks delicious." He gave her a polite smile as he passed by.

"Master Stephen." Sarah curtsied before returning to tidying up the kitchen.

Again something bothered me. Something I was supposed to be doing right then. Probably my resumé.

We ate breakfast as a family. My father talked about his latest class, and my mother shared news about a new company she'd started. She was painting murals for corporations, and her waiting list was twelve months long. At the mention of murals, an unpleasant sensation trailed down the back of my neck, similar to having ice dumped down my collar, though I couldn't place why.

It wasn't until I'd plowed my way through my third

helping of pancakes that the back door opened and a man walked into the room carrying a black bag. "Good morning, St. James Family!"

"We're so glad you came, Dr. Evans." Stephen rose to his feet to shake the doctor's hand.

Dr. Evans smiled as he took the chair next to me. The more I stared at him, the more familiar he seemed. My head throbbed from the effort of trying to remember.

"Kellen." He inclined his head to the side and suddenly my temporarily displaced memories came rushing back into my mind.

Cali. Arawn. The second part of the prophecy.

I leaned forward in my seat and my mother's pendant spilled over my collar to rest on the front of my shirt.

His benign expression slipped for an instant, but it was enough for me to glimpse greed and longing. His eyes never left the pendant, and neither did my mother's.

"That's an interesting piece of jewelry. Where did you get it, honey?" She tugged at her ponytail. Her previously fresh-faced appearance became somewhat blurry and her voice sounded frazzled.

"I got it from you, in a letter I received from you after you died."

She stared hard at me, as though she didn't compute the words I'd spoken. "Died? But, honey, I'm fine. I'm right here."

"No, you aren't." My heart ached with the knowledge that I'd been tricked. Every one of us knew it. "All of this," I gestured around the room, "is an illusion. You've been trying to keep me from Cali, to make me forget how I came to be here."

I turned to Dr. Evans. "Hello, William."

The scene before me quickly changed from the most wonderful dream into a terrible nightmare as the perfect setting melted away before my eyes like a watercolor painting struck by a jet of water. In mere moments, the beautiful sunlit morning shifted into the darkness of night, and I went from sitting across from my beloved mother to sitting across from her rotting, stinking corpse.

CHAPTER 54
CALI

The moment I turned from my savior, I found the portal. The swirling vortex of fire and blackness stood out before me. Occasionally other colors would burst from the opening. Hues of purple, red, yellow, and blue, among others.

Hesitantly I took two steps forward when the man in the white robes appeared directly in front of me. He seemed even older than when we'd met moments ago, as though the very effort of appearing on the mountaintop had aged him.

Standing tall, I placed my hands on my hips. Gabriel had informed me this made me look tough. "Who are you?"

He didn't rush to answer. He only stared, regarding me as though I was a product available for purchase. I tipped my chin, refusing to shy away, waiting for the explanation I deserved. "I am Ainmire. I am certain your sister has mentioned me."

"Rowan?" What did Rowan have to do with this strange creature? Perhaps my immortal memory would have provided more clues, but my mortal one chose not to. Impatience shot through me. "She did not. That name means nothing to me.

My family and I are the only immortals other than the Children of Danu."

Disappointment flashed across his face but didn't linger. He cocked an eyebrow. "That's quite a self-absorbed point of view, Princess. There are many who roam alternative planes that are destined to live forever. I am one such being, but there are others."

Ainmire's eyes glowed an unusual violet color. I'd never seen anything like them before. They would be almost hypnotic if the man wasn't so obviously evil.

He inspected his white cloak and focused on removing a fleck of dirt and smoothing the material.

"I'm the one you call self-absorbed?" I laughed. "Perhaps you'd like a mirror to continue your primping."

His purple irises glinted. "I came here to offer you a boon, Princess."

"I am no princess, and I want nothing from you," I spat, backing away from him. He'd delayed me long enough.

"You know nothing." He smiled, but there was no kindness in the expression. It was coated in bitterness and hate. "I, on the other hand, make it my business to know everything—all the stories, all the players. I know the truth about the prophecy."

I froze, hating that his words had any impact on me. Everyone knew about the prophecy, but no one had ever known what it meant. Not even my father.

"Partner with me and I will share all I know. Even the whereabouts of Kellen St. James." A slow smile filled his face. "Ready to join me now?"

Oh, he had me now—or at least he thought he did.

Kellen would tell me there was another way. That there was always another option beyond siding with evil. I had to trust that.

"I am afraid you are to be disappointed." I thrust my

hands out before me and let loose the fire that waited within me. The flames encircled my adversary. Then, turning toward the sky I shouted, "Open!"

Not only did the portal not open, no help came.

With a smug grin, Ainmire got to his feet. "Were you under the impression someone was coming to rescue you, Princess? Well I have news. No one's coming." He sent the wave of fire that surrounded him back in my direction, but it merely singed me. Ainmire could kill me in a heartbeat. Instead he chose to torment me, as though I was his entertainment.

In the distance, the sounds of fighting rang out. The faerie battle raged on, continuing up the mountain. My legs shook as I readied myself for another attack from Ainmire. He'd been toying with me. If he chose to meet me in true combat, I wouldn't last.

"Open!" My cry sounded louder this time, but still nothing happened.

One more time, I promised myself as Ainmire regrouped.

"Open!" This time I screamed the word as loud as I could, my cry piercing the night. But no portal came.

The fire within me petered out. My mortal state, which had never been designed to wield Fire, could not sustain it. Ainmire sent another wave of flames toward me, then pulled them back almost immediately, but not before the flames singed my hair and lightly burned my skin.

I let out a cry, which echoed weakly across the mountaintop as my gift bounded back on me, throwing me to the ground.

Ainmire walked toward me, laughing. "Oh, what a mistake you made in denying our alliance, Princess. You will pay for your own poor choice."

My body burned as a thousand pinpricks pierced my skin. Something flew past my periphery. No, these weren't pinpricks at all. They were arrows. A swarm of the tiniest, most delicate faeries flew overhead, raining arrows down upon me.

I watched in horror as blood began to seep from tiny wounds on my skin. I fell to my knees, not yet defeated but unable to stand another moment.

Suddenly, a word formed in my mind. Carefully, I whispered, "*Oscail.*"

Ainmire came to stand before me. "You are valiant, young one, but you will not win in that mortal body. You are all alone."

Refusing to look away, I met Ainmire's eyes. "I am *never* alone."

"No, she is not." A new voice broke the tension of the moment.

A rush of warm air shot at me, followed by the scent of fresh grass and sunshine as the portal opened and my brother, Cabhan, charged through, looking every bit the warrior angel. A full army of angels followed from behind, swords at the ready. The angels surrounded Ainmire. He appeared taken aback for the slightest of moments before he held his hand aloft. With a soft pop, a sword appeared in his grip.

The blood from my puncture wounds dripped to the ground and vanished when it landed on the dark earth. Wind slammed into me, making my ears burn from the cold. My mud-covered body had had enough.

Cabhan flew to my side and took my hand in his. "Sister, are you all right?"

I looked up into his eyes. I didn't need to say that I wasn't. This had all gone horribly wrong. "Block him, all right? I need to get through the portal." I had to get help for Kellen, even if that meant I'd die after I reached the Green Lands.

"You're sure? Sister, you are weak." He cupped my cheek in his hand.

"If it is my time to leave this plane, I will, but I will not do so until I've finished my job." That's what The Protector had called it, and I found I liked the sound.

My brother pressed a swift kiss to my forehead. "Then do as you must, Sister. All my love to you."

Turning, Cabhan flew toward the battlefield, sword swinging. Faeries scattered across the ground as they fell from the angels' attack.

As quickly as I could, I crawled toward the portal.

"Cali, go!" Cabhan's voice spurred me on as an arrow whizzed past my head.

The clash of sword against sword rang in my ears. Forcing myself to my feet, I drew a deep breath and backed up a couple of steps. Then, running as quickly as my broken body would allow, I launched myself into the air and jumped off the side of Cadillac Mountain.

CHAPTER 55

KELLEN

My stomach heaved and I leaped from the chair, biting my lip to keep from vomiting. The corpse, which was more skeleton than flesh, held no trace of my mother's soul. I had no idea whether it belonged to her or if it was that of a random person who'd gotten in the way. When I finally turned back, William had lost the white doctor's coat and returned to his general uniform of jeans, flannel shirt, and barn coat.

Even though he'd lied to us, even though his intention had been to get me here all along, William's presence didn't upset me nearly as much as Stephen's absence. For where Stephen had been standing, I found a man who wasn't a man at all, but the Lord of Faerie. Arawn. Every muscle in my body locked. I'd known all along that the Lord of Faerie could come back, but I thought I'd have more time. Yet here I was, barely two weeks after our last encounter, and I was staring down the evil bastard again.

"Greetings, young St. James." Arawn spoke in a gravelly voice.

This vile immortal gave new meaning to the word jerk.

After all, he was the one responsible for trapping Cali's family, the Children of Danu (version 1.0), in Faerie.

He stood over six feet tall with two long jagged antlers protruding from his head. His face had no discernible features except for the glowing red eyes with no pupils. Despite the tiny fractures of light that shone through him, Arawn was more shadow than man, giving the impression that he might disappear at any moment. I knew I wouldn't be that lucky.

"So, we meet again. It was inevitable. I arranged it, after all." The evil lord clasped his blackened hands together. "I enjoyed the connection we shared through your dreams, Kellen. It was a great way to spy on you, as it were. Pity you're such a light sleeper."

Shock coursed through me. I'd never suspected Arawn. That seemed foolish now. "So that was you. As far as dreams go, those were pretty vague."

"When have you ever known dreams to be clear? I simply needed to get a sense of your true desires, and I achieved that with my servant's help." He gestured to William.

As he turned away from William, pure and unadulterated hatred filled the other man's face. The emotion was so intense and unexpected that I couldn't stop staring.

Catching me watching, William jerked his head in Arawn's direction. *Pay attention to everything he says. Follow my lead.*

I stumbled and caught myself in time to avoid falling over. William, it seemed, could communicate telepathically. *Didn't see that one coming.*

"Careful there, young Kellen. Your weary legs fail you. Come, we must sit." Arawn frowned as he glanced around the room. "This is a rather unpleasant scene, don't you think?" He gestured to the corpse almost impatiently and waved his hand.

In the next instant, Arawn, William, and I were sitting in

the study. The "Addison and Stephen—A Forever Love" sign was centered directly above his head.

"Yes, yes, much better." Arawn clapped his hands in approval. "I do apologize for having your mother's body exhumed, but I had little choice in the matter. It was the best possible way to bring her back for my purposes."

Pure, unadulterated rage filled me as I shot to my feet and lunged for him. I didn't get far. Two steps in and an unseen force knocked me back ten feet and directly into the doorframe. Pain sliced down one side of my back like a knife, and a red haze blurred my vision. An impossible ringing filled my ears as though I sat on the inside of a bell that had tolled.

Quit arguing with him. If you want to get back to Cali, you need to play nice. Again, William's voice filled my mind. *I can't help you if you're dead.*

I'd believed William was all Team Arawn, but that wasn't the vibe I was getting now. Why was William even interested in helping me? I was right where he wanted me. Yet there had to be a reason he wasn't speaking to me in front of Arawn. I'd have to go with my instincts.

I performed a quick scan of my body. Nothing was broken. I wasn't bleeding, and no bones had been jerked from alignment. I inclined my head in Arawn's direction. "My apologies, my lord. You took me by surprise."

Arawn chuckled and William soon joined in.

"Dear boy. Understandable given the circumstances." Arawn gestured to an armless chair across from him. "Please, take a seat, Kellen."

Once I joined him, he leaned forward. "Apologies for your father. I took his soul, or what was left of it."

"You killed my father?" The image from my dream, of Arawn standing over Stephen's convulsing body, flooded my mind.

"He was a bit of a bastard. The exact opposite of the real Stephen St. James."

Granda's sorrow, his complete desolation at losing his son came back to me. I swallowed my anger. I wouldn't get anywhere by losing it. "The real Stephen? I'm afraid I don't know that story."

"Allow me to educate you, then." Arawn rubbed his palms together as though truly delighted to be speaking to me. "I'm not unlike other men, Kellen. Once I reached two hundred thousand years of age, I started thinking about a family. I wanted children, but Danu refused. Danu and I were lovers, you see."

Shock sent every question flying from my mind. I stared hard at this creature. I couldn't imagine it ever touching the beautiful Danu, the woman I'd once seen forever frozen in the art along a cave wall.

Arawn laughed. "Ah! You should see your visage, Kellen. It betrays your thoughts! Yes, I was once a god on the side of the light. Can you even imagine? I was handsome, the most handsome god ever. Yet though I was created for her, Danu would not consent to be my wife and have a family with me. Eventually I took her life and trapped her children. And one night, eons later, Stephen St. James snuck into my *rath*."

"You kept the real Stephen St. James and sent a false one in his place, didn't you? My father was nothing more than a changeling."

I hadn't wanted it to be true, though I knew in my heart it was. It explained so much. His callousness in sending me away and my mother's death. I had a changeling's blood in my veins. No wonder the second part of the prophecy claimed I would turn against the light.

Arawn's eyes popped open wider so that they encompassed his entire face, twin red lasers against a sea of darkness. "Well done, Kellen! You are quite intelligent, aren't you?

I only sent the imposter aboveground when that moaning Taiclaigh started showing up every night with offerings. It was annoying, truly, so I sent him a copy of his boy." Arawn steepled his shadowy fingers. "Most changelings are weak, not even people at all. This one was an exact replica. Except for his soul."

"Yeah. He didn't have one." Memories of Stephen and all of the ugliness in this house pressed down on me as though Arawn were forcing it to.

Arawn's mouth split into a wide grin, yet I could see no teeth, as though his mouth were a black hole. "In truth, the father you knew had a small piece of one, the barest sliver of soul from the original." He clapped his hands together. "Because the true Stephen was filled with so much light, even the tiniest sliver of his soul could command the changeling's darkness. Of course, this changeling's most important job was to fit in."

Fit in. Stephen had always done his duty. I always wondered why he'd taken care of Gran and visited her so often, even as he seemed to hate her.

Though my heart raced inside my chest, I forced myself to calm. If I wanted to learn about the family that was even more of a mystery than it had been before, I'd need to play it cool. If Arawn knew the information mattered to me, he'd make sure I didn't get it.

He frowned, leaning forward to inspect me. "I must say, I was surprised to find out about you and your brother. I've never known any of them to have families before. Then again, the man who fathered you wasn't a normal changeling."

It had been bad enough thinking my father was an ass. Finding out he wasn't even human—a man who wasn't a man —made it a thousand times worse. "Where is he? The real Stephen?"

Let it go. William's insistent voice pushed into my thoughts.

A cloud seemed to settle over Arawn. "Why does his location matter? He is nothing to you."

I thought about the people that would want to know. Granda and Gran, even my mother, but they were all gone. Even though I'd met them all in the Green Lands and the Cusp, there was no guarantee I'd be able to pass anything I learned on to them now. "It's nothing."

"We aren't here to discuss Stephen. We're here to talk about the amulet."

Forcing myself to look directly at Arawn wasn't an easy task, but I managed. I would be strong, for myself and for Cali.

"I'm guessing you mean Danu's amulet?"

"Why, yes!" Arawn spread his arms wide, as though preaching to the pulpit. "When I murdered Danu and her fool of a husband Bilé, I forced her power into the amulet she wore about her neck. Me being me, I had the foresight to recognize that there was too much light in Danu's magick for me to absorb, so I wrapped the stone in a magickal cloth. Even drawing on the stone's power from afar was enough to injure me. It weakened me so that only the darkest parts of my person remained." Arawn gestured to himself as though he were a model showing off the latest fashion. "In the end, I found a way to extract the power I needed to control her children." A biting coldness crept into his tone that reminded me what a ruthless bastard Arawn was.

"Although I appreciate the history lesson," I said, sitting back in my chair as though this were a casual conversation between friends, "I still have no idea what this amulet has to do with me."

Arawn nodded, his red eyes seeming to scan me. "It was stolen from me."

It felt like a million years ago that Cana had landed in the middle of my wedding and accused me of having something I shouldn't. "I don't have Danu's amulet."

"I already know this. That fool Dillion stole it from me. Stole it right from my very house!" Arawn slammed his fist down onto nothing—empty air—though I could have sworn I felt a vibration.

"Why do you want it so badly? I've heard it's cursed." Again, I did my best to keep things conversational.

"Quite right you are, Kellen. If anyone other than Danu herself so much as holds it, it owns them. If they use it, the amulet extracts a piece of their life-force with each use. The instant they release it, it kills them. The only reason I stand before you is because I had the foresight to use the protective cloth to take the amulet from Danu's body. Without it, there would be even less of me left than there is now. When I used its magick I did so at great risk, so I only used it once, to construct The Call—the magick that has kept the Children of Danu imprisoned all these years."

Sounded like just another day with faeries. But then Arawn's explanation sank in. *It extracts a piece of their life-force with each use.* Dillion had looked much older when he showed up in Maine. The theft of the amulet would also explain his intense power at the wedding when he blasted Cana and the C.O.D. away.

I had to get back to Cali and Dillion, to warn them. Maybe we could even go to Dillion's library and I could research a solution. There had to be magick that could save him.

"If Dillion has that thing, he'll never give it to you."

Silence followed for several moments as a sly smile filled Arawn's face. He turned to William. "Do you have something you'd like to show Kellen?"

William's jaw flinched as he reached into his pocket and

withdrew a glowing green stone on a chain. The stone pulsed as though it were alive. But even as I longed for a closer look, I knew what this meant, and I didn't need William's voice inside my head to confirm it.

Dillion is dead.

CHAPTER 56

CALI

B racing myself, I prepared for a rough landing on the other side of the portal. I hoped I'd end up rolling across the lush grass of the Green Lands and not down the cold, hard rock of Cadillac Mountain. But though I launched myself forward, I didn't pass through the portal. Instead, I bounced off the portal's surface and fell back onto the rocks.

I cried out as hot, burning pain radiated from my shoulder.

Why couldn't I pass through? I'd opened the portal. Even now I could glimpse green grass on the other side, beckoning me. The only explanation was that someone had sealed it again.

The instant I located Ainmire in the crowd, his eyes found mine and he roared with laughter, confirming my fears. "There's no need to go so soon, Princess. Join us!"

The battle raged on around me, but I had no weapons and was in no condition to fight. I could flee, but to where? Gabriel's house? I couldn't remember how to get back, and my job was to open this portal. I'd managed that, but not long enough to save myself.

My head throbbed and I winced as I attempted to move my shoulder. Cabhan and the other angels, of which there were twelve, appeared to be weakening. Ainmire looked as though he was merely out for a stroll on a summer's day. He was glowing, and he fought all twelve one-handed, as though they were children.

Not only was he winning, but he was growing younger. The white faded from his hair, replaced by black strands the color of midnight.

White-hot pain exploded all over me as another battalion of winged faeries attacked from above. Tiny arrows rained down on me. What they lacked in size they made up for in velocity and force. They only pinched when they struck me. Still, the projectiles punctured my flesh hard and at odd angles so that they drew blood and wore me down. I soon fell to my knees.

"Fire, come to me," I begged in a hoarse whisper that I'd intended as a shout. Yet there was nothing. The magick I'd called to stop Cana was gone. No awareness of power, no warming of my fingers. Maybe it was supposed to be temporary, but it felt as though I'd been abandoned. I was on my own.

With my muscles weakened and my body weary, I fell forward, slamming my chin on a rock. I bit my own tongue and blood seeped from my mouth, leaving the taste of rust and salt behind. The impact sent shockwaves through me as arrow after arrow dug into my skin.

I closed my eyes and imagined Kellen kneeling beside me, holding my hand. Yet the dreams I'd held close to my heart were beginning to blur. Dreams of marrying Kellen and, though I'd never admitted as much to him, ruling by his side . . . forever. I would never have those experiences with Kellen, and I would never be his.

Something flashed in my periphery and I peered at the

horizon, trying to make out what it was. Yet the scene playing out made little sense through eyes strained past their breaking point.

The closer they came, my vision snapped into focus. A fleet of magnificent ships floated toward us, their flags flapping proudly in the wind. Some were merchant boats with cargo tied down. Others pirate ships sailing under ominous skull-and-crossbones flags. One small fishing vessel came closest to me. A fisherman stood on its deck brandishing a shotgun. He raised a fist in the air and shouted, "Onward! Onward!"

As the boat approached, it looked like it might strike me. I tried to raise my hand out of instinct but couldn't. Yet the moment I expected pain, an icy chill crawled over my skin and the ship sailed *through* me.

They were spirits. Ghosts of the sea come to rescue us.

Each member of the ghost fleet had writing on his or her back. Squinting, I tried to read it, though the dark and the distance made interpreting the words on the transparent beings a challenge. Then another ship passed directly by me and I made out *CORNWALLIS 1944* on the back of a crewman.

Our saviors brandished weaponry of all kinds. They fired shots from aged rifles and smaller pistols of varying shapes and sizes. Some let loose flaming arrows, Fire first a beacon in the night and then a fierce warrior as she sent faeries scattering. Still others leaped from the boats to their feet, wielding swords and sabers.

The first cannon fire sent faeries scurrying for cover as a cannonball lodged itself in the ground beside Ainmire. He did not stop brandishing his blade at Cabhan, but my weakened brother parried every effort.

The faeries turned their attention from me and I sagged to the rocky ground, only able to look on as they launched an intense counterattack on the ghost ships. Yet their magick had little or no effect. The dead would not be stopped.

The faeries fled in droves, taking to the wood or popping out of existence. Yet, their damage had been done. I'd lost quite a bit of my mortal blood, and though I couldn't be certain, it felt like an impossible amount.

The pain took over again, and my eyelids slid shut as sleep claimed me.

CHAPTER 57

KELLEN

Sadness coursed through me as William held the amulet aloft. Dillion and I had never been close, but I'd respected him, and he'd helped me on more than one occasion. Beyond that, I hurt for Cali who had few family members left in her life.

I took it from him. I had to be the one to do it.

William's voice filled my head, once again leaving me with more questions than answers. If only I could question him without Arawn knowing. Yet the *whys* must have lingered in my eyes, because he continued.

I'm not William, the caretaker. I'm Willock, Dillion's son.

My mind reeling, I stared hard at the man I now knew as Willock. This man was Dillion's son?

I had to take the amulet from him, Kellen. He was already dying. I couldn't let the others find it.

Willock's mental confirmation sent my heart aching all the more, yet it was also torn. "So, you brought it right to Arawn."

Slowly, Willock gave a half nod of his head. *No, I brought it right to you.*

Before I could react, Arawn chimed in. "He did. Like a good servant would."

I focused on the stone as I listened, using my false fascination with it as a guide to process all that William—no *Willock*—had shared.

But soon, a yearning rose within me. I could imagine how warm the stone would feel in my hand. I wanted to hold it, wanted to wield its power. I leaned in closer despite myself, taking in the hypnotic green of its surface, smooth, but for the embossing at its center.

Arawn moved in beside me, jarring me from whatever hold the amulet had over me. "That impression in the stone appeared after Danu's death. Initially, I thought it to be a watermark or a family crest. It wasn't until the amulet continued to weaken me that I realized it is the most important part—a missing piece that stabilizes Danu's powers."

The amulet pulsed, as though it had a life of its own. Truthfully, as much as I longed to hold it, the thing made me uncomfortable.

"Where's the missing piece?" Then the answer rose up as clearly as if I'd known it all along. The way Willock had eyed my pendant and had even asked to see it . . .

"Why, Kellen, you wear the last component around your neck!" His laughter filled the room, sending shivers across my skin.

And Lugh had sworn my pendant only had sentimental value. Had he truly believed that, or had he been trying to protect me?

"So why not have your lapdog here take it from me?" I gestured to Willock. "It would have been easy enough to do." We'd eaten dinner at his house, after all.

Arawn's voice took on a tone of mild annoyance. "The wardings around you were great, so much so that in my weakened form, I could not destroy them."

Wardings? Where had I heard that before? In Faerie. Cali had said there were wardings in place to protect me against immortals. She had to be invited into Gran's house before she could cross them. Did that mean there were wardings at Alastrom? Why did those matter? Willock had been invited in. He could have taken the pendant from me at any time and he didn't. He could have brought me to Arawn any time, yet he didn't.

Trust me. I have a plan, and if you blow it, we're both going to end up dead. Willock's voice whispered in my head.

Fine, but if Warlock Boy had been more forthcoming with the details, I wouldn't have to work for answers.

"But no matter," Arawn continued, having no idea of my one-sided mental exchange with Willock. "As any good servant would, Willock waited, and he brought you to me."

"And what's the rest? There has to be more. Why do you need me, apart from wanting revenge because I weakened you with a sword?"

The Lord of Faerie's eyes flared for a moment, only to return to their normal size in the next instant. "You have to be the one to control the amulet for me. You are its master. Without you, I can only access a portion of its power."

"Me? But why?"

Arawn moved in and I suppressed a shudder as he came too close to my personal bubble for comfort. "Does the why of it matter? The object of great import is what possessing the amulet will *give you.*"

He snapped his fingers and my mother, Gran, Alistair, Gabe, Dillion, Lugh, and Brigid stood in front of me. Even Stephen himself stood in the group, though this version looked infinitely kinder than the one I'd grown up with. Each one smiled and waved. Gabe dipped his head behind the others, as though not to draw too much attention to himself.

Then, impossibly, Cali stepped out from behind the

group, a broad smile widening her face. She crossed the room and slid her arms around me. There was no hesitation in her movements and the rightness I always felt when I was with her returned. I knew she couldn't be real, but that didn't stop me from catching her up in my arms.

"If you partner with me, Kellen," Arawn spoke in his roughened voice, "you could have this life every day. Everyone you've ever cared about will be with you always. You'll never be alone again."

"Kellen." Cali sighed against me, her voice a slice of heaven as her cheek met mine.

Yet before I could touch my lips to hers, she turned to ash and fell in a pile at my feet.

Sighing, I looked on as the same thing happened to the rest. One after the other they disintegrated in turn. They'd been nothing more than Arawn's creations. Granda had warned me Arawn had a talent for this.

Nothing was real except Arawn, Willock, and myself. Even that I couldn't be sure of.

Arawn waved his hand and the room transformed from the comfortable color scheme to the dark maroon color that had dominated the version of the home I remembered. Dread pooled in my stomach, an intense unease that always followed me when I so much as thought about this place.

When I faced Arawn once more, he was hunched over, leaning against the arm of the chair for support. More fractures of light appeared across his person.

"That's why you want me. You don't just want access to power. You're dying."

Neither he nor Willock spoke.

"I don't want anything to do with you. I should have killed you the right way the first time." Standing, I headed for the door.

Yet I'd hardly taken a handful of steps when pain surged

through me, running straight up my spine. I gritted my teeth as my body began to turn on its own, away from the exit and toward Arawn.

"I did suspect you might want to go in that direction, Kellen." Arawn's voice rang out in the large room. "Forgive me, but I made sure to bring insurance."

With a wave of his hand, a door opened to my right. I'd never gone through it as a boy, having avoided Stephen's study as much as possible. Carefully, I moved toward the opening, casting a sideways glance at Willock as I passed. He met my eye, then just as quickly looked away.

Finally, I reached the doorway. It didn't lead to a room, but a closet. It wasn't empty either. Staring hard, I fought to make out the outline of the thing that hung upside down from the ceiling. It was impossible to see. I wasn't sure I wanted to feel around in there for a light switch, either, if more corpses awaited me.

Arawn waved his hand and a small light switched on in the room. I backed up, then froze as I met the eyes of my brother Roger.

His body was emaciated. His ribs poked out against the filthy T-shirt he wore. Even at twenty-three, he would have had a boyish quality if not for his withered state. An IV was inserted into his arm, and the bag on the other end glowed with a semi-translucent substance. Roger raised his head and peered at me for a long moment before he spat in my direction. His aim fell short, which increased the loathing in his eyes.

Arawn moved to stand beside me, and as he touched my arm, the sensation that a million tiny insects skittered across my skin filled me. "He, like you, carries changeling blood in his veins."

Paralyzed, I could only stand there, staring at Roger. How long had he been like this?

"When I found Roger, I began the process of extracting his humanity. The changeling half of him will take over and he will be even less human soon. Unless you choose to side with me. Then only you will be the one to lose your humanity. I can't have a little thing like your conscience getting in the way if we are to work together. The choice is yours."

Oh, why had I thought the perfect home montage was all that Arawn would throw my way? It would be wrong of me to abandon Roger. It didn't matter that we'd never been close. This was what Granda had meant by an offer I couldn't refuse.

My brother continued to stare with the same evil glint in his eye. Regardless of how Roger had treated me, his actions were a reflection of his own origins. I could no more condemn him to a life with Arawn than walk over there and murder him myself.

Go along with him for now. Do as I say. Willock's thoughts reinforced the decision I'd already made.

"If I join you, then Roger becomes human and you free him."

"Of course." Arawn smiled.

"He'll be sent back to school with no memory of any of this," I continued, remembering Granda's words about specifics. "No recurring nightmares, not the slightest hint that it ever happened." I idly toyed with my mother's pendant, which had begun to heat against my skin. It had almost grown too uncomfortable to wear.

"Agreed."

"What will happen to Calienta?"

"Oh, the lovely Calienta." His voice implied she was anything but lovely, and the memory of Cali encasing Arawn's hell hounds in ice came back to me.

Arawn shrugged. "Dead, I'm afraid. Unable to protect that mortal body of hers."

My legs shook, threatening to give out. I screamed inside my mind. *Cali. No.*

It was as if someone had reached inside my chest and squeezed my heart.

Cali was dead. We would never spend our lives together.

Suddenly, I had no future at all.

"You won't touch Gabe. No one goes near him or my grandfather. *Ever.* Or Cali's family. No more vendettas, no more trickery. We're done."

Arawn extended a blackened hand from beneath the sleeve of his robe. "You have my word."

"Then we have a deal. I'll join you." Grasping Arawn's skeletal hand in a firm grip, we shook on it.

CHAPTER 58
CALI

Ainmire continued to battle angels and ghost ships alike as though it did not tire him at all. He appeared to grow more youthful the longer the battle proceeded. Eventually the ghost ships faded away and the angels sank to their knees, exhausted.

When the last warrior lowered her sword, Ainmire jumped atop a large boulder and clapped his hands to call the group to order.

"Friends. Let us put a stop to this madness. I have news. Lord Arawn lives! What's more, St. James has joined him! The second part of the prophecy has been fulfilled."

No! Kellen would never turn to the darkness. He was good to his core.

Alternating cries of "Hooray!" and "No!" came from the battlefield. The expressions of the faeries and angels varied from horror to curiosity to relief.

I attempted to crawl to my knees but found myself paralyzed within the next instant. Ainmire didn't even glance my way.

"Perhaps our opponents should go home to their families and take this time to say . . . farewell."

My heart ached as mental anguish added to the physical pain I'd been suffering all along. I wanted to curl myself into a ball and sob, to be absorbed into the stone where I could forget everything. As I attempted to fold in on myself, however, sharp stabbing pains took over my body. Even if there was a solution for my injuries, a way to heal me, I could not live in a world where Kellen was evil.

"Kellen." My voice didn't rise above the sound of the dispersing fighters. Others remained, whispering excitedly about Ainmire's plans. No one looked to me. They knew I no longer posed a threat.

When I opened my eyes, Cabhan sat down on the ground next to me and stroked my hair. The pain that filled up my body only a moment ago eased slightly. His weak smile conveyed a world of sadness.

Cab kept his eyes trained on me. "If I know Kellen at all, he probably thought he might be able to stop Arawn if he aligned with him. Cali, it would not have been a simple choice." Cab shook his head, his brow furrowed while the wind picked up tufts of his blond hair. It reminded me of the days when we would run together in the sunlight through the hills and valleys of our home. His hair would dance as he ran. He always waited for me. Always made sure I was right there with him.

"I know."

"No matter what choice Kellen made, he would have been sacrificing himself."

Willock's words came back to me. *There's no future for you with either of us. Surely you must know that.* He'd known that this would happen.

"You sided with Arawn once. Is there anything you can do

or say to help Kellen?" I hated to ask this of him, but if it would help Kellen, I had no choice.

Cabhan winced at the reminder. "It was not the same. I went . . . willingly."

I tried to sit up, but again my limbs wouldn't obey. I shook my head. "I'm sorry I reminded you. I shouldn't have."

"It is all right. My past is of my own making. I can only hope now to remake the future." Cabhan stared at me, tears falling from his eyes. "You have to come with me, dear Sister." Cabhan's voice soothed me, as though covering me with a warm blanket.

"Why? Where are we going?" But as I searched his eyes, I received my answer. The time for my death was at hand. I was no longer an immortal. Cab was my angel come to take me home. "Oh."

I scanned what little I could of the mountaintop, looking everywhere but at Cabhan. "If I go with you now, I'll never see him. I'll never see Kell—" My throat closed. I couldn't finish.

Cabhan lifted his hands from my head and pain claimed me again. I cried out, and Cabhan quickly replaced his hands, sending it away.

"You have sustained too many injuries. I've been masking your pain." He frowned as though he wished it could be different. "Someday, you will see him again."

The tears came as I squeezed my eyes shut against the pain. A brilliant white light shone behind my eyelids. It glided toward me. It didn't matter what was coming, not anymore. All the fight within me had disappeared.

Good-bye, my love.

CHAPTER 59

KELLEN

The need for sleep pummeled me, urging me to give in and collapse from exhaustion. My muscles ached, my head hurt—everything hurt. Despite this, I stood on the deck that overlooked the rolling backyard of Stephen's estate and stared into the night, trying to look every inch a man Arawn would respect. I'd asked for a moment alone to collect my thoughts, yet they represented a jumble of emotions, with sadness taking the lead.

Cali was gone.

Gabe was somewhere.

We didn't win.

Nothing I did from this point on would have any meaning. I'd suffered too much loss. Too much pain. Now my father had died, and I'd been orphaned. Technically I'd never had a true father, but that didn't make me mourn any less for what might have been. Placing my head in my hands, I tried to block it out, to make it all go away.

"Master Kellen." Willock interrupted my reverie.

A chill went through me at hearing myself addressed like

that. Though I supposed the title would become my identity. I was the master of Danu's amulet, or at least I would be.

"Where are the servants, Willock? The staff that used to work here? Sarah, Bea, Jane . . ." Stephen had probably hired others in my absence, but those were the people I remembered.

"I fired them." Willock's voice sounded even. "All except one. I wasn't fast enough to save the cook."

"Sarah." So that was why she'd appeared in Arawn's dream world. Her body was likely somewhere in the house, waiting to be discovered. I swallowed hard and silently thanked her for her hard work, for the kindness she'd shown me as a child.

"You convinced him to keep Roger alive." When he nodded, I continued. "There's so much about you that I don't understand. Are you on Arawn's side or mine or Cana's? Or are you waiting to see who wins?"

Willock shook his head, furiously. "You don't understand what you're talking about, Arawn—"

"You thought to hold a discussion outside of my presence, Willock?" Arawn's gravelly voice broke into the moment, sending my already frayed nerves jangling.

I spoke up, keeping my voice self-assured. "I tried to escape. I panicked. Willock convinced me of your power and that I should stay."

Goddess, but you are a terrible liar. Willock's voice filled my head.

"Are we going to save my brother or not?" I kept my tone confident, focusing on hiding the fear inside.

"He is prepared. This way." Arawn waved a hand and I followed him into the house. Without Arawn to distract me, I got a better look at the inside. The place had fallen into a dismal state of disrepair. Curtains hung at odd angles, the rods broken or falling from wall brackets. Chairs lay sideways on the floor and newspapers covered every surface. The kitchen was littered with spoiled food. My stomach turned and I held my breath to keep from being sick.

Back in the study, however, a clean-cut Roger sat fully dressed on the couch, a suitcase on the floor beside him. Without the influence of the changeling blood in his veins, he looked like a different person. His eyes were closed, but I couldn't tell if he was asleep or unconscious.

Arawn snapped his fingers and Roger opened his eyes, much like at the end of a hypnosis session. I assumed he couldn't see Arawn, because he surely would have gaped at the Lord of Faerie's impossible form. He looked around until his eyes landed on me.

"Kellen?" Roger's voice sounded as though he hadn't used it in months.

"Hey, Roge." The nickname sounded foreign on my lips. We'd never had childhood nicknames for each other. At least not ones that were nice. "Dog Breath" didn't seem to fit the moment.

"I didn't know you were home. Where's Dad?" Roger asked, frowning.

My head began to ache when Roger called Stephen "Dad." They'd had a closer relationship, yet Stephen had also been cruel to Roger on occasion. Roger never seemed to mind. Maybe their shared bloodline meant it didn't matter.

"I'm sorry, Roge, but he died. Remember? We went to the funeral." I allowed myself a sideways glance at Arawn, mentally willing him to plant memories of the funeral in Roger's mind.

It must have worked, because after a moment of what appeared to be furious pondering, Roger spoke. "Oh yeah. I forgot."

"You probably tried to put it out of your mind. I know I'll be doing the same." I forced a sigh. "You're going back to school tonight, huh?" I prodded, testing him out after his de-changeling process.

"Right." Roger glanced at the bags all around him. "Looks that way."

"Have a safe trip." I made for the front door, hoping he'd follow and there would be a taxi waiting. Roger needed to leave before Arawn changed his mind.

"Kellen." Roger's voice stopped me and I hooked my thumb in my back pocket so I'd seem more casual and less anxious. As if it weren't of the utmost importance that Roger get out of there for his own safety.

"Thanks for the letters from Mom." He frowned again, as though he remembered them, but didn't. "I haven't read them yet, but I will."

Maybe that was better. Learning your father imprisoned your mother and was a murderer never went over well.

"Sure. And when you do read them, call me if you need to talk."

Roger nodded, paling. "Sure. Can I have your number?"

I gave it to him. Roger had just finished entering the last digit when Arawn waved a hand and Roger was gone, luggage and all.

"He'd better have made it back to school."

"That he did." Arawn's voice no longer held the silky, amused tone he'd used with me earlier. His impatience and weariness were seeping through, along with more of the pinpricks of light that dotted his cloak. "Willock!"

Willock stalked into the room. "Yes, Masters."

"It is time for Kellen here to lose his humanity." Arawn chuckled, the deep rumbling signaling the end of it all.

I would not think about who I had been. I would think about who I had to become. Cali would have wanted me to protect Mortal Earth and save her family. If I owned the amulet, then I could keep others from falling victim to Arawn. My heart steeled under my own resolve.

Willock led me to a chair in the middle of the room. He stood before me and placed his hands on my shoulders. "We'll start the process in a moment. Give me time to prepare."

What did losing my humanity entail? Immortality? If there was any truth to the prophecy it would seem so. *The one who refuses immortality in light will receive it in darkness.*

Willock closed his eyes and breathed in and out, his breath steady and sure despite the hollows beneath his eyes. Soon his voice filled my head.

I am going to relax you. When I give you the sign, start twitching about like you're in pain and try to look evil.

A wash of warmth passed over my body as though I'd been filled with molten gold. The heat coated my skin on the outside then filled me up on the inside. My muscles unclenched and I didn't have to pretend to be relaxed when I slumped in the chair. My breath lowered to a slow, even pace.

"Kellen." At the sound of Arawn's voice I opened my eyes. "This is going to hurt."

Now, Kellen! Willock's voice sounded inside my head.

I grabbed my midsection and moaned, flailing my legs. I even made a point of falling onto the floor. It wasn't difficult to fake pain. I already felt it whenever I thought of Cali.

Cali was dead. I choked back tears. "Noooo!"

Curling into the fetal position, I twitched erratically and rolled about on the floor. Just when I thought things had gone on too long, Willock's voice filled my head.

Overact much? Slow it down. Not as intense now.

I eased the fake spasms until they were almost nonexistent. With my shouts no longer filling the room, the silence overwhelmed me.

We are finished. Still, now.

Willock beamed. "That went perfectly. Kellen will make a fine partner."

Arawn's voice broke the quiet. "Kellen. Get up."

Quickly I stood, my back to Arawn. I called to mind every horrible thing that had ever happened to me and slowly turned to the Lord of Faerie. Meeting his eyes, I willed him to believe me.

"Willock has given me the amulet." Arawn spoke in a gravelly voice. "You will now hand over the pendant from your neck, and I will merge the two."

I chanced a glance at Willock and found that the warlock's color had gone. He clutched the back of a chair for support. Arawn seemed not to notice his servant's condition.

My brow furrowed, but then I remembered that I was supposed to look evil. "Master, should I not be the one to do that? You said you needed me to wield the amulet's power."

"Yes, but Willock has guaranteed that if I join the two, I will be restored to my original body. The one that the amulet stole from me all those years ago." Arawn let out a low chuckle coated in evil. "What do you mortals call it? An insurance policy?"

Willock's voice was there again in my head. *Give it to him, Kellen. It's the only way.*

As though it didn't matter, I removed my mother's pendant from around my neck and thrust it at him.

Arawn snapped it roughly from my hand, making me want to stop him, to reclaim what was mine. Greedily, he held my mother's pendant up to the light, inspecting it. "So this is the piece that almost ended me. Fascinating. How odd that the item that helped ensure my almost-demise will now be my path to ultimate power."

He brought the pendant closer to the amulet. He aligned the impression in the stone with the pendant. Then, ever so carefully, he brought the pendant down on top of the amulet.

For a moment, nothing happened. Then Arawn began to transform before my eyes. His antlers faded and his hair sprouted and lengthened into long blond tresses. His skin transformed from shadow to a healthy bronze hue, which spread out over his ripped muscles.

He regarded me with the same piercing blue eyes all of the immortals shared. They were alight with both triumph and—despite his beauty—evil. Then he smiled, showing a set of gleaming white teeth.

"I own you now, Kellen St. James."

Take cover! Willock's astounded cry broke my concentration, but I still wasn't fast enough.

The explosion slammed me against the wall with a resounding thud. Flames blew out the glass in the windows and incinerated furniture. Walls collapsed. I shielded my eyes, taking cover as best I could even as rubble rained down around me and the lights winked out.

CHAPTER 60

KELLEN

I burst through the French doors and onto the back deck, gasping for air. The urge to puke rose up on me, and I bit my tongue to keep from vomiting. My clothes were covered in filth and blood. My body throbbed from where I'd slammed into the wall, not once, but twice. I didn't care. The pain grounded me. It reminded me that I was me and my blood didn't define me.

Willock walked out onto the deck. His face and hair were tinged with soot, but otherwise he seemed unharmed. He stopped at the railing beside me and frowned.

I whirled around to confront him. "What the hell happened?"

Willock beamed. "Arawn was given misinformation. He thought that if he joined the amulet with your pendant it would heal him instantly."

"And that wasn't true?"

"It might have worked. It just didn't. The joining was . . . *rejected*." Willock shrugged and waved his hand in an arc. Instantly, air swirled around me, magnifying the cold until finally the breeze settled. When it stopped, the blood and soot had vanished from my skin and I wore new clothes—poufy coat, flannel shirt, and jeans.

"Wow. Thanks."

"That's the last time I'm dressing you." His serious expression clashed with his words.

"That's a shame. This is much warmer." I zipped up the new coat, and some of the chill left me. There was so much I wanted to ask Willock that I didn't know where to begin. "How thoughtful. You even got my size right."

He shrugged. "I pay attention."

The pair of us stood in silence, the frosty New York air battering us from our places on the wide deck. I had questions for Willock, but the warlock had gone through something back in the house. He needed to be the one to break the silence first. He didn't disappoint.

"You asked me whose side I was on. I started out on Arawn's—he was in many ways like a father to me. But the truth is that Arawn took me from my family, just as he did the true Stephen St. James. We grew up together. We were brothers. Arawn created a glamour of this perfect family—a fairy tale story. It's easy to forget you had another life, another purpose, when you're given perfection."

Arawn had referred to Willock as his servant. I wasn't sure I wanted to imagine that kind of perfection.

"When this began, I only engaged Cana as a backup strategy, in case I failed to find you, but then the strangest thing happened. I came to the house and met Gabriel, you, and Cali." His Adam's apple bobbed as he kept his eyes on mine. "You have to understand. Arawn showed me pictures of Calienta. He told me one day we would be together. That she and I would rule Faerie. When we met in this world . . ."

"You were already in love with her." Of course Willock, who would've only known love as a manipulative tool, had immediately used his magick on Cali. "But then you realized she was in love with me." My words were intended to convince me as much as him.

"She never pretended any differently." He shook his head, a million miles away, yet with me. "Even when I kissed her, her thoughts stayed on you."

Jealousy surged within me, but I forced myself to tamp it down as Willock stared off at something I couldn't see. Reliving the moment, no doubt.

"Seeing Cali and her reaction to me made me doubt Arawn again. I'd felt that way once before, but Arawn had manipulated me with magick so I'd forget. Seeing Cali brought back all the times he'd lied to me."

"How did you know he lied at all? If you were spelled . . ."

"Stephen and I were both content for decades until I found Arawn's journal and realized our world was fabricated. A product of magick." Sadness stole across Willock's features.

"Arawn wrote all that down in a journal?" I'd never taken him for the sentimental type.

Willock's eyes held years of torment. "I think he enjoyed reliving the ways in which he tortured others."

A shudder passed through me. *That* I had no problem believing.

"When I told Stephen the truth about Arawn, we made a plan and escaped. Stephen made it aboveground, but Arawn caught me. Stephen spent a week on Mortal Earth. I'm sure you can imagine who he met there."

"My mother." I suddenly remembered the story about how my mother had left Stephen. How he'd followed her to Ireland, and she thought he'd changed.

Except Stephen hadn't followed her to Ireland. He'd never left.

"Arawn lured him home and locked him up, and I forgot it all again until I saw my father, Dillion. The past I'd forgotten in my years with Arawn came charging back. My father and I had been working for Danu. She had foreseen Arawn's betrayal and enlisted us to help her." Tears pooled in the corners of Willock's eyes, though he continued to speak. "I'd forgotten that."

"You were a kid." If I'd been offered the same things Arawn presented me with tonight when I'd been small, I wasn't convinced I wouldn't have done the same.

"Don't make excuses for me, Kellen. I turned against the light." He swiped at his tears, suddenly seeming older than he had these past few days.

"Did you? You saved me. You saved everyone here. That doesn't sound like joining the Dark Side. I'm pretty sure you set Arawn up with the amulet too."

"I did, and it might have worked for him if he'd been you." He shrugged. "Only one person can join the two. Danu wanted it to be you."

"Danu did?"

Willock nodded in agreement.

"But if I have changeling blood in me, why would she want me to have control over it? I'm not human." I was missing part of my soul, just like my vile father.

"You've got it wrong. The Stephen that you knew, that you lived with, wasn't your father."

My stomach dropped out and I swayed with the wind, the deck boards creaking beneath me as I processed this. "How can that be? Roger—"

"The changeling fathered your brother, but not you. The false Stephen was placed here to make sure you didn't exist. Arawn's been charting the prophecy since he discovered it. He never intended the changeling to marry your mother, it just happened. Perhaps it was that sliver of the real Stephen's soul within him that made him seek her out." Willock stuffed his hands into his pockets, the crisp breeze blowing back his curly brown hair as he stood against the wind.

"Then you asked me why I didn't turn you in. I'd started out with plans to simply wait for my real father, Dillion, to show, but I began putting things together the moment we met. You looked so much like Stephen—the real Stephen—and you acted like him. You're smart, sure, but you're kind and good too. You always want to do the right thing, to make sure everyone's taken care of—just like him."

Finally, he turned toward me, his blue-gray eyes more open and calmer than I'd ever seen them. The Willock that had come before had been nothing more than a facade. "I don't believe that Stephen knows you exist, but I do know he's your father."

"How? Looks and mannerisms don't equate to DNA."

"They don't." Willock laughed lightly. "But when I was faking the ceremony in there to remove your humanity, it wasn't changeling blood I sensed inside you, but faerie. If I had any doubts before, they were erased then."

"So, you're saying the real Stephen is my father and I have faerie blood inside me? How is that even possible?"

The Stephen who'd gotten lost in Faerie, the one Granda talked about, was *my father*. I forced myself to breathe deeply, but regaining any sense of calm was impossible.

"*Half*-faerie blood, and yes, it's a long story." Willock gripped the deck and winced as though in pain. He'd had to hand over the amulet to Arawn a moment ago. Willock's pocket glowed gold, indicating he'd gotten it back, but was he too late?

"Kellen, listen to me. You need to take the amulet and then go to Faerie to rescue Stephen. It's not just because he's trapped there. There's no one in charge, and Faerie will fall into chaos without a ruler. Your father is the rightful king, half-mortal, half-faerie on his mother's side, one of the last in the line of faerie royalty. He will need to ascend the throne quickly."

His mother's side. *Gran.* "Gran was part faerie?" I thought back to all of the stories, to her combined interest and fear in the Good People. Maybe she'd always been afraid they would come for her just as they had her son.

"That's probably the real reason Arawn stole him. His faerie blood." I shoved a hand through my hair, unable to process as Willock's last phenomenon struck me. "So, if my father is the king, then that makes me . . ."

"The *Prince* of Faerie." Willock slowly sank to one knee before me and bowed his head. "Your Highness."

"I am *not* a prince. I'm just a guy from New York."

Willock rose to his feet and withdrew the amulet from his pocket before offering it to me. "There's so much more to tell you, but you have to leave immediately. You have only to claim your birthright and you will enter onto a course that will allow you to change many things."

The green stone pulsed the way it had back in the house. My hands itched to pick it up, but I knew the consequences. "You'll die if you turn it over."

Willock hadn't always been my favorite person, but I didn't want his life to end over a stone I didn't even want.

Willock's eyes filled with an emotion I didn't need to sense to read. Resolve. "I'm already dead. It will steal my life-force every day until it claims it, because it was never mine to begin with."

Before I could argue, Willock grabbed my palm and rested the amulet atop it, all the while keeping his fingers in contact with its surface. With his other hand he held out my mother's pendant, familiar and gleaming. "You are the child of Mortal Earth and Faerie, born of lost man and lost woman. This is yours to wield."

The instant the amulet touched my skin, a feeling of rightness that I had only ever experienced when I was with Cali took me over. *Cali, oh Cali.* I couldn't bear to think she was gone. I didn't know what she would say about my true father or what I'd learned, but she would tell me that the amulet could not fall into another's control again. She would tell me I had to step up, and she would be right. It didn't matter that I didn't want to own it. It was the life I'd been given, and the sooner I accepted it, the sooner the Children of Danu would be freed.

"Focus, Kellen. The pendant."

With a heavy heart, I took the pendant from Willock. Both objects began to vibrate the closer they came in contact with one another.

Willock began to sweat profusely despite the cold. "On the count of three. One . . . two . . . three!" He removed his hand from the amulet.

Without hesitation, I pressed the pendant against the grooves in the amulet. Slowly, the pieces fused until they became one.

That was it. There were no fireworks or light shows. Talk about anticlimactic.

But a moment later, an indescribable feeling of power burst forth from the amulet and flooded my body. The energy shot through me, healing the cut the bird had left on the back of my neck and my bruises and aches and pains. It reminded me of my brief experience as an immortal, when Síl had granted me High Kingship. The power had been overwhelming. Irresistible.

With Danu's amulet, the temptation could easily be described as twenty times that—no, two hundred times more. My fingers twitched as though to drop it.

"Don't let go of it. Don't let it out of your sight." Willock swallowed, lowering himself to the floor of the deck. He'd gone ashen and his body shook. "Can I make a request?"

"Of course. Anything. What can I do?"

"I need to see her one last time."

I didn't need a name to know who "her" was. Willock was responsible for saving my life. I couldn't let him die without granting his last request. Nodding, I held the amulet out before me, knowing I needed the chance for a final farewell as much as Willock.

I slid my eyes closed and brought Cali to the front of my mind. I didn't know how the stone worked, but it felt right to envision her hair, her eyes, her body, her mind, her heart—they were all parts of Cali that popped into my head when I thought of her. "Show me Cali."

The amulet glowed a rich golden color as I opened my eyes. Then something spiraled in the air, spinning round and round until a window formed above me. Its twin panes swung open and through it I glimpsed Cali.

I fell backward onto my butt as I stared at her. I'd expected to find her as a spirit or angel, yet she was alive and with Cabhan. She'd been hurt badly, but she lived. Her wide, beautiful blue eyes filled the window until the image faded and the amulet ceased its glowing.

"Did you see that, Willock? Cali's—" But the rest of my words didn't matter.

Willock sat dead on the ground beside me. His empty eyes still stared ahead, and a peaceful smile lingered on his face.

Reaching down, I gently slid Willock's eyes closed. "Good-bye, my friend."

I'd barely completed the motion when his body vanished as though Willock had never existed, leaving me alone, outside my father's house with far too many ghosts.

CHAPTER 61

Light burned against the backs of my eyelids as I peered out from behind my hooded lids. A brilliant light shone from the portal and lit the sky, bringing closure to an endless night. The wind stilled, and the air calmed. The portal flickered and Síl, my family's creator, stepped through.

"You've come to take her then, Síl." Relief filled Cabhan's voice. It would have been painful for Cab to guide me to the mortal heavens, despite the knowledge that we'd see one another more. Not that I understood the workings of the place. I was supposed to live forever . . . once.

Síl opened his hands at his sides. "If she wishes. Though I came to offer her another option."

"What do you . . . ?" But I fought to speak. My time in this mortal body was almost at an end.

Síl smiled, the act filled with distant compassion. "I can restore you to a goddess, if you wish. You have done everything within your power to help our cause, Calienta. This is my reward to you, should you choose to accept it."

My mind flashed to Kellen. He was not dead, but he'd

chosen a different side. If I became an immortal again, I might have a chance at turning him back to the light.

"I accept." The voice did not sound like my own. I'd used the last breath left in my lungs to respond.

Cabhan squeezed my shoulders. His sigh brushed my cheek as his relief shifted to sadness.

Síl bent down and touched my forehead. I cried out as Cabhan's hands went away and the pain returned to take me over. In every part of me. Too much.

Síl spoke softly, his words floating through my brain. "*Tar ar ais.*"

My thoughts scattered as though my mind and body were separate elements and I was witnessing the ceremony from afar. I couldn't focus on anything Síl said or did. It was easier, in this quiet space, to *be*. There was no pain here, no worry or fear, only existence.

Calienta, I miss you so much. My memory of Kellen's voice was so sharp that it was as if he stood beside me. They were ghost memories. Lingering thoughts he'd had when I visited his dreams in his youth. They'd meant everything to me once.

Snap! In a rush the world slammed back into focus. Síl's calm demeanor, Cabhan's furrowed brow, the near-empty mountaintop. I'd become rooted to my body and the earth once more.

Four golden strands of light wound their way down from the sky and dove into my solar plexus. When the light disappeared, I sat up, shaky, but *me*. Me as I'd always been —immortal.

The pain disappeared and I felt good. Better than I had inside my mortal skin. With a resounding snap, my consciousness and my body became one again. And my memories, my knowledge, came pouring back into my brain. Including everything about the prophecy, Kellen, the old ones and *Gabriel.* "Oh." I covered my mouth with my hand as the revelations poured into me. Things I hadn't yet shared with Kellen because it hadn't been the right time.

"How do you feel?" Síl asked, laughter in his eyes. Then he glanced down at my person. "You might consider a clean-up when you're ready."

At his prodding, I took in my clothes and found them covered in blood—my own or someone else's. I waved a hand over myself, conjuring a sweatsuit like the one Kellen had bought for me at Walmart.

Cabhan shook his head and laughed. "Sister, I see you are yourself once more."

I couldn't help grinning, despite Kellen, despite everything. "I am, Brother, but I've one more thing to do." I waved a hand at the last fragments of night and lit the few remaining stars that clung to the sky, ones that appeared to me as gray shadows. Now they winked more brightly than even the sliver of moon that barely hung on amongst them.

"Now everything is almost as it should be." Turning quickly to Cab, I wrapped my arms around him in a fierce hug. "I love you."

"And I you, dear Sister. Give my love to our parents." He smiled as he drew back from me. He took several slow steps backward before he finally faded into the approaching dawn.

Síl gestured to the portal. "Let us go to your parents. They have been filled with worry."

It seemed as if my insides lit up at the prospect of seeing my parents. They would be able to help me, and they might even know something about Ainmire. For even though my memories had returned, any facts about my almost-captor remained strangely absent. I still had no idea who he was, only that he had some connection to my sister.

"Yes, then we must find Kellen." Determination coursed through my veins as we moved toward the portal.

The instant I thought the words "Take me to Cali," the grounds of my father's empty estate disappeared and the Maine woods took their place. Impossibly tall pine trees were everywhere, shadowing the steep path before me. The smell of salt water and earth filled my nostrils.

There was no sign of Calienta, but as I cast out my senses, her answering emotions crashed into me. Worry. Fear. Triumph. There were others but worry topped the list. I had to reach her.

The amulet pulsated in my hand as though it were alive and knew I'd attached the pendant to it.

Use me, it said.

Even though the amulet's power was no longer unstable, merely restrained, I shoved it into my pocket. I'd run on my own before. I didn't need magick to do it now.

Climbing the hill, I reached the mountain's peak and froze. A ring of fire hovered in the air, the kind that would have done Johnny Cash credit. It shimmered, clearer for a moment, before fading to become only partially visible in the growing light.

Yet the fiery ring itself was not what entranced me. It was who stood at its entrance.

"Cali!" Though the distance between us wasn't large, it felt as if she stood miles away.

A smile broke across her face. "Kellen!"

I sprinted across the flat rocky mountaintop, imagining how it would feel to catch her up in my arms and kiss her. Then panic filled her eyes and pummeled me as her emotions burst forth. An invisible force yanked her backward and through the fiery ring.

The ring had to have been a portal. I had to get to her before it closed. I could run and jump toward it and then use the amulet to open it again and get through to Cali.

That was it. I could use it *this once*—or really a second time—to open the portal and go after Cali.

This time, I visualized nothing. I took off running, the only other sound a bird's cry as my feet pounded across the rock. I'd almost reached the spot. A few more steps and the flat plateau would give way to a dark ravine.

Taking a deep breath, I launched myself into the air in the direction of the portal at the precise instant it disappeared.

CHAPTER 63

CALI

No matter how many times I tried to propel myself through the portal, its energy pulled me back and away from Kellen. My heart threatened to burst from my chest.

"Kellen!" I cried his name to no one.

Yet, despite our separation, my heart sang. Kellen had come to find me! If he had turned to the darkness, I wouldn't have mattered to him. Which meant we had a chance.

Before I could contemplate further, the counterforce of the portal knocked me down and I landed roughly on my backside. "Ouch."

"Oh, I do hope you are not hurt, Calienta?" a voice boomed from somewhere nearby.

Síl. Síl could help me get to Kellen!

I spun around and realized that I stood, not in my beloved Green Lands, but in a place made of . . . white. White tiles, white walls, even high white ceilings. I stood at the intersection of two hallways, and the portal was now nowhere to be found.

Something wasn't right.

"You need to open the portal again. Kellen is out there." I had to get back to him.

Síl appeared then and smiled, but there was something off about him. "It does not matter where St. James is, for you will never see him again."

In the blink of a mortal eye, Síl transformed from the creator I'd cared for and respected to the being that I'd come to fear the most in a short space of time.

"Ainmire."

The odd man tipped back his head and laughed. "What do you think of the trick I employed to get you here? Was it all not inspired?"

If he wanted compliments, this ass would be waiting a millennium.

"Where are we?"

"A hidden place of my own creation. I call it my Fortress of Solitude." He frowned and shook his head just as quickly. "No, I do believe that one's been taken. I'll need to come up with something more original."

"And where is Kellen?"

He waved me off. "Oh, losing his mind over the loss of his love, I'd imagine." He jutted out his bottom lip in a pout.

Without thinking, I shot fire from my palms. The flames stretched out in long bright lines of heat that headed directly for Ainmire, yet he easily deflected my attack. With a wave of his hand, the fire turned to ice, then shattered into shards that scattered across the white beneath us.

Ainmire chuckled. "Eager to use your gifts again so soon, Princess? I don't blame you. I would be." With a flick of his wrist, he slammed me face first against the floor.

Scowling, I leaped to my feet, prepared to keep the duel going all night if need be. If I could wage a battle as a mortal and fight to the end, nothing would stop me as an immortal.

"What is it you want? Who are you?"

"I have use for you, Princess. As I have told you, I am Ainmire, the Star Catcher."

"I am no Princess." Why did he keep calling me that?

Before I could ask, he vanished in a whirl of his cloak, leaving me alone.

I sank to the floor. I'd been so close to Kellen. He'd been right there and alive. If only I could see him once more, even for a moment.

But I was kidding myself. Even a million moments would never be enough.

Closing my eyes, I concentrated on Gabriel with everything I had. Impossible though it might be, I had to get a message to Kellen, and Gabe might be my last chance.

CHAPTER 64

KELLEN

Steel-like hands gripped my arms, pulling me back before I would have leaped off the side of the mountain. They set me down gently on my feet and I spun around.

Gabe grinned. "That was a close one, man."

Laughter erupted from my chest. "Gabe!" I lunged at my best friend, hugging him with everything I had in me. "I never thought I'd see you again."

"Yeah, dude. Those faerie losers ran me off the freaking road. That car rental company is gonna be pissed." He shook his head. "I'm gonna have to call my mom and —whoa."

Something fluttered from the sky then. A piece of parchment. It drifted downward and hovered in the air briefly in front of us as though it wanted to be seen. Then it sank to the ground and landed at our feet.

"Oh no. It has writing on it. Another message." When would it end?

Gabe's brow furrowed into a million questions. "Dude, you seem to get these a lot."

"No kidding?" I picked it up and unfurled the parchment.

I've been taken by Ainmire, the Star Catcher. Only Rowan will know what to do.

—Cali

Goddess, I was an idiot. I'd doubted Cali. I'd let my own trust issues come between us and now she was gone. Technically we'd made up, but things were still... *fragile*. We didn't have time to work through it all and there was no getting those moments back.

I had to find Cali. I needed to tell her that I was all in. That I would always be on her side—no matter what choices she made. The truth was, she's always been on mine. I was just too afraid to let myself believe it.

"K, what's wrong?" Gabe held out his hand, as if ready to somehow blight the contents of the paper from my mind.

"They have Cali." My voice was unsteady as I offered the slip of paper to Gabe.

No sooner had he accepted the paper than waves of emotion slammed into me, but they weren't my own. With a shock I realized they were Gabe's.

Worry and confusion. Who was Rowan? Relief at seeing me, but concern for Cali. Something more too. Something that he deliberately wasn't telling me.

I drew the paper back, my hands shaking. "What were you just thinking? What are you feeling? Be honest."

"I don't know that this is exactly the right time for a sharing circle, K." Gabe cocked one sandy eyebrow and relief hit me again. My best friend was alive. "But if you seriously need to know, I'm super worried about Cali, and I want to know who the hell this Rowan person is."

"Great. Now I'm sensing *your* emotions?" My legs shook. Was this the half-faerie thing? The ability to experience the emotions of others—not just Cali's?

Gabe's eyebrows shot skyward. "K, that's a little too much, if you know what I mean."

"For me too."

Was it some sort of cosmic joke? I'd experienced so little emotion in my life, that I was now getting to live the feelings of others? Honestly, I didn't have time to investigate.

"We need to go to Connecticut. Now. I have zero idea where in Connecticut Rowan lives, but it's a start."

"Road trip!" Gabe extended his pointer and pinky fingers in the air. Yet he'd no sooner "rocked on" once when his smile faltered. "Wait, I totaled the car, remember?"

Well, I had promised to be honest with Gabe, but between the amulet, my new father, and learning I was some kind of half-faerie prince, there was a lot to process. Even for me. I'd learned my lesson about keeping secrets though.

"K, don't take this the wrong way, but your pocket. It's . . . glowing."

I locked my fingers around the amulet and withdrew the stone. It didn't seem any less imposing in the light of day.

Gabe's mouth dropped open. "Dude, what the holy freaking heck is that?" He blinked furiously, but there was no way he'd ever clear this from his vision.

The amulet heated in the palm of my hand as I stared hard at my friend. "You're probably going to freak out about this, but I think I can get us to Connecticut . . . *without* a car."

Gabe's eyes widened like saucers. "And you're going to freak out just as much, K, but I can too." He grimaced as though he feared the big reveal of whatever secret he'd been hiding more than the journey to find Rowan.

I stared into the eyes of my best friend, familiar in so many ways yet a stranger in others. "Wow. We do have a lot to catch up on."

"Yeah." Gabe nodded staring out at the sea that seemed to separate use from the rest of the world. "You could say that."

The rain had washed the world clean, just like on the day of my wedding. This time I stood on the opposite side of the Atlantic, and I wasn't waiting for Cali to walk toward me. I would run toward Cali and find her no matter where she'd gone.

Someone had the girl I loved, and I *would* get her back. Screw the odds.

THE MUSIC

If you had the chance to read the first book in this series, *The Star Child*, you'll know that music plays an incredibly important role in character development for me. I always write melodies for characters in my head and that helps me to get under their skin, so to speak. As with the first book, these are not meant to be major symphonic works, but instead provide insight into my creative process.

Cali

Gabriel Stewart

Maine

S. Keyes

YOUR NEXT FREE READ!

The most wonderful thing about writing is connecting with readers! I occasionally send out newsletters with details on new releases, as well as special offers and other news related to my books.

And if you sign up for my mailing list I'll send you another book for FREE.

Steph

DOWNLOAD YOUR FREE BOOK >
http://bit.ly/fall-stars-free

ABOUT THE AUTHOR

Stephanie Keyes is the author of over a dozen other titles for teens and adults. The Spellbinder's Sonata, her Beauty and the Beast meets Phantom mash-up, was an Amazon #1 new release. Spellbinder's was awarded the RONE Award for Best Young Adult Book of 2019 and took 2nd place in the Athena Awards for Excellence in YA and NA Books (Paranormal Category). She also writes contemporary romance.

Keyes has spoken at events throughout the US and the UK, and was a featured artist at Pittsburgh's First Night 2019. She is a member of The Society of Children's Book Writers and Illustrators (SCBWI) and Pennwriters.

Keyes is a technical writer and content strategist, teacher, and speaker. She lives in Pittsburgh, Pennsylvania with her husband and her boys, Hip-Hop and Bam-Bam, and dog, Duncan MacLeod.

BB bookbub.com/authors/stephanie-keyes
f facebook.com/StephanieKeyesAuthor
instagram.com/stephkeyes38

Young Adult Fantasy

The Star Child

Seventeen-year-old Kellen St. James has been haunted by the same girl for half of his life. When they finally meet outside of his dreams, he's thrust into the world of faeries, gods and goddesses—and all at his college graduation.

The Spellbinder's Sonata

A brilliant concert pianist, a clarinetist with a history of magic, and a haunted house. Beauty and the Beast meets The Phantom of the Opera in a tale of magic, music, and one dark curse.

The Boy in the Trees

Part of the Blood In the Shadows anthology, Jemma's sketched the same boy hundreds of times. The only problem? They've never met.

New Adult Romance

The Internship of Pippa Darling

Pippa's one Irish internship away from graduation, unfortunately it's with Finn Burke, the one author whose work she hates.

The Education of Uma Gallagher

Uma Gallagher's thrilled to land a teaching position in Dublin, but the last thing she expects is to find rock star Caden Hannigan in the back of her class.

ACKNOWLEDGMENTS

I originally wrote this book in the summer of 2012. It was a time filled with excitement and promise. I had my first book under my belt, a new baby, and a new life...

Quite a contrast to the next time I pulled up this manuscript nine years later, five days after my grandmother died. I wasn't even sure I had it in me to write at all, let alone tackle another editing project. Gran was the inspiration for Kellen's Gran and my first best friend.

When I first wrote *The Star Child* series my father was dying of Cancer. It pulled me from a dark place and helped me cope. This time, it was *The Fallen Stars* that led me out of my head and away from my grief.

Maybe it's the characters—there is something remarkable about normal people who achieve extraordinary things. That's what this series has always been about for me. Putting a teenage boy who seems ordinary into extraordinary circumstances and waiting to see what he'll do.

Before you say that I'm writing him and I should know what he'll do, keep in mind that I'll argue with you. Kellen, Cali, and Gabe have always been in the driver's seat. It doesn't matter what I plan. More often than not, these characters take over and lead the story elsewhere. Of course half the fun is, and always has been, the journey.

Hugs to the members of my Facebook Readers Group. You are one amazing bunch and I'm honored that you came to stay and that you love my stories as much as I do. Particularly Annie Amsden, Taryn Frye, and Lauren Shalek for your time as beta readers.

Thank you, Laura Parnam, for being an amazing editor who took this manuscript and made it fit for readers everywhere. I'm happy to have you on Team Keyes!

An enormous round of hugs to Najla Qamber, who completely reimagined *The Star Child* series covers. I love the new cover for *The Fallen Stars,* and I'm grateful for your creativity and enthusiasm for the project.

Hugs and more hugs to Mary Jo Glover for convincing me this revised version was ready to go out into the world. Thanks to the Rt. 19 Writers for your constant support and love. As Gran used to say: A friend is like a four-leaf clover—hard to find and lucky to have.

To my boys, I love you both. You guys are the best sons I could ever hope for, and I'm blessed to have you in my life.

And finally, to Aaron, without whom none of this would be possible. I am blessed every day to have you in my life. I'm pretty sure 2020 was one of the hardest we've gone through yet. You are the angel that always rushes to my side. Thanks for having my back, A. I love you.

CPSIA information can be obtained
at www.ICGtesting.com
Printed in the USA
LVHW030126090421
683894LV00010B/229